WINTER'S FIRE

Giles Kristian

CORGI BOOKS

TRANSWORLD PUBLISHERS
61–63 Uxbridge Road, London W5 5SA
www.penguin.co.uk

Transworld is part of the Penguin Random House group of companies
whose addresses can be found at global.penguinrandomhouse.com

Penguin
Random House
UK

First published in Great Britain in 2016 by Bantam Press
an imprint of Transworld Publishers
Corgi edition published 2016

A CIP catalogue record for this book
is available from the British Library.

ISBN 9780552171328

Typeset in 11/14 pt Meridien by Thomson Digital Pvt Ltd, Noida, Delhi.
Printed and bound by Clays Ltd, Bungay, Suffolk.

Penguin Random House is committed to a sustainable
future for our business, our readers and our planet. This book
is made from Forest Stewardship Council® certified paper.

MIX
Paper from
responsible sources
FSC® C018179

1 3 5 7 9 10 8 6 4 2

Winter's Fire is for Chris Cornell, whose voice and music has seeped into this saga like mead into the feasting table.

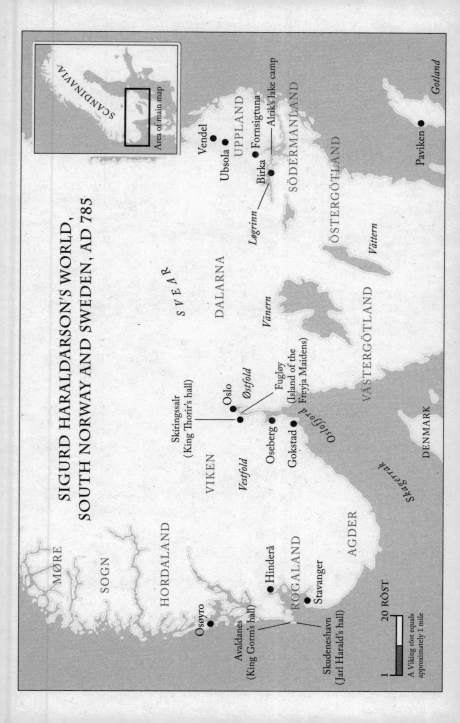

SIGURD HARALDARSON'S WORLD,
SOUTH NORWAY AND SWEDEN, AD 785

SCANDINAVIA

Area of main map

Gotland

Vendel

Ubsola

UPPLAND

Fornsigtuna

Birka

Alrik's lake camp

SÖDERMANLAND

Paviken

Lagrinn

SVEAR

DALARNA

ÖSTERGÖTLAND

Vänern

Vättern

Skíringssalr
(King Thorir's hall)

Oslo

Østfold

Fugløy
(Island of the Freyja Maidens)

VÄSTERGÖTLAND

VIKEN

Vestfold

Oseberg

Gokstad

Oslofjord

DENMARK

MØRE

SOGN

HORDALAND

Hinderå

ROGALAND

Stavanger

AGDER

Skagerrak

Osøyro

Avaldanes
(King Gorm's hall)

Skudeneshavn
(Jarl Harald's hall)

20 RÖST

A Viking röst equals
approximately 1 mile

The maidens of death came riding
To claim his battle-slain kin
But Sigurd was Óðin-kissed, men said,
And the fire burnt within.
A boy no more, he killed a jarl
And fled with half a crew.
So swore his vengeance on the king
As young men often do.

Sigurd Haraldarson's Saga

CHAPTER ONE

_____

THE TRACKS WERE FRESH BUT THE SNOW WAS OLD. DEEP too, so that it was impossible to know how many animals there were, for each was using the same tracks as the one in front. The trail they made through the pines was narrow and straight. Or as straight as it could be in a forest.

'Wolves waste no energy when they're on the move. Not like dogs,' Olaf had explained when they set out into the night with spears and bellies full of ale.

'Aye, but a dog wouldn't waste a nice warm fire,' Svein had said, shuddering at the sudden cold and pressing a thick finger against one nostril to expel a wad of smoke-blackened snot on to the snow. 'So I am thinking that maybe dogs have more clever in them than wolves.' He glanced back towards the hall as though already regretting his decision to go with Olaf and Sigurd. 'More clever than us too,' he added, clearing his other nostril and pulling the wool back over his face, blinking smoke-stung eyes in the frigid air.

They had wrapped their legs and hands with wool too and wore the same sheepskin or fur and leather hats that they had pulled on to their heads when the snows had come, and which they had rarely taken off since, even inside Jarl Hakon Burner's old hall. For that place was huge and there were never enough bodies inside to warm its edges, even with both hearths burning day and night.

'Compared to wolves dogs walk as if they are drunk,' Olaf had gone on, cinching his cloak tight at his neck. 'Tend to drag their toes as well, whereas wolves have a cleaner stride. Leave neater tracks, see.'

He had been right about that, Sigurd thought now as a shaft of moonglow arrowed through the trees, lighting the trail before them and threading the brittle mantle with silver, like wire inlay on a blade. The left and right paw prints were only slightly offset and it was clear that the wolves were making much lighter work of it than Sigurd and his friends. Sigurd could see where the lead wolf's body had carved a track through the snow like a karvi's sleek bow through a heavy sea. By contrast he and his companions laboured and puffed and sweated now despite the chill. For the pine canopy above had not prevented the snow settling deep in places, nor stopped the prevailing south-westerly wind piling it up in drifts against trunks, making it hard going.

'Bollocks, but the lad's blowing like Völund's own bellows!' Olaf said a while later, pulling the woollen wrap below his chin and planting his spear butt in the snow as he and Sigurd turned to look at Svein who had fallen behind. 'The beasts'll smell his mead-breath five rôsts off and we'll never catch a glimpse of them.'

Olaf had been Sigurd's father's closest friend and now he treated them all as a man will who thinks his having a few more years on his back is the same as having twice as much sense. Perhaps it was, too. And yet Sigurd knew that Olaf would take a spear in the gut or an arrow in the throat for him, and where was the sense in that? Olaf would say he owed it to Sigurd's father Harald – hard to gainsay, for you could count the dead jarl's still breathing hearthmen on one hand these days. On three fingers actually.

Now, though, Olaf's own mead-breath was clouding around his face as though his beard were on fire and Sigurd suspected his stopping to moan about Svein had more to do with Olaf catching his own wind than it had to do with their big friend. Sigurd found himself smiling. He was a long way off Olaf's age and whilst he might have been clumsy compared to their prey he nevertheless felt a wolf's stamina thrum in his blood, felt the beast's vigour in his flesh, and believed he could keep this pace up all night if need be.

'Better being out here with the silence in our ears than back there with them full of Crow-Song,' Sigurd said.

'True enough,' Olaf agreed. 'By the time he has spun your killing of that treacherous, over-reaching crab bait Jarl Randver into your saga tale he will have you sharing kinship with the Allfather himself and I will be some troll-slayer with a dwarf-forged sword.' One of his eyebrows curved like Bifröst the rainbow-bridge. 'Fucking skalds, eh?'

Sigurd felt the cold air on his teeth. 'He says the truth is as welcome in a good story as a fart under the furs.'

They could have waited until morning before setting out, but Asgot had smelt new snow in the air, or seen it in his runes perhaps, and Sigurd would not risk another fall covering the tracks. Besides which he welcomed any excuse to get out of Hakon Burner's hall.

They had gone up to Osøyro the first time harbouring the hope that Jarl Hakon Brandingi, who had earned his reputation as a hall-burner many times over, might help them fight the oath-breaker King Gorm. But arriving at Brandingi's hall they had found the jarl himself a living corpse and his son, Thengil, lording it around the place instead. Thengil had been a soft, slimy nithing, and perhaps that had been all to the good because he had died piss-soaked and strung up from the rafters, and the corpse jarl's last hearthmen, proper warriors to a man, had seen in Sigurd one last chance to live and die as men should. They had sworn loyalty to him, which was a heavy thing, they being warriors of so many fights and Sigurd being grass-green by comparison.

He could still see those greybeards in the eye of his mind, standing there in their last shieldwall by Jarl Randver's hall in Hinderå, facing the jarl's warriors who, though younger and undoubtedly stronger, must have learnt a thing or two that day. For those old Sword-Norse had stood their ground so that Sigurd and the others could get to the sea and take ship away. Not that the greybeards' legs could have carried them fast enough even if they had wanted to live.

After that steel-storm by the Nilsavika headland in which Sigurd killed Jarl Randver, whose bones now sat in the cold dark at the bottom of the fjord, they had sailed back up to Osøyro, to Jarl Hakon Brandingi's old hall. There, their ears had been full of the curses of those old women who blamed Sigurd that their men were now in the afterlife without them; and all Sigurd could do was give each a handful of silver, which the women took off to live out the rest of their lives in some village elsewhere, not wanting to dwell with their menfolk's ghosts nor with Sigurd's crew.

But dead as Randver was, he yet had living sons and the eldest of them, Hrani, now had ships and men and a thirst for revenge. And then there was

King Gorm and all the Sword-Norse he could call upon, and the oath-breaker would never have a better chance to rid himself of Sigurd. So like a hunted wolf, Sigurd had taken to his den to wait out the winter. But that huge hall, bigger than any Sigurd had ever seen or heard of, was a forsaken place. Its ancient soot-blackened timbers were corpse-cold. Its corners, in which men and women once fumbled, now writhed with rats. Its mead-stained benches lay up in the roof beams swathed in spiders' web thick as wool, and of the hangings on the walls keeping out the draughts, a few had been spun in recent years but most were old, faded and threadbare. It was a hall of ghosts and no amount of lamp or hearth flame could breathe life into it.

Which was why Sigurd would rather be knee-deep in snow hunting wolves. For if they could find the creatures' den they could come back with more spears and dogs and traps.

The beasts had dug their way into the sheep pen and killed two ewes; but there would have been little point trying to follow them had there not been snow on the ground and had the wolves not dragged one of the ewes off, which meant they were not moving as fast as they could have been. It also meant there was a chance that their den was nearby, and as Olaf had said, best to deal with them now – or else pay dearly for it in the summer when there would be no tracks to follow.

'There,' Sigurd said, pointing to a patch of disturbed snow up ahead from which tracks radiated like spokes on a cart wheel. In the middle was the ewe, or rather what was left of it, and as they drew closer the little moonlight permeating the forest canopy turned the gore-smeared snow darker still.

'Eyes sharp then,' Olaf murmured, lifting his spear a little higher, his own eyes scouring the trees around them. Knowing that spear-armed men followed them, the wolves had eaten what they could before vanishing like sea mist. 'I'd wager they're three rôsts away by now,' Olaf said, then nodded at the deeper forest which was gloomy as Hel's own hall, the pines like pillars beyond counting. 'But there's always a chance they're out there watching us and will risk a spear in the ribs to protect this kill.'

'Well, that is it then. We turn back,' Svein said, 'get back to a fire.' He stamped his fur-lined boots in the snow, trying to put some warmth back in his feet.

'May as well,' Olaf agreed. 'No point in freezing our balls off for we will not find the den now.'

Sigurd did not want to go back yet, not while his blood was still thrumming with the thrill of having found the ewe. Not while the wolves might yet be close, for their kill was steaming where it lay in the bloody snow, the hot contents of its stomach meeting the night air, meaning that part of it was only recently ripped open. He was about to say as much when a wolf's howl cut through the night like a blade through flesh. Immediately other beasts joined the chorus and for a cold heartbeat the sound reminded Sigurd of the many war horns whose thin notes – all different in pitch – had pierced the day in the Karmsund Strait when his father had been betrayed by King Gorm and the fjord had turned red.

'We didn't bring enough spears,' Svein said, peering north and rolling his great shoulders, for the howling filled the forest around them so that it seemed there must be a score or more animals.

'That's the trick of it,' Olaf said, 'to make other packs think there are more of them than there are.'

'It is a good trick,' Sigurd said, eyeing the tracks leading away from the kill.

'Aye, low cunning,' Olaf agreed, 'but Svein is right that there are still more than we had bargained for.' He sniffed and hawked phlegm into the snow. 'Might be as well for us to leave them to it and set our traps near the pens rather than trudging all the way out here into their territory. Like fools pissing up against a neighbouring jarl's hall.'

The howling was cut with *yip yipping* now as though the wolves were summoning their own bloodlust and encouraging each other to bold and reckless acts the way young warriors do in the shieldwall before a fight. It was a sound to turn your bone marrow to ice and none of the men needed to say as much to know that each thought it.

'Could be those that took our ewe are back with the pack, meaning their den is close,' Sigurd suggested, still eager to do what they had come out there to do. 'We find their den and mark it. Come back in daylight. Or they attack us and we kill a few of them and the rest leave this place. Leaving our animals in peace.'

Olaf and Svein looked at each other, their breath clouding before their faces. 'I suppose if they go for us and get their teeth into Svein they will be eating him for a week, giving us plenty of time to get away,' Olaf suggested, earning himself a growled insult from the red-haired giant. 'So, we ignore the beasts' warning and walk right up to their den, of which they are bound to be as protective as you would be of *Reinen* or your own hall.' He flapped a big hand. 'I don't include Burner's hall in that for I know you don't much care for the place, which is the real reason we're out here pissing icicles.'

Sigurd had not known his dislike of Jarl Hakon's old place was so obvious.

He pointed his spear into the forest. 'Does that not sound like a challenge to you, Uncle?'

'Aye,' Olaf admitted, 'and you are your father's son.'

Turning their backs on the slaughtered ewe they set off along the new trail, eyes sharp as rivet points, hearts hammering against their breastbones because it was no easy thing to walk towards that bowel-loosening clamour.

'Remind me to tell you the saga of the ram which men called the Terror,' Olaf said, then glanced at

Svein. 'Your father and Slagfid were both up to their necks in that mischief and all because we were young and stupid and could not turn away from a challenge.' With that he stopped and gestured with his spear, inviting Sigurd to lead the way. 'After you, Haraldarson.'

Sigurd trudged ahead, putting his feet in the wolves' tracks, a wolf's grin on his own face. 'I am happy to lead the way, Uncle,' he said, 'for it is well known that wolves will go for the one lagging behind. They can easily tell which of their prey is old and will be less trouble to bring down.'

'Ha! It is not difficult to see why you have so many enemies and so few friends,' Olaf said, nevertheless glancing behind him as they walked.

But as they progressed along the track into a part of the forest where the trees were closer together and the snow was more shallow because of it, it was Svein who realized that although the howling might be the beasts issuing a challenge, the way one war band will hurl a spear over the heads of another, that challenge was not aimed at the three men lumbering through the snow after them.

'Down!' he hissed, pulling Sigurd's cloak. The three of them crouched, which felt to Sigurd like a foolish thing to do, giving away their advantage of height to put their faces level with a wolf's jaws. But his eyes picked out the shapes in the gloom, told him that the wolves were not facing in their direction. Since they had turned off the original path where they had found the dead ewe, what little breeze there was carried their own scent eastward away from the wolves, so that there was a chance, albeit a slim one, that the creatures did not even know they were so close, particularly given all the noise they were themselves making.

'They have some animal cornered,' Svein whispered.

Above them a bird flapped in the snow-laden canopy: a raven perhaps, following the pack, waiting for it to kill again, and Sigurd saw Olaf touch the Thór's hammer amulet at his neck because where there was blood and death there were always ravens.

'An elk. Or a bear,' Olaf suggested. The pack had surrounded its prey and Sigurd looked from one beast to another, trying to get a grip on their number in the half-light. Ten? Maybe more. He could not say, other than there were enough to bring down a bear, if Olaf was right and that was what had got the wolves baying for blood. But all Sigurd could see was the pack, the crouching beasts all snarl and noise and bristle.

'Are you sure we should get involved in this fight?' Svein asked Sigurd, for if the wolves *had* cornered a bear the three men might be better off away from the tooth and claw of it all.

'Unless you can tell me that you have heard a bear singing the galdr before, then I think we have walked into something else here,' Sigurd murmured, tapping his ear which was turned towards the howling chaos among the trees a spear's throw away.

21

'Óðin's arse!' Olaf hissed.

It was no easy thing to pick the human voice out of all that wolf singing, but once Sigurd had found the thread of it there was no doubt. And it was a woman too, though what a woman was doing alone out in the woods at night was itself a question to make a man's neck hairs stand up like a wolf's hackles.

'I didn't come out here to tangle with a seiðr-witch,' Oláf said, flexing his hand around his spear's shaft to get some warmth into his fingers. The wolves were snarling more than howling now and it was a sound that Sigurd felt in his very guts like a rockfall in a cave.

'She cannot be much of a witch or else she would have concealed herself from them,' Svein said, which was more sense than they were used to hearing from him.

'There's not a spell I ever heard of that could fool a wolf's nose,' Olaf countered.

'There,' Sigurd said, pointing to a dim shape which his eyes had sifted from the earth-packed root ball of a fallen tree. Against the dark of it he had not seen the woman before but now he had picked her out, standing there with her back to the roots, facing the snarling beasts. Chanting.

'Aye, I see her,' Olaf said.

'Have you thought that maybe she is speaking to them?' Svein said. 'That she is their master? For they have not eaten her yet.'

'Keep watching, Red, and you'll have your answer to that,' Olaf told him, and Sigurd agreed with him, for though the witch's galdr was keeping the beasts at bay, some of them were edging closer, their bellies touching the snow. One wolf, a huge male standing well over three foot high at the shoulder, was now a mere spear-length from the witch, close enough to leap and snarling his threats, making it clear to the pack that he would draw first blood. Then the pack would join the kill and it would be a frenzy of feeding, those wicked sharp teeth shearing flesh from bone which the beasts would swallow in bloody lumps.

'Ready?' Sigurd said and did not need to see them nod. Witch or no, none of them would crouch spear-armed in the dark and watch a woman ripped apart.

'Don't let them get behind you,' Olaf said, as Sigurd stood, roaring, and the three of them lumbered through the snow towards the witch, and the wolves turned, their yellow eyes catching the moonlight, their lips hitched back to show those scramasax-sharp teeth.

The pack leader bowed its body, throwing its great head over its left shoulder to growl at Sigurd who did not stop but tramped towards it and thrust his spear, but the blade missed its target as the big male twisted aside. Then it leapt and Sigurd brought the spear across though not fast enough and the beast's jaws, twice as strong as the biggest hound's, clamped round Sigurd's forearm as the bristling mass of muscle and bone barrelled into his chest, knocking him backwards into the snow. It was as if Völund's own anvil was crushing his arm. Those yellow eyes bored into his but Sigurd was roaring his own challenge into the beast's hot acrid breath, the fog of it the only thing between him and the wolf's muzzle. The weight of the creature pressed the spear shaft against Sigurd's chest as he struggled now for every breath to scream defiance. Yet as the beast sought to crush the bone and get to the marrow in his arm Sigurd managed to slip his right hand beneath the thick belly fur and haul the scramasax from its scabbard.

The wolf was snarling death, a berserking fury shaking its head now so that Sigurd thought it would rip his arm from its socket, but to think was to die and so he punched the blade into the beast's side and felt the iron grate against a rib before tearing into the flesh. The wolf showed no sign of knowing it had a foot of blade inside it, gripped as it was by its own bloodlust, wrenching Sigurd's arm this way and that as Sigurd twisted the scramasax, trying to force the blade deeper and do even more damage. He thought he could hear laughter. Some god, perhaps, amused to see him on his back in the snow, his own limb the only thing between him and having his throat torn out. Then Sigurd pulled the scramasax from its fleshy sheath between the wolf's ribs and plunged it in again, screaming into that pointed muzzle, defying the wolf as Týr

lord of battle must have done in the same heartbeat
that the mighty Fenrir bit off his arm.

Fast as an owl swooping from an oak bough, the
thought crossed Sigurd's mind that the others must
be fighting, too, for why else were they not helping
him? Then his right hand and arm felt somehow
on fire but he realized it must be the beast's blood,
hot and sticky as pitch, and so he struck again and
again, screaming death to the wolf, working the
blade deep into its chest to slice into its thumping
heart.

The snarling stopped. Those great jaws weakened
for all that the wolf tried to champ down still, was
likely confused as to why it had not bitten through
the bone. A shudder went through the beast, its
muscles thrumming like a ship's rigging in a storm,
and Sigurd watched its eyes roll back in its head.
Then the huge head fell sidewards and the life went
out of it and somewhere another wolf howled as
though it knew its leader was dead, while Sigurd lay
there under the weight of it: all that bristle, muscle,
sinew and bone that was now only lifeless carcass.

Then Olaf was there at last and he heaved the dead
wolf off Sigurd, his worry plain to see by the light
reflecting off the snow.

'Your arm,' he said.

'Is still mine,' Sigurd said, 'no thanks to you.'
Olaf offered his hand and Sigurd took it in his right,
letting Olaf pull him to his feet, his chest heaving
for breath, his head wreathed in his own warm fog.

Olaf toed the huge beast to make sure it was dead, as Sigurd looked around. The other wolves had gone and Svein was standing guard, spear raised after them. Besides the one Sigurd had killed there were two more beasts lying in the snow, one of them dead and the other still panting, its legs twitching as though it thought it were running.

'Your arm,' Olaf said again, nodding at the limb. Sigurd lifted his left hand, clenching and unclenching his fist to make sure the tendons and muscles still did what they were supposed to, though his arm was full of pain. He bent and thrust his scramasax into the snow and when he pulled it out most of the blood was off the blade. Then he sheathed the thing and, gritting his teeth, shoved the sleeves of his tunics up to reveal the place around which the wolf's jaws had been locked moments before.

A grin spread in Olaf's beard because there was no torn flesh, no sharp slivers of broken bone sticking out of a bloody mess. Instead there was the greave that Sigurd usually wore on his shin: the leather wrap with its iron splints and some of those splints with dents in them now, teeth marks that were better there than in Sigurd's arm bones. A man called Ofeig Grettir had bought the greaves off Sigurd with information, but Black Floki had slaughtered Grettir along with the man who had kept him on the end of a chain and Sigurd had been glad to have the greaves back. Never more glad than now.

'A raging dog will always go for your arm if you offer it,' Sigurd said, wincing as he made a fist again. 'I thought a wolf might do the same if it came to it.'

'Loki's own cunning,' Olaf said, turning to the witch now who stood in the shadows against the uprooted tree, watching and silent. 'And who are you, woman? That my young friend here nearly got himself on the inside of a wolf for.'

The woman glanced at Olaf but then settled her eyes back on Sigurd where they had been before. Her right hand gripped the knob of a staff and she leant the thing towards Sigurd.

'I am the then, the now and the may be,' she said and even hooded as she was her voice betrayed her many years, though there was no stoop or crookedness in her so far as Sigurd could see.

'You are a seiðr-kona,' Sigurd said. More of an accusation than a question, and in his peripheral vision he saw both Svein and Olaf touch the Thór's hammers at their necks because a seiðr-wife was not someone you wanted to meet out in the forest by the light of a sliver of moon.

'Not much of one,' Svein dared, 'or you would have used some dark magic to hide yourself from those wolves.'

The head inside that lambskin hood turned to Svein, the hood's lining – catskin by the looks – as white as the snow they stood in.

'I could make *you* vanish, giant,' she said, which was as good an admission as they could have hoped,

27

or not hoped for. Because a seiðr-wife was as dangerous as the knife you can't see. They had all heard tales of such women hurling spells that addled their victim's mind by illusion or madness. And yet Sigurd had just wrestled with a wolf and the fight-thrill of that was still in him so that he was not going to be afraid of an old woman, especially a crone who would have been wolf food if not for him.

'I am not surprised they came for you,' he said, nodding at the big wolf lying there on the snow, its mouth frozen in a snarl, those flesh-ripping teeth looking dangerous even now. 'With all the skins you are wearing.' Over a dark blue mantle the witch wore the fur of a forest cat and her legs were wrapped in fleece. She had on catskin gloves and shoes of shaggy calfskin, and the wolves must have reckoned they were in for an easy feast, for all that they would have thought her a strange creature.

'And yet I am unharmed,' she said, and though he could not see her face in the shadow of that hood Sigurd knew those words had come through a smile.

'You did not summon us here by some spell, if that is what you want us to think,' Olaf said, and that hooded head turned back towards him so that Olaf, who was braver than Týr himself, almost flinched. 'We were hunting them,' he said.

'Because Sigurd does not like his new hall,' Svein put in, tramping through the snow to get a look at Sigurd's wolf because it was so much bigger than the ones he and Olaf had speared.

'Which one of you heard the galdr?' she asked. She was looking at Sigurd, or at least her head was turned towards him.

'We heard the beasts,' Olaf said, 'howling like their tails were on fire. The dead would have heard it.'

'None of you heard my galdr?' she said.

There was a silence, the kind that there can only be in a forest with deep snow on the ground and more swathing the boughs above. Then a bird flapped somewhere in the high branches and a stream of snow tumbled to the ground near the witch.

So the raven would feed on the wolf, Sigurd thought, wondering at the strange omen in that.

'I heard it, witch,' he said.

'Ah yes, Fenrir-killer,' she said, and again Sigurd heard the smile in that.

'It is good for you that he did kill the beast, old woman,' Svein said, 'or it would be snapping your bones like dry sticks by now.'

'So you say.' The seiðr-wife took two steps and slowly brought the staff across, at which Olaf and Svein both lifted their own spears as if to defend themselves. But instead of hurling some spell at them the witch prodded the big wolf with the staff and looked up at Sigurd, her head cocked. A shaft of moonlight cut across half of her face, giving Sigurd a glimpse of white skin and the dark glossed jet of an eye.

'What is your name?' he asked.

'Ha!' The fog of that utterance hung in the moonlight for a heartbeat. 'You would more often hear a cat's footfall or the breath of a fish,' she said, then leant the staff towards Sigurd, who fought every impulse to put his own spear between them. 'Does a fox need gills? Or a mouse horns?' she asked. 'Folk call me witch.' Somewhere to the east the wolves were howling again and it sent a shiver scuttling up the back of Sigurd's neck because it reminded him of the wailing of the womenfolk when he had set fire to his father's hall, burning those of his village who had been slaughtered by Jarl Randver's men. 'But you have asked, wolf-killer,' the witch said, 'and so I will tell you. I was called Bergljot once. Aye, Bergljot,' she repeated the name, barely loud enough for him to hear, as if she had intrigued herself by speaking it aloud.

'What are you doing out here alone, Bergljot?' Sigurd asked. He pointed his spear back along the tracks which they had made. 'We have come far. But you have come further by my reckoning.'

He knew there were no villages for ten rôsts in any direction and that even had there been, this woman had not come from one of them. Then again, such as she probably lived alone in some herb-crammed hovel with only mice, birds and spiders for company.

'It is safer for me to travel at night,' she said.

'Oh yes, you have shown how that is so,' Olaf said, nodding at the dead beast nearest him, but

Sigurd knew what the woman had meant and Olaf knew too, for some folk would sooner throw a sack over a seiðr-wife's head and fill her with spears than risk her dark magic shrivelling their manhood or sending them mad.

'Do you see a scratch on me, Olaf Ollersson?'

Sigurd and Svein looked at Olaf who looked at them, heavy-browed beyond the fog of his own breath, though it was not impossible that a witch should possess enough seiðr craft to know his name and his father's name.

'Whereas these poor creatures are quite dead,' she said, crouching and thrusting a gloved hand into the thick fur of the wolf's ruff. 'As dead as your brothers, young Sigurd.'

'Where are you bound?' Sigurd asked her, beginning to feel about as comfortable as a man whose breeks are running with fleas.

'You know where, young Sigurd,' she said, standing, her face in the shadows now but the eyes in him like a cat's claws.

'We came out here to hunt, woman,' Olaf said, 'not stand here freezing our bollocks off talking to some seiðr-wife, regretting robbing a wolf of his feast.'

Even Svein, who was a mountain next to the old woman, tensed at those words. But the woman laughed. She laughed and you would have thought she had been rinsing her guts with mead all night, not tramping through knee-deep snow and being

31

beset by beasts that would have ripped her to shreds had she not been saved by men's spears.

'What is so funny?' Sigurd asked her, his own ire pricked to be laughed at by the crone.

'Aye, share it with us, for nothing warms the belly like a good laugh,' Olaf said.

'Nothing but spiced mead,' Svein rumbled. 'Which we ought to be drinking now instead of standing here growing snot icicles.'

The witch lifted her staff and pointed the knobbed end at each of them in turn. 'You are out here hunting,' she said, the laughter gone now, vanished like breath in the air. 'You are hunting and yet you are the ones being hunted.'

Sigurd felt dread's ice blade slide into his heart then, yet he shrugged her warning off like snowflakes before they could seep into the wool. 'I have enemies, old woman. What of it?'

'Enemies,' she said. Sigurd thought he heard the creak of her brow warping as she said the word. 'You have enemies the way a herring has a whale.' She lifted one fur-clad arm and pointed at him, the catskin gloves white as the snow. 'I see you, Haraldarson. I see you well.'

'What else do you see, woman?' Sigurd asked.

'I see a flaming hearth and a plate of hot food,' she said.

That got a laugh even from Olaf, but Sigurd was still snared by what some wandering seiðr-wife seemed to know about him. He stared at her and she stared back and no one spoke, so that the silence lay as heavy as the white mantle weighing down the spruce boughs above them.

Then Sigurd thrust his spear into the snow and trudged over to the big wolf he had killed, squatting to get a hold of the beast, his face almost in the snow so as to heft the dead weight up and over and on to his shoulders. *Gods, you are heavy*, he thought. But the wolf was warm too and Sigurd welcomed the feel of that last shadow of its life on his shoulders and against the back of his neck, even as the copper tang of its blood and the pungent stink of the shit which had leaked from it in death filled his nose.

Olaf and Svein hefted their own beasts and the three of them turned back to follow their boot-tracks home again.

And the witch went with them.

CHAPTER TWO

———

'DO I HAVE TO EAT IN THE DARK NOW?' THE KING YELLED, backhanding his bowl across the bench, its hot contents flying everywhere and even striking one of his hirðmen in the face. The warrior let the pottage scald his skin rather than be seen to wipe it away.

'You, get some oil into that,' Moldof growled at a thrall standing nearby, pointing at the nearest iron dish on its three long legs. 'Before I take a brand from the hearth and shove it up your arse to see my food by.'

The thrall was already moving amongst the benches and the bodies crammed on them, for such threats from the king's former champion were as good as promises these days. Perhaps they always had been, but ever since he had lost his sword hand, and with it his arm up to the elbow, fighting Jarl Harald of Skudeneshavn the previous summer, Moldof had become as sour in mood as his face was to look at. Even wolf-jointed and using a blade left-handed, the giant was still more than a match for most of the king's hearthmen, but he was no longer Gorm's champion, could no longer claim the honour of standing at the king's prow, and the shame came off him like a stink.

'I should chain one or two of them to the rock and let them drink the fucking tide!' King Gorm yelled, like a pot simmering over after being left too long above the flame, and his people tensed at their benches, hirðmen glancing at each other while their women looked for their children in the corners to make sure they were not making a nuisance of themselves with the king being in such foul temper.

A big man named Hreidar leant over and snatched up his king's empty drinking horn, then stood and plunged it into a bucket at the end of the table. He passed it back to Gorm, licking what he had spilled from the back of his hand, then raised his own horn to the king.

'Death to your enemies, lord.' He grinned. 'But not before their pricks shrivel and their women see them begging for a sharp blade and a good swing behind it.'

This got a chorus of cheers but nothing from Moldof other than a muttered curse that escaped his lips like a weak fart, for he hated Hreidar and of course he would, Hreidar being the king's new champion. But Moldof held his tongue because he was one arm short of being able to beat the man if an insult grew to a fight.

As for the king himself, he could not find a smile to bend the steel line of his lips but nodded and raised his horn at Hreidar, putting the thing to his mouth and drinking as though he had just swum across the fjord and had a throat as salty as Óðin's seed.

Then he looked to the dark end of the hall at the figure sitting on the end of a bench, hunched over his cup, talking to no one. Looking at no one. The man had given his name as Fionn, a name which Gorm had never had in his ears before and so did not know what it meant, but the man had said he was from Alba in the west, and no doubt that explained his warped, jumbled Norse and the fact that no one knew him, his kin or how he had come to be in Avaldsnes. And yet he'd sought an audience with Gorm and perhaps out of curiosity Gorm had listened to what he had to say. Fionn had heard about the king's . . . problem. Could solve it for a price, he said. The nerve! Did he not think the king could clean up his own mess? Should have thrown the arrogant little shit out on his arse. But he hadn't.

And there he is, under my roof for some reason. Drinking my mead.

At a gesture from Queen Kadlin, a birch-thin man named Galti took the bukkehorn from his belt and began playing the liveliest tune he knew. The queen nodded and swept an arm out to signal that everyone should fall back to their food and drink, which they did, rekindling conversations and leaving Gorm Shield-Shaker to steep in his own ire, as he had done for weeks now. The king felt the ill-mood on his face from the moment he awoke to the last drop of mead when he fell back into his bed skins and snored the night away or, more often, lay looking up at the beams, listening to the mice scratching away in the reeds. It was like an ache, like an old blade wound or mended bone that nagged whenever rain threatened. And there was nothing he could do to shake it off. Neither women nor mead could make him forget.

Haraldarson.

'Why would you bring that up now, Hreidar?' he asked, dropping those words on to the hall's thrum like a flat rock on to water.

Hreidar frowned, recalling the last thing he had said. 'About killing your enemies?' He jutted his chin. 'The boy Sigurd needs to die.'

'That *boy* slaughtered Jarl Randver,' Moldof growled, his ugly mouth and a bucket's worth of ale warping the words.

The king said nothing.

Hreidar shrugged. 'We know where he is hiding,' he said, 'and we know that he does not have even half a crew with him.' He glanced at some of the other big-bearded, blade-scarred men sitting at their king's mead bench. 'It would be no more trouble than shaking out a fur to rid it of fleas. Let us sail up there and squash this Sigurd Haraldarson before we snug *Storm-Bison* up in her naust for the winter.'

Fionn from Alba looked up at this, though his dark eyes revealed nothing.

King Gorm eyeballed Hreidar, feeling the muscles beneath his beard – more iron than copper his beard these days, he knew – bouncing with the anger he fought to contain.

'You are not my prow man for the wits in your skull, Hreidar, but because you are big and ugly and yet have two hands on the ends of your arms. I would sooner ask my hounds for advice than you.'

This was no light insult but Hreidar was still flush with pride at being made Gorm's champion and so his lord's words slid off him like water off a gull's wing.

'Still, he is right if you ask me,' Moldof put in, which had Hreidar's brows bending because that was the last place from which he expected support. 'If you leave a rats' nest alone for any length of time, when you uncover it again you will be up to your knees in the creatures. So it may be with this young man, if we do not deal with him now while he is weak. While he has nothing but the skin on his own back and an ambition that might as well sit at the top of Yggdrasil for all the chance he has of getting his hands on it.'

'His ambition is to see me dead,' the king muttered into his beard, fingering the new torc of gold which he wore at his neck.

'That it is,' Moldof said, 'and who can blame him for thirsting after it, given how things played out?' The king would not answer that.

'He has a fine ship, let us not forget,' a man named Otkel said, 'a fine ship and barely the men to sail it let alone wet the oars and get its wings beating. *Reinen* would look good in your berth, lord. It would make even *Storm-Bison* crave new paint and an arse scraping.'

'We should spear the lad while he's licking his wounds,' a big-bellied, ruddy-faced warrior called Ham said. 'With two crews we'll pick the bones of Jarl Burner's old hall clean.'

'Aye, there must be plunder worth having up there, for unless I missed it, Burner's son never came here to pay his silver dues,' Hreidar said.

'That's because Thengil Hakonarson had nothing,' Moldof said. 'Never raided a day in his worthless life, that one. Which is the only reason we left him squirming up there in his father's shadow like a worm in a dung heap.'

'You are all full of advice sitting here in my hall with my food in your bellies and my mead on your breath,' the king told them, 'knowing that the only fight you will have tonight is to get your women's legs open when you crawl to bed.' He fluttered thick fingers at them, his rings glinting in the light of the newly lit lamp nearby. 'You crow about fighting but you see only a part of the thing. Like mackerel swimming around the keel never knowing that there is a whole ship above them. Bilge and ballast and thwarts full of men.'

'And those men full of thoughts and fears, hopes and doubts,' someone said, but no one was interested in poetry now.

'But it would not be a fight,' Ham countered, sucking at a bone he had fished from his bowl, 'more like slaughtering a few pigs for the Jól feast.' He licked his fingers and wiped them in the bush of his beard. 'Let me take some of the youngens up there. There are a few that could do with being blooded.' He looked at Hreidar and shrugged, and the king's champion nodded.

'There will never be a better time to finish this and be done with the last of Jarl Harald's litter,' he said. Others nodded and growled their agreement and they were like men poking sticks into the embers to raise a flame.

'The young man is Óðin-favoured!' the king blurted, then grimaced as though wishing he could take the words back, as if by saying them it confirmed their truth. But then this thing had been gnawing at him for so long that maybe it was just as well to get it out there now. Maybe someone could put his mind at ease. Looking at the faces around him he doubted it.

'It is true young Sigurd has been lucky,' Otkel said. 'He has kept his head afloat on a sea of blood that should have drowned him along with his father and brothers and all of Jarl Harald's hirðmen.' He scratched his cheek. 'Perhaps it *is* more than luck.'

'He has avoided death the way smoke avoids the fist which tries to grip it,' Moldof said.

'Aye, and then there is that business with the tree,' King Gorm said, as if the words tasted rancid.

No one spoke for a few moments then, for they all had heard the tale of how Sigurd had walked in the Allfather's footsteps, sacrificing himself as the hanged god had, tied amongst the branches of a tree and left to starve. And yet the young man had not starved. He endured for nine days, men said, and in that time was shown visions of his own future. He earned himself the Hangaguð's attention and with it his favour so that perhaps only a fool would try to fight him now. Even Jarl Randver, a powerful jarl who could call on hundreds of spears, had been unable to beat him in the end, had failed to turn aside the death which Sigurd had brazenly brought to the man's own hall. There were always whispers stirring like dry floor rushes in the king's hall, that the young warrior Sigurd Haraldarson was beloved of the Æsir. And King Gorm, who feared no man, did fear old One-Eye and had no wish to anger the gods.

'It is no small thing to have an Óðin-favoured man for an enemy,' King Gorm said and none of them could disagree with that. He stabbed a finger against his temple where a big vein throbbed beneath the skin. 'It has been at me like Nídhögg at the roots of

Yggdrasil that what we did to Jarl Harald has turned the lords of Asgard against us. That I have poisoned my own wyrd with that—' He chewed his lip rather than say the word *betrayal*, though there was not a man there who did not know what he had bitten back.

'If the gods had not wanted Jarl Harald dead they would not have made it so easy for us to kill him,' Hreidar said, almost smiling.

'Ha! Easy, you say?' Moldof spat, sweeping his wolf-joint through the hearth smoke. 'I do not recall you fighting the man, Hreidar. Nor do I recall it being so easy.'

He spoke truly: Hreidar, Otkel, Ham and many other warriors in that hall remembered Moldof's fight with Harald, just as Gorm himself did. How could they not? Even men who were not there on the day talked of it. It had been like the clash of two giant bull elks, neither man giving or asking for quarter, and it was already the stuff of skald songs. Not that that made up for losing half an arm and his place at his king's prow as far as Moldof was concerned, which he made plain by his constant sulking.

'Still, Harald and all but one of his sons are dead,' Hreidar said. 'His wife is dead and his hall is ashes and we have got not even a scratch from this god-favoured runt.' He raised his hands, their palms all callus, tough as boiled leather from the oar and sword and shield work. 'Yes the boy somehow beat Jarl

42

Randver,' he went on, 'but before his sword dried he flew the coop as though his feathers were on fire. Even now Randver's son's arse polishes his father's high seat, the man waiting for your permission to wear the jarl torc.' He gestured eastward with his mead horn. 'The waters are smooth again over in Hinderå and what does Sigurd have to show for it?'

'Hrani will fill Randver's boots well enough,' an older man called Alfgeir affirmed with a nod. Alfgeir had been quiet up to now but King Gorm nodded at him, acknowledging his opinion as one which was actually worth something.

Ham gave a great belch then held up a fat finger. 'Then why don't we stay out of the mire of it all and let Hrani Randversson deal with young Sigurd? No one can say he does not have a debt to settle with the lad.' He took a hunk of bread and ran it around the inside of his bowl. 'Let the Hinderå men mop up the last of this mess while we drink the winter away.'

'You would like that, hey, Ham?' Hreidar said. 'Sitting on your fat arse while other men do the work for you.'

Ham shrugged. Why wouldn't he like it?

'Haraldarson's attack on Jarl Randver was an attack on us all. He insults us,' Moldof said. 'He insults the king!' The folk of Avaldsnes had not heard the former champion raise his voice above a growl since he had lost his sword arm, and so they looked up now and it just happened that the music stopped, Galti taking the bukkehorn from his lips and watching the king's table like everyone else.

'Let me go and finish it, lord,' Moldof said. 'I will find the young wolf and gut him. I will put rocks where his gut rope was and sink him in the fjord.' He tapped his own temple where an old scar puckered the skin. 'You will never need to have him in your thought box again.'

'But you are needed here, Moldof, to protect the women and growl at children to help mothers get them into bed,' Hreidar said, which got some grins though no one dared to laugh.

'Watch your tongue, Hreidar,' Moldof gnarred, 'unless you want to dig your own burial mound with it.'

Hreidar's teeth flashed in his beard. 'That might have had my mouth dry as one of old Hroald's farts once.' He shook his head. 'But I have never seen a man with one arm scare anything other than the broth in the pot.'

Moldof's ill-favoured face twisted and he hauled his great bulk out from the mead bench, drawing up to his full height like a dragon ship's sail hauled up the mast.

With a word King Gorm might have smothered the flames of this before they grew. Instead he lifted the mead horn to his lips and sat back in his chair, relieved to see men's attentions shift from his burdens regarding his wyrd and the son of the man he had betrayed, to the two warriors, who now drained their own horns and set them on the mead-stained boards.

'Sit down, you hot-headed bulls,' Alfgeir said, flapping his arm up and down like a cormorant's wing. 'Before someone gives offence that can only be repaid in blood.'

'I will sit when Moldof admits that his glory days are wake ripples off the stern,' Hreidar said, as the others around the table, but for the king himself, stood and pushed back the benches so that they could get out of the way. And perhaps Hreidar had been waiting for this moment to fully step out of the former champion's shadow, which was still long these days one arm or no. For it would be easier for Moldof to sprout a new limb than to ignore this challenge. He threw himself at Hreidar, who twisted aside as Moldof's left fist flew wide, the momentum carrying the bigger man forward so that he turned and fell hard on to the rush-strewn floor. A collective gasp rose to the rafters of King Gorm's hall as folk who had always held Moldof in awe now beheld him lying at another man's feet in the spilled mead and mouse turds.

'Sigurd Haraldarson will piss his breeks with fear when he hears that you are coming for him,' Hreidar said, shaking his head. He stepped back to give Moldof the space to rise and those standing behind him moved back as one, like a wave. Moldof swung again but Hreidar threw up both forearms to block the blow then lashed out with his right fist, hammering it against Moldof's left cheek. Moldof instinctively swung his own right arm but it was just a stump and it looked pathetic waving about like that, not even nearly reaching the king's champion. Then he strode forward and rammed his shoulder into Hreidar's chest, his great mass irresistible so that Hreidar was thrown backwards, the breath driven from his lungs as Moldof brought his left fist up, the knuckles gouging the skin from Hreidar's forehead. But the king's champion grinned and threw himself forward, leading with his right elbow, and Moldof, who was like an ill-ballasted boat for he had yet to learn the new balance of his one-armed self, took the blow and stumbled, the back of his knees hitting a bench so that he tipped over it and landed in a heap.

King Gorm shook his head, ashamed to see the once great warrior bested so easily. 'Might have been a different matter if they'd used blades,' he rumbled under his breath to the man beside him.

'Stay down, man!' Alfgeir told Moldof, 'for you will piss on your own saga and be remembered as a wolf-jointed fool.' But the one-armed warrior spat a curse and made to rise.

'Enough of this,' King Gorm said at last, giving Hreidar cold eyes. 'I would expect this from new beards trying to impress my bed slaves, but not from you.'

Hreidar looked from Moldof to his king, then nodded and showed Gorm his palm by way of an apology. He extended the same hand to Moldof, happy as he was to help him up now that he had filled every eye in that hall with the humiliation of the king's former prow man.

Moldof spat on to the floor rushes, eyeballing Hreidar who shrugged and climbed back on to the bench, swiping at the blood on his forehead and licking it from his hand before washing it down with more mead.

'I will bring you Sigurd's head and slaughter those who are loyal to him,' Moldof told the king.

'Ha! I would like to see you rowing round in circles trying to find him,' Hreidar said, and this got some laughter from men who spun the picture of that in their minds, though not from the king who was half sorry for his former champion and half ashamed of him.

'I stood at our king's prow when you were still learning one end of a spear from the other,' Moldof growled at Hreidar, turning those small boar's eyes on the other men at the king's table, men with whom he had not only endured the steel-storm often, but above whom his own legend had risen long ago. 'I have killed more men than you have had fucks.' This got some muttering but nothing out loud, for no one felt able to argue with Moldof on this point, which was saying something given the women of Avaldsnes. The king smiled, though, to show his appreciation of Moldof's insult and, more importantly, to show that he knew the man could not possibly have aimed that barb about fucking in his direction.

'Keep your feet by the fire this winter,' Moldof told them, 'and I will go and get this thing done with half the arms but twice the balls.' With that he called for more mead and the hum of the hall flowed back over the whole thing like the sea over a blood offering. Talk at the benches turned to ship maintenance and the mead supply and the taxes which King Gorm could expect from skippers wanting to sail north up the narrow channel below their hilltop perch. Shield-Shaker himself went back to his brooding, the thread of this Sigurd problem too tangled for him to find the end of it. Should he leave the young man alone and hope the whole storm of it calmed in time, but risk Sigurd coming back to bite him? Or would it be better to go after him now and kill him, but in doing so risk angering the gods further, for surely all men could see that Haraldarson was Óðin-favoured?

These dark thoughts were a mire from which King Gorm with all his silver and sharp steel could not free himself.

And whilst the king brooded, Moldof drank, getting used to holding the horn in his left hand, because it was always a good thing to fill your belly with mead before going hunting.

CHAPTER THREE

'DO YOU BELIEVE HER, ASGOT?' SIGURD ASKED. HE TOOK the fur off his shoulders and leant over to put it around his sister, who had been doing a poor job of trying not to shiver, even near the fire as she was. Runa nestled into the fur and smiled at Sigurd, though his eyes were back on the godi who for once had undone his beard rope in order to pull his comb through it and strip it of its crew of lice. He might have the gods' whispers in his ears with every other breeze, but the man looked older with his greying beard splayed out like that, Sigurd thought.

'Do I believe that men are coming to kill you?' Asgot asked, staring at the witch who sat alone by the other hearth staring into the flames as though they were tongues whose speech she could hear. 'Or do I believe that this seiðr-wife learnt all about you from the Norns? That those spinners of men's wyrds

49

Urd, Verdandi and Skuld revealed you to this witch and told her to seek you out with this warning?'

Sigurd frowned and shrugged. 'Any of it,' he said.

Asgot's thin lips twisted. 'You do not need knowledge of seiðr-craft to know that you have made enemies and that those men want you dead.'

'She knew my name.'

'You have a reputation, Haraldarson,' Asgot said.

'Aye,' Olaf put in, 'yet we were out there up to our balls in snow, fur-clad and freezing our arses off, not lording it in silver torcs and skald song. The cold forest doesn't give a toss about reputation.'

Now it was Asgot who shrugged. 'A cat does not care about the sea and yet it can smell it on the air.'

'It seems to me,' Runa said, 'that what is more important than *how* she knew my brother and that he was up here in this old hall, is that she knew at all.' She looked at the other faces around the fire, at Svein, Bram and Valgerd the shieldmaiden, Black Floki, Bjarni, Bjorn and the others. 'For if she knew it then there is every chance that others know it too.'

'Knowing it and doing something about it are two different things,' Bram said. 'Men don't go raiding in winter.'

Black Floki looked at him. 'Do you call it raiding when you slaughter a horse for the Jól feast?' he asked.

'Floki is right,' Olaf said. 'For a man like Biflindi, or even Jarl Randver's son Hrani, coming up here to finish us would be more like a little hunting trip than going a-Viking.'

'Well, I for one am happier at the thought of fighting King Gorm or Randver's strutting son than living under the same roof as that witch,' Bjarni said, nodding towards the seiðr-wife, who was whispering to herself now. Or perhaps she was answering the flames.

'That is easy to say when old Shield-Shaker is not banging on our door with all his spears standing behind him like a fucking forest,' Olaf told him before turning back to Sigurd. 'Still, young Runa is right about this. If the old crone knew we were here then it is likely that others know it, be it the Norns told them or some other flapping tongue.' A deep rumble came from his throat, as though he would rather swallow his next words down than say them. 'We should leave,' he said, looking from Svein to Sigurd. 'Fill *Reinen* with what we can get together quickly and off we go. Like a bear we disappear into some hole for the winter and we hope the hunters forget about us.'

Asgot glared at him. 'You think Sigurd won himself the Allfather's attention just to piss it away now? Once earned such a boon must not be allowed to run through one's fingers,' he said, making a fist of his bony hand. 'Only bold action will keep Óðin's one eye turned towards Sigurd and keep us in his favour.'

'Favour?' Olaf blurted. At the same moment some wood in the fire cracked fiercely as though to echo the bull-shouldered warrior. 'Try telling that to those sword-brothers who fought beside us little more than two moons past, those we burnt or who lie rotting at Hinderå. Or even our kinsmen who were carried away on the blood-sea when this whole thing began.'

These words were as a knife twisting in Sigurd's guts, a blade that had been in him a while now, ever since they had come to Osøyro and Hakon Burner's hall. For in the calm after the storm of swords Sigurd had faced another more insidious enemy, which was the guilt he felt at having led so many brave companions to their deaths. There was Hauk and his greybeards, men who had lived in this very hall when they were young and broad and drinking Jarl Hakon's mead. There were the men from the Lysefjord: Agnar Hunter, big Ubba and Karsten Ríkr who had been as good at the helm as old Solmund. There was Kætil Kartr and Hendil and Sigurd's friend Loker whom he had killed with his own hands to prove he was a man worth following and not some boy shivering in his father's long shadow. A loom weight in Sigurd's guts, that one. Loker had wanted to kill Valgerd for taking off his arm with her scramasax, had soured over it enough to challenge Sigurd himself, which was a thing Sigurd could not ignore what with everyone's eyes on them. Not if he was to lead them all. And so he had fought and killed Loker and Svein had dropped Loker over *Reinen*'s side into the sea. Just like that.

All those men had given Sigurd their oath and in return he had given them death.

'They drink in the Spear God's hall,' Bram said, as though that was reward enough for any man worth the sword at his hip.

Svein nodded. 'There are none who deserved their benches in Valhöll more,' he said. 'While we shiver our arses off, they feast on Óðin's meat and mead.'

And while Sigurd nodded that this was so, he yet felt the weight of their loss and he could not imagine being able to unburden himself of it while he remained under Jarl Burner's roof and lived amongst the benches upon which he suspected Hauk and his brave warriors' ghosts still lingered.

Bjorn looked at Olaf, all bristles and frown. 'You want us to trade this roof for the snow and the ice without knowing where we are to go?'

'I would rather be out there than in this place of ghosts,' Valgerd put in.

'Me too,' Runa said bravely, though she was rubbing her hands together and spreading the fingers wide before the hearthfire.

Bjorn's brother Bjarni sniffed, dragging a hand across his red nose. 'There is ice across some of the narrow channels and creeping around *Reinen*. This morning I watched a dog run across it and cock its leg to piss on her rudder.'

'I hope you speared the mongrel, Bjarni,' old Solmund said, horrified by the thought. He loved that ship more than anything in the world.

'He would have answered to me if he had, seeing as it is my dog,' Runa said, which had the helmsman mumbling into his white beard. Sigurd knew that his sister had been feeding the hound scraps ever since it had first come sniffing around the hall.

'To stay here is to invite a fight we cannot win,' Olaf said.

'Aye, would you rather be cold or dead, youngen?' Solmund asked Bjorn, who had no answer to that, or not one he wished to share.

'We stay here,' Sigurd said, surprising himself. Olaf was giving him the opportunity he had craved since the first snows, to leave this draughty hall, its cobweb-slung corners and its ghosts. And yet he was choosing to stay. Perhaps it had something to do with the seiðr-wife whom they had found in the snow. Who had found them, he reflected, somehow knowing that was the way of it. Or perhaps it was Asgot's talk of showing the Allfather that he was worthy of his favour, which old One-Eye might begin to doubt were Sigurd to scarper at the first mention of his enemies searching for him. Besides, where would they go? However much he wanted to weigh anchor and leave this place of the dead there was no safe bay that he knew of. No jarl who would take him in and play the host. There was no wind either, had not been for weeks, the air hanging cold and heavy and still, meaning *Reinen* would have to be rowed and there were not enough of them to do that. Not for any distance anyway.

'We stay here a little while longer,' he said, still as if needing to convince himself. 'We eat whatever meat we can hunt and we stay strong and warm.'

Some of them nodded and others spoke softly to each other. Over by the other hearth the witch laughed and it sounded like a hen's clucking, which had some of them touching the Thór's hammers at their necks or the hilts of knives or swords, for they all kept their war gear in reach.

'Well then, we'd better have a pair of eyes always watching the sea,' Olaf said, 'for I will not have some king or would-be jarl burning this hall with me sleeping in it.'

'From tomorrow we will take turns keeping watch,' Bram said and they all seemed content with this, because for all their talk the idea of setting out into the freezing world was not a comforting one. The snow lay thick beyond those old timbers, while the flames in both hearths crackled and spat, illuminating the darkness and chasing shadows.

'And if anyone comes, we kill them,' Valgerd said, as though it would be as easy as that, and Black Floki, who liked the shieldmaiden even less than he liked most people, grinned.

Six days later somebody came.

It had not snowed again since the night Sigurd had killed the wolf, but the white mantle lay heavy and thick and untouched by any thaw. A bright cold sun shone in a bright blue sky, which was in itself so rare that it more or less proved that the man cared not at all about being seen. It was that time of the year when daylight was fleeting as youth, but while it reigned the fjord glittered like a polished brynja and the untrodden snow sparkled like the silver inlay on a war god's axe head. The air was crisp and there was no wind.

And the man came.

'He is making hard work of it,' Olaf said.

'Hard work? My mother could handle oars better than that when she had a beard longer than mine,' Solmund said.

Having been fetched by Valgerd who had been on watch since dawn, they gathered on the rocks by the winding path which led from the shore up through the birch and tall spruce. All but for Asgot who was tending the fire up in the hall. They came shivering in furs, sword- and spear-armed but their helmets and shields left in the hall, blinking and coughing woodsmoke out of their lungs, their breath fogging around their faces. Below them sat the rotten old jetty against which *Reinen* was moored, sitting as still as the dead on that sleeping sea. But they were not looking at *Reinen*. Their eyes were riveted to the small craft being rowed badly towards the shore, and the figure in her thwarts, who looked more like a bear than a man from that distance in his furs and shaggy hat.

'If he is aiming for our jetty then I am thinking he is either blind or drunk,' Hagal Crow-Song said, huffing into the cup he had made of his hands.

'Or both,' Bram suggested.

Which was not impossible, Sigurd thought, for the little boat was tending to larboard, so much so that for every fourth stroke the man pushed the opposite oar blade clear of the water, so letting his left arm work alone to point the bow back towards the jetty.

'It is painful to watch,' Bjorn said.

'Who is he then, witch?' Olaf asked the old woman, who did not look quite so strange in all her cat skins now, since Sigurd, Olaf and Svein wore their wolf pelts against the cold, the beasts' heads upon their own, the eyes gone but the teeth locked in an everlasting snarl.

'He is one of those hunting you,' she said to Sigurd, two hands and chin resting on her long staff as she watched the skiff.

Svein chuckled at this. 'Well then, we had better make a shieldwall, hey, Uncle,' he said.

'Forget about our saga tale, Red,' Bjarni said, holding out a hand and making it tremble, 'we should jump on to *Reinen* and row for our lives.' He grinned at Aslak who grinned back. But Sigurd was not smiling. This man rowing towards them was likely further proof that folk knew where he and his last few oathsworn warriors were holed up for the winter, which was what Olaf was thinking too judging by the frown.

'It was only a matter of time,' Olaf murmured, scratching amongst his beard.

Like the wolves they had hunted, they all used the same tracks in the snow when they set off foraging or to collect firewood; there was a trail leading down to the shore as well as several others which spider-webbed off from the hall. But for Sigurd's wolves it was about more than ease of passage: it was so that they would know if they had visitors by the new tracks they made. With *Reinen* snugged up under a thick layer of pine resin, her thwarts sheathed in greased animal skins underneath a blanket of snow, the only prints as yet on the jetty itself had been made by fox paws, Runa's dog and the gulls. But now it seemed a stranger would be tramping across the ancient boards, and even if the man did not already know that Sigurd Haraldarson would be there to greet him, he would carry that news away with him when he left again.

'Perhaps it is the king himself come to make amends for being a slimy lump of snail snot,' Solmund said.

'Aye, it's Biflindi come to offer Sigurd Jarl Randver's torc and his hall at Hinderå,' Svein said, 'so long as Sigurd agrees not to go down to Avaldsnes and bury an axe in his skull for being an oath-breaking piece of troll shit.'

'Troll shit he may be, but he did not get the name Shield-Shaker for being afraid of a fight,' Hagal pointed out, for the byname Biflindi suited King Gorm the way a ship suited Solmund.

'Whoever it is he'll be lucky to get here at all, even on a sleeping sea like that,' Bjorn said as they watched the boat limp – if a boat could limp – towards the mooring.

'All the luck a man can carry will not help him if we do not like him,' Olaf gnarred, 'for any man so bad at rowing cannot be good at swimming. Just give me the word, Sigurd, and I'll sink him. Send the sod down into the cold wet dark and it'll be one less thing to worry us.'

But Sigurd had a sense of cold foreboding himself now because he suddenly saw the reason for the little boat's wanderings and knew the man leaning back in the thwarts. 'Moldof,' he said.

'You sure?' Olaf said, but even he knew the truth of it now.

'Isn't Moldof the king's prow man Father fought that day when the king betrayed him?' Runa asked.

'Aye, lass, and your father lopped the ugly turd's sword arm off, which I wish I had seen with my own eyes,' Olaf said. For Sigurd was the only one amongst them standing on that rock who had seen Jarl Harald fight King Gorm's champion and still lived with the memory of it.

The sour despair of that memory flooded over Sigurd now, making the breath snag in his chest like a fishhook amongst the weed. The blood in his veins seemed to slow and he felt the hairs rise on the back of his neck at the sight of the man rowing towards them. Towards him. Sigurd had watched his father

GILES KRISTIAN

slaughtered that day along with the last of Harald's brave and loyal hirðmen. Sigurd would have been slaughtered himself had his brother Sorli and two other men, Asbjorn and Finn, not charged at the king, screaming death to the traitor and giving Sigurd the chance to run for his life. Not that Moldof had played any part in that red murder, what with Harald having cut off his arm in a bout of single combat which must have had the gods themselves wide-eyed.

'I'll wager he brings a message from the king,' Crow-Song said, no doubt thinking this was all good stuff for the saga tale about Sigurd which he claimed he was weaving.

'I doubt it,' Olaf said. 'Why would the king send half a man like Moldof? Doesn't do his reputation much good.'

'Skalds sing of Moldof,' Crow-Song said. 'He may lack an arm but he does not lack reputation.'

'Let us take his other arm then,' Valgerd said, her golden braids like Runa's piled up beneath a fox-skin hat to help keep the warmth in her skull, 'and Crow-Song can weave him a new reputation as a man who rows with his cock.' This got some chuckles. No one doubted that the shieldmaiden would lop off Moldof's good arm without so much as blinking. Just as she had lopped off Loker's before joining Sigurd's crew and swearing the oath to him.

Moldof leant back in the stroke, clumsy but relentless, coming on, one oar stave lashed to the

60

stump of his right arm, which could not have been an easy thing to do, as Svein pointed out.

'Are we going to stand here freezing our arse hairs off, or shall we go and greet our guest?' Olaf asked.

'Don't kill him until we have heard what he has to say,' Sigurd said, and Olaf held up a hand as if to say *Would I do such a thing?* And with that they tramped through the snow, slipping on the ice which sheathed the rocks, down to the jetty, which was so slippery once their feet had sunk through the snow that Svein fell on his arse and cursed loud enough to send a cormorant croaking up towards the low sun. The others laughed, which did not help, and neither did Hagal by saying that you wouldn't catch heroes like Moldof falling on their backsides at moments like this.

'Hold your tongue, skald, unless you want to sing your tales to the fish,' Svein growled, which had them laughing even more, until Sigurd stilled them with a hand. It was no laughing matter to meet Moldof again, this man who, before he had fought Harald, had tried to rouse the jarl's anger with foul insults about Sigurd's brothers who had died in the red slaughter of the ship battle in the Karmsund Strait.

'Haraldarson.' Moldof's gruff voice carried across the flat water. Sigurd did not reply but took three paces forward by way of acknowledgement.

There was a palpable silence then while Moldof brought the little boat up to the jetty and half held on to it while he sought to untie the rope which lashed the oar to his half arm. No one moved to help him, neither did they offer to tie off the skiff, and the whole thing seemed to take an age, but at last the king's former champion unloaded his war gear – two spears and his shield – and clambered up on to the boards.

'What do you want, Moldof?' Sigurd said.

In his bear skin and fur hat Moldof looked massive, bigger than Svein, and Sigurd knew that the shoulders, chest and arms beneath all the fur were heavily muscled and battle-hardened. Gorm's man was still puffing from the rowing and his face and wild beard were greasy with sweat.

'I am here to kill you, Sigurd Haraldarson, and take your head back to my king.'

For a moment no one said a word, but neither did anyone laugh. It took guts for a man to say such a thing in front of eleven armed warriors.

'Did my jarl skewer your brain, Moldof?' Olaf asked. 'Did Harald prise it from your thought box like a mussel from a shell?'

'Aye, Moldof, it is hard to take threats seriously from a man who can't braid his own beard,' Bram said.

But Moldof had come for a fight. Sigurd caught a glimpse of the brynja rings at his neck as he bent to pick up the two big spears from the snow.

'I will take your head too, Olaf,' Moldof said, 'though I might throw that to the crabs because it is worth nothing.'

Svein stepped forward but Olaf grabbed a handful of the wolf pelt on his back and he stopped.

'You did not lose your ambition then when you lost your arm,' Olaf said, 'but you will have to wait until you are full grown before you are ready to fight me, Moldof son of . . .' he shrugged, '. . . nobody.'

This was well said and Moldof didn't much care for it. He rolled his great shoulders and hefted one of the spears in his left hand.

'Careful now!' Bram told his companions, gesturing that they should step away from Sigurd and Olaf. 'If he throws a spear anything like he rows, he's likely to skewer one of us by mistake.'

There was more laughing at this but Sigurd cut it short. 'You have come here to die then, Moldof?' he asked, though there was more than enough statement in it. 'For even in your two-armed days you would be killed here in the time it takes a crow to flap its wings twice.' He forced a smile. 'Are you so worthless to that oath-breaker that he would not care if you threw yourself on my sword here today?'

'I am no longer the king's prow man,' Moldof said.

'That is hardly surprising, you fucking lump,' Bram said, eyeballing Moldof, wanting nothing more than to fight him there and then. 'You are not useful enough now to empty his piss bucket.'

Moldof regarded Bram and there was no fear in his eyes for all his missing arm. Sigurd noted this well. He had seen this man pierce his father's shield with a one-handed spear thrust. He had seen him throw his own shield and knock Finn Yngvarsson to the ground who was standing twenty feet away.

'Hagal Crow-Song tells me that skalds have saga tales about you, Moldof,' Sigurd said and the big man's eyes glinted at that. *The hook is in then*, Sigurd thought. 'I think now that I recall hearing one of them when I was a boy. Some story about you taking your axe to the mast of some karl's ship and felling it like an oak, dropping the sail on to your enemies so that all Gorm's hirðmen had to do was club them through the wool.'

Moldof almost smiled at the memory. 'I fought at the king's prow more times than you have years in you, Haraldarson,' he said.

'Then it is a shame that you will be remembered not as a champion and prow man but as a nithing who came to me to be slaughtered because you could not live with the shame of it.'

'He did not like that,' Olaf murmured in Sigurd's ear.

'The skalds will forget your name, Moldof,' Sigurd said, 'and into those tales that were once about you they will stick some other warrior's name. Perhaps in years to come it will be King Gorm's new champion who cut down that mast.'

Moldof shrugged. 'That is the way of it with skalds,' he said as though he cared nothing about it, though the eyes below that shaggy hat told Sigurd a different tale.

'You want me to melt the snow with his guts?'
Black Floki asked Sigurd, gesturing at Moldof with
his hand axe.

'Not yet, Floki,' Sigurd said and now Moldof
laughed, his breath pluming in the still, frigid air,
the sound deadened by the snow all around yet also
carrying across the sleeping sea.

'You?' Moldof asked, pointing his spear at Floki.
'The turd I laid this morning was bigger than you.'
Then his eyes were back on Sigurd. 'You have
gathered a strange crew, Haraldarson. Boys, old
men and even a woman, I see. They talk about her.'
He looked at Valgerd. 'But I did not believe it. And
yet here you are.' He hawked and spat a gobbet into
the snow, his eyes on Valgerd. 'They say you are a
valkyrie.'

'That is the way of it with skalds,' Valgerd said,
smiling.

'I have an offer for you, Moldof,' Sigurd said.

'It is not for you to offer me anything, boy,'
Moldof said. 'I am here to kill you, but find that you
are trying to talk me to death. I have a wife for that.'

This got a grin from Olaf.

'I will not raise my sword to you, Moldof,' Sigurd
said, 'but will keep it snugged in its scabbard and
so you will not have the honour . . . the pleasure
of fighting me.' He gestured at the warriors behind
him. 'Instead, my friends here will make a spear
ring around you where you stand and they will
each take a bit of your flesh but none will give you

a death wound. When the snow is red with your blood and you can no longer stand I will piss on you, then have my sister Runa roll you off the jetty.' He turned to Runa then so that she would become the subject of Moldof's gaze and he would see her fresh young face and know how few years she had on her back. 'You will have a drowning death, given to you by a girl, and instead of drinking mead with those of your line in the Allfather's hall you will linger in Rán's cold embrace.' He cocked his head but spoke then to Hagal at his left shoulder. 'Do you think you can work that into my saga tale, Crow-Song?'

'I am weaving it as I stand here, Sigurd,' Hagal replied.

'All good stories must have those bits which set folk laughing,' Svein said.

Sigurd let the blade of his words sink into Moldof then, almost pitying King Gorm's former champion. The man had come alone up to Osøyro to kill the king's enemy and prove himself a great warrior still, or perhaps more likely to earn a good death that would gain him a bench in Valhöll. Instead, and before he had even cast his spear, Moldof's ambition – likely the last thing he clung to in this life – had been pissed on with just a few words from Sigurd. A warrior like Moldof knew all too well that a man's reputation is the most valuable thing he leaves behind him in death. Now, after all his brave deeds in the sword-song, he would leave nothing of worth behind. Nothing but a sorry tale, the ring of it in his ears as he sank to the slime and weed of the fjord bed, dragged down by his brynja and silver arm rings and staining the sea with his blood.

'Now will you hear my offer?' Sigurd asked him. Moldof did not say yes, but he did not say no, either. 'Join me. Fight with me against the oath-breaker. Earn more fame and silver and die a warrior's death instead of being pecked at by the fish in a sea grave.' Sigurd smiled at the man then, which was not easy when that man was Moldof and, as such, a living memory of that day in the pine woods near Avaldsnes when Sigurd's life had been savagely overturned like a boat in a storm. 'I am Óðin-favoured. You have heard men say it. Perhaps you have even heard the oath-breaker say it?'

'You have been lucky,' Moldof said. 'But trying to hold on to luck is like trying to keep water in your fist.'

'And yet my luck has rubbed off on to you, Moldof,' Sigurd said, 'for you are alive and have received a generous offer from me when you could otherwise have been busy tripping over your own gut rope.'

'We don't want him, Sigurd,' Svein said.

'That ugly swine was killing men before you were born, lad,' Olaf growled at Svein.

'I will not make you swear an oath to me yet,' Sigurd said, 'for I will wait to see if you are still of any use without your sword arm. I have seen your rowing and am not so sure.'

Moldof put the butt of his spear into the snow on the jetty.

'I've seen it all now,' old Solmund said.

'Others will come for you, Haraldarson,' Moldof said.

Sigurd nodded. 'But not today. So let us go up to my hall and get some warmth into our bones.' He turned his back on the huge warrior and tramped towards the path which led up to shelter, a hearth and the iron pot of horse broth that hung above the flames. There was ale too, bought from the nearest village with some of the silver that Sigurd had dug up from its safe place amongst the pines on the island south of Røtinga.

'He's not coming, Sigurd,' Aslak hissed, having looked over his shoulder. Sigurd kept walking, his back to *Reinen* and the warrior beside her.

'He'll come, lad,' Olaf answered for him.

And Moldof did.

CHAPTER FOUR

THE DAYS PASSED BUT THE WINTER HELD ON AND THE SUN, when it could be seen, never rose properly into the sky but hung low, pallid and cold. Shadows lay long across the snow and the air bit still, eking in through the unseen cracks high up in the old hall's timbers to ruffle the hangings lining the staves behind the benches. It had lamp flames dancing, throwing their shadow monsters across the walls of dead oak and working their shape-shifting seiðr on the faces of the living.

The two hearths burnt day and night and Sigurd's crew were either huddled around them or else out hunting deer and squirrel or buying provisions from the folk who lived beyond the woods west of Hakon's hall. On the hillside overlooking the sea they had cut a swathe through the trees – which had been allowed to grow tall in Thengil Hakonarson's time – so that they would see ships when they came. They watched the land too where they could, in case their enemies tried to come unannounced, and the hall was so huge that they trained with sword, shield and spear beneath its ancient beams. Olaf reminded them that only a fool, and a soon-to-be-dead fool at that, thinks that he will still be fast and strong even though he has long sat on his arse by the fire.

Olaf himself trained with Moldof often, the giant working with his one arm until the sweat poured off him and he could hardly lift his spear. Sigurd sparred mostly with Floki, who was Týr-blessed with weapons, and those two seemed like reflections of each other, their wool-wrapped blades a blur in the flame-licked gloom.

The winter endured and they waited. And then one morning Runa threw open the great flame-singed door and ran up the hall's central aisle to where Sigurd and Olaf sat talking.

'They are here!' she said, bent double, drawing smoky air into her lungs.

'Who is here, sister?' Sigurd asked, though he had no need.

'The king,' Runa said. 'Or his men anyway.'

'How do you know it's Biflindi?' Olaf asked.

She scowled at him. 'I know the ship, Uncle,' she said and Olaf nodded, for Runa had stood with Sigurd on the cliffs that day of the ship fight in the Karmsund Strait, when King Gorm had revealed his treachery by not coming to their father's aid against Jarl Randver.

'How many ships?' Moldof asked before Sigurd could.

'Just one,' Runa said.

'Then he has not come to fight you, Haraldarson,' Moldof said, 'or he would have brought three crews at least.' A grin spread in that huge, unkempt beard of his. 'You are Óðin-touched, Sigurd. And the king loses sleep over it.'

The rest had gathered up the thread of it and were arming themselves, shrugging into brynjur, tightening belts, huffing on to helmets and scrubbing them to a shine with their tunic sleeves or the legs of their breeks.

'Hey, Sigurd, maybe King Gorm wants to join your crew too,' Bram called, tying a leather thong around a long braid of hair.

'I would not have him in the bilge with a bailing bucket,' Sigurd said, making sure that he looked like a war god in his own gear. Over his brynja and helmet he wore the great wolf's pelt, the beast's lower jaw fixed on the helmet's spike, its teeth promising death to his enemies. He strapped the greaves on to his shins over the fur-lined boots and hitched his cloak over the pommel of the sword at his left hip. There was a scramasax sheathed above his groin and a hand axe tucked into his belt. Then he took up his spear and strode from the great hall and his hirðmen went with him.

'Sigurd, wait a moment.' The voice was dry and old and he turned back to look at the witch who was in her dark corner of the hall where she could spend days unnoticed by anyone.

'What do you have to say to me, seiðr-wife?' Sigurd asked, gesturing at the others to go on ahead. 'Be quick about it.'

'I have a riddle for you.'

'Now is not the time for riddles, old woman,' Sigurd said, yet he did not walk away.

'Who are the two who ride to the ting?' she asked him anyway. 'Three eyes have they together, ten feet, and one tail: and thus they travel through the lands.'

Sigurd could not help but smile. 'Óðin and Sleipnir his eight-legged steed, of course,' he said, because that was one of the first riddles every child learnt from their elders. 'You will have to do better than that,' he dared.

'Óðin is the Wild Huntsman,' the witch said with a smile, a hand raised as if pointing at the god's flying, fleeting charge through the sky upon the snorting beast's back, 'and his passing raises such a rush and roar of the wind as will waft away the souls of the dead. And with it Haraldarson too,' she said, now pointing a finger at Sigurd.

He blamed the shiver which ran up his spine on the cold air that was a shock to his body standing there half in the hall and half out of it.

'Back to your sleep, witch, and next time set a riddle that I have not heard a hundred times before,' he said, ignoring the rest of what she had said, and with that he turned his back on her and walked out into the day.

'The wild hunt! The raging host!' the witch called after him. 'You cannot escape it, Haraldarson. You cannot escape the wings of the storm!' She laughed then and the sound of it was like claws in Sigurd's back as he tramped through the snow, walking in the prints which the others had made.

The king's ship did not come up to the jetty. Instead she lowered her sail and her crew took up the oars, rowing her to within a good arrow-shot from the shore. Her skipper dropped the anchor stone and two men climbed into a tender tethered off the stern.

'It seems they do not trust us with their ship,' Bjarni said.

'Be fools if they did,' Solmund said.

Sigurd waited on the snow-covered jetty where they had met Moldof those weeks before. One man was rowing the tender while the other sat stiff-backed and proud, though even at a distance Sigurd could tell that it was not King Gorm. This was a much younger man, whose loose golden hair was probably getting caught in the rings of his brynja, though he looked vain enough not to care.

'You were right, Moldof, the oath-breaker has a message for me,' Sigurd said.

'The pretty one is called Freystein,' Moldof said, jutting his chin towards the man sitting facing the shore while the other rowed. 'Thinks he's good with a sword.'

'Is he?' Sigurd asked, but the curl of Moldof's lip was answer enough.

They watched the men climb up on to the planks and Sigurd left them standing there huffing into cold hands and striking their upper arms for warmth. The one who had rowed had a nestbaggin slung over his shoulder and eyes that jumped around like fleas on a fur.

'Who are you?' Sigurd asked eventually. He aimed the question at the young warrior with hair as golden as his own, wanting to hear this Freystein introduce himself. The man nodded respectfully and came forward, until Olaf growled at him that if he took another step he would be dead.

The man stopped.

'I am Freystein who men call Quick-Sword,' he said, as though it was a name which ought to impress.

'Did your woman give you that name?' Olaf asked and the others chuckled at that.

'Why don't you find out?' Freystein said to Olaf, which showed just how vain he was, for he could have had the quickest sword in the world but he would still be a dead man if Sigurd gave the word.

'Let us first hear what the oath-breaker has sent his dog to bark at us,' Olaf replied, a smile bending his lips.

Freystein nodded and looked at Sigurd. 'Sigurd Haraldarson?' he said, wanting it confirmed. Sigurd dipped his head and with it the wolf's head impaled on his helmet.

Freystein regarded him for a long moment. 'My lord is willing to bury the issue of your attacking Jarl Randver and killing him. Even though you surely knew that by making war on the jarl you were making war on the king.' He looked beyond Sigurd and must have seen Moldof then for his brows arched and there was a glint of teeth in his fair beard, though he said nothing about it.

'The oath-breaker betrayed my father,' Sigurd said. 'King Gorm and the worm Randver between them killed my brothers and my mother and many of our kinsfolk. They plotted their treachery well, buying off jarls far and wide to ensure there would be nothing to take the shine off their new alliance.' He threw both arms out as if to accept a great silver hoard which he had been offered. 'But now he is willing to overlook my killing of the worm?' He smiled. 'How generous of him.'

Freystein nodded, running a hand through his long golden hair. 'As I said, he'll bury it.'

'But I don't want the thing buried for I have not finished with it yet,' Sigurd said. 'Your king and Jarl Randver wove their own wyrds.' Freystein frowned, not liking what he was hearing. 'Randver has paid the price,' Sigurd said. 'The sheep's dropping who sits on the high seat at Avaldsnes who you call king will pay next.'

Freystein held up a finger. 'You have not heard the rest of it, Haraldarson,' he said. 'King Gorm is not only willing to be merciful. He would be generous

75

too, even to you. He strives to build peace these days, at least with those within five days' sailing of Avaldsnes, and he would have peace between you and him.'

'Because he knows I am Óðin-favoured,' Sigurd said.

'Because war is expensive,' Freystein countered, as though he were giving away information he should not be, though Sigurd knew he was merely changing tack to steer off the whole god-favoured business. 'If you will swear an oath to my king he will give you lands and silver. He will even give you another ship so that you can go raiding properly in the spring.'

'Do I look like I have the crew for two ships, Freystein?' Sigurd asked.

'The king will lend you men and arms. The ship will be yours to keep. You will raid the Danes and keep two thirds of the plunder. The rest you will give to Biflindi.'

'Would he make me jarl in Hinderå and give me Randver's high seat?' Sigurd asked him.

'Aye, it's not as if the worm has any use for it now,' Olaf rumbled.

Freystein shook his head. 'King Gorm cannot give you what is not his to give. Randver's son Hrani sits in his father's seat now. He has already sent silver to the king and the king will support his claim.' Sigurd was about to speak but Freystein raised a hand. 'You will keep this hall if you want it,' he said, looking up the hillside to the tree line which hid Jarl Hakon's hall. 'I have heard it is twice the size of the king's.' He shrugged. 'Or perhaps you may build another where your father's was at Skudeneshavn. A hall even greater than Eik-hjálmr was.'

'I could,' Sigurd agreed. 'But I would rather kill your king.'

Freystein took that in good part, smiling broadly though his companion did not seem so comfortable. There was a man who looked as if he would rather jump into the tender and row back to his ship faster than a mackerel could swim it.

'Come now, Sigurd,' Freystein said, 'this is not an opportunity to turn your back on. Not if you want to live as long as your father did.' He reached an arm out to his companion who nodded and took the nestbaggin from his shoulder. He gave it to Freystein who loosened the draw string and plunged a hand inside. When he pulled it out again there was a murmur from those around Sigurd.

Sigurd himself felt as if Thór had swung the hammer Mjöllnir into his chest.

'Óðin's arse,' Olaf growled.

'That is a sight to rouse the blood,' Svein said.

Freystein held up a great neck ring of twisted silver thicker than a man's thumb and glinting like a fish's scales. The last time its lustre had winked in Sigurd's eyes had been in the wet woods near Avaldsnes when it had been round his father's neck. Harald had fought like a champion from some saga tale that day, but in the end he had been cut down and someone, perhaps King Gorm himself, must have pulled that silver torc from the jarl's corpse. And now here it was again, within Sigurd's reach, whispering to him to take it back for the sake of his father and his brothers, for his mother and even for Runa who stood wrapped in furs on the rocks nearby.

'My king sends this, your father's torc, as a gift and a sign of his respect.'

'I would like to see that round your neck, Sigurd,' Svein said.

'Aye, it's a foul thing to see it in this nithing's hand,' Olaf said, and far from seeming offended by this Freystein held the torc out, though it was clear that if Sigurd wanted it he would have to go and get it.

'Do you think I should take it, Uncle?' Sigurd asked.

'I think it's yours, Sigurd,' he said. Then he edged closer, leaning in to Sigurd's right ear. 'I think men like to see silver at the neck of the man they've sworn oaths to.' Sigurd recognized the truth in this. Such a torc around a man's neck could draw new men too, like cold hands to the hearth, because a man who owns silver is one who can also give it.

'What do the gods tell you?' Sigurd called to Asgot.

His stick-thin body wrapped tightly in skins and grey furs, the godi looked like one of the silver birch trees amongst which he stood. 'They watch,' Asgot said, giving no more answer than that.

Sigurd nodded. He considered asking the seiðr-witch if she had foreseen this meeting with King Gorm's man. Did she already know what the outcome would be? Would he lay his hands on his father's neck ring and shine its lustre upon his own reputation?

He looked over his shoulder at the witch and she grinned inside her catskin hood.

'Are you a fighting man, Freystein?' he asked. 'Or just the king's tongue thrall, earning your meat and mead with words while other men pay in sweat and blood?'

This ruffled the preening cock's feathers and his hand fell to his sword's hilt. 'I am a hirðman,' he said, clearly thinking this was answer enough. And it was too. For all that King Gorm made his silver from taxes these days more than from raiding, this Freystein would not have got the two silver rings on his arms without at least once or twice staining his shoes with the slaughter's dew.

'Good.' Sigurd nodded. 'Then you will know that now is the time to pull your sword from its scabbard.'

Freystein flicked his loose golden hair back over his shoulders. 'I am my king's hearthman,' he said, 'but today I am here to talk, Haraldarson, not fight.' He looked suddenly nervous and well he might.

'Unless your words can deflect steel and iron, unless your tongue can slice flesh and bone, you would be better off drawing your sword, Freystein,' Sigurd said.

'Sigurd?' Olaf said, but Sigurd was already walking towards Freystein and pulling his own sword, Troll-Tickler, from its scabbard as he went.

'Hold, man!' Freystein blurted, even as his sword hissed into the bleak, grey day.

'No more talking, kingsman,' Sigurd said and his first swing would have cleaved Freystein's head in half had the man not got his own blade in the way. Yet he staggered back under the blow, his feet slipping on the brittle snow and ice sheathing the jetty's planks. He glanced back to his ship anchored out there in the bay, but those aboard her could not help him now. His companion stepped back, shaking his head and throwing up his arms to show that he wanted no part of it. Another step would put him in the sea.

Freystein parried again and this time swung his sword, but there was not enough muscle behind it and Troll-Tickler turned it aside easily.

'This is dishonourable, Sigurd! The king will spit fury if you kill me!' Freystein managed, eyes bulging. His face, which had no doubt brought women to his bed, was fear-warped and ugly now.

'The king can spit lightning and fart thunder for all I care,' Sigurd said. 'That slithering prick has no right to offer me what is already mine. I will take these things back when I choose.' With that he strode forward again and swung Troll-Tickler high, but as Freystein brought his own sword up to block, Sigurd twisted, stepping back on to his left foot, and brought Troll-Tickler down across his own body before scything it up into Freystein's belly above his right hip. The blade tore up through the rings of the man's brynja and he screeched with the shock of it as a dozen broken rings fell on to the jetty.

Sigurd hauled the blade free and took a step back. Freystein stood there still as a rock, as though waiting to see if he had been dealt a death wound, for there was not yet blood in the torn flesh.

'Sometimes happens like that on a cold day,' Bram rumbled from somewhere behind as Sigurd walked up to Freystein and took hold of his shoulder, turning the stunned man around so that he faced out to sea. So that the men in King Gorm's ship had eyes full of it. Then, gripping Freystein's left shoulder he put Troll-Tickler's point against the small of the man's back and forced the blade in, grimacing as it broke through mail and wool, leather, linen, skin and flesh. The steel scraped off bone, held for a heartbeat, then broke through the last resistance and erupted from Freystein's belly, and Sigurd held him close, his mouth against the man's ear so that to those on Biflindi's ship it must look as if Freystein was being savaged by a wolf. The king's man was mewing.

'This is the answer I give to your king,' Sigurd roared across the water, as Freystein's high-pitched cry ended in a soft sigh and his legs gave way so that he fell to his knees. Sigurd hauled his blade free and stood looking at the ship in the bay, ignoring Gorm's other man who was pissing down his own leg, the liquid steaming in the cold air.

To his credit Freystein still gripped his sword. He had dropped the jarl torc, though, and Sigurd bent to pick it out of the snow. He opened the ring wider and put it around Freystein's neck as the man knelt, coming to terms with his own death. But before Sigurd had finished squeezing the two bulging ends together, Freystein pitched forward into the snow, his golden hair splayed across the icy crust.

'That is that then,' Olaf said.

They stood there for a moment. Just looking. 'Svein, help this piss-soaked huglausi get Freystein into the boat,' Olaf said, glaring at Freystein's companion, who was corpse-pale himself and trembling like an old dog.

'Take this worthless pile of pig shit back to your king,' Sigurd said. 'Tell the oath-breaker that Sigurd Haraldarson says there will be no peace between us. Tell the maggot-arsed nithing to start digging his own burial mound for he will need it soon enough.' The man nodded, as Svein and Bram took hold of Freystein and lifted him, and still there was no blood to be seen, not a drop staining the snow. 'And leave the torc where it is,' Sigurd warned the Avaldsnes man. 'Tell your king that he may keep my father's torc a little longer yet. Until such time as I decide to take it back.' He bored his eyes into the man. 'But I *will* have it back.'

'I will tell him . . . lord,' the man said, hoping his flattery would be well received.

Sigurd looked over at Runa. Her eyes betrayed no fear or horror at what they had just seen. But her jaw was tight and her cold-reddened hands were knots at her sides and Sigurd knew that his killing of Freystein must have shocked her. He wanted to tell her that all would be well, that he knew what he was doing. But just as no blood had come to Freystein's torn flesh, so no reassuring words would come to Sigurd's lips. In truth he did not know what he was doing, only that he had followed where instinct led. That would do for now.

Of the others on that shoreline watching Gorm's man clamber into his boat beside the bloodless corpse, most had granite-hard faces and cold eyes. They knew now, if they had not already known, that there could be no peace, and that they were up to their knees in this blood feud until the end. Valgerd and Aslak, Crow-Song and old Solmund and the others. They would sail into this storm together.

Asgot caught Sigurd's eye and gave a slight nod. Sigurd had once again proved himself worthy of the Allfather's one-eyed gaze. Black Floki was grinning like a wolf. Olaf was frowning, though even he would not say that Sigurd had been wrong to decline the king's offer, so Sigurd bent and picked up a handful of snow, running it along his blade to remove any bit of Freystein that might be caught on it, and watching the king's men out there in the bay who were yelling curses, threats and insults at him. Bjarni and Bram hurled their own insults back, calling the Avaldsnes men cowards and inviting them to come ashore and fight. But the yard was already being hauled up the mast and the oars were clunking into their ports and there would be no more fighting today. Freystein's piss-wet friend rowed the little boat back to his ship and Sigurd watched him go.

And in Valhöll the roof beams shook with the gods' laughter.

'He said what?' Gorm knew he was yelling. He knew his thralls were scuttling away like crabs off a rock, suddenly seeking outside jobs because freezing was preferable to being near his blazing rage. 'The insolent, swaggering shit! The strutting, cocksure, lording puddle of rancid pus!'

Groa flinched as a gobbet of Gorm's spittle struck his lip.

'I'll rip his throat out!' No. A better idea. 'I'll cut the runt. I'll open him up and pull out his gut rope. Feed it to my pigs and make him watch as they gobble it up.' Gorm backhanded a cup off the table and it bounced in the rushes by the hearth. His hound was whining, sad to see its master agitated. Gorm closed his eyes and took a breath. 'Who does that haughty son of a nobody jarl think he is?'

'He's an animal, lord,' Groa said, putting a hand to his lip. 'They all are.'

In that deep, slow breath Gorm caught the tang of stale piss. It was coming from Groa. He felt his lip curl at the thought that the man might have pissed himself with fear in front of Haraldarson and his crew. *Mouse piss in the floor rushes*, he told himself, preferring that explanation.

'I should have cut him down there and then, lord,' Groa said. 'I nearly did.' He put a hand to the hilt of the sword at his left hip. 'But then we would never have brought Freystein's body home.' Groa looked around, peering through the smoke, relieved that no one who had been on the ship watching Freystein die was in the hall to hear the lies spilling like goat turds from his mouth.

Gorm looked down at Freystein's body. At Jarl Harald's torc which was still round his blue-white neck. Even that was a big thing. All that silver. Harald had been too self-important. Doubtless that's where his runt got it from.

'He didn't bleed?' the king asked. You could not miss Freystein's death wound, but his breeks, tunic and mail were clean.

'It was cold,' Groa said with a shrug.

'Arse,' Gorm muttered, wishing Freystein were alive to know how disappointed his king was with him. He looked back to Groa. *What did you do then*, he thought, glaring at Groa, disgusted by the sight of him. *What did you do when Haraldarson was opening*

Freystein up from hip to chest? When he was putting that rope of twisted silver round Freystein's neck? Other than piss yourself.

'He said there will be no peace between you, lord. That you should dig your burial mound,' Groa said, filling the silence, using words like a shield to deflect the king's obvious revulsion.

'My burial mound?' The rage came again and Gorm turned to look at the hearth flames, drawing the sweet birch smoke deep into his lungs. 'Hmm . . .' He swallowed another clutch of curses and listened to the fuel cracking and popping. Outside, Kadlin was yelling at a thrall. As if getting the stain out of a kyrtill hem was important.

'And Moldof?' Gorm said. He watched the flames still. He did not want to see Groa's annoying face. He could almost hear the man squirming.

'He was there, lord,' Groa said.

'I know he was there,' Gorm said. 'He didn't give you a sign of any sort?'

'A sign, lord?'

Gorm turned round and fixed the man with his eyes. *This spineless toad sits at my table*, he thought. 'Moldof went up to Osøyro to put a sword in Haraldarson. Yet there he was on that jetty, standing with those treacherous dogs watching Haraldarson kill my hearthman. Listening to Haraldarson pile insults upon me.' This was perhaps the worst part of all. Worse than Freystein being split open anyway. Quick-Sword. Ha! Not quick enough. 'Perhaps

Moldof gave you some secret sign that he still intends to do what he promised.'

'I saw no sign, lord,' Groa said. 'He watched Freystein die and did nothing. Together we might have killed a handful of them.' His hand went towards his sword grip again then he thought better of it and scratched his side instead. 'Maybe Moldof has joined them because he cannot face the shame of what he is nowadays.'

The smell of piss was stronger now. The heat from the hearth getting into the weave of Groa's breeks.

'Get this out of my sight,' Gorm said, waving a hand at the bloodless corpse in the rushes. 'But give me that first.' By 'that' he meant the torc, which Groa bent and prised off Freystein's neck, no doubt relieved that Quick-Sword's eyes were closed, and gave to his king.

I offer this to the man and he turns it down? Well, he will regret that.

'Fetch Fionn,' he told Groa.

'Fionn? That little pale man who looks like a stoat?'

'Bring him to me.'

'Is he still here? If so I don't know where,' Groa said. 'But I'll find him,' he added with a curt nod, having seen the rage flare in Gorm's eyes again.

'You will,' Gorm said. Then he turned back to the hearth to watch the flames dance.

*

'So you've changed your mind, lord,' the man said.

Gorm grunted. He had not changed his mind. He had not made up his mind where this outlander was concerned. He had just sent for the man and there was nothing more to it than that. Yet.

'I knew you would. Just a matter of waiting.' The man wasn't smug about it, simply matter of fact.

Gorm winced as his stomach griped. He had woken that morning just in time to get to the latrine pit but his bowels were full of dark, stinking water again. He could feel it churning. 'Spiced ale?' he said.

'Keeps the cold out,' the man said in his strange accent.

Gorm gestured to a thrall who was stirring the pot hanging over the hearth. The thrall took two cups and dipped them into the steaming juniper ale.

Groa was right, Fionn did look like a stoat. Or a pine marten perhaps. And he was as pale as poor Freystein too, ill-looking really, all sinew and vein and sunken eyes like piss holes in snow. To look at him Gorm did not know why he had sent for the man. Certainly Fionn did not look much of a warrior, even less so in the company of Hreidar and Alfgeir and his other hirðmen. Third or fourth rank in the shieldwall perhaps.

But then again . . .

There *was* something about him. Something in those dark eyes: to look at them was like peering into the fjord on a dark winter's day and hoping to see the fish on the bottom taking your hook. They showed nothing of what lay beneath, those eyes, and maybe that was a common trait in men from Alba in the west. Who could say?

'What makes you think you can do it?' Gorm asked. 'He has friends. Not many of course. But good fighters.'

'You want them all dead? Or just this Sigurd Haraldarson?'

'Just him. For now.'

Fionn nodded. 'Then I can do it.'

'Others have tried. Others have failed. Most are dead,' Gorm said as the thrall gave them their cups and slipped away like a wraith.

'I'll kill him,' Fionn said.

Gorm lifted the cup to his nose and breathed in the fragrant brew. Fionn was confident. He'd give him that. But maybe he was deluded. Maybe he was mad without seeming it.

Fionn's brow lifted a touch. 'If you have a rotten tooth that is hurting, you do not ask the smith to knock it out with his hammer. You use—' He mimed the action in the absence of the Norse word.

'Pliers,' Gorm said, annoyed with himself for playing the game.

Fionn nodded. 'You pull it out like a bent nail.'

Gorm knew full well what the man meant by this but gave him more frown anyway.

'Sigurd Haraldarson will be expecting the hammer. Not the pliers,' Fionn said, blowing into the steaming cup before slurping at the ale.

'Still, you must reckon yourself a great fighter, Fionn of Alba,' Gorm said, trying to draw the man into a boast or two. Anything to suggest he was a warrior after all.

Fionn shrugged. 'I fight when I need to. But you don't need to fight to kill.'

Was the man talking about poison? Hemlock in Haraldarson's ale? Gorm didn't think so. *He loves his blades, this little man.* A good-looking sword at his hip. Not a big cleaver – he didn't have the muscle for it – but a well-made weapon if the hilt was anything to go by with its lobed pommel and grip inlaid with fine silver wire. A bone-handled scramasax hanging above his groin and another long knife scabbarded at his right hip. No brynja that Gorm had seen. Nor a helmet. Blades in the dark then. Or in the back, rather than a toe-to-toe fight. No honour in that. Not that Gorm cared where Harald's son was concerned. That golden puffed-up boy did not deserve a good death.

'They say you are from Alba in the west,' Gorm said. Fionn nodded. 'Why are you not in Alba now?'

'A man paid me to kill his king,' Fionn said.

This was a brave thing to admit, Gorm thought.

'And his king's wife too,' Fionn went on. 'She being with child.' His lip curled. 'Then the man decided he wanted his silver back and tried to have me killed.' He held the king's eye. 'That did not go well for him.'

'And yet you had to flee the land of your birth? You wash up here on my shore,' Gorm said.

'It became complicated,' Fionn said with a shrug.

Gorm did not doubt it. 'If you do it—' he began.

'*When* I do it, lord king,' Fionn interrupted. The stoaty little shit.

'How much will it cost me?' Gorm asked, not that he cared. He drank, feeling the ale course down his throat to bloom hot in his empty belly. He had not eaten yet today with his guts being sour. Gods, what a feast he would give when Harald's runt was dead. When that thorn was out of his flesh.

'Looking at that torc at your neck,' Fionn said, 'I think I will have the same weight in silver.'

Gorm touched the twisted rope of gold at his neck. Thick as his forefinger, it was the kind of neck ring which skalds put in their songs of the ancient heroes, its dragon-head terminals facing each other across the hollow between his collar bones.

'That is a lot of silver,' Gorm said.

'You will give me silver for my journey, and food. I will keep Haraldarson's sword and any silver I find on him. Same goes for any of the others if it turns out I have to kill them too.'

Gorm kept his face smooth as a sleeping sea. He would have given this stranger *Storm-Bison*, his favourite ship, in return for Haraldarson's head on a spear. He nodded at the cup in Fionn's hand. 'I'll fill that with hacksilver if you open Moldof's belly too,' he said. 'If it turns out that he is now Haraldarson's man.'

91

Fionn shook his head. 'I would be doing that one-armed fool a favour and will kill him for nothing,' he said.

Gorm studied him. What did he have to lose by sending him after Haraldarson? Nothing so long as he kept it to himself, in case the man made a mess of it and it reflected badly on him.

'Tell no one,' he said, tilting his cup at the Alba man. 'As far as anyone else is concerned, you have moved on.'

Fionn nodded. 'I do not hunger to live for ever in some fireside saga,' he said. 'Nor do I need Haraldarson's friends coming after me. No one will know it was me.'

'Good,' Gorm said, frowning as his guts bubbled and he felt the pressure of their foul contents as a dull ache; for a terrifying moment he feared he might shit himself in front of this man. 'Now leave me,' he said. 'And do not return here until it is done.'

Fionn nodded again, downing the rest of his ale in one go before putting the empty cup on the end of the long table and preparing to leave.

'Wait,' Gorm said and Fionn turned back to face him. 'What happened to this king in Alba? You killed him?'

'Yes,' Fionn said.

'And his wife whose belly was full of child?'

'Her too,' the man said.

Gorm nodded. Fionn turned and walked away and Gorm watched him go, feeling the rush of cold air sweep into the hall as the Alba man opened the door and went out into the day.

Gorm grunted at his clenching guts, finished his ale, then hurried off to the latrine pit, imagining the relief he would feel when Harald's son was no longer in the world.

'We have the sea to ourselves and can there be a better feeling than that?' Solmund asked, gripping the loom of the tiller like the hand of a lover. His eyes, like Sigurd's own, were watery in the frigid air and his nose was red as a rowan berry. 'This is better than being stoppered up in Burner's old hall like stale beer in a flask, hey!' A drop quivered at the end of the helmsman's nose and his bones must have been as cold as icicles for he did not have much flesh over them these days, but rarely had Sigurd seen him so happy.

'It's colder than Hel's arse cheeks,' Olaf said, clapping his hands as he stepped up to join them on the steering platform and watched the ragged coast slip by *Reinen*'s steerboard side. 'There's a reason crews don't go raiding in winter. Why we trade the sea-road for the roaring hearth.'

'Now who is the skald?' Hagal Crow-Song said through a grin.

'It doesn't take much to be a better skald than you, Crow-Song,' Olaf replied, and Sigurd felt the cold air on his own teeth as Hagal muttered curses into his beard.

In truth Olaf too was happy to be at sea again, even in this biting cold and with barely a fart's worth of wind playing on *Reinen*'s sail to push them south into the Bjørnafjord. It was better than waiting for your enemies to turn up, like a shipwrecked man treading water before inevitably sinking to the sea bed, as Solmund himself had put it.

'The king will come. Your insult will give him no choice,' Moldof had said. 'And he will come with four or five crews to make sure he stamps you out properly. He'll bring enough spears to beat you even were Týr and Óðin themselves stood in your shieldwall.'

Sigurd had known this was the truth, that his refusal of Biflindi's offer and his killing of the messenger Freystein would be to the king's reputation as salt water is to a sword or brynja: it would eat away at it like iron rot. Gorm had no choice now but to kill Sigurd and have the world see him do it. Which was why they had hauled the snow-crusted skins from *Reinen*'s thwarts, thumbed new tarred horsehair between some of the strakes, bailed out the seep water from the bilge, knocked open those oarhole covers which had frozen stuck and hefted their sea chests aboard. They had piled spears in the bow and stern, shields midships, water barrels in the small open hold, along with dry kindling, spare cloaks, tools, ropes and rivets, their brynjur and as much smoked meat and fish as they could get their hands on. But most of this space was taken up by bales of bear furs, wolf, fox and squirrel pelts, sheep skins, otter skins and even reindeer hides, which Thengil Hakonarson had hoarded up in the rafters of his hall. It had taken them half a day to bring all the bales down, and from the look of the bird shit and old nest material on the top bales, and the mice nests on the bottom furs, they must have been up there for years. And yet most of them were in fine condition and the whole lot was worth a good deal of silver.

'Seems that fat toad Thengil was a raider in his way,' Olaf had said, when the others started to carry the bales down to the jetty, Svein making a show of taking one under each arm. 'If you had four legs and a hairy back you were as good as dead.'

'Then it is just as well Bram was not born in these parts,' Bjarni said, nodding at Bram who was bynamed Bear because he was all beard and bluster and shared a good many similarities with that animal.

'Ha!' Bram said, patting the top fur of the bale he was about to heft. 'And I was just about to ask you and your brother if either of you recognize this pelt, for the last time I saw it it was between your mother's legs.'

The brothers appreciated the insult and grinned at one another as they lifted their own bales and followed Bram out of the dark smoky hall.

'Thengil must have traded with the Sámi for the reindeer hides,' Sigurd said.

'Unless they were left over from his father's time,' Olaf suggested. 'Old Hakon Burner used to collect tribute far and wide. Wouldn't surprise me if he raided in the wastelands to the east just for the damned mischief in it.'

However they had got there, those pelts would have been better used lining the planks of Burner's old hall which was as big as Bilskírnir, Thór's own dwelling place, and draughty as Svein's backside, as Crow-Song had put it. Now the bales accounted for almost all of Sigurd's wealth. He could not pay his hirðmen with skins, but he could trade those skins for food or silver and seeing as he was crew-light, those bales were more than worth the space they took up aboard *Reinen*.

'So where will we go?' Olaf had asked that night after they had watched King Gorm's man row the torc-wearing corpse back to the waiting ship, and that ship had turned its stern post on them and sailed away.

'South,' Sigurd said, 'then east.' He shrugged.

'Aye, so long as we sail beyond Biflindi's reach – Hrani Randversson's reach too come to that – it doesn't matter where we go.' Olaf had fixed those sea-grey eyes on Sigurd's own then and his next words were heavy things, like loom weights in Sigurd's ears. 'But you will need to give them silver,' he said.

'I know my duties, Uncle,' Sigurd had replied, prickling under the older man's gaze, resentful of being reminded of his responsibilities. He had not forgotten that those warriors freezing in *Reinen*'s thwarts, all but for Moldof, had sworn an oath to him, their lips touching the pommel of his sword, their words spoken over the blade. They would fight for him, had sworn sword and shield, flesh and bone, to not flee one step from the battle as long as the sun shines and the world endures, henceforth and for evermore. But an oath was weighed in the scales of honour and must be found to balance or else it was nothing more than chaff in the wind. To balance those scales Sigurd must give them meat, shelter and silver.

There was not much in the way of shelter now, though, out there aboard *Reinen*.

'Still, I am no jarl,' Sigurd said. 'And they are not like any húskarlar I have seen. We are all of us outlaws now.' He gestured at the ship beneath them and the fjord around them. 'Whoever wants more than this is free to jump overboard. I will not stop them.'

Olaf raised an eyebrow at Solmund and Sigurd turned his back on them both to look out across the fjord, which was rippled and iron grey and cold as death.

CHAPTER FIVE

THEY HAD ALL KNOWN THAT THEY WOULD GO SOUTH BECAUSE where else was there to go? They could have sailed north up to Kaupangen where Solmund said there was a small settlement from which some supplies might be got. But beyond that there was likely nothing but jagged, empty coast and unless you wanted to raid for the wind-dried cod and smoked herring that the folk up there lived on, there was no reason to go there.

'Fish is not the sort of silver we need,' Svein had said when old Solmund had talked of his exploits in the north. Besides which, it was not the time of year to be going north. It was one thing to be at sea when most sensible men were snugged up by their hearths and jarls and kings had hauled their dragon ships from the water and tucked them up in their nausts; it was altogether another to venture into the freezing unknown, especially crew-light in a ship which had not been given the love and attention it would have had if pulled aground over winter. For that was the time to re-clink the ship, replace old strakes, sew sail rents and give the woollen cloth a new coating of pine resin and sheep's fat to help it hold the wind better. The hull could be scraped of slime and of the mussels that cluster where the keel meets the belly. New horsehair string could be pushed into any cracks and the whole ship, from thwarts to mast, to the rigging and oars, could be coated in sticky resin to shield it from rain and salt water. But there had been little opportunity to treat *Reinen* so kindly and now they would make do with things as they were. And at least they were not going north.

They had all known that they would go south, and no one doubted the dangers in that, so none was surprised when, on the third day out of Osøyro, they saw another ship ploughing its furrow through the wide sea.

'If the witch were here we could have asked her who they were,' Svein said, mainly to rankle Asgot who had not liked having a seiðr-wife around the place. But all he got from the godi was a sneer and he shrugged as if to suggest it was worth a try. The witch had left the previous dawn, trudging off into the brittle snow and being swallowed by the woods as though she had never been.

'Wolves are one thing, Sigurd Haraldarson, but boats are another,' she had said, the corners of her eyes creasing like well-used leather. 'I have done what the gods asked of me. At least where you are concerned. Perhaps we will meet again.'

But none of them, not even Sigurd whom she had come to warn, had been sorry to see the back of her and her cat skins.

'My cock has been hiding since the day she arrived,' Bjarni had said, but only when he was sure she was out of earshot, which was a full day after she had left.

'You worry for nothing, brother,' Bjorn had said, 'for even a seiðr-wife cannot put a spell on something she cannot see. It would be like trying to hit a louse with a spear-throw.'

The others had laughed at that and it was a good sound if a small one in Jarl Hakon's vast old hall.

'Bollocks but they really want us dead,' Olaf said now, for who else but King Gorm would have a ship out there in the rough water west of Karmøy in the heart of winter?

'Wanting it is not the same as having it,' Sigurd reminded him as they stood at the prow. Some of the others were shrugging into their brynjur and grabbing spears though the ship was still a good distance off, having come round a headland like a hawk swooping from a branch.

'Treat them like you would a dog turd in the street,' Sigurd called back to Solmund at the helm.

'We'll give them a wide berth if we can,' Solmund called back, 'but that would be easier if you would all get back to work instead of puffing up your damn chests and laying your cocks over the side.'

'You heard him! Back to the ropes!' Olaf yelled, and they swapped spear shafts for tarred lines again. It had been hard work all morning, tacking *Reinen* into the wind, Olaf shouting commands and setting the sail from the feel of the gusts on his cheeks. Solmund would drive the steerboard hard to one side until *Reinen* turned so far into the wind that the wind on the front of the sail halted her and then blew her backwards. With one corner of the sail released and lines freed at bow, midships and stern, Bram and Svein would haul on the ropes stretching to each end of the yard in order to draw the sail to the other side of the boat, catching the wind to move forward once again. When they got it right *Reinen* would lurch forward and fly like an arrow from a bow. But it was hard work and mostly silent work too, each crew member playing their part with Olaf's the only voice in their ears.

Despite Solmund's cautious optimism, Sigurd was not so sure they would get past the other ship before it came across their bows. Not against the wind. Not when all the other ship had to do was turn her bows towards the north and run with the wind.

He was still watching the other ship when Runa came to stand with him, clutching the sheer strake as *Reinen*'s sail snapped full of wind and she set off at the gallop on the new tack.

'Are you two friends now?' Sigurd asked, patting the rail beside his sister's hand. Runa had not spent much time at sea and was still getting used to the way *Reinen* flexed through the water like a fish. Like all good ships her hull had been built to ride the waves and the current, not to muscle through the sea like a drunk man through a crowded hall.

'We are on speaking terms,' Runa said, her gaze, like his, fixed on the other ship that looked to be making its turn now in order to come at them like a spear with the wind behind it. Out here in the open water that wind whipped white spume off the waves and *Reinen* was flexing through her length; Sigurd hoped that the rivets would not begin to work themselves free of the strakes. She was a fine ship, but she was not made to endure the open sea for long and he could feel her trying to agree terms with winds and currents which were arguing amongst themselves.

'How can you be sure they are our enemies?' Runa asked. Her golden hair had worked free of her fur hat and was streaming and fluttering in the gusts, and she had one hand at her throat clutching the Freyja amulet which brought her luck.

'Because we have no friends, sister,' Sigurd said, for there was not a jarl or wealthy karl anywhere who would side with him these days. The only allies he had in the world were in that belly of oak, heaving and hauling on ropes, driving *Reinen* on, beating against the wind. 'That is one of Biflindi's ships and its skipper has been waiting for us.'

Sailing down through the sheltered waters of the Karmsund Strait had not been an option. No ships could pass through the channel below Avaldsnes without paying the king for the privilege, and seeing as the king wanted Sigurd dead more than he wanted all the taxes in the world, it would have been impossible to slip through the net that way. So they had taken the sea-road west of Karmøy. There had been a chance that they would not meet any of King Gorm's crews out there. For even though the king was bound to set the trap, a sea fog or sheeting rain might conceal their passing. Or the king's skippers might prefer to keep their ships moored in some safe harbour than be patrolling amongst Rán's white-haired daughters with the wind freezing their cheeks and numbing their hands.

In the event, though, there had been no fog and no veil of rain to hide *Reinen*. The king's ships must have flown from Avaldsnes the moment he laid eyes on Freystein's torc-wearing corpse and knew there could be no peace with Sigurd.

'That's *Wave-Thunder*,' Moldof said, confirming it. 'I thought it earlier but wanted to be sure. Her skipper is called Bjalki. I know him.'

'Is he any good?' Sigurd asked.

'You're asking his opinion now?' Aslak said. 'It was not long ago that he showed up meaning to hew off your head, toss it in his little boat and row it back to the oath-breaker.'

'Winds change,' Sigurd said, glancing at Moldof, who with Valgerd was putting spare shields in the rack on *Reinen*'s larboard side to form a higher rampart against spears and arrows and to make it more difficult for the enemy to clamber aboard.

'Bjalki rarely eats at the king's table,' Moldof said. 'But he's ambitious. He'll be hungry for this chance.'

Sigurd nodded. How ambitious your enemy was was always a thing worth knowing.

'It's going to be close,' Olaf called.

'Close enough to smell the whoresons,' Bram said.

Asgot had a short axe in either hand, ready to cut the ropes of any grappling hooks that were thrown into the thwarts. The rest worked the ship.

'Be ready with your compliments!' Solmund bellowed from the tiller. 'We'll be cosy enough to share fleas and if you haven't pissed yet you'll have to wait.'

Wave-Thunder had got her bows round now and was coming fast with the wind in her sail. *Reinen* was on her westward tack, heading out into the open sea, and would have time for one, maybe two more turns before the enemy was upon them. Sigurd was torn. He could take his crew from their work and have them arm themselves properly, but this would stop *Reinen* dead in the water and make the fight unavoidable. A fight they could not win, judging by the spears, long axes and shield-bearing men crammed in the belly of the king's ship. Or he could have them work the sail and maybe they would edge past, but maybe they would be caught like a hare in the eagle's talons and then they would die quickly because they were too few and not ready for the fight.

'Go aft, Runa,' Sigurd said. 'Take a shield and stay near Solmund, but get down amongst the ribs.' The first arrows streaked from the enemy ship now, one of them clattering into *Reinen*'s thwarts but most falling short into the wave furrows.

Runa shook her head. 'I can fight. You know I can. Valgerd has taught me the ways to kill a man. It is not so hard as one might think.'

Sigurd did not doubt that his sister could fight. He had watched her and Valgerd training together and had been as surprised as he was impressed by Runa's resilience and determination. The inevitable cuts and bruises had, if anything, spurred her to greater efforts and she was a quick learner too.

'What did you expect? She's Harald and Grimhild's daughter,' Olaf had said one day, when he and Sigurd had sat by the hearth watching Runa, her teeth gritted, grunting with effort as she hammered Valgerd's shield with wild sword blows. 'Besides, she had to put up with you and your brothers growing up,' Olaf said, and Sigurd had smiled, though his mood had inevitably soured as he thought of his brothers Thorvard, Sigmund and

Sorli: all dead now, like their mother and father and so many others.

'I won't hide like a mouse in the floor rushes,' Runa said now.

Sigurd sighed. 'Fetch a shield *and* a spear. But keep your head down.'

He could see the enemy crew's leader now, a barrel-chested man who stood at the prow of his ship tying the helmet strap under his chin as he barked commands at his men. Beside him was a broad-shouldered warrior with a long axe who had the look of a prow man. He loomed beside the carved dragon head making sure that his enemies could see more of him than they could of anyone else aboard his ship. He was yelling something, insults probably, but whatever it was got lost in the wind.

'Sigurd?' Olaf called after a while, wanting the younger man to make the final decision about whether to stay at their stations or prepare for a fight.

They had completed another tack and were heading out to sea again, so that it seemed they must collide with the enemy, that *Wave-Thunder*'s bows would strike *Reinen* midships or aft. Then the king's men would hurl their hooks and haul the ships together hull to hull and when they were as close as lovers the killing would begin.

'Hold your positions!' Sigurd yelled, raising his shield to knock an arrow out of the air into the sea.

Olaf nodded, the order good enough for him.

Then the sea air was thick with the noise of their enemies' war cries and Sigurd's nose was full of their stench and a spear thunked into *Reinen*'s mast, where it quivered like a branch in the wind.

'Tell your king that I proclaim him an oath-breaker and a coward!' Sigurd yelled over the side. He was close enough to his enemies to see the blood-hunger in their eyes and the snarl of their teeth. He could see the Thór's hammers at their throats, the rings of the prow man's brynja beneath his furs and the patches of grey in the skipper Bjalki's beard. 'Gorm is a pile of vomit!' he bellowed. 'A spineless tax collector who has forgotten how to please the gods. He is a nithing!' And then Sigurd laughed, even as an arrow whipped past his head and another thunked into the free board where he stood, because the enemy prow had all but kissed *Reinen*'s stern post yet *Reinen* had slipped by just beyond reach. Bjalki was red-faced and yelling but Sigurd was laughing too hard to hear the words coming out of his mouth.

Then a grappling hook clumped into the thwarts, but before it could bite into a rib or snag on the sheer strake Asgot hacked through the rope and the frayed end slithered harmlessly away.

Those on the ropes cheered and yelled insults at the other crew, who bristled helplessly, their chance missed. The grin in old Solmund's beard was so wide its corners might have met at the nape of his neck, and Sigurd shared a look with Olaf that said more than words could. Gods but it had been close.

Her sail full of wind, the king's ship flew past, her skipper already yelling at his men to lower the sail so that he could turn her back into the wind and give chase.

'Now we will see what kind of a crew they are!' Solmund called, leaning to spit over the side in disgust. It wasn't long before they got their answer. Sigurd had made his way aft, slapping the grinning brothers Bjorn and Bjarni on their shoulders and declaring that even half a crew they were more than a match for any other. Now he stood at *Reinen*'s stern, watching Gorm's men run out their oars and begin to row after them.

'All muscle and no craft,' Solmund said, unimpressed because it seemed their enemy had no confidence in their own ability to tack into the wind.

'This skipper Bjalki has crammed his thwarts with fighting men and left no room to work the sail,' Sigurd said.

Solmund's lip curled. 'Either way they won't catch us now.'

And yet, after the time it takes to sharpen a knife, Sigurd and Olaf were exchanging concerned looks again. 'What the pig-swivers lack in sea craft they make up in brawn,' Olaf said, for with so many oars in the water *Wave-Thunder* was coming on at a frightening speed, so that it was not impossible that with *Reinen*'s long tacks their enemies might eventually catch them. It did not help that now and then Olaf would misjudge the wind, or one of the men would take too long to tie off a rope and *Reinen* would be blown backwards, losing much of the distance they had previously fought so hard for.

And they were getting tired now.

'They are like shit clinging to a sheep's arse,' Olaf growled as they came to the end of the landward tack and everyone prepared for the well-practised fury of movement that would bring the sail across and take *Reinen* back out to sea.

'Bjalki is trying to make a name for himself,' Crow-Song said, dragging an arm across his sweat-slick face.

'No storm-driver to swell his sail
He yet carves the wave with his prow.
His men lash the sea with their oars
But poor Bjalki cannot catch us now.'

There were smiles at that for it was rare to hear Hagal word-weaving these days, and they enjoyed it, even if no one admitted as much to Crow-Song.

They were off the coast of Åkra now, could see the smoke hanging in the wan sky above the village like unspun sheep's wool. It was a cold, dull, slate-grey day, yet most of them had taken off their furs and cloaks and worked in tunics and breeks, though they would begin to shiver between each setting of the sail.

'We should turn around and fight them, Sigurd,' Black Floki called, his crow-black braids hanging either side of his lean, glistening face as he and Svein heaved that great log, the bietas, across the beam of the ship.

'It would not be a fair fight for they will be too tired to lift their shields,' Svein said, wedging one end of the log into *Reinen*'s side ribs and threading a rope through a notch in the other end which now hung out over the windward edge of the boat. The giant's own braids danced like red ropes as he worked and Sigurd thought how much he looked like his father Styrbiorn these days. Styrbiorn who had slaughtered Jarl Harald's enemies with his long-hafted axe, until by some bad luck the axe head had caught on *Sea-Eagle*'s prow beast and some nithing had plunged his spear into the champion's belly. That had been Styrbiorn's death wound and Sigurd and Svein had watched him fall back into the thwarts like a felled oak.

'It would be worth turning round for a little fight just to have a taste of the wind on our side,' Bram said. 'Gods this is thirsty work.'

'So what are you thinking?' Olaf asked Sigurd, his eyes little more than slits, perhaps remembering the last time they had turned *Reinen* around to face the enemy. That enemy had been Jarl Randver of Hinderå, and having fled across the froth-crested sound Sigurd had felt Óðin's one-eyed glare on him like the heat from a forge. They had chosen to end that business one way or another and, turning *Reinen* and dropping the sail, they had waited for Randver and the slaughter that came with him.

'I have an idea, Uncle,' Sigurd said, watching a gull dive down to snatch something from the waves.

'So long as it does not involve losing half this half crew – unless you want Solmund hauling on ropes with his arms and steering us with his feet.'

But while having an enemy ship half up their arse was nothing to be happy about, Olaf knew that it was better to deal with that threat than risk running into another of Gorm's crews and having to fight two ships together.

'Well, lad?' he said, having given the command to move the sail across for the next turn. 'Let's hear it.'

They made a mess of two out of the next five tacks. On these failed attempts the wind blew them back and Solmund and Olaf waved their arms and yelled insults at those working the sail. Then they let the wind spill from the great woollen sail so that *Reinen* rocked in complaint, her mast swinging from side to side, before they made headway again.

Sigurd watched the ragged coast with its snow-sheathed pines slide slowly past then looked at *Wave-Thunder* and smiled because his plan was working. Her oars were beating even faster now, cutting neatly into the fjord and biting well, because Bjalki knew he might actually catch up with *Reinen* and make his fame.

'The turds must think we have broken out the ale and are up to our eyebrows in it,' Olaf said.

'Aye and it's painful as a knife in the ribs,' Solmund moaned, 'letting those king's men think we've got no sea craft.'

'They won't think it for much longer,' Sigurd told him. They were some twenty boat lengths ahead of *Wave-Thunder* now and he locked eyes again with the enemy skipper, though this time he did not hurl any insults, wanting Bjalki to think his confidence had leaked like the wind from *Reinen*'s sail.

'Ugly bollock,' Olaf said, grimacing beside Sigurd, because *Wave-Thunder*'s skipper was all grin now, imagining the silver arm ring he would earn and the feast which King Gorm would lay on in his honour. His men's oars beat like wings, the plunge and lift relentless and inevitable. With muscle and spruce those Avaldsnes men were weaving their own saga and it was only a matter of time before they lashed their hull to *Reinen*, spilled over her side in a wave of sharp steel, and slaughtered their king's most hated enemy.

'Now!' Sigurd yelled, and snarling like wolves his crew went to work, Solmund driving the tiller across to turn them into the wind. It was a storm of muscle and rope and *Reinen* gave herself to her skipper.

'Like a lover on a summer's night!' Solmund called.

'You've a good memory, old man,' Bjarni said, getting an insult back for his trouble.

Then Svein and Bram and the others trimmed and tightened the sail which cracked loudly as, at last, the wind bellied it, the wool stretching with the sudden force, and *Reinen* bolted like the creature for which she was named.

Now it was down to Solmund, who was old and not as keen-eyed as he once was, but who loved being at *Reinen*'s helm more than he loved anything in the world.

'Remember this for your saga tale, skald,' Sigurd called to Hagal as they grabbed spears and Svein took up his long axe and Valgerd nocked an arrow to her bow string.

Bjalki was so shocked by *Reinen*'s about turn that he was too slow in giving any commands that might have changed things, and Solmund aimed *Reinen*'s prow beast at that of the enemy.

'If he gets this wrong we'll all be swimming,' Olaf muttered.

Then Solmund pushed the tiller and *Reinen*'s bow turned. The king's men had no time to unship their oars and *Reinen*'s sweeping chest smashed into them in a thunder of splintering, snapping wood cut with screams as men were crushed in the thwarts by their own oar shafts.

'Kill them!' Sigurd bellowed, casting his spear which took a man in his chest, hurling him back into his companions. Valgerd's first arrow plunged into a grizzled-looking warrior's open mouth and the second planted itself in a young man's eye and he screamed like a vixen. Bram's spear had taken their prow man in the shoulder and now he stood impaled, his mouth gaping like a fish as he stared in disbelief. Svein could not reach anyone with his long axe and so stood with his arms wide, roaring at the enemy that they were cowards and the sons of shit-stinking sows.

Then, the insults still hanging in the air like a fart, it was all over, *Reinen* having left *Wave-Thunder* reeling in her wake.

'Óðin!' Asgot screamed, arms raised, fingers grasping at the leaden sky. 'Óðin spear-lord! We kill in your name, Raven god!'

Sigurd strode up the deck, pulling a silver ring from his arm. 'Solmund Sigðir!' he said, but the old man batted away the name Victory-giver as though it was a cloud of gnats and Sigurd laughed. 'Here, take this.' He held out the arm ring but the helmsman shook his head with a smile that was all worn teeth and gaps.

'What would I do with that, young Sigurd?' he asked. 'I'm too old for all that strutting and boasting. Besides which, I have all that I need.' He patted the tiller where the wood was worn smooth and shiny. 'Beats all the silver you could give me.'

Sigurd nodded and clamped a hand on the helmsman's shoulder. 'You did well, old man.'

'She's a fine ship,' Solmund said, 'and has a half-decent crew.'

'Don't tell them that,' Sigurd said. He turned and tossed the ring to Bjorn who caught it in one hand. 'Cut it. Everyone gets a share,' Sigurd said, 'but for Olaf and Asgot. We'll let the godi sacrifice something.'

'And Olaf?' Bjorn asked.

'He'll be happy with a horn of mead. When we can find some.' Sigurd caught Olaf's eye and the older man nodded, which was approval enough. An arm ring cut into nine pieces would not make any of them rich, but it was silver and they had earned it. Yet even so its lustre was nothing compared to the sight of Bjalki's crew floundering against the wind with neither enough oars or sea craft to make headway out there amongst the froth-whipped waves.

'Now that is an unhappy ship, I think,' Svein said, his red beard slashed by teeth.

A ship of splintered oars, broken bones and blood, Sigurd thought. But even a few corpses in the thwarts would be as nothing against the damage done to their pride, and Sigurd continued to gaze at his enemy as Olaf and the others went to work turning *Reinen* back into the wind and beginning to tack once again.

'The gods love you, brother,' Runa said, the breath of those words fogging around her face.

'Aye, girl, they do,' Olaf said, 'but the gods change their minds more often than my wife. They are as fickle as the wind and we'd do well to keep that in mind before we try a trick like that again.' He gestured towards Solmund behind him. 'I'm not even sure the old goat did not mean to pass those swines on their larboard side.'

'I heard that,' Solmund called, proving that his ears still worked.

Sigurd took Runa's hand in his. 'Uncle is right, sister, the gods are fickle. But the Allfather loves chaos.' He smiled at her. 'And so we shall give him chaos.'

CHAPTER SIX

WHEN THEY ROUNDED THE SOUTHERN TIP OF THE ISLAND IT was as though the low leaden sky had sunk down to drape itself over *Reinen* and her crew. It was not raining but the air itself was wet and everything aboard was clammy and greasy to the touch, though that in itself did not account for the dark mood that weighed on Sigurd like a ship's anchor. And neither was he alone in this mind mire. Olaf, Svein, Aslak, Solmund and Asgot were as gloomy as the day and had withdrawn into the cave of their own memories like bears in their winter dens.

Runa sat weeping at the bow and Sigurd did nothing to comfort her. Instead he peered through the mist-hazed air towards the shore. He could barely make out the jetty and perhaps that was just as well. If the day had been clear and he had been able to see the rocks and the path that led up to Eik-hjálmr his father's hall – no more than blackened rotting timbers now – his mind would have fashioned his mother standing there, her beaded necklace and her silver brooch outshone by her graceful beauty. He would imagine his brothers Thorvard, Sigmund and Sorli challenging each other to see who could jump from the boards and be the first to swim to one of the islands. Their father Harald would be there calling them young fools, making a show of not being interested, but watching all the same with pride in his eyes.

They were all gone now. All of it was gone. Their lives, their ambitions, their bonds one to another had all been washed away by a tide of blood. By what the skalds called the red war.

And yet, even death cannot break some bonds. For in the hereafter, in Óðin's hall, men may have the chance to feast with their kinsmen once again and for the rest of time, or at least until the final chaos and the gods' doom. Sigurd clung to those bonds now, be they invisible as a bird's spittle or a fish's breath, as was Gleipnir, the binding which held the wolf Fenrir. He would answer the demands of his own blood kinship with the blood of his enemies.

But not yet.

'We could sneak into Gorm's hall in the dead of night and gut him in his bed,' Svein had suggested back when they were deciding where to go from Hakon Burner's hall. 'Why wait when that turd's death is long overdue?'

'I will not do it in the dark, Svein,' Sigurd had said. 'I will do it in the full light of the day, when all men can see. I will blow the horns to announce the oath-breaker's doom. He will get the end he has spun for himself, my friend, but neither our slain kin nor the gods will miss it.'

But to take his revenge like that Sigurd needed men and spears. He needed silver and he needed reputation, for reputation is a weapon in itself, a thin cold blade which worms into your enemy's guts when he is trying to sleep at night. All this would take time, and so for now they were sailing away from Avaldsnes and King Gorm and the ambition that burnt inside Sigurd. Yet he would keep that fire inside his chest. He would fan its flames with deeds worthy of the Spear-God's one-eyed gaze and one day, when he was ready, he would go north again to claim what he was owed.

'Gods but I miss 'em,' Olaf said now, coming to stand at Sigurd's shoulder.

'If my brothers were with us now I would almost pity the king,' Sigurd said.

Olaf nodded. 'Thorvard had the makings of a saga hero. Even Slagfid admitted that Thorvard was going to be a great warrior. Said the lad was one of the best he'd seen.' Slagfid had been Jarl Harald's champion and as fierce a warrior as Sigurd had ever known.

'And Sigmund had enough clever in him for two men,' Olaf went on. 'Your father envied the lad that, you know. Sigmund could put a rock and raven's feather in the scales and find a way to make them balance.'

This talk of the past was like a fist around Sigurd's heart, clenching it so that he could barely breathe. But he did not stop Olaf talking.

'As for Sorli, he was trouble that boy . . .'

Sigurd's eyes were still grasping at the shore but he could hear the smile on Olaf's lips.

'Lad had balls like boulders. I remember when you were youngens and Thorvard, who was built like a man even then, got carried away with the training spears one day. Gave you an eye as black as Hel's arsehole.' Sigurd remembered it well, as if it had been yesterday. 'When Sorli laid eyes on you he strode right up to Thorvard and put a fist in his mouth.' Olaf chuckled. 'Blood everywhere. Knocked out a tooth as I recall, which was something seeing as he'd been balancing on his tiptoes to give the blow. Ah, Sorli. He'd march across the rainbow-bridge and kick Óðin in the bollocks if the gods upset you or your brothers.' Olaf shook his head. 'I miss 'em.'

Sigurd could not have spoken then even if he had wanted to.

Olaf's big hand gripped his shoulder. 'They're drinking Óðin's mead now, lad, and they're proud of you. All of them, your mother and Harald too,' he said, then he turned and gazed towards the land sliding by on *Reinen*'s larboard. 'But they're no prouder than I am,' he said. 'Let's get that straight here and now.'

Sigurd stared through the sea mist at the shore. But he could see even less now than before.

It had made it worse that the wind had died away, making progress past Skudeneshavn so slow that it had been impossible not to dwell on the village's fate. Even though the place meant nothing to Bjarni and Bjorn, Valgerd, Black Floki and the rest, the Skudeneshavn men's mood had got into them too, like seep water in the bilge.

'Are you sure you do not want to put in, Uncle?' Sigurd had asked, for Olaf had family still living there, his wife Ragnhild and his sons Harek and the white-haired bairn Eric.

Olaf shook his head. 'Skudeneshavn is Randver's son's pissing post now,' he said. 'If the lad has any brains in his skull he'll have men here flashing silver around the place and feeding our womenfolk,' he spat, 'bedding them too likely as not, but mainly waiting for us to show our faces.'

'Hrani Randversson is jarl in all but name now,' Svein said.

The thought that Hrani's men would be sniffing round the daughters and wives of Jarl Harald's dead hirðmen sickened Sigurd. But he knew that was the way of things. If you kill a man you can take what is his. Maybe you hold on to it. Maybe not.

Olaf shook his head again, as if trying to convince himself. 'No, we can't risk it. As much as I'd give every bit of silver I owned to see my kin again, even have Ragnhild chew my ear off, for a while at least.' He grinned but it was a sad grin. 'It's the kind of bone-headed thing you'd do, Sigurd, but those of us with a few years on our backs are supposed to know better.'

And so they had sailed past Sigurd's old home on into the Skude Fjord, into the gloomy damp day, and when the wind finally died altogether they took the oars down from their trees and rowed. Sigurd rowed too because *Reinen* needed every available blade in the water to move her, and even Moldof managed well enough with one arm and one oar.

'If a woman can row . . .' he had growled, snatching the oar that Aslak had been handing to Bjorn, for Valgerd had already taken hers and passed it through an oar port by her sea chest on the steerboard side midships. The only ones not bending their backs at the benches were Solmund, because he was at the tiller, and Runa, whose young eyes were watching over the bows for rocks because it was low tide. She made a strange sight standing there at the prow man's place: a young golden-haired woman treading the boards where Slagfid, her father's champion, had stood and smote men with his great axe. Where Svein himself had stood in the gore-stained chaos of the blood-fray. And now and then Sigurd looked over his shoulder at her as he rowed, thinking how precious she was and how he would never let harm befall her.

'And what if you get an itch on your nose or have to scratch your arse?' Bjarni asked Moldof. 'Then what will you do, one-arm?'

Sigurd suspected Bjarni had chosen the bench behind the giant just so that he could nettle him, from here to the world's edge if his wyrd allowed.

'Or a gull craps on your ugly head?' Bjarni added.

'Then you can wipe it off for me, little man,' Moldof said, his one huge hand gripping the stave as he heaved it back, leaning so far that his lank hair dripped sweat on to Bjarni's breeks.

The moon was still near full that night and enough of its cold glow bled through the cloud that, with the Skudeneshavn men's knowledge of the sea around those parts, they were confident rowing. Sigurd lost himself in the cadence of it, every stroke the same as the last, each like a stitch in some god's tunic, or a ring in a giant's brynja. He was sure he heard Bram snoring for a while, and there were times when he himself was more asleep than awake, though the rhythm of the oars beat on.

There was some magic about rowing at night, about sharing the silence, when the dark-dwellers are abroad and you wonder what beasts writhe beneath your feet, beneath the thin strakes which are all that separates you from the depths. When the only sound is the clump of the oars in their ports and the strike and hiss of the blades hitting the water.

Yet rowing at night was not without risks and Sigurd had them take turns at the watch, two at a time even though that meant two less at the oars. The coast and the islands and the small rocks standing proud of the sea with which they were so familiar in the daylight looked completely different at night, so that there was a constant fear that simply mistaking one marker for another could see them run aground and drowned. Even so, Sigurd had decided it was better to row under night's veil when they could. Because they were heading south-east to Rennisøy and could only have been in more dangerous waters had they been heading up the Karmsund Strait beneath King Gorm's hall on the hill at Avaldsnes. This fjord was now Hrani Randversson's hunting ground and the young would-be jarl was bound to have crews out looking for the man who killed his father, just as King Gorm had ships waiting like owls in the high boughs.

'What better way to show that his arse is the best fit for his father's seat perched up there in Örngarð than to catch the men who fed Randver to the crabs,' Olaf had suggested when they had laid out the dangers of sailing south.

'And yet we do not know what kind of man this Hrani is,' Asgot had said. 'Perhaps he is a careful man, one who would rather stay in his hall and rut with his father's bed thralls than be drawn deeper into the mire of a feud with a god-favoured killer.'

But Runa had shaken her head and Sigurd had invited her to speak even though she was a girl barely on the cusp of womanhood and amongst warriors.

'Hrani is cruel,' she said, 'and whilst I think he lacks his father's wisdom—'

'Ha! Look what good his wisdom did him,' Bram put in, but Sigurd gestured for his sister to continue.

'The men respect Hrani as a warrior,' Runa said, and she should know. When Hrani had raided Skudeneshavn, knowing Jarl Harald was walking up to his death at Avaldsnes, he had taken Runa hostage. The idea was that she would marry Amleth, Hrani's younger brother, thus turning the ground over the whole bloody affair so that new seeds could grow from the alliance between Randver's people and Harald's. Sigurd had made sure that the marriage between Runa and Amleth never happened, of course, though not before Runa had lived awhile under Jarl Randver's roof and come to know a thing or two about Hrani.

'He will be thirsting to prove himself and will give little thought to whom the gods favour and whom they do not,' she said now.

'He will think of it when he comes face to face with me,' Sigurd said.

Hrani had led the war band that had brought steel and death to Skudeneshavn. One of his

warriors had killed Sigurd's mother, though not
before Grimhild had given a man named Andvett
his death-wound. She had opened his guts with a
scramasax, and Runa, who had been taken prisoner,
had watched Andvett bleed to death, writhing in
the thwarts of Randver's ship.

And now Sigurd wanted to kill Hrani as much as
he had wanted to kill the man's father.

Örn-garð, the Eagle's Dwelling-place. That was
the name of Hrani's hall and Sigurd thought about
that now as he leant back in the stroke, pulling the
black sea past *Reinen*'s hull. Like his father, Hrani
doubtless considered himself a lord of land and sea.
And like an eagle he would be hunting.

Sigurd did not have enough men to win if it came
to a fight. There would be a time, but that time was
not now.

So they rowed at night.

The next morning they found a quiet cove on the
south side of Mosterøy, the island south of Rennisøy,
where they dropped the anchor and moored to get
some rest. It was damp but not so cold and they
hunkered up in the thwarts between *Reinen*'s ribs,
most of them asleep and snoring before the first watch
was set. They slept on a sleeping sea, the sound of it
caressing the shore like a lover breathing nearby, only
broken by the occasional coarse call of a cormorant,
that bark travelling far across the still water.

When they woke they ate some smoked meat and
cheese, washed it down with weak ale and went once

more to their benches to thread the oars back through their ports. And then came rain. Not the soft drizzle which you did not even notice, though your clothes were soaked through, but a fierce, cruel, driving rain. It hammered the fjord, dimpling the surface at first and then seeming to come in long shafts which arrowed through so that Aslak remarked that the next fish they caught would be full of holes.

'This is good for us,' Olaf said, rain dripping from his beard.

'How so?' Svein asked. He had braided his beard into a thick red rope and water streamed from the end of it.

'Because anyone out looking for us will not look so hard with the rain pissing down their necks,' Bram answered for Olaf as the oars plunged and rose, the blades dripping before they fell again.

'Well, I would rather fight and be dry than sit here as wet as an otter's cunny,' Bjarni said, which got some grunts of agreement from the benches around him, and Sigurd glanced at Valgerd and saw her lips constrict with the ghost of a smile. She caught his eye and he looked away.

And they had been wrong when they thought the rain would help them pass unnoticed through Hrani Randversson's fjord.

There were two ships and they came from the south, their oar banks beating like eagle's wings, swooping up past the pine-bristled coast. There was no doubting that they were coming for *Reinen*.

'Randver's?' Solmund asked, his brow more furrowed than the fjord as his old eyes tried to pick any identifying details from the craft.

'Hrani's now,' Sigurd reminded him and Crow-Song confirmed it, for as a skald he had sold his craft to kings and jarls and anyone with silver and mead, before he had joined Sigurd's crew. Before Sigurd had told Hagal that he would either crew-up with them or else Sigurd would cut open his back, pull out his lungs and nail them to the wall of a barn belonging to a farmer named Roldar, whose guests they were.

'You see the prow beast on the lead ship?' the skald asked, having pulled in his oar to stand with Sigurd at the prow.

'A yellow dragon?' Sigurd said.

Crow-Song nodded. 'You're meant to think it's gold,' he said.

'Perhaps I would if it looked like gold,' Sigurd said.

'*Golden-Fire*,' Olaf said, recalling the vessel's name, then curled his lips and scratched his great beard. 'Sigurd's right. Ought to be called *Dragon's-Piss*.'

'Want me to fit our beast, Sigurd?' Svein offered from his row bench. *Reinen*'s prow beast was a snarling creature with fierce eyes and it was the prow man's honour to fit the massive reindeer antlers either side of its head. Not that anyone thought it looked like a reindeer, but that only added to the terror of it. Or so Jarl Harald had explained it.

'Not yet, Svein,' Sigurd replied. 'Solmund, hold this course.'

'Well, we can't out-row them,' Olaf said.

Runa looked at her brother, teeth worrying her bottom lip which glistened with rain. 'We could make landfall before they reach us,' she said, eyes wide and hopeful.

Olaf seemed to consider this, then nodded. 'See that beach there, Sigurd?' He pointed to a break in the rocks where the surf rolled up, depositing masses of scummy foam on the pebbles and grit. 'We could run her up the shingle and leg it.'

'And give them *Reinen*? No, Uncle.' Sigurd shook his head. 'I won't do that.'

'Well, we can't fight two crews,' Olaf said. 'They'll come up nice and cosy, one on either side of us, and that will be that. We'd last longer by jumping overboard in our brynjur.' Sigurd had seen men go overboard in their brynjur. They thrashed for maybe two or three heartbeats and then they were gone.

He looked at his crew, all of them rowing towards the enemy, and he knew they would keep up that rhythm until he told them otherwise. They had given him their oath but what could he give them in return? There would be no glory in this fight. It would barely even be a fight. Murder would be a more fitting word.

'Well, lad?' Olaf said. 'At least let them die with their war gear on.'

Sigurd's heart was beating five times for every oar stroke. His stomach felt as if it were full of snakes, the creatures writhing and rolling over each other. Above him gulls shrieked in the rain. He breathed in the scent of the pines on the shore and wondered if these were his last moments. If he would soon be with his father and brothers again. His mother too, for she had been as brave and proud as any warrior and would not be refused entry to Valhöll.

'Moldof, come here,' he said.

With his one massive arm the giant lifted the wooden blade from the water and worked the oar stave out of the port. Bjarni pulled his own oar in as far as it would go and Bram put his foot on the end, pressing it against the deck while Bjarni helped Moldof bring his oar back over the top strake into the ship. Then King Gorm's former champion came to Sigurd, rolled his huge shoulders and nodded.

'I have an idea, Moldof,' Sigurd said.

'You want to share it with me?' Olaf said. 'Or shall I have them get their mail on and prepare to drink mead with their grandfathers?'

Sigurd ignored Olaf's question, his gaze riveted to Moldof. 'You will do exactly what I tell you,' he said, 'because if you do not, Olaf will take off your other arm and throw you over the side and I doubt even Rán will want you in her cold kingdom. You will wander Niflheim and Hel's beasts will feed on what's left of you.'

Moldof looked from Sigurd to Olaf, who nodded as though what Sigurd had suggested would be no more trouble than drawing his sword.

The vein in Moldof's neck seemed to throb and a deep growl rolled in his throat but never made it past his lips. 'Talk quickly then, Haraldarson,' he said.

With so few oars in the fjord they would never outrun *Golden-Fire* and the other ship, which Hagal now recognized as *Storm-Steed*. Both of Hrani's ships were full-crewed and sleeker than *Reinen*, and as Solmund pointed out, you did not name a ship *Storm-Steed* if it was slow.

'We've got both feet in this snare and there's no slipping out of it now,' Bram said, leaning right back in the stroke. 'I would rather fight with a sword than an oar, if it's all the same to you, Olaf.'

This got some *ayes* from those who did not have much confidence in Sigurd's plan.

'Killing a man with an oar cannot be so difficult,' Floki suggested.

'And doing it from a distance means you won't get his shit on your shoes,' Svein put in, having given it some thought.

'In the last fight I am sure we killed some men with their own oars, which is hardly a good death if you ask me,' Aslak said.

'If you ladies could row as well as you talk we would not be in this mess to begin with,' Olaf said, hauling his own spruce blade through the water. 'Now keep this pace and try to look like you know what you are doing, hey!'

Bjorn was the stroke man and it was his shoulders they all watched to ensure they kept the rhythm and that their oars bit the fjord together.

'Almost there. Put us between them, Solmund,' Moldof said.

'You don't tell me my business,' the helmsman gnarred, aiming to thread *Reinen* through the gap between Hrani's ships in order to show that they had no intention of trying to skirt around the trap those skippers had set.

A man at *Golden-Fire*'s prow was lifting his arm up and down in a gesture that told *Reinen* to slow, and there were other men along her sides ready with oars to make sure the ships did not come together too aggressively. Moldof had taken up the biggest spear he could find, a ten-foot-long boar-killer, and now stood in all his war gear by Solmund on the steering platform gripping the thick ash shaft and looking like a champion but for his being an arm short.

'Oars in!' he bellowed, rain dripping from his helmet's nasal, and *Reinen*'s crew obeyed, pulling the staves into the ship so that they would not break against *Golden-Fire*'s hull as *Reinen* came alongside. Rope ends were hurled across and Bjarni, Aslak and Floki passed them through the oar ports to lash both ships together.

The other ship, *Storm-Steed*, held water off *Reinen*'s larboard side but close enough that her crew could rain spears and arrows into *Reinen*'s thwarts should her skipper give the order. Both *Golden-Fire* and *Storm-Steed*'s sides were lined with warriors whose shields made brightly painted ramparts, the iron blades of their spears dull against the rain-flayed murk. Thunder rumbled across the eastern sky and men touched the hammers at their necks because somewhere Thór was slaying his enemies, and Sigurd feared it was a bad omen, a warning that he should have been fighting now. And yet he did not have so much as an eating knife within reach.

'I know this ship,' *Golden-Fire*'s skipper called across before any other greeting. He wore a helmet and mail but had not drawn the sword which hung at his right hip. 'Even without her prow beast mounted I know her. This is *Reinen*, which belonged to Jarl Harald of Skudeneshavn.'

'You have that right,' Moldof said, stepping down from the steering platform and striding across the deck towards the man. The rain hissed like dragon's breath and they would have to get close to hear each other above it. 'And who are you?'

The skipper was a short man and must have been impressed by Moldof though he gave no sign of it. 'I am Estrith whom men call the Left-Handed.'

'Why do they call you that?' Moldof asked, his face as straight as its ugliness would allow.

Estrith frowned as though deciding whether Moldof was teasing him or was just as stupid as he looked. 'I think you might suit the name even better,' he said, cocking an eyebrow.

'You can keep it,' Moldof said, unimpressed with the byname.

'This is *Golden-Fire*,' Estrith said, slapping the ship's sheer strake, 'and we are Jarl Hrani's men.'

'I did not know Randver's son wore the jarl torc now,' Moldof said.

Estrith glared up at the giant. 'He will soon enough,' he said, 'and he will be a great jarl. As great as his father perhaps.'

'That should not be hard,' Moldof said, which could have brought him trouble if Estrith had not chosen to ignore it.

The warrior next to *Golden-Fire*'s skipper leant in close to Estrith and whispered in his ear while Moldof waited patiently, rain sheeting down his brynja like water down a cliff.

Estrith stiffened and waved the man away. 'I know who you are,' he said, raising his voice above the seething of the sea. The fjord looked like it was coming to the boil. 'You are Moldof, King Gorm's champion.'

Moldof nodded but said nothing.

'Well met, Moldof,' Estrith said, 'I am honoured to meet the man who almost beat Jarl Harald.' He was a cocky one, this Estrith, as small men often are, but Moldof was wise enough not to pick the insult out

of that. 'What are you doing here?' Estrith asked.
'The last I heard, the outlaw Haraldarson was riding
Rán's daughters in this very ship. We have been
looking for him.' He scratched his short-cropped
beard. 'I don't mind telling you I thought the Norns
had spun me a silver wyrd when I saw this ship
and recognized her. I've seen her gallop under sail,
though I'd wager *Golden-Fire* has her for speed.' He
nodded towards the other ship off *Reinen*'s larboard
side. '*Storm-Steed* would leave us both behind, I fear,'
he said, crossing his arms over his chest, 'but under
oar I'd put my men against any crew in the world.'
He frowned. 'So, Moldof King's Champion, what
are you doing in Sigurd Haraldarson's ship?'

Moldof raked the men of *Golden-Fire*'s shieldwall
with his eyes, then looked back down at their
skipper.

'I am the king's man and do not have to explain
myself to you, Estrith Shit-Hand,' he said.

Estrith's eyes bulged at that but he kept his
anger stoppered like ale in a flask. 'You would be
unwise to throw insults around, Moldof, for all your
reputation,' he said. 'It strikes me that you have
barely half a crew there, and are yourself perhaps
only half the man you used to be.'

'And yet I am still twice the man you are,' Moldof
said, and Olaf, who sat on his bench near *Reinen*'s
stern so that all Estrith could see of him was the
back of his rain-soaked head, gave a low grunt of
disapproval.

135

Some of Estrith's warriors growled insults but none were loud enough to be heard above the sibilance of the rain on the sea. In truth Moldof knew he could stand there and tell them each in turn that they were the shit-smeared runts of rancid boars and they would almost certainly do nothing about it, for their lord was a nearly-jarl whereas Moldof's was a king, and Hrani would only wear the jarl's torc if King Gorm all but placed it round his neck.

'So where is Sigurd Haraldarson?' Estrith asked, changing tack to save face.

'What is it to you?' Moldof replied and this time Estrith sighed.

'We are allies, Moldof, and we all seek the outlaw's death.' He held out his palms. 'If you can tell me that Sigurd is dead I will be grateful. We will row back to Hinderå and get out of this pissing rain. The gods know we would all welcome a fire and some hot food.' He gestured at the men in *Reinen*'s thwarts. 'None of us should be out here at this time of year.'

Now Moldof nodded his head, the rain still cascading from his helmet's rim and dripping from his wild beard. 'I found Sigurd and what was left of his crew skulking in Jarl Hakon Burner's great hall up in Osøyro,' he said. 'I challenged the lad to a fight and to his credit he accepted. We fought. I killed him.'

Estrith's brows arched at that, though he did not dispute the account. Even one-armed, he must have thought that Moldof was fierce and experienced enough to beat a young man, for all the talk of Sigurd being god-favoured.

'Did the lad fight well?' he asked.

'Not as well as his father,' Moldof said.

'Lucky for you,' Estrith said, 'or else you would have no arms left and would eat your dinner like a dog.'

'Men are always brave when standing in their own ship,' Moldof said.

Estrith ignored him. 'Where is the body? I am sure the king will want to see Harald's whelp's corpse with his own eyes.'

Moldof stared at Estrith. The rain hammered down and both crews were soaked and miserable-looking and longed to get under a roof. Then Moldof shrugged his massive shoulders, shook his head and looked over his shoulder. 'Bjorn, Bjarni, bring the body here so that Estrith can get a bone in his breeks and we can be on our way.'

The brothers left their benches and went to the open hold. After some grunting and cursing they struggled over to *Reinen*'s side with a burden wrapped in animal skins. 'Over there,' Moldof said and they nodded, hefting the burden over to the mast step where they laid it down. 'Careful,' Moldof growled. 'My king won't be able to drink his mead from the lad's skull if you put a fucking hole in it.'

Bjorn cut the ropes tying the bundle and Bjarni pulled the skins away from the head end and Estrith murmured something to the men around him. They all leant forward, crowding up to *Golden-Fire*'s side to get a better look at the young warrior who had killed their jarl and defied their king.

And there he was. Sigurd Haraldarson, corpse-pale and naked, the rain bouncing off his face and chest, running in rivulets through the dark blood that was smeared across his flesh.

And Sigurd held his breath, which was a joy compared with breathing in the stink of the fish guts which Svein had slapped over him before they had tied him up in those skins.

'That is him,' Estrith confirmed. 'I saw him once when he came with Jarl Harald to Örn-garð.' His eyes narrowed. 'Where are you taking him? I am sure Jarl Hrani—' he corrected himself, 'soon-to-be Jarl Hrani, that is, will be grateful to see the corpse for himself. It would be my honour to escort you to my lord's hall.'

Moldof shook his head. 'My orders are to take the body to some witch in Stavanger.'

'Ah,' Estrith said as if he understood.

Moldof laid it out for him anyway. 'All that talk about the lad being Óðin-kissed,' he said. 'Bollocks if you ask me. He died easily enough. And I'm sure my king does not believe a word of it either. But some people see the gods' work in a wet fart. These people will only be satisfied after this Stavanger witch has worked her seiðr on the corpse.' He made a show of touching the iron of his spear blade then, which suggested he still had his fears despite his brave talk. 'She will weave some spell that will make him unrecognizable when he enters Óðin's dwelling place.' He grinned for the first time since meeting Estrith. 'The Allfather can't favour him if he doesn't even know where he is.' Then he turned his head and spat into the thwarts. 'And even if the witch's magic does not work . . .' He turned and looked at the still body by the mast step. 'If I meet the lad when I go to Valhöll I will kill him again.'

Sigurd was glad of the small motion of the ships as they clumped together, for it was unlikely that anyone would notice his shallow breathing, though he wished Bjarni would throw the skin back over his face. A man like Estrith had likely seen enough corpses to know the difference between a dead face and one trying to look dead.

'So these are Sigurd's men?' Estrith said, jerking a finger towards those taking their rest at *Reinen*'s benches.

'*Were* Sigurd's men,' Moldof corrected him.

'Then they too are outlaws and must answer for the killing of Jarl Randver.' For the first time since the hulls had come together Estrith's left hand fell across his body to the sword at his hip.

'My king has spared their lives in return for the oath they will swear to him,' Moldof said, as if the words tasted foul on his tongue. 'What else was there for them? They are King Gorm's men now.'

'That will be a sour draught for my lord Hrani to swallow,' Estrith said, putting his hand back on the sheer strake.

Moldof shrugged. 'My men have rested enough. Heave away so that I can go and find this witch. I'll wager you will want to get home to tell your lord that he may sleep easy in his bed now knowing that the Óðin-favoured boy is dead.'

Estrith bristled at the implication that Hrani had been afraid of Sigurd. 'It will be good to get out of this rain,' he said, as another peal of thunder rolled across the grey sky. Then he gave the order for his men to release the lines and waved to the skipper of *Storm-Steed*, assuring him that all was well. Bjarni covered Sigurd's face, tying the skins up again, then he and Bjorn hefted Sigurd back to the hold whilst Aslak and Floki untied the ropes and threw them across to *Golden-Fire*.

The ships started to move apart and *Reinen*'s crew got their oars back in the water to hold her prow pointing south until they were given the order to row.

'Pay my respects to the king,' Estrith called as the grey sea spread between the hulls and the rain lashed down upon it.

'Why?' Moldof called back. 'Does the dog care for the respect of a flea?'

Estrith spat a curse at him then, emboldened by the distance between himself and the great spear in the giant's hand. But Moldof had already turned his back on the man and was telling Solmund to renew their previous course.

And inside his fish-gut-stinking skins Sigurd lay as still as a dead man, listening to the plunge of the oars, the creak of the timbers, and the thunder god raging in the east.

CHAPTER SEVEN

WHEN THERE WAS ENOUGH WIND THEY HAULED *REINEN*'S
sail up the stout pine mast and when there was no
wind they bent their backs to oars, rowing under
the waning moon until the nights were dark as
pitch again and the risk of tearing open the hull was
too great. On those nights they snugged up to the
coast, running mooring ropes from *Reinen*'s bow to
trees or rocks on the shore while keeping her off
those rocks by dropping two anchor stones over the
stern. They ate little in order to save what they had,
though whoever was on watch would sit with a line
and hook in the water, so there was almost always
fresh fish the next day. They huddled under skins
and furs and Crow-Song told them tales to help
the long nights pass: stories of long-dead kings and
heroes, of monsters and great hoards of silver, and
more often than not these tales were about the few
or the brave defeating their more powerful enemies.

With the cold and damp burrowed deep into the marrow of their bones they would set off again into the dawn, long before the first pale light spread its wings over the eastern horizon.

It was slow and arduous, wet, cold and miserable, but every wave they put between themselves and their enemies was to the good. On the fifth day after the encounter with Hrani's ships, Sigurd had them run *Reinen* up a secluded beach, the scrape of the keel on the shingle a welcome sound to all.

The beach was short, the pebbles giving way to rocks that rose steeply to a thick wood, yet it was all but hidden by a gull-thronged outcrop which stretched out into the fjord and it was as good a place as any to light a fire and get a broth bubbling over it.

'It's too late,' Bjarni said, rubbing his hands and staring at them, shaking his head. 'Cold as a frost giant's bollocks. I'll never get the feeling back in them.' He held them to the fire over which an iron cauldron full of herring, shellfish and garlic bubbled, its steam making Sigurd's mouth water. 'It is a pity for all the girls who will never again know the pleasure that these hands can give.'

'I think I can hear them weeping,' Bram said, frowning, then scratched his bearded cheek and let out a raging fart. 'No, no. My mistake.'

Bjarni stretched his neck to look over at Valgerd, who sat hugging her legs on the other side of the fire. 'Though I am willing to give them one last try, if you are interested, shieldmaiden,' he said, wiggling his fingers and grinning.

'Why not try me?' Valgerd said, then winked at Runa beside her. 'For I was just thinking that this stew would be improved by some meat.'

'It would only be kind to leave him one finger,' Runa said, 'so that he can still pick his nose.'

'He can use this,' Valgerd said, pulling her wicked sharp scramasax from the sheath in the small of her back. It was the same knife with which she had taken off Loker's arm up in the Lysefjord.

'It's funny but I think they are thawing after all,' Bjarni said, clenching his fists, still smiling.

'Unlike some around here, hey brother,' Bjorn said, nodding towards Valgerd. This got some low chuckles from those around the flames, though the shieldmaiden did not seem to mind.

Sigurd was relieved, if not a little surprised, by how readily the men had accepted Valgerd into the crew. They were all guilty of letting their eyes linger a little too long on her, none more than Sigurd himself, but no man had let lust get the better of him. Partly this was out of respect for Sigurd, he knew, but partly it was because Valgerd had earned her place amongst them. For all her beauty she was no less a warrior than any of them. She had fought and killed with them, and perhaps bonds forged in the blood-fray could be stronger than men's desires. Or perhaps they feared her, and if so they were wiser than they looked, for Valgerd was a killer.

And yet Sigurd wanted her. If their eyes met he would look away more often than not, but now and then he held her gaze and on those times he would feel the blood rush to his groin and his breeks would seem to shrink.

'Look away, Sigurd. No good can come of it, lad,' Olaf murmured by his ear now, leaning forward to feed more sticks into the fire.

Sigurd felt the rush of heat in his cheeks but did not bother to deny it. Olaf had been around long enough to see such things without even looking. Still, Sigurd hoped it was not so obvious to the others as well.

'I'll fetch more wood,' Sigurd said, climbing to his feet, avoiding Valgerd's eye as though his life depended on it. He walked back down the shingle to look for driftwood, knowing that whatever there was had already been gathered. Then he stood at the land's edge, where the sea lapped at the rocks and seethed down amongst the shingle after each gentle swell. Beside him *Reinen* loomed in the dark, her scent, of pitch and pine and foul bilge water, overpowering the tang of the salt-encrusted wrack which the sea had coughed up on to the beach. He felt the breeze on his right cheek and knew that the clouds were thin enough that they could have left the oars in their trees and sailed east by the light of the stars.

Not tonight, he thought. *Let them enjoy the fire and the hot food in their bellies. They deserve it.* And in any case, Solmund and Olaf must have felt that breeze even before him, having ploughed the sea-road more often than he, and yet neither had mentioned it.

'The fire reminds them of home,' a voice said. 'Of the past.'

He turned and there was Valgerd standing there looking out across the dark water, her loose golden hair catching what little light there was. Sigurd wondered how he had not heard her walk across the small stones but put it down to the shieldmaiden's soft boots and the breathing of the sea.

'I think Bjarni has his eye on you,' he said, cringing inwardly at his own words because he remembered that Valgerd's tastes lay elsewhere. Her last lover had been a woman, the völva from the sacred spring whom she had been sworn to protect.

She raised an eyebrow, a half smile on her lips. 'Bjarni is more in love with his own right hand, I think,' she said, then nodded towards *Reinen* sitting beyond the sea's reach above the high-tide line. 'It is hard to sleep sometimes for the beat of his hand beneath the furs.'

Sigurd had no answer to that.

'His are not the only eyes I feel on me,' she said after a while. Sigurd wondered if the water lapping on to the beach was deep enough to drown himself in. 'Runa would like you to marry me, I think,' she said.

'And what does Runa know of such things?' Sigurd managed.

'Whereas you know all there is to know about such things,' she said.

He did not bite on that hook. Besides, she was right. He had more experience of the blood-fray and the vagaries of the gods than he had of women.

'I know that when I am jarl I will be expected to take a wife who brings an alliance as her dowry,' he said.

'Is that what you want? A peace cow and a high seat in your own hall?'

What he wanted was Valgerd but he did not say it.

'I want to kill my enemies and avenge my kin,' he said. Which was also true. He shrugged, watching a far-off patch of sea which shimmered like molten iron beneath a gap in the cloud. 'If I end my days in a hall surrounded by sons and daughters and loyal hearthmen I will be surprised.'

Valgerd said nothing to that and he looked at her. Gods she was beautiful: golden and strong like Runa, but different in every other way. Whereas Runa still had a girl's features, the rounded, slightly upturned nose, the full cheeks and the smooth high forehead, Valgerd's beauty had a fierceness about it. Her cheekbones were high and sharp as scramasax blades. Her nose was straight and strong and her eyes were like those of the big cats which dwelt in the forests and were beloved of the goddess Freyja.

'Did you come down here alone to talk to the gods?' she asked. 'Because you are more likely to get answers from the fish.'

'You are brave to mock the gods,' he said.

She shrugged. 'They mock us.'

He said nothing to that.

'So, Sigurd Heppinn, where will we go?' she asked. 'Where will the threads of your wyrd lead us?'

'Sigurd the Lucky?'

'That is what they are calling you now,' she said. 'Since we wriggled through Hrani Randversson's net.'

He thought about his family and all the blood through which he had waded since King Gorm had betrayed his father.

'If I am lucky it does not say much for those who are unlucky,' he said.

'You are free and you have a fine ship,' she said and chose not to argue the difference between being free and being a hunted outlaw.

'We'll go south,' he said, returning to her earlier question. 'We'll follow the coast and try not to get killed by some Svear king. Perhaps we'll cross the sea to raid the Danes like my father used to. We need silver.' And they did, for with silver Sigurd could buy spears, warriors who were not already oath-tied to some other lord. Without silver, or at least the promise of it, he would be lucky to hold on to the half crew he had. 'So long as we are out of the oath-breaker's reach. Hrani Randversson's too.'

Valgerd nodded. A movement on the stones caught Sigurd's eye and he watched a brown crab edging along the tideline. At the onset of winter most of the crabs retreated to warmer, deeper waters. Not this one apparently, and it was large enough to make good eating.

'Why did you leave the fire?' he asked Valgerd.

By way of answer she stepped down on to the shingle, dropped her breeks and squatted to piss on to the smooth stones. 'It was not so that I could talk to the gods,' she said. And Sigurd kept his gaze on the sea, smiling to himself. Thinking himself a fool.

When she had finished she walked to the sea's edge where the stones glistened.

'So we are going raiding,' she said, picking up the crab by its back legs. The creature had survived the winter but it would not survive the cook pot.

Sigurd shrugged. 'No one will expect it at this time of year,' he said.

And he hoped that was true.

Hrani Randversson stood on the hill at Avaldsnes overlooking the channel of dark water and mumbled the foulest of curses. It was clear to everyone gathered there in the snow below King Gorm's hall that Estrith Left-Handed was as dead as a man could be. Worse, he was naked and blue

149

as the veins in a woman's wrists as he lay there on that rock, pathetic and shamed, given up as the tide retreated. As if not even Rán, Mother of the Waves, who takes the drowned into her cold embrace, had wanted him.

'Try not to look so sour about it, husband,' Herkja said. 'What's done is done.'

'It should not have been done at all,' Hrani growled. 'Not like this. Not by him.'

Herkja gave him a disapproving look and clapped her mittened hands together for warmth before rejoining the conversation she had been having with Queen Kadlin and a gaggle of Avaldsnes women, all of them far more interested in the talk of spring weddings than in the fate of some skipper from Hinderå.

Hrani looked back at the flat rock and the body on it, thinking that at least Estrith was not being picked at by crabs as he would be were it summer.

'Oh don't mind him,' Herkja told the queen, dismissing Hrani with a flutter of her ringed fingers. 'Some old wound. He is too proud to admit that it still pains him and so we must all suffer for it.' She shook her head. 'But you know what men are like.'

'They are all the same in that regard,' Queen Kadlin said, 'but at least your husband is still a young man, my dear.' She leant in close to Herkja, though did not lower her voice. 'Imagine how many wounds my husband *doesn't* complain about,' she said and Herkja laughed.

Hrani shook his head and cursed again. They had married at the Jól feast because Hrani had been keen to play the part of a jarl after his father's death, which meant having a good wife to run his hall and bear his cup. And whilst Herkja was a beauty, the daughter of a wealthy karl from Sandnessjøen on the island of Alsten south of Hinderå, her tongue was a little too free with her advice given how her neck could hardly have warmed the silver he had put around it. Furthermore, it was unseemly that she should be laughing now, while Estrith Left-Handed lay drowned on that flat rock for all to see.

If it had been down to Hrani, which it should have been, *Golden-Fire*'s skipper would have been punished. Certainly outlawed. Perhaps even killed, though not in such a foul way as this. For he had let Sigurd Haraldarson slip through the net. He had been close enough to that hag-ridden, murdering, hall-less fiend to put a spear in him and yet he had fallen for Sigurd's trick, believing him dead. Now who knew where Sigurd and the dregs of his crew might be, or where they were headed? Yes, Estrith had failed him and by doing so had brought this poor end upon himself. But it was down to Hrani as the man's jarl to punish him. King Gorm had had no business sending his men to Örn-garð to pull Estrith from his jarl's hall like a mussel from a shell.

'He is doing it to make a point,' Hrani's brother Amleth had said as they feasted the king's hirðmen with meat and mead and Hrani had sat in the jarl's seat with Herkja on his left hissing at him to paint more smile and less grimace on his face.

'I know why he is doing it, little brother,' Hrani had said. 'Our king wants to remind me who holds the power. Who has the longest claws. And he is using my hall as his scratching post to do it.'

And now Hrani was supposed to stand there on that hill freezing his balls off and be reminded what happens to those who fail in their duty.

'Well, Hrani, I hope the next skipper of *Golden-Fire* is not a man so easily fooled, hey!' King Gorm said, trudging across the slope and striking Hrani's fur-clad back with a big hand.

'Your man Moldof must possess more Loki-cunning than anyone gave him credit for, lord,' Hrani said, unable to resist, 'for from what my men tell me it was he that spun the trick of it all, claiming that he had killed Sigurd himself.' The king's face darkened but Hrani pushed on. 'What punishment have you in mind for him, should you ever lay your hands on him?'

The king removed his arm from Hrani's shoulder and Hrani knew that his mention of Moldof was like a flea in Gorm's ear. 'I am thinking that Moldof must be biding his time,' the king said, irritated. 'Like a smith who must judge the right time to strike the glowing iron.'

'And yet when the opportunity came along to be rid of Sigurd and his half crew, your prow man turned his back on it. Strange,' Hrani said, shaking his head as though he could not fathom it. 'At Moldof's word Estrith and my men would have boarded Haraldarson's ship and cut the dogs down beside their own sea chests.'

His eyes still on the drowned corpse out in the channel, the king shrugged broad shoulders, scratching his beard which was greyer than it had been the last time Hrani had seen him. 'Moldof was my prow man and champion for many years. He lost all that and an arm when he fought Jarl Harald in those woods,' he gestured to the south, 'but the man still has his pride. He left my hall to bring me Sigurd Haraldarson's head. He will do that or die trying. Moldof would not betray me. He is made like an ox but he has more wits in him than that.'

This last was aimed like a spear at Hrani, who nodded, knowing he had nettled the king enough, though the sight of Estrith out there on that flat rock goaded him on. A big herring gull had swept down to the skerry and now stood perched on Estrith's blueish chest, its yellow bill wide open as it gave its loud laughing call.

'A warrior can expect to be pecked by crows and ravens. But gulls?' Hrani shook his head.

'A warrior would have killed Sigurd Haraldarson when he had the chance,' King Gorm said. 'Come, Jarl Hrani,' he said, turning away from the sea and walking back up the snow-covered slope towards his hall, at which point his attending warriors and the women gathered there did the same. 'Let us get by the fire and rinse our insides with some warm mead. Forget about your man. I never understood how he worked a tiller with his left hand anyway.'

For a little while Hrani stood waiting to see if that gull would start picking at Estrith, or whether it was simply using him as a bench while it considered its coming meal of small fish or slick weed yielded up by the retreating tide. Then he turned and trudged up the hill after his king.

The farmstead was a modest affair comprising a longhouse, grain store, byre, animal pens and several other small outbuildings, the whole lot enclosed by a decent enough fence that would keep out wolves till Ragnarök and a man with an axe till noon. Beyond that was grazing land cut by a stream, the line of it showing like a black vein across the mantle of brittle snow. But it was the byre which interested Sigurd and the five others who had followed him along the track leading from the shore up through the trees to the arable land beyond. They were hungry and it was the kind of hunger that fish can never truly satisfy.

'If there's fresh meat for the taking we'd be fools to deny ourselves,' Svein had said when Bjorn and Bjarni had returned to the ship with news of what lay up on the high ground beyond sight of the sea. They had all seen the tarnish of smoke against the sky but Bjorn and Bjarni had been the first to volunteer to go ashore and investigate, their faces lit with the predatory lust which all raiding men recognize and all those who have been raided learn to fear.

It was a cold but clear and dry day, a rare enough thing itself for that time of the year, and the sky was the brilliant, flawless blue of Freyja's eyes, which meant that any smoke against it was visible for as far as the eye could see.

'See what's there and come straight back,' Sigurd had told the brothers.

'That means you don't so much as drink a drop or sniff a skirt before getting your arses back here, understand?' Olaf had warned them, and to give them their due the pair did as they were told, though they had all but licked their lips at the telling of the byre within which the cattle lowed as if pleading to be eaten, as Bjorn had put it.

'We could just buy a cow from this farmer,' Runa suggested now as they stood on the south side of the steading, looking across the hilly, snow-covered land and wondering how they could get what they wanted with the least amount of effort.

'What is the point in having swords and axes if you still have to pay for everything?' Bjorn asked, which few of the others could argue with.

'But why kill the man?' Runa asked, at which Bjorn looked at Sigurd with raised brows as if to say this is what you get when you bring your sister along.

She had pleaded with Sigurd that she be allowed to come, saying that if she did not remind her legs what it felt like to stand on solid rock again she feared she would spend the rest of her life walking like Crow-Song after two horns of mead.

'I may not have an endless capacity for mead, young Runa,' Hagal had put in, unable to let that slur slide by unanswered, 'but I do know when to stop and that is to my advantage. A man can neither observe the conspiracies of the mead hall clearly nor weave a fine tale if he is face down in his pottage.'

'I am just teasing, Hagal,' Runa said, giving one of Hagal's braids a gentle tug which was all it took to wipe the frown off the skald's face.

'You can come,' Sigurd had said, smiling to see his sister's eyes light up at something so simple as the prospect of going ashore for a short while. From the report of what awaited them Sigurd did not expect danger – though he insisted she wore brynja and helmet and carried a shield and spear.

Runa had suffered as much as he and yet the world was not blighted for her. Her spirit was a flame which Sigurd had promised himself he would fan whenever he could. 'It will do us all good to stretch our legs,' he'd said in a low voice so as not to incite the jealousy of those who would remain with *Reinen*.

'If they give us no trouble we won't hurt them,' Sigurd said now for the benefit of Bjorn, Svein, Floki and Aslak.

'No point in taking the edge off a blade if it can be avoided easily enough,' Svein agreed, for he had always had a soft spot for Runa, which was the only possible explanation for him advocating peaceableness that Sigurd could see.

'So what is the plan?' Aslak asked, huffing breath into his hands. 'It looks as if they are all snugged up by their hearth. No one is coming to invite us inside.' It was that kind of cold where if you were to leave an axe carelessly on the ground, it would freeze to it so completely that the haft would snap off at the head if you tried to lever it free. Anything left in mud, like a shoe or a loom weight, became a part of it until the thaw.

Somewhere within the steading a dog was barking, which may or may not have been because it sensed strangers nearby. Some hooded crows were pecking amongst the snow at the stream's edge. Beyond the farmstead to the north and east, stands of birch and pine, looking troubled by their white burden, played host to a clamour of rooks whose raucous cawing rose into the sky.

'Floki will go over the wall and open the gate,' Sigurd said. 'Then we will tell whoever lives here that we are taking a cow or maybe a bull and whatever else we like the look of.' He shrugged. 'We'll butcher the meat here, making sure no one runs off to their jarl, but we'll cook it on the shore in case we have to move on.'

157

'Who is the jarl round here?' Aslak asked, but no one knew. Not that it mattered, for jarls did not stray far from their hearths in the winter and were more likely to stay wrapped in furs and bed slaves than come trudging out because of the theft of one cow and a cheese or two.

Everyone nodded, happy with that plan, then they set off across the rolling snow-covered hills and toiled up the slope towards the farm, their war gear jangling and clumping and their breath clouding ghost-like. Theirs were the only tracks through the snow. Not that they could blame these folk for staying indoors if they had the supplies to see them through. If anything the clear sky had turned it even colder. The faraway white sun had all the heat of week-old hearth ash, so that ear rims tingled and burnt, noses glowed red and, inside his boots, Sigurd's toes would have curled right under his feet if they could.

'Looks like we're not the only ones wanting inside this place,' Bjorn said, pointing his spear to the oval spoor of a big dog fox, the animal's single-file prints stitching the snow along the white-topped perimeter fence. Sigurd thought he caught the scent of the fox's urine on the morning air but he doubted the creature had found a way in to the hen coop.

His shield slung over his back, Floki kicked his boots against the timbers to get the worst of the snow off them, then stepped into the stirrup of Svein's hands. Svein straightened and up Floki went, grabbing hold of the top of the fence so that he could haul himself over, which he did as nimbly as a squirrel before disappearing from view. They heard the crump of him landing in the drifts on the other side and Sigurd asked if there was any sign of the folk who lived there.

'All quiet,' came the reply, though Floki was not referring to the dog which was barking continuously now – the poor creature having been left outside to stand guard – or to the cattle in the byre which were lowing.

Floki opened the gate and the others passed through into the farmstead, standing a moment to familiarize themselves with the layout. Then, hefting spears and raising their shields, they tramped towards the longhouse from whose thatch smoke poured up in stark contrast to the clean sky. But no arrows streaked from between the outbuildings and neither did any blade-wielding men step out into the day to defend their home, and it was left to Sigurd to thump the butt of his spear against the longhouse door as though he were a cousin come to share a cup of ale and some news of the world beyond the wooden wall.

They waited, stamping their feet and getting cold. Svein looked at Sigurd with watery eyes and a heavy frown. 'This is not how a raid is supposed to be,' he said.

Before Sigurd could ask his friend what usually happened, seeing as Svein was such an old hand at this raiding life, they heard a muffled voice from within.

'Who is it? We are not expecting guests.'

'Open this door,' Sigurd said.

'No,' came the reply.

Bjorn mumbled a curse. Runa laughed.

'I can't decide whether to burn this house and kill all of your cattle,' Sigurd said, 'or take just one animal and leave you to your hearth and furs. It is strange but I find I make better decisions when my feet are not freezing.'

There was more muffled conversation on the other side of the door but then they heard the clump of the locking bar being removed and it swung ajar.

A man's face appeared in the crack.

'Who are you?' he said.

Svein kicked the door open, sending the man flying on to the hay-strewn floor. They walked into the flame-lit house, coughing on the smoke which the open door drew, their eyes adjusting to the dark.

'Who are you?' the man asked again, gathering up the hand axe he had dropped and climbing to his feet.

'What does it matter?' Sigurd asked him, looking around the room. The people living there had pulled their beds up to surround the hearth. Three of those six beds had people in them, old folk, their terror-stricken faces the only parts of them showing beyond the piles of pelts beneath which they cowered from winter.

'You've come to raid us?' a woman asked. She stood behind a roof post, but had it been three times as thick it would not have come close to hiding her. Sigurd looked beyond the hearth flames and saw the pale face of a boy up in the loft, peering down with round eyes.

'We've come for meat,' Sigurd said. His eyes stung from the smoke which was so thick in the room that he thought should the woman drop dead there and then her flesh would still be good to eat in twenty years or more. 'Just meat,' he assured her.

The man edged closer to his enormous wife, still holding that hand axe, though what he thought he was going to do with that against five battle-hardened men who were armed like war gods, Sigurd could not imagine.

'The only raiding we've had has been from the wind, the rain and this damned cold,' the woman said, stepping out from behind the post and taking a key from the hook on her belt. 'This will get you in the byre,' she said. Sigurd nodded and took the key, giving it to Svein.

'We'll find the fattest one,' Svein said through a grin, nodding at Aslak and Bjorn to go with him.

'We've salt fish if you want?' the woman said.

'We've got more than enough of that,' Sigurd said.

'Cheese?' she offered. Sigurd nodded. 'Skyr?' she said. 'I made enough to last Fimbulvetr. My husband says it is the best batch I have made for years.'

'I have not had good skyr for such a long time,' Runa said, and so Sigurd gestured for the woman to fetch some.

'Strange time of year to be out raiding,' the woman's husband said, scratching his bearded chin with the blunt edge of his axe.

'And yet look how easy it is,' Sigurd said. 'I am surprised everyone is not doing it.'

The man had no answer to that, as Sigurd went over to join Floki who was already warming his hands above the hearth, those three in their beds – two old women and an ancient man by the looks, though it was hard to know for sure – staring at him as if he had fallen from the sky. Runa followed her brother towards the fireplace and the golden promise of its flames, leaning her spear against a post so that she could flex and make fists of her pink hands to get the blood gushing into them. 'Thank you for your hospitality,' she said to the farmer's wife who had returned with a large wooden bowl full of skyr.

The woman nodded, giving the skyr to Runa who could not resist scooping three fingers' worth of the thick, curdled milk out of the bowl and into her mouth.

'This is as good as our mother used to make,' Runa told her, which might have put a smile on those full lips had the woman's thought box not been full of how to get her family through this raid alive and with minimal loss to their livelihood.

'You are welcome to it, girl,' the woman said, waving a hand at her husband that he should put that axe down before it caused someone offence. The man frowned and squatted, placing the axe on the floor behind the hearth stones as if he believed he might have got away without anyone seeing it.

'You came by sea,' the man said, more of a statement than a question, which was a fair assumption on his part since he had not recognized any of his visitors and must suppose they had come some considerable way. 'Must be quiet as the grave out there.'

'There are not many boats out,' Sigurd said, wondering how Svein and the others were getting on with the slaughtering and butchering. It would not be easy carrying so much meat back to the ship but at least the frigid air would keep the meat fresh on their continued journey and there would be no flies to bother it. Yes, this winter raiding had its benefits, he thought.

'Who is the jarl here?' he asked the farmer.

'Ebbi Eggilsson,' he said, glancing at his wife who was stuffing two cheeses into a sack for Runa.

'And which king does Jarl Ebbi swear fealty to?' Sigurd asked. For though they had sailed far south to the arse end of Norway and were now following the coast eastward, they had yet to come into the Jutland Sea. Who knew if King Gorm's power reached as far south as this?

163

The farmer frowned. 'King Svarin, I think,' he said, seeming far from sure and looking to the skull-faced old man in the bed nearest. But he got no help from him.

'Not King Gorm?' Sigurd asked.

'Maybe,' the man said. 'We have little to do with such things. We've no sons to send the jarl should he be dragged off to go fighting with the king.'

Sigurd did not mention the boy peering down at him from the loft, who looked a good few years from fighting age anyway.

'And where are you headed?' the farmer asked.

'Birka,' Sigurd said. It was not as though this man would come after them, nor would his jarl. Not for the sake of one cow.

'Been there twice,' the farmer said, 'and twice was one too many times. Folk crammed together like sheep in a pen. It's not for me.'

The door opened again, drawing the hearth smoke and letting cold air into the room like another unwanted guest, and Sigurd gestured at Aslak to come in quickly and shut it behind him. The farmer and his wife had been good hosts up to now and the old folk in their beds looked frail enough that a cold blast could finish them off.

'We are ready,' Aslak said. He had a handful of snow and was rubbing it against his other hand to get the blood off. He smiled at the farmer's wife. 'You keep your cattle well fed,' he said, 'and we thank you for it.'

The woman did her best to smile back, as the old man in the bed muttered something about the indignity of being robbed by men barely into their beards and even a girl, and that he might as well die now that he had seen everything.

'You only have to ask,' Floki told him, pulling his long knife from its sheath and letting the hearth flames dance along its polished length.

'What are your men doing now?' the farmer asked. Sigurd frowned but a heartbeat later he heard what had got the man worried. It was the unmistakable sound of an axe hacking into timbers. 'Won't you leave us in peace now that you have what you want?'

'Aslak?' Sigurd said. Aslak frowned and shook his head.

The door thumped open again and this time it was Bjorn standing there and he had that look.

'Visitors,' he said.

'Jarl Ebbi?' Runa suggested. Her shield was slung across her back. She had given her spear to Floki to carry so that she could bring the sack with the cheeses and the skyr in it.

'Why would the jarl ruin this man's gate?' Sigurd said. 'You have enemies?' he asked the farmer. The man shook his head and Sigurd cursed under his breath. He had been thinking this winter raiding was easy and that it was strange more men did not do it. It seemed more men did do it. He stepped outside and there stood Svein facing the gate, his long axe in his hands, the butchered meat in a pile on the snow beside him.

'Seen anyone yet?' he called.

'Not yet,' Svein replied over his shoulder, 'but they're making a mess of that gate.'

The head of the axe doing the work was coming through the planks now and catching so that the man wielding it had to work hard to free the blade before pulling it out for another swing.

'We could go over the back wall,' Aslak suggested, looking back past the longhouse between the grain store and the pig pen. 'Whoever it is, they've not come for us.'

Aslak was right. These men, whoever they were, most likely wanted provisions: meat and grain, cheese and ale to stave off the cold in lean times. It was just this farmstead's bad luck that they were being raided twice in one day. This was not Sigurd's fight. They could take their meat and get out over the back wall before these others broke down the gate, though why these others hadn't simply climbed over to open it Sigurd could not say. Perhaps they were breaking the gate to keep warm or, more likely, just because they could.

'Sigurd?' Svein said, still facing the gate, waiting for Sigurd to give some command.

So what if these new men slaughtered another beast or two? So what if they slaughtered the farmer and his wife and the three hoary old folk in their beds? Sigurd had his own responsibilities. Then he thought of the boy up in the loft, imagined those blue eyes of his wide with fear as some growler took a fistful of his yellow hair and cut his throat.

Maybe these raiders would not find the boy. And then what? It was a dark, foul thing to see your kin die, to watch bloodlines end, severed by steel. Such a thing could poison you. Or it could set you on a road of blood and vengeance. Fire and sword.

Let the boy be a boy.

'Shieldwall!' Sigurd called, tramping through the snow to stand with Svein. The others hurried to join them, and for a moment the axe man stopped his work and Sigurd saw men's faces through the holes, those peering men no doubt wondering what kind of farmer they had come across who had enough war-trained sons that they could present a skjaldborg. Then the axe was cutting again and soon it was joined by booted feet as the attackers kicked away the last splintered resistance. Then they poured in through the wreckage, all eyes and beard and done up like the fur bales Sigurd's men had stowed aboard *Reinen*.

'Stay behind me, Runa,' Sigurd growled over his shoulder, then saw the farmer trudging towards him, his axe back in his hand and an old shield in the other. 'Get back inside and see to your family,' Sigurd said, and the man nodded, not needing to be told twice. But Sigurd was not being kind. A skjaldborg was only as strong as its weakest man and Sigurd did not want a man more practised at feeding cows than crows beside him if it came to a fight. Which it probably would looking at the thirteen men who stood facing them in a loose line a good spear-throw away.

'Who are you?' one of them called, his breath pluming round his red-bearded face. The newcomers were armed mostly with axes and spears and all had shields. Who could say how many wore brynjur under all those furs, but the chances were that none of them did, seeing as none of them owned a helmet.

'We are the men who got here before you,' Sigurd called back. 'Find another farm.'

The man pointed his spear to the joints of meat lying in the snow beside Sigurd's shieldwall. 'It looks to me as if you have what you came for. More than enough to feed the six of you.' He was a handsome man but not a rich one by the looks of him and what little war gear was visible. In this situation most warriors would proudly display whatever fine gear they had for that could sometimes be enough to win the fight before it started. 'Why don't you fuck off and we'll just take our share?'

Sigurd made a show of considering this offer. 'I think that if we walk away this time what is to say you will not beat us to the prize next time? And if we keep going like this, eventually these people will have nothing left worth stealing.' Sigurd shook his head. 'Better to kill you now and keep this farm going a little longer.' With that Svein lifted his massive axe and rolled his shoulders, loosening off in readiness. Really Svein was just showing these men the full extent of his size.

The farmer's dog was once more barking continuously, straining at the end of its tether as it ran back and forth. And this gave one amongst the other raiding party an opportunity to show off. Armed with a bow he walked a few paces ahead of his companions, pulling an arrow from the quiver at his waist and nocking it. The next time Sigurd saw that arrow it was in the dog's eye and the dog was dead, which was no bad thing as far as he was concerned. But whilst it had shut the animal up, it also showed that the bowman was a very good shot.

'Uncle's going to say we can't do one simple job without getting into a fight,' Bjorn rumbled, pushing his helmet down tight. Some of them had taken to calling Olaf Uncle because he was older than they and more experienced in women, war and the whale road, having been Sigurd's father's best friend. Olaf did not seem to mind.

'So we are going to fight over this?' the leader of the other band asked.

'Do not forget your sister is here,' Svein growled out of the corner of his mouth.

Sigurd had not forgotten, but he did not know what to do about that now. 'You can turn round and walk back through the mess you made,' he called, pointing at the splintered planks lying in the gateway.

But the other man shook his head. 'No, I don't think we will,' he shouted back, gesturing with his spear. 'Not now we have come all this way.'

Sigurd nodded, as if he understood perfectly well. Both men knew there was pride at stake now. Knew too that men can be such fools when it comes to pride.

Perhaps it is another test, Sigurd thought. *Perhaps the Æsir have a hand in this.* For was it not ill luck that another raiding party had turned up at the same farmstead at more or less the same time? And even if these other men walked away now, they would more than likely come back after Sigurd had gone, and take out their frustration on the farmer's family. They would make a slaughter of man and beast and then they would burn down the stead and warm themselves by the flames.

Sigurd would not let that happen. And so there would have to be a fight.

'Well then, let's get on with it for I am getting cold standing here like a fucking tree,' Svein said.

'Come, then,' Sigurd invited the men strung out across the snow facing him.

At their leader's command they drew together until their shields overlapped and they had made their own wall of wood and iron, their spears protruding over the tops of their shields.

'Who has the horn?' Sigurd asked his men.

'Here,' Aslak said.

'Blow it, then,' Sigurd said and Aslak put the big horn to his lips. The note was deep and long and

Aslak sounded the horn twice more so that those down at the shore with *Reinen* would hear it.

'Do not tell me we have to wait for the others,' Svein said.

But they could not wait even if they wanted to, for the other shieldwall was moving towards them now, those men perhaps fearing what that horn signal meant and wanting to kill the five men facing them before reinforcements arrived.

'We're going to piss on your corpses,' a man yelled across the mostly smooth snow between them.

'I can see that golden-haired bitch hiding behind you,' another warrior shouted at Sigurd. 'I'm going to split her open but not with my sword, hey!'

'Come out, come out, my pretty!' a man with a long, black beard rope bellowed, all gap-toothed grin above the rim of his shield.

'Arrow!' Bjorn called and two heartbeats later a shaft thunked into Svein's shield.

'I feel like stretching my legs, Sigurd,' Floki said, and Sigurd nodded, knowing full well what the young man meant by that. Floki stepped out of the skjaldborg, not that you could really call it a shieldwall with only four men now standing in it.

'Where in Frigg's cunny does he think he's going?' Bjorn asked, barely flinching as an arrow struck his shield, the point lifting a sliver from the inside of a limewood plank but not piercing it fully.

'That is what those goat turds will be wondering,' Sigurd said, watching Floki, light-footed through the snow, as he walked round the opposing shieldwall's right flank, causing some of them to turn with him. Which gave Sigurd an idea.

'Are you sure you want to die today?' their red-bearded leader asked, not needing to shout now because they were close enough to see the lice in each other's beards and smell the mustiness of the furs under which they were all buried.

'Break,' Sigurd said to those standing with him. 'Runa, stay with me.' Bjorn and Aslak stalked out on his left and Svein tramped out on his right, leaving Sigurd in space with Runa at his back. Sigurd did not know if the thirteen men facing them were good fighters, but even if they were not, they would have wrapped their shieldwall round Sigurd's and even an unskilled spearman can kill a man from behind who is busy fighting another in front. Besides which, when Svein began swinging that big axe of his it was a good idea to be somewhere else.

'You are a lucky man,' Sigurd said, smiling at the warrior who had halted his men, unsure what to do now that there was no longer a skjaldborg facing him.

'And why is that?' he asked, buying time as his mind whirred.

'Because before I am eating this farmer's meat on the shore beside my ship, you will be drinking mead with your ancestors.' Sigurd rolled his right shoulder in its socket, wondering if his muscles and bones would be too cold to obey him now. 'If you see my father and my brothers, tell them I look forward to joining them at Óðin's high table. But it will not be today.' With that he pulled his arm back and hurled the spear, which streaked like an iron lightning bolt and perhaps the man's shield was rotten, or perhaps it was weakened in some previous fight, but Sigurd's spear punched through the wood and into his chest, pinning the shield to him. He fell, the men beside him stepping away, looking at him with incredulity, expecting him to stand and cast the ruined shield aside. But dead men did not stand.

And it was into this cauldron of shock that Svein poured chaos. He bellowed, cursing his enemies as he strode towards them, looping his long-hafted axe whose crescent blade promised cold death on that cold day. Those men backed away from him, instinct telling them that they must escape that smiting weapon, yet honour forcing them to stand their ground.

Roaring their deaths, Svein brought the axe down in an overhead cut and it cleaved the shield raised against it, cut through the arm beneath and on into the fur-snugged head, only stopping its dreadful descent when it snagged in the cradle of its victim's hips. Svein ripped it free of the splintered bone, the two halves of the man falling apart in a flood of blood and glistening intestines, as that wicked-sharp blade flew up as fast as a grouse, looping back over the red-haired giant's head before scything in from the side to take another man's head off his shoulders before he could scramble out of range. That blade was a living thing in Svein's hands, never still now but soaring through the air around him, tracing invisible ship's knots, thirsting to drink more blood as the big man gave himself to the battle lust.

Floki turned a spear jab aside with his own shaft, then slashed his spear blade across his opponent's throat before dancing out of the path of an arcing sword and stepping forward to thrust the spear through fur and skins into a warrior's belly. Aslak and Bjorn were moving fast, stabbing and slashing with their spears, whilst Sigurd faced the man with the long beard rope, taking a succession of heavy blows on his shield before sheathing Troll-Tickler in the man's gullet and drawing it out in a crimson spray which spattered the snow.

This other raiding party had not begun their day expecting anything like this and had probably thought they would just need to growl a little to leave this farmstead with everything they had it in mind to steal. Now they were being butchered where they stood and the hard truth of it must have been a blow as savage as any from Svein's axe.

'Fall back! Regroup!' one of them yelled, and that was a good plan, but it is hard to put plans into practice when you are busy being killed. Still, five of them closed together like a fist, trudging back through the snow to join the bowman who had kept his distance all along. Panting and wide-eyed, their shields raised but no longer overlapping, they backed away, and even if it had not yet sunk into their skulls that six of their friends would never drink with them again, they must nevertheless have seen the mess of those butchered men lying there before them.

The one other raider still standing chose instead to run and Bjorn made a grab for him but fell in the snow, and Aslak hurled his spear, missing by a finger length, and the man's fear carried him like wings over the snow. Bjorn got to his feet, cursing.

'Any luck and the others'll get him,' Svein said.

'We have had enough,' another of those thunderstruck men told Sigurd. 'Let us walk away. Let us go and you can keep whatever plunder you find on our dead.'

'Let you go?' Sigurd said. 'If I did that, my friends would not be happy.' He pointed his sword beyond them to the ruined gate. 'They have trudged up here through the snow to fight you and now you are done with fighting?' He shook his head. 'That is no way to behave.'

Olaf, Bram and Moldof picked their way through the broken timbers, and Sigurd was glad that it was only those who had come, for as it had turned out this band of doomed men was not worth leaving *Reinen* unguarded for.

'I see you did not wait for us,' Olaf yelled, his chest rising and falling heavily beneath his furs and ringmail. 'But at least we have not come all the way up here for nothing.' His breath fogged the air above his head and he rolled his shoulders, hefting his shield and spear as he walked towards the six men, Bram on his right and Moldof on his left.

'Did you get the runner?' Aslak called to Olaf.

'Did we bollocks! Ran like a scalded dog that one,' Olaf replied.

'We yield!' a man from the other crew called, thrusting his spear into the snow.

'That's up to you, lad,' Olaf said, not breaking stride. 'But if it were me I'd rather die with a weapon in my hands than on my knees in the ice.'

The man knew beyond doubt then that the Norns, those three spinners who weave men's past, present and future, had cut the threads of his wyrd and all that was left to him now was to choose the manner of his death. He chose well, pulling the spear from the snow and thrusting it at Olaf who parried with his own spear and threw his weight behind his shield, slamming it into his opponent's and knocking him on to his arse in the snow.

'Up you get,' Olaf said, as Moldof hammered his sword into another man's shield, splintering it with one blow before twisting to his left and lopping the man's spear in two. Then he thrust his sword into the man's chest and hauled it out, already turning to seek his next kill. 'Now's the time to pull that scramasax,' Olaf told his man, who was scrambling to his feet, puffing like forge bellows so that he had half disappeared in his own cloud. And perhaps he did not even see the blade that killed him, though he bled out with a good-looking long knife in his hand.

Bram squared up to a man with a long loose beard who was a full head taller than him and perhaps as broad in the shoulder, but before they could fight each other the tall man grunted and fell face down in the snow, one of Floki's short axes lodged between his shoulder blades.

'You selfish little runt,' Bram growled at Floki, who stood twenty paces away grinning like a wolf.

Then the bowman ran. He plunged off through the crisp mantle and Bram remarked that it was not worth the effort of chasing him seeing as to be haring off like that he could not possibly be wearing a brynja or any silver worth getting out of breath for.

Aslak, Bjorn and Svein made light work of the last two and set to pilfering the dead for rings, blades and anything of worth, while Sigurd surveyed the slaughteryard that had been made of the steading. Around each of the dead the snow was stained crimson. Pools of blood were melting the ice and spatters could be seen as far as ten paces from the body, prompting Aslak to observe that it was only in such conditions that you realized how far the battle-sweat could fly in a fight.

'Who *are* you?' The farmer stood behind them in the open doorway of his longhouse, grey hearth smoke leaking out into the day around him. He stared at Sigurd as he might at a god who had come down from Asgard to Midgard.

'We are the men who have killed one of your beasts and left you with eleven corpses to deal with,' he said.

'But at least we did not smash your gate in,' Svein said, plunging his axe blade into the snow to clean it.

'Who were this lot?' Olaf asked, coming to join Sigurd and Runa.

Sigurd shrugged. 'Raiders,' he said, 'who would have been better off staying by their hearth this morning.'

'Aye, well there's no sign of a ship out there so they must have come the hard way,' Olaf said, nodding inland towards the higher ground. And that was when they saw the plume of black smoke rising from the stone tower which stood on the ridge to the north of the farmstead.

'You let this farmer send someone to light his beacon?' Olaf asked, for the stone tower clearly belonged to this steading.

'I did not see anyone leave the place,' Runa said. 'Those old folk could not have done it, surely.'

But Sigurd could see the small figure with the shock of yellow hair standing up there on the skyline beside the smoke-belching fire. It was the boy he had spotted up in the loft. The lad must have snuck out and run up the hill and perhaps the farmer had sent him or perhaps the man had not known he had gone, but none of that mattered now.

'How long will it be before your neighbours put a war party together?' he asked the farmer, who looked more frightened now than he had before, perhaps expecting Sigurd to kill his family for lighting the beacon to summon help.

'I hope they don't come, lord,' the man said, using that title as a sign of respect, and what he meant was that he knew that his fellow farmers would die unless they came in great numbers.

'How long?' Sigurd asked again. It would be getting dark soon and Sigurd had it in mind to roast a share of that meat on the shore before sailing from this place.

'They will gather before nightfall but they will want to wait for Jarl Ebbi and his men before they attack. He can bring thirty or more warriors if he chooses. As for the karls around here who are sworn to come to each other's aid,' he scratched his short beard, 'I would say there'll be forty men if they manage to drag all their sons along. But I will tell them you came here in peace. That I gave you a good hearth welcome and in return you killed these other men.'

The man's wife pushed past him now, coming outside to get a look at the mess, but the farmer grabbed hold of her arm, warning her that the issue was not yet fully resolved. Whatever he said was enough to get her back inside and the door shut, leaving her husband standing there shivering beside his own log pile.

Sigurd smiled. 'Your boy did well to get all the way up there so quickly.'

For a moment the man seemed unsure how to answer that. Then he nodded. 'He's fast as the wind, lord,' he said.

'We've lingered here long enough,' Olaf called. Svein told the farmer to find him some sacks for all the cuts of meat, and the others having pilfered what they could from the dead gathered their spears and shields and set off out of the steading. Sigurd stood for a moment, watching them go.

'It is sad, don't you think?' Runa said, looking at the red-bearded man Sigurd had killed. Sigurd had retrieved his spear and Svein had stripped the man of his furs and tunic, looking for silver stashed against his skin, so that now the pale corpse made for a pathetic sight lying there half naked. He did not look handsome now. Just dead. 'These eleven men will not be returning to their wives and children. If they are from far away perhaps their kin will never know what became of them.'

'They had the chance to walk away,' Sigurd said.

'They would have taken it if they'd known who they were facing,' Runa said. And she was right. Sigurd might not have many warriors at his command, certainly not enough to take on a jarl let alone a king. But those warriors he had were killers. Each was worthy of his or her own saga for their skill and courage and for their arrogance too, for they seemed to think they were unbeatable. But together they were savage as winter. They were a wolfpack.

'These men are dead but that family still lives,' Sigurd said, looking up at the boy who was still up there by the pillar of smoke which rose straight in the still air, tall as a roof beam in Valhöll. 'Come, sister, or they will feast on that meat without us.'

Together they walked through the ruined gateway and followed the others back down the slope across the rolling snow-covered meadows. And neither of them saw the arrow until it had streaked past their heads.

Sigurd spun, cursing himself for not having killed that bowman when he'd had the chance. And there he was, standing by the rock behind which he had hidden from the rest, nocking another arrow to his bow string. Clearly it was Sigurd he wanted.

'Go, Runa,' Sigurd said, as the next arrow thumped into his shield which he had lifted to protect his face.

'No,' she said, and Sigurd cursed again, striding towards the man to put distance between himself and Runa.

'You're a dead man,' Sigurd told the archer, watching him over the rim of his shield, close enough to see the grimace of hatred on his face. The man took another arrow from the quiver on his belt, turned his head to spit into the snow, put the arrow to the string, drew, held, then loosed. Sigurd did not see this arrow fly but he felt it glance off his helmet with a *tonk*. A finger's breadth lower and he would have seen the arrow very well for it would have passed through his helmet's left eye guard on its way into his skull.

He heard one of his men yell Runa's name and he looked over his shoulder to see them lumbering back through the snow towards Runa who was on her knees, clutching her face.

'Runa!' he screamed, then shook the shield off his arm and cast his spear aside, turned back to the archer and ran at him. The man stood rooted to the spot for another three heartbeats; long enough to shoot another arrow, this one thumping into Sigurd's shoulder, but seeing that it did not even slow Sigurd, he turned and fled and Sigurd flew after him.

Plunging through the deep snow, Sigurd threw off his helmet then fumbled at his belt until that too fell away with his scabbarded sword and was left behind. Still, the archer was even less cumbered, having no brynja, and he had a spear-throw's worth of head start. Moreover he ran with a swiftness born of fear, clutching his bow in one hand and his arrows in the other lest they fly out of the quiver with his plunging stride.

It was true that fear could make a man fast on his feet. But so could rage, and Sigurd burnt with rage. It pumped blood into his limbs and pounded in his ears. It rasped in his throat like a hateful beast and it shut out the world so that all he could see was his prey in front of him, a desperate and pathetic creature that was too dim-witted to know there was no escape from death.

The bowman ran for the trees, hoping he could lose his pursuer amongst them. He never made it. With six feet of ground between them, Sigurd threw himself at the man, grabbing hold of his furs and bringing him down with a grunt as the air was forced from their lungs. Then Sigurd was on him, clawing at the man's face, forcing his thumbs into the eye sockets so that the archer screamed. Then the thin bone at the back of the man's eyes gave way and Sigurd's thumbs plunged into the hot mush of his brain. The body jerked and convulsed beneath him and finally went still and Sigurd wiped his thumbs on the dead man's furs before standing, gasping for each scalding breath, his pulse in his ears like the beating of a sword on the inside of a shield.

He did not bother to see if the dead man had anything worth taking.

'Wander the afterlife blind, you nithing piece of troll shit,' he growled at the dead man, whose eyes were little wells of blood from which the crows would drink before nightfall. Then he turned and ran back along his own tracks.

To Runa.

CHAPTER EIGHT

'SHE'S SLEEPING,' VALGERD SAID, PLACING BLOOD-SOAKED rags into the fire which burnt on the muddy sand of the shore. 'I was careful but there will be no missing the scar.'

Sigurd looked over her shoulder at Runa who was lying amongst a pile of skins and furs above the tideline. He was relieved to see her asleep though not surprised, for he had poured a bucket full of mead down her throat to numb the pain. The arrow which had glanced off Sigurd's helmet had slashed open her face from just below her left eye to her ear. It had bled and it had hurt, but Valgerd had washed the wound with sea water and stitched it closed, and so long as there was no wound rot Runa would come out of it well enough. And yet Sigurd was in a foul mood and had hardly touched the plate of succulent beef which Olaf had put in front of him.

'We go to the trouble of killing a dozen men and you can't bring yourself to eat?' Olaf had growled, sitting down beside Sigurd who had left Valgerd to dress the wound with linens. They had decided to spend the night on the shore beside *Reinen*, with lookouts posted in case Jarl Ebbi came looking for them. They would weigh anchor and be gone at first light, but first they would eat.

'It is my fault she is lying there with her face torn open. I should have killed that whoreson back at that farm.'

Olaf nodded. 'Yes, we should never have let him run off like that. But we had already made the mistake before that.'

Sigurd looked up into his friend's eyes.

'Runa shouldn't have been there, Sigurd,' Olaf said. 'Even had those turds not shown up at the same steading at the same time, you might have expected a fight of some sort. Or else why go armed like Týr himself?' He shrugged. 'There were blades and arrows flying around. People get hurt on days like today. There are twelve poker-stiff bodies up there that are proof of that, lad. Runa shouldn't have been there.'

'I know that,' Sigurd said. What made it worse was that the others had known it before the first blood was spilled, which was why Svein was barely talking to Sigurd now. He was angry with Sigurd and it came off him like a stink.

'What man takes his little sister raiding?' was all he had said, which had been more than enough as far as Sigurd was concerned.

'What if there is more to it than that?' Sigurd had asked Olaf, who had frowned, not understanding where he was going with that. 'The arrow was meant for me. It hit my helmet, which changed its flight.'

'You think the gods want to punish you?' Olaf asked. 'That they would hurt Runa to hurt you?'

Sigurd thought about that. 'Perhaps they cannot let me die,' he said. 'I am Óðin-favoured. So maybe they go after my family instead. Maybe they want me to watch everyone I love suffer. Until I am the last.'

'Has *he* been filling your head with this?' Olaf asked, nodding towards Asgot who sat cross-legged on a flat rock nearby, savaging a hunk of meat whose bloody juice was dripping into his beard.

'I have not spoken to him about it,' Sigurd said.

Olaf nodded. 'Good. Keep it that way.' He picked up the plate of meat and offered it to Sigurd, who took it and put it down beside him. 'Look, Sigurd, what happened out there with that arrow was an accident. Bad luck at worst.'

'But I shouldn't have put Runa at risk,' Sigurd said.

'*We* shouldn't have put Runa at risk,' Olaf corrected him. 'And seeing as there's bound to be plenty more fighting before this is all over, we ought to think about what we can do with the girl to keep her safe.' He shook his head and scratched his thickly bearded cheek. Ideas were not exactly bursting from him. After a little while he got up and walked up the strand to check on those men who were coming to the end of their watch.

'Well, I won't abandon her,' Sigurd said. Not that anyone was listening. Then he went over to Runa and sat down beside her, leaning against the rock and looking out across the still black water. Holding her hand as she slept.

Hrani had to admit that for all King Gorm's taste for chaining his enemies to the rocks and watching them drown, he was a generous host in his own hall. There were trenchers of pork and beef and whale meat and rabbit. There were plates of fish and cheese and freshly baked bread and pots of honey, all of it washed down with buckets of mead flavoured with apple, juniper berries, dried fruit blossoms and warmed by hot stones.

'If this is how you celebrate drowning a nithing skipper, I hope Jarl Hrani and I are fortunate enough to be here when you kill Sigurd Haraldarson, my lord,' Herkja said to the king beside her, flashing him a smile and eyes which must have had his old snake stirring in his breeks.

The king nodded, lifting his cup towards Herkja and Hrani beside her. 'That will be a feast to tempt the gods down from Asgard,' he said, 'which brings me to the question of what we should do to bring such a night to pass. Your husband and I must discuss how we are going to pay young Sigurd in kind for his treatment of my hirðman Freystein, and for his many other offences.'

Being perched on the hill as it was, the royal farmstead was subject to the winds which blew up and down the Karmsund Strait. But the walls of the king's longhall were hung with thick tapestries which kept out all but the most determined gusts.

'Is it true that Sigurd sent your man's corpse back to you wearing his father's jarl torc?' Herkja asked, knowing it *was* true but savouring the gore of the story, as she had when Hrani had first told it to her.

The king frowned and Queen Kadlin leant forward, fixing Herkja with eyes like rivet heads in the fire-licked dark.

'This Sigurd is a savage,' she said. 'He could have had power and wealth. Instead he insults us all.'

I wonder what power. I wonder whose wealth, Hrani thought but did not say, for whilst being jarl at Hinderå he was now jarl at Skudeneshavn too, where Sigurd's father had been jarl. He would like to know what the king had been prepared to offer Sigurd in return for his fealty, though he knew he would get no answer about that now. Besides which, Sigurd had made it all moot by putting his blade through this Freystein and sending Harald's torc back to the king round his messenger's neck.

'He may be a savage, my lady,' Herkja said, 'but I almost pity him for having made enemies of our husbands. He must feel like the woodlouse that finds itself on the end of the log in the middle of the hearth with flame all around.'

Queen Kadlin laughed at that. 'My girl, you have the imagination of a skald,' she said, 'but your stomach is too weak if you pity such a man.' Now her face had all the charm of a granite cliff. 'Sigurd and any fools who follow him will die. They will die and be denied the Allfather's mead.' She held Herkja's gaze an uncomfortable moment, then forced a smile, wafting away her talk of death with a pale hand. 'Come now. Sit by me,' she said, beckoning Herkja and patting the bench beside her. 'Let us leave the men to discuss how they are going to pay the savage what they owe him. I would hear about your life at Hinderå and how you find raising that boy.' She leant in close. 'They say his mother was a thrall?' she said in the voice of someone whispering to be heard.

Herkja planted a kiss on Hrani's cheek, then dutifully climbed out from the bench to do as her queen bid and talk about the son she had inherited. Not that Hrani cared what they talked about, but the sooner his new wife had her own boy growing in her belly the better. He pointed to his cup so that one of the pretty thralls would come over and fill it with warm mead. He was comfortable, his stomach was full and he had even put behind him that business about the king killing Estrith Left-Handed. Almost. And now his night was going to get even better. Because they were going to talk of killing their common enemy, a man Hrani hated to the very marrow in his bones.

'Did you get the name of their leader?' Fionn asked, warming his hands over the fire. Clenching and unclenching his fists to help the heat get into them. The man had done well to get a fire going at all, what with all that snow and ice. But Fionn supposed it was either that or die out there like a lame beast, for the only dwelling Fionn had seen since yesterday was five rôsts to the north and it was already too dark to make that sort of distance and seek hospitality which might or might not be forthcoming.

'No,' the man said. 'He was young though. Well, younger than me.'

The pine branches crackled and spluttered but there was enough flame to warm their faces as the two of them crouched over the fire. And yet it was the smoke, not the flame, which had led Fionn inland, over a hill and across a valley, straight to the man as surely as if he could see him through trees, rock, earth and the blackness of night. It was the smoke which had killed the man, even if he did not know it yet.

'Was there a one-armed man with them? A big wolf-jointed bastard.'

The man shook his head. He was shivering. Looked as if he hadn't eaten for days. 'There was a red-bearded giant. Had a long axe. Of course.'

Fionn had known already that it was Haraldarson's crew who had got the better of this man's raiding band, but it was good to have it confirmed. 'And you were the only one to escape?' he asked.

The man turned to look at him now, his eyes narrow, reflecting the flame glow. 'What's it to you? Why the questions?'

Tethered in the trees nearby, one of Fionn's two ponies nickered and snorted.

'I'm looking for the men who killed your friends,' Fionn said. No harm in telling this man that. No harm in telling him anything.

'Why?'

'I'm going to kill the young golden-haired man who made you shit yourself and run away. Made you abandon your friends when they needed you.'

The man stood then, clutching the hilt of his sword and glaring at Fionn as the pine branches hissed and spat.

'Peace, friend,' Fionn said, raising a hand to show he meant no harm. Smiling even. 'I'm thankful for the fire. Your friends stayed and made a fight of it and look where it got them. You were wise to run.'

The man frowned, not liking that much either, but he huffed into his hands and crouched by the fire again so that it lit the side of his gaunt, shadow-pooled face.

'So where was this farm you mentioned?' Fionn asked. He picked up the nestbaggin from where he had left it on a bed of pine branches to keep it off the snow, then opened it and took out a dead hare which he had snared that morning.

The man jutted his chin towards the south. 'Two days' walk. Got a decent fence around it. Did have a gate but we broke it in.' He was eyeing the hare with round, greedy eyes. 'I doubt the farmer will be able to tell you much. They were just there to steal his food, same as us.'

'They might still be there, enjoying the hearth and a roof over their heads. All the meat they could want, a little crew like that,' Fionn said. 'And even if they didn't stay long, tracks will lead off from there. I'll find them.' Tracks in the snow perhaps, but other tracks too. A word spoken here. A name mentioned. Signs which a man could follow if he knew his business. He laid the hare on the snow beside the fire. Its dead eye glinted in the flamelight. It was a slow business, this tracking his prey through the snow, and at some point it was likely he would have to take ship again or fall too far behind. But he had still been at Avaldsnes when the news had been brought to the king that his ship *Wave-Thunder* and her skipper Bjalki had run into Haraldarson and his ship *Reinen* off the coast of Åkra in the open sea. Sigurd had smashed Bjalki's oars and fled into the south leaving *Wave-Thunder* all but crippled, like a bird with a broken wing, and her benches strewn with dead and dying men. King Gorm had raged and thundered and Fionn had set off southward, buying passage here and there to cross the water, asking questions. Threading together sightings of *Reinen* by fishermen and coast-dwellers and the whispers of the mackerel in the sea.

Gods knew what would become of Bjalki, though in fairness he had at least tried to fight.

And yet Sigurd might be even now sitting by some farmer's hearth, his ship hidden in some island cove while her crew warmed their bones.

'You going to skin that and get it cooked or not?' the man asked, nodding at the hare.

Fionn drew his knife and looked along its edge which reflected the fire's glow, then tested its sharpness against his thumbnail.

Haraldarson and his crew were ahead of him but they would need to come ashore often, to hunt or raid and to cook their food. It was only a matter of time before Fionn caught up with them, and he did not mind the wait, for he was a patient man.

'Not much meat on it,' he said. 'Even the hares can't find much to eat with all this snow.'

The man looked down at the hare. 'I'll take whatever you can spare,' he said. Then he shrugged and shivered. 'I have shared my fire with you,' he reminded Fionn.

Fionn nodded. 'We will need a good green stick for a spit,' he said, standing and moving towards the trees.

'We should eat one of your horses,' the man said. He began to say something else but it came out as a gurgle because his throat was cut, the rent of it spraying blood across the snow and into the fire where it sizzled.

When the man's legs had stopped shaking and his heart had stopped beating, Fionn laid him on his back in the snow, then cleaned his knife on the man's tunic. Then he went to fetch his hand axe from the horse and cut himself a stick from a pine branch. Nice and straight, it was, and green enough not to burn, if he was careful.

Then he came back and sat down again beside the fire, and began to skin the hare.

'There may be a place,' Valgerd said. She had come to stand beside Sigurd at the prow and she kept her voice low so that the others would not hear. 'Somewhere Runa can stay where she will be safe until this blood feud runs dry.'

'Olaf told you?' Sigurd said. He did not like the idea of them talking about Runa and what to do about her behind his back.

'And he's right. A shieldwall is no place for the girl,' she said. 'We cannot protect her when we are so few. And you will end up making the wrong decision in a fight because you are thinking about what might happen to her.'

Sigurd thought about this for a while, though he needn't have. He knew what she said was true. Still, he didn't have to like it.

'Where?' he asked.

'There is an island. Fugløy,' the shieldmaiden said, which did not help Sigurd much for only the gods could say how many islands shared that name. He knew of three Bird Islands within a day's sailing from Skudeneshavn! 'It's a sacred place,' Valgerd went on, 'an island upon which men are forbidden to live for it is the home of the Maidens of Freyja.'

Sigurd gave a slight shake of his head to show that he had never heard of these women.

'Freyja the daughter of Njörd and Skadi was born in Vanheim,' Valgerd said and this time Sigurd nodded. He recalled the stories of the Vanir, those gods associated with fertility and magic, and their long ago war against the Æsir. 'When Freyja reached Asgard the gods were so impressed by her beauty and grace that they gave her Sessrymnir, a hall so vast that she could accommodate as many guests as she wanted.'

Valgerd reached out to trace a finger over the intricate carving which ran up the stem post, her lips bowed in a sad smile so that it seemed to Sigurd her thoughts were caught up in the person who had told her this story rather than in the story itself. 'But for all her beauty Freyja was not satisfied to sit in her hall like some soft, pleasure-loving queen,' she said, 'which is why she often leads the Valkyries down to the battlefields, choosing and claiming one half of the heroes slain.'

'As much as half the slain?' Sigurd said, struck by a sudden fear. What if in death he was claimed not by Óðin but by Freyja? If he were taken to this hall Sessrymnir he would never drink with his brothers and father again, for they were surely in Valhöll, Óðin being the god of jarls. Another reason for me to die wearing the jarl's torc, he thought.

'I am just telling it as it was told to me,' Valgerd said, looking at him.

'So Freyja the golden-haired and blue-eyed is no stranger to the sword-song. What has this to do with Runa?' he asked, though he knew what they were coming round to.

'The Freyja Maidens devote their lives wholly to the goddess,' Valgerd said. 'They live on Fugløy and take no husbands. They spend their days training for war.'

'What war?' Sigurd asked.

Valgerd looked out across the water and shrugged. 'The end of days,' she said.

'Ragnarök,' Sigurd said, the word itself heavy as a stone anchor.

'They will fight at Freyja's side in the last battle,' the shieldmaiden said. It was hard to tell whether Valgerd admired these women or thought them fools. For as a shieldmaiden she had given her life to the gods in a way, protecting the völva and the sacred spring at which folk made their offerings.

And yet since the witch had died, and taken a long and miserable time doing it, so Valgerd had said, the shieldmaiden had seemed to have nothing but scorn for the gods.

A herring gull shrieked in the wan sky above them and Sigurd watched it wheel away into the west.

'You want me to take Runa to this Fugløy,' Sigurd said. An icy wind thrummed the lines and whistled through the blocks. It ruffled beards and made eyes water.

'The maidens may take her in,' Valgerd said.

'How do you know all this? I thought you lived in a waterfall with the spirits and your völva down at the arse end of the Lysefjord.'

'My mother told me of the maidens when I was a little girl,' she said.

Sigurd's thoughts were buzzing like the shrouds with the gusts in them. *Runa must stay with me and I must stay with her,* he told himself.

'Why would they take her?' he said.

'Because you will pay them well,' Valgerd said, watching the sleeping, snow-covered land slide by. 'And because my mother's mother lived amongst them.'

Sigurd turned to her but she kept her eyes fixed to the skeletal birch and the snow-laden pines and the cold rocks of the shoreline.

'She was a Freyja Maiden for many years.'

'You said they could not take a husband,' Sigurd said.

Valgerd's lips pursed into what was almost a proper smile. 'Some do,' she said. 'If the prophetess deems the man a worthy match. If he is a strong jarl or a powerful king.' One of her eyebrows arched like Bifröst. 'Or sometimes a warrior of reputation can earn himself one of the Freyja Maidens as a wife, as happened in my grandmother's case. For the issue of such a match may be gods-favoured and will surely fight beside the Æsir and the Vanir at the twilight of the world.' She pointed to the shore and Sigurd looked up just in time to see an otter slip from the smooth rock into the water. 'Away from the Freyja Maidens Ingun brought my mother up as a warrior. That was always to be her wyrd with the parents she had.'

'And your mother was a guardian of the spring before you,' Sigurd said, looking at her fierce beauty but seeing beyond it.

She nodded, then turned to look at Runa who sat on a sea chest on the steerboard side before the sail, which had enough wind in it to save the oars getting wet. The girl was looking out to sea, her face still swathed in bandages and her eyes still full of shame. She blamed herself for the injury, which to Sigurd was worse than her blaming him.

'I should have had my shield up,' she had told him.

'I should have caught the arrow with my own shield instead of letting it hit my helmet,' he had said. But Runa believed she had let them all down through her own carelessness. And worse, she worried that the others thought she brought the crew bad luck, for in every other sense the raid had gone as smoothly as could be.

'You think she would be safe with these corpse-maidens?' Sigurd said, for what were these island women if not Valkyries in training? And Valkyries were not necessarily to be trusted, he knew. It was said they shared some powers with the Norns and could not only prophesy the outcome of a battle but sometimes weave a victory or a defeat with their own hands. They possessed the art of the war-fetter, too, and could bind a warrior with terror or release him from those same bonds.

'Safer than she'd be with us,' Valgerd said, which was not quite the same thing in Sigurd's mind. 'The Freyja Maidens are not sworn to any king,' Valgerd said. 'Nor do they pay tribute to any man.' She smiled at the saying of that. 'In my grandmother's day it was the opposite. The local jarls would make offerings at their temple. They'd even give them bairns sometimes, to be brought up as one of them, thinking it bought them the Goddess's favour, in this life and the next.'

'Where is this island?' Sigurd asked.

Valgerd shook her head. 'Somewhere not far from Skíringssalr in Vestfold. That's all I know.'

Sigurd had heard of Skíringssalr. It meant *shining hall*, being named after the king's hall on the hill behind it, though he did not know which king, only that Skíringssalr was a trading outpost which sailors had talked about over the years in his father's hall. He did know that the Vestfold was under Danish control and had been for as long as anyone could remember. The royal estate there levied taxes from every trader who set up at the kaupang, the trading place, in summer to sell their wares.

He and Valgerd both looked out over the sweep of the sheer strake, their hair whipping around their faces, breathing in the fresh sea air, letting it fill them. Letting it clean them. Not that sea or wind, rain or snow could scour away all stains, Sigurd thought. He had killed his friend Loker for Valgerd and that was one such stain. And yet there were few people he would not kill for her, he realized now, knowing that he was getting the terms of the oath they had sworn to each other back to front. She had sworn on his sword to kill *his* enemies and in return he would reward her with silver as if he were her jarl. Ha! Try telling that to Loker! There are bears in the forests that have more jarl about them than I, he thought, turning into the wind to look at his half crew of outlaws and homeless men.

'If Runa is agreeable we will seek out these Freyja Maidens and ask them to take her in,' he said, drawing the words out of himself like an arrow from the flesh.

'And if she is not?' Valgerd said, that eyebrow cocked again.

'Then we will do it anyway,' he said, hating the thought. But he would not lose Runa. That was one death in which he would play no part. No matter what.

Then he turned to make his way to Solmund, to ask the old skipper if he had ever sailed to Vestfold and knew where to find this Skíringssalr and the king who lived there.

Fionn was enjoying the work. Having sat on his horse for the last two days it was good to get his body moving, get the blood flowing through his limbs again. He bent and lifted the split timber, knowing that the farmer would be surprised at how strong he was, then he held it in place against the new gate as the farmer hammered in the nails. There was little talking, just the rhythmic thump of the hammer on the iron heads, the sound chasing across the meadow and its white mantle, echoing back off the trunks of the trees where the woods began.

Haraldarson was not here. That had been obvious, but the farmer had said Fionn looked in need of a proper meal and Fionn had offered to help the man repair his gate in return for a hot dinner and somewhere warm to sleep. The man used to have thralls, three of them, he said, but he had sold them after a poor harvest.

'No trouble round here for eight or nine years, then I sell my thralls this summer past and get raided twice this winter. Twice on the same damned day,' the farmer said through lips clenched on a nail.

'What can you tell me about the men who raided you?' Fionn said. The hammer struck once more and went still. 'Not the ones who died,' Fionn added. 'The ones that did the killing.'

'Why?' the farmer asked. 'They friends of yours?'

Fionn said nothing.

The farmer shrugged. 'You're from somewhere off across the sea. These men were Norse.'

The hammer came down once, twice, three times.

'What are they to you?'

'The leader of these men is called Sigurd Haraldarson,' Fionn said. 'I am going to kill him, which should please you seeing as he stole from you that which you can ill afford to lose.'

The farmer grunted. 'Butchered my best cow. Took some cheeses and most of my ale.'

There were tracks all over the place, which did not help. But some jarl called Ebbi had come with a war party the previous day, having seen the smoke from this farmer's signal fire up on the hill. There were other footprints too, because men from the nearest four or five farms had also come to show their support. None had helped this man fix his gate though.

'I'll say this for 'em, they never laid a finger on my family, which I'm thankful for. Whereas you should have seen what they did to the other crew. The ones as showed up just after them. Those shits who broke in my gate. Killed my dog too.'

'Dangerous men, then?' Fionn said, realizing that it might not be a straightforward thing this fishing for clues, because it seemed that, far from wanting his vengeance against Haraldarson and his crew, the farmer was grateful to them for dealing with the other raiders.

'So how is it you're out to kill the man?' the farmer asked. He had sunk the last nail into that supporting plank and now stood back to see how straight it was.

'He has a powerful enemy in the north.'

'Namely?'

'Namely King Gorm of Avaldsnes, whom men call Shield-Shaker.'

The farmer *hoom*ed in the back of his throat. 'Explains why they're on the run I suppose. But you're a brave man if you mean to fight them alone. Never seen blade skill like it. Carved that other crew up as easily as they butchered my cow.'

A murder of crows was making a clamour at the far tree line and the farmer looked up. Nervous these days no doubt. 'Hands are getting cold,' he said, huffing warm air into them. 'You're a young man but just you wait. Skin gets thin. Blood too. The cold sinks right in and once it's in the only thing for it is hot broth and a seat by the fire.' He picked a spare plank out of the snow and leant it against the fence. 'Come on, let's eat. We'll finish this later.'

They trudged up to the longhouse and were joined by the farmer's boy who had been into the byre to feed Fionn's horses. A handsome young lad, his eyes were drawn to Fionn's sword and knives the way crows are drawn to the dead. Only normal for a lad that age, and yet there was something about young Roe that told Fionn he had no intention of following the furrow which his father ploughed. *He'll join a crew soon as he's strong enough to pull an oar,* Fionn thought to himself as they stamped the snow off their shoes and went inside the smoky house. The farmer's fat wife was clucking over the broth she was preparing. An old woman was squatting over a bucket with the help of an old man who was himself bent as a bow. Another old woman lay snoring in her bed by the hearth.

The farmer told his boy to fetch them some water and cheese to nibble on while they waited for the meat in the broth to soften.

'Did Sigurd Haraldarson tell you where he was going?' Fionn asked the man. No point in delaying it.

The man shook his head. 'Why would he tell me that?' he asked, watching his boy disappear behind the woollen hangings.

He's lying, Fionn thought. *That is a shame.* 'None of them mentioned where they might be headed?' he said, looking from the man to his wife, who kept her eyes on the broth she was stirring.

'Not that I heard,' the farmer said.

Roe came back with two cups and a jug. When he had poured the water he went off again for the cheese.

Fionn smiled. 'You are not protecting him, are you, Rognvald? This is not some misplaced loyalty because he killed that other crew?' His eyes were into the farmer's face like grit from the quern stone in the loaf.

'I told you, they killed my cow. My best milker.'

Fionn shrugged. 'They likely saved your lives. Who can say what that other crew would have done to your family? To your wife,' he added, nodding towards the woman.

The farmer squirmed in his own skin.

'Like to see the whoresons try it on with me,' the farmer's wife said, all belly and breasts behind the steam rising from the cauldron. 'As you can see, friend, I am no wisp of a girl.'

Roe returned with a wedge of cheese on a plate and set it on the table in front of his father and their guest.

'Wake your mormor, boy, and tell her the stew is nearly ready,' Rognvald said.

'Would you like to see my knife, boy?' Fionn asked before the boy turned back towards the hearth and the beds round it.

The boy nodded, glancing at his father who gave a slight shake of his head, but the boy came closer anyway and Fionn drew the long knife and flipped it over to offer him the stag-antler handle. 'Careful now, it's wicked sharp.'

Roe closed his fingers round the grip, relishing the feel of the ridged antler, looking from Fionn to the blade, eyes wide with the grim curiosity that comes from having seen what such blades can do to a man's flesh.

'Back where I come from we call it a scían. Two sharp edges here, see,' Fionn said, 'leading to a point which'll slide right into a man's eye and out the back of his head before he even knows you're there. Not like the long knives your people use, which are good for slashing a throat or hacking off a hand. I've heard it called a thrusting sax.'

'Wake your mormor, boy,' the farmer said again, his face darkening, rubbing the fingers of his right hand together as he stood there.

'Ah, let the boy look awhile longer,' Fionn said, ruffling Roe's golden head. 'He'll be able to tell his friends he's held a real scían all the way from Alba across the sea to the west.' He grinned at the boy. 'Beautiful, isn't she?'

The boy nodded and grinned back.

'So you are sure Haraldarson and his men said nothing, gave nothing away of their intentions?'

The farmer looked at his wife, who gave him a look that would melt snow. Her fat neck trembled but still her husband kept his teeth together. He was afraid that to speak up now was to admit the earlier lie.

'Have you killed men with it?' Roe asked, looking right into Fionn's eyes. No games with this young lad. As straight as an arrow, and so Fionn would be straight back.

'Oh yes, I've killed many men with this blade. More than I can remember.' He held out his hand and the boy gave the knife back to him, hilt first. Good boy. Fionn turned the long blade in the firelight. 'She is a soul stealer. A lean, hungry bitch.' Roe was under the knife's spell and he seemed to have forgotten his task of waking the old crone whose every snore ended in a wheeze and crackle.

'I can't be sure,' the farmer's wife said, glancing from her husband to Fionn, 'for I was seeing to the old ones, you see, and fetching some of my skyr for the girl. Must be this Sigurd's sister from the looks of 'em both. Pretty things the pair of 'em. Not what you expect from raiders. Anyway . . . when this Haraldarson was talking to his friends he might have mentioned Birka.' She looked at Rognvald. 'What do you say, husband? Did you catch mention of Birka?'

Rognvald muttered that it was possible, though why anyone would want to go to that shit hole was a mystery to him.

Haraldarson being Birka-bound made perfect sense to Fionn, though, for it was a place famed for attracting the dispossessed and men on the make, outlaws, traders and warriors looking for a ring giver. Perhaps Sigurd had the silver to buy himself a proper crew. Or perhaps he would offer his sword to some jarl, thinking he could escape King Gorm's wrath that way. Hiding behind new oaths in some faraway mead hall. Starting again like a damaged sword which is reforged.

Fionn nodded. He would find Haraldarson in Birka then.

His scían had split brynja rings before, with intent behind it. The blade had passed through the rings and the tough leather and wool beneath to kill men who were all sinew and muscle and fat.

It slipped into the boy like a whisper into an ear. Between the ribs, brushing the bones then into his eager heart which fluttered through the blade. His eyes flared, would never close again, and piss ran down his leg on to the floor. Not enough of it to puddle.

It was the woman, not the man, who moved first. Shrieking, she ran through the smoke and threw herself on the long knife, flailing with the ladle and foaming at the mouth as she died. While Rognvald came at him with a hand axe. Bravely enough, though is it courage when a man has already lost everything? Fionn wondered as he twisted out of the axe's path and put the scían through Rognvald's neck, letting the farmer's dead weight pull him off the blade to land in a heap across his wife's huge body.

The old man was half out of his bed and cursing when he died, and as with the two skeletal women there was no pleasure in it, but they would die anyway soon enough without the hand that fed them. No pleasure in killing the boy either. He had not lied as his parents had. But the boy had spirit and might have grown into a killer. A hunter like Fionn. Only a fool would wound a young boar then turn his back on it and walk away. So it was done.

He left the dead where they lay and went over to the broth. It smelt good.

It tasted even better.

CHAPTER NINE

THE KAUPANG AT SKÍRINGSSALR SAT IN A PROTECTED BAY IN Viksfjord by the main sailing route along the coast. Not that there were any trading vessels or fighting ships out there now. The only boats out on the dark water were the odd færing in which brave or hungry men sat swathed in pelts and hunched into themselves, their weighted lines running down and down into the deep.

'That sod deserves whatever he can pull up,' Olaf had said about one such man they had passed. When they had first seen him he was still in the lee of a gull-crowned island, but now he was drifting with the waves towards the rocks. He would need to wind in his line – never a pleasant thing for the hands in this cold – and row back out before he risked holing his boat.

As *Reinen* passed within an arrow-shot the fisherman waved in greeting. No doubt he was surprised to see a ship like *Reinen*, even lightly crewed as she was, coming into Skíringssalr at this time of year and he was testing to see whether he ought to drop his block and line and row for his life. To save him the trouble, Olaf raised a hand and nodded back, putting the man at ease so that he smiled and called across, asking Njörd to give Olaf fair winds and kind seas.

'This is good farming country,' Solmund said at the tiller, looking out across the land as the others took the oars from their trees and threaded them through the ports. There was little wind anyway and they had already lowered the yard and furled the sail on it in readiness to manoeuvre *Reinen* into her berth. 'But more important is the mouth of the river to the west of here. Crews sail inland for the iron. Whetstone and soapstone too.'

'Maybe we should raid inland then?' Svein suggested, leaning back in the stroke.

'You want to row upriver with not even half a crew?' Olaf asked him, those words pissing out the flame of Svein's idea before it could take hold amongst them, for rowing against the current was not something which anyone enjoyed, for all that there were few better ways to stay warm.

'Besides which, we are not here to raid at all,' Sigurd reminded them, his eyes running along the rows of small houses and workshops strung out along the water's edge, his nose full of the sweet scent of the birch smoke rising into the sky. Around the bay several wharves and smaller jetties jutted out into the water, some with færings or knörrs snugged up against them, but most bare but for the odd gull, and on one a group of children standing on the edge with lines in the water.

Sigurd tried to imagine what Skíringssalr looked like in high summer, thronged with all manner of boats and buzzing like a beehive with craftsmen, traders and seafarers from all over. As it was now, the place was a ghost of itself, blanketed with snow and as quiet as the burial mounds which could be seen beyond the settlement, on promontories and on the low heights along the fjord's edges.

Then Solmund pointed to the north and the ridge of high land overlooking the bay and Sigurd did not need the old steersman to explain what they were looking at.

'Skíringssalr itself,' Sigurd said, though there was no clue as to how it had got the name shining hall, what with it looking like any other jarl or king's mead hall, albeit the place was easily as big as Eik-hjálmr, Sigurd's father's old hall, had been. Before Sigurd himself had placed the Skudeneshavn dead inside it and burnt it to the ground.

'And you're sure it's a good idea, paying your respects to some Danish king?' Solmund asked him, pushing the tiller to turn *Reinen* towards the shore as Olaf ordered the steerboard side rowers to lift their oars. Those on the larboard made several more strokes and the ship turned neatly, the steerboard blades biting the water again before she had swung fully round. Then, the oars dipping and lifting in perfect unison again, *Reinen* glided like a swan towards the berth Olaf had chosen, her bows pointing back out into the fjord in case they should have to leave in haste.

Sigurd had not answered Solmund and now he took a mooring rope and jumped up on to the sheer strake as some of the others lined the sides ready to grab hold of the jetty and see to it that they landed as smoothly as a sword sliding into its scabbard.

'Here they come,' Aslak said, taking another rope, from the stern now, and lashing it to the mooring rail as Sigurd tied his off.

Men in mail and helmets and carrying shields were trudging down the hill from the king's hall, the fog around their beards and heads no doubt full of the curses they were uttering at having to leave a cosy warm hall to growl at some crew that had arrived unannounced. With *Reinen*'s prow beast safely stowed in the hold and the oar strokes unhurried, even languid, they had not come into Skíringssalr looking like some raiding party of eager young men seeking to attack the place with the surprise of a lightning strike. Nevertheless, the Danes would have been watching them like a hawk from its roost, wondering who they were and why they were out in the Viksfjord in winter, and now they were coming, a great wave of Spear-Danes rolling down the hill.

'Whoresons are trying to scare us,' Svein said, standing on the wharf leaning on the head of his long-hafted axe.

'Then they should have sent at least three times as many,' Bram Bear said, which raised a laugh because there must have been forty Danes spilling down that ridge from their king's hall.

'Still, that's a lot of hearthmen to keep in your hall over winter,' Olaf observed. 'This Danish king must have plenty of mead.'

'And a decent skald,' Svein said, meaning to irk Hagal, who was hardly earning his keep as a skald these days, if he ever had.

Sigurd had them all in their war gear, in brynjur and helmets, their furs left in the thwarts so that their mail and arms were on display, for it was important to make the right impression. But he did not have them make a shieldwall across that wharf, and that again was deliberately done. Instead his warriors stood in a loose pack in all their war glory, so that each looked like the hero of their own saga. Svein loomed. Bram glowered. Black Floki stood at Sigurd's right shoulder, as silent as the fjord, his shield in one hand and a short axe in the other.

When they had come almost to the shore, a spear's throw from Sigurd, the Danes stopped and formed a skjaldborg, catching their breath and glaring from beneath the rims of their helmets. One of them came forward and planted the butt of his spear into the snow. He was not a tall man, nor a young man, but Sigurd had never seen a broader man. His shoulders, under his fine-looking brynja, were as square as a sailcloth. His beard was a silver rope which fell to his chest and his eyes were small and grey as the sky.

'Who are you?' he asked.

'I am Sigurd Haraldarson,' Sigurd said, 'who killed Jarl Randver of Hinderå and who will kill King Gorm of Avaldsnes when I decide that the worms need a good feast.'

The man laughed at that. 'A Norseman who kills other Norsemen. That is a good start. And a jarl-killer no less.' Then the smile was gone and those small eyes sharpened to spear tips. 'You are an ambitious young man it seems to me. Have you come here to kill the king who lives in that hall?' he asked, thumbing back the way they had come. He lifted the spear then thrust it back into the crisp mantle. 'There must be some hungry worms under here somewhere.' The man's eyes flicked across to Valgerd and lingered there a moment, though Sigurd could not blame him for that, and not just because she was a woman dressed for war.

'I have no quarrel with your king,' Sigurd said. 'To tell you the truth I do not even know his name.' He looked up and down the shoreline. 'I would have asked someone but . . .' He shrugged. 'Everyone must be sitting by a warm fire indoors.'

'Everyone except us,' the man said, his accent as thick as the snow they stood in. He gestured at the boarded-up store houses and workshops along the beachfront. 'You must have noticed that there is little in the way of trading being done at this time of year. But then a man who has not heard of King Thorir Gapthrosnir is clearly a man who knows as much as a herring about what goes on in this world.'

'We live to the west, many weeks' sailing from here,' Sigurd said, wondering how the king on that hill had got the byname *the one in gaping frenzy*. 'And as you well know, there are more men who call themselves king than there are pretty girls in all of Denmark.'

The man did not know how to take that. Was Sigurd saying that the man's king was nothing special? Or that Danish girls were ugly? Or both?

'Well, at least there will be one less king when you kill this Gorm of Avaldsnes,' the man said, his tone a hair's breadth from open mockery. 'Why are you here if not to trade?' He nodded at *Reinen*. 'She is a handsome ship. Perhaps a gift for King Thorir?'

Sigurd smiled. 'I have come to ask a favour of your king. A favour for which I will pay very well.'

A stout, big-bearded warrior who must have been this man's son growled in the warrior's ear and the broad man nodded, never taking his eyes from Sigurd. 'You want a favour from a king you had never heard of until a moment ago?' he said.

'I do,' Sigurd said.

The man swept his gaze across the crew standing on the wharf before him and he seemed impressed by what he saw. He could hardly be anything else, Sigurd thought, for whilst they might be only half a crew they looked like war gods come down from Asgard.

'Well then,' the man said, 'you and your friends had better come up to my king's hall so that we may all learn what you want from Thorir Gapthrosnir. I will have my men watch your ship, not that there is anyone around to steal her.' With that the short but impossibly wide man turned and marched back up the hill and Sigurd and his crew followed, the Danish warriors closing around them with shields and spears and reeking of woodsmoke and honey.

Skíringssalr, the shining hall. The very moment Sigurd walked into the place there was no more wondering how it had got the name. For it was brighter inside the hall than outside in the grey day. It was a golden, blazing, flame-burnished hall the likes of which neither Sigurd nor his companions had ever seen.

'Welcome to Skíringssalr,' the square-shouldered Dane said, removing his helmet as he led Sigurd and the others past the great hearth whose flames flapped like war banners in the wind. They had left their weapons outside with the stewards, which none of them had liked doing, though they knew they must observe the custom or stand outside in the cold.

'Even a Dane would not murder his own guests,' Olaf had growled to Svein under his breath. And yet they remembered only too well that a rich farmer called Guthorm had tried to do just that, and would have too, had Floki, who was his thrall at the time, not slaughtered Guthorm and his kin before they could carry out their murder.

'I will have mead brought so that we may drink to the jarl-killer,' the man said, gesturing at the raised wooden benches lining the walls where Sigurd and his crew should sit. And then the man stepped up on to the low platform and sat in one of the big chairs beside two women: one of them a wizened old crone who could only have been his mother by how short she was, and the other an ageing beauty with the proud eyes and bearing of a queen. Her greying fair hair was intricately braided and pinned in a coil atop her head. The oval brooches pinned on the shoulder straps of her apron-skirt were the size of her fists and made of gold, and between them were several strings of glass and amber beads which glowed in the candlelight.

'The crafty sod,' Olaf mumbled, and Sigurd knew they had been tricked and that the short, broad-shouldered man was no hirðman but King Thorir himself. His hair was thinning and cropped short so that the only braid he wore was the one hanging from his chin, which would make an impressive beard if loose. But he was a man who had good, strong years still in him.

'Sigurd Haraldarson, Queen Halla,' the king said, gesturing at the younger of the two women on his left.

'It is an honour, lady,' Sigurd said.

The queen nodded. 'I am intrigued to know what brings you up the Viksfjord at this time of year, young Sigurd Haraldarson,' she said.

Now Sigurd nodded but said no more about it, knowing you did not go straight into the matter but must wait until mead was flowing and the fire's warmth had got into the warp and weft of their tunics and breeks. Instead, he introduced Olaf and Asgot, Solmund and Svein and all his crew, which was easily enough done as there were not many of them, and he finished with Runa, at whom Queen Halla smiled with a mixture of kindness and pity. For the scar on Runa's face was raw and livid, and she wore it with the clumsiness of a boy into his first beard fluff.

The king had nodded to each of them in turn and even complimented Svein on his size, though he had looked a little ill at ease when Sigurd introduced Asgot, which was not unusual for men were always wary when they knew they had a godi under their roof.

There were no hounds in the hall that Sigurd could see, but there were at least a dozen cats. The creatures were curling themselves round folks' legs and benches, sharpening their claws on roof posts, or sleeping under tables, which had struck Sigurd as odd until Asgot muttered that the whole place reeked of Freyja seiðr.

Pretty girls moved through the hall, filling horns and cups as the king's hearthmen took to their benches and tables and made themselves comfortable amongst the women already in their cups, which gave Sigurd a moment to fill his eyes with this shining place. As well as the chain-hung and tall free-standing iron oil lamps you would find in any hall, there were candles everywhere. Hundreds of candles, and they were of beeswax, which accounted for the honey Sigurd had smelt on the Danes who had come down to the shore. They burnt cleanly and with little smoke because their wicks did not yet need trimming, which meant they had been lit recently, perhaps when *Reinen* had been spotted coming into the bay. If this king's aim was to impress his guests then he had succeeded, for beeswax candles were rare and expensive, scarcely seen amongst the western isles. And yet they were not so rare as the fabrics which hung from Skíringssalr's raftered ceiling, scores of them, from one end of the hall to the other, floating as lightly as summer clouds on the draughts. Only these fabrics were not white like clouds but gold.

'Looks like a golden sea, upon which Óðin far-wanderer might sail his ship Skíthblathnir, which receives fair winds whenever the sail is set,' Hagal said, which was a better description than Sigurd could have come up with.

'And that's why you're a skald. Or used to be, anyway,' Solmund told Crow-Song, looking up with awe at the shimmering drapes, which all but hid the dark roof timbers and hung there like the hem of some goddess's wedding kyrtill, as Runa said, which Hagal agreed was an even better word picture than his.

'Silks,' King Thorir said, looking up at the wafting gold fabrics as though he were still in awe of them himself. The only part of the roof not festooned with this glimmering gold was that part directly above the central hearth by the smoke hole. 'No good for keeping the cold out, but the sight alone is enough to warm a man who appreciates beauty. From across the Baltic sea. You would think it too fragile to make the journey and yet there it is, shimmering like the golden tears of Valfreyja herself.'

That mention of Freyja as the Lady of the Slain was a good start, Sigurd thought, hoping that it hinted at King Thorir's dedication to the goddess, which would in turn suggest he might be familiar with the Freyja Maidens whom Valgerd had talked of. Had Thorir and his men not stared at Valgerd? Perhaps there was more to their interest in the shieldmaiden than her fierce beauty.

'The candles I get from Karl the king of the Franks,' King Thorir said. 'He sends his priests with chests full of them, thinking that he can buy me for his nailed god. For his White Christ.'

'These priests say all my husband need do is let them bathe him,' Queen Halla said. 'He would say

221

some words, whatever these priests told him to say, I suppose, and that would gain him entry into their god's kingdom.' She stretched out her arms, both palms uppermost. 'They send us candles and ask that the king at least thinks about their offer.'

'I tell him I am thinking about it,' King Thorir said, drinking from a great horn.

'And are you?' Sigurd asked, wanting to know more about this Frankish king and the god he worshipped.

King Thorir shrugged those massive shoulders of his. 'As far as I can see, the Franks' god is nothing compared with our own. A god favoured by weaklings and cowards.' He tipped his horn towards Sigurd. 'And yet King Karl is neither. He is more powerful than all your Norse kings put together. So you can see it is an issue I must think on. As I have been doing for many years now.' He grinned, clearly satisfied with the arrangement he had struck with these Frankish priests. 'Besides, this is a place of trade. Ships come here from all over, so I am a friend to all. It has done me no harm,' he said, sweeping an arm out which caused one of his candles to gutter.

'So you like our hall?' Queen Halla asked Sigurd, her brooches gleaming like plunder from Fáfnir's hoard.

'I have never seen its like, lady,' Sigurd said.

She laughed at that. 'You don't look old enough to have seen much of anything, Sigurd Haraldarson.'

'I have seen what the gods have chosen to show me, lady,' Sigurd said, at which Asgot nodded for it was a good answer, saying little and yet much. And it was enough to narrow the king's eyes.

'Why did you kill this Jarl Randver? And why *will* you kill King Gorm?' King Thorir asked, again pointing his drinking horn at Sigurd.

So Sigurd told him the story, leaving out none of the gore, even telling of his days spent hanging on that tree in the fetid swamp, and the deaths of those brave greybeards from Osøyro who earned their places in Valhöll at the last, due to their pride and the fact that they had been too old to run from the fight. All in all it was a good story – everyone in that shining hall must have thought so – and one that even a skald would enjoy the telling of what with all the mention of murder and revenge and the gods. And when Sigurd had finished, King Thorir raised his mead horn in recognition of a tale well told, as the thralls began to bring bowls of steaming meat stew to his guests.

'Óðin-favoured, hey?' the king said, his mouth moving as though chewing on a thought.

'So men say,' Sigurd replied, sitting back against the wall. The telling of all that had befallen him had been tiring. And yet it had felt good laying it all out like a massive pelt for all to appreciate.

'That is quite something, for I am Freyja-favoured.' King Thorir swung his gaze on to Valgerd then, but the shieldmaiden's face gave nothing away.

'Then we both have powerful allies, lord,' Sigurd said.

'Perhaps. Though it sounds as if you are in need of more allies, Sigurd,' King Thorir said, 'and if that is the reason why you have come here, you will be disappointed. For as I have told you, I am finding more profit in trade and taxes than in war.'

'As much as I would welcome your help against King Gorm, I do not think that even with all your Spear-Danes we would be enough,' Sigurd said. 'No, I am not ready to feed the oath-breaker to the worms just yet. I have come here to Skíringssalr on another matter. I have heard of an island which is home to a band of warrior women, Freyja Maidens, who train for the sword-song that will ring out across the worlds of men and gods come Ragnarök.'

King Thorir glanced at his wife then looked back to Sigurd. 'So you had not heard of King Thorir Gapthrosnir but you know about the Maidens? Even though few men have ever laid eyes on this island you speak of?' He looked at Valgerd again.

'I told Sigurd of the Freyja Maidens, lord,' Valgerd said.

'You were one of them?' he asked, his frown suggesting that if that were so, he did not recognize her.

'My mother's mother was,' Valgerd said. 'Until she left the island. The High Mother had taken a lover for herself. A young warrior who had made his reputation fighting for King Audun.'

'A piss bucket king,' King Thorir growled, for his father had more than likely fought against Audun who had been king to the north of Skíringssalr until he had fallen off his boat and drowned. That was a story which had flown far.

'But this young man fell in love with my grandmother and she with him. The High Mother wanted him killed and her banished but the Prophetess forbade it. Instead she let them leave the island and even blessed their marriage.'

'I remember some talk of it,' the king said, waving a hand through the smoke. 'What do you want with the Maidens, Haraldarson?' There was a steel edge in his voice which was hardly surprising if, as Valgerd had said, the king of Skíringssalr was sworn to protect the island and its women warriors.

'I want Runa to live on the island with these Freyja Maidens,' Sigurd said, 'where she will be safe.' He gestured at the warriors around him. 'We will follow the coast east but not until I know that Runa is out of danger. Where we are going there is bound to be fighting.'

'You will raid?'

'Perhaps.'

'Not my lands.'

'Not your lands,' Sigurd agreed. Though that promise was easier given than kept.

'I see that someone has already tried to ruin your great beauty, girl,' King Thorir said to Runa, 'but

225

we are thankful that they failed. I trust that your brother avenged you?'

'He did, my lord,' Runa said, turning her livid scar away from their hosts.

For a moment Sigurd felt again the savage, hot hatred in his belly that had filled him as he killed the archer whose arrow had torn open Runa's face.

'And you would not consider an arrangement with me?' the king said. 'We could look after young Runa here, in this hall. She would be safe with us.'

'And what would stop you coming to a subsequent agreement with my enemies, who are even now searching for me?' Sigurd asked.

'I could give you my oath,' King Thorir said.

Sigurd grinned. 'In my experience, kings are no less likely to break their oaths than the thralls who empty their piss pots.'

Thorir bristled at that, though there was a half smile on Queen Halla's lips, Sigurd noticed.

'Careful, lad,' Olaf hissed out of the corner of his mouth.

The king looked at Valgerd. 'You know where to find the Freyja Maidens?' he asked.

'No, King Thorir,' she said. 'My mother told me of their island but I have never been there.'

'Ah, so you want me to show you the place, Sigurd,' the king said.

'I will pay you,' Sigurd said.

But the king shook his head. 'No. I will not show you where it is. Not even if I wanted to, which I do not. For it is forbidden.' He raised a hand before Sigurd could speak again. 'However, perhaps I will arrange for your sister's safe conduct to the island. For a fair price. I have business with the Maidens from time to time. I send them gifts. Mail coats. Helmets. Swords.' He glanced up at the golden silks that were set shimmering in the draughts by the light of all those candles whose burning sweetened the usual fug of a hall. 'I help the Maidens where I can and in return they will see that I am taken to Freyja's hall, Sessrymnir, when the day of my death comes, and no matter the manner of it. My wife, too, will enjoy the Goddess's hospitality.'

'You would not rather be received in Valhöll, King Thorir?' Olaf said.

Thorir's face darkened like a fjord where two currents meet. 'I have sons. Fine sons. But we had a daughter once. Our beautiful Hallveig died when she was just a girl. She waits for us now in Sessrymnir. We will see her again.' He glanced at his wife. 'Freyja willing.'

Olaf nodded. 'A hard loss, King Thorir,' he said, 'I am sorry to hear of it.' The king nodded back before downing a belly-full of mead.

'My lord, if Olaf and I may speak a moment about your offer?' Sigurd asked, at which the king dipped his head and held out a big hand, inviting them to talk amongst themselves.

'There would be nothing to stop him taking payment from us and then sending word to King

Gorm or Hrani Randversson, offering them Runa for a price,' Olaf said. 'We would be gone up the coast and none the wiser.'

Sigurd shook his head. 'I will not leave without knowing that Runa is safe with these Freyja Maidens.' As much as he was determined that his sister should not face the dangers of any coming fights, he was also reluctant to trust a Danish king he had not heard of until this very day. 'So what do we do, Uncle?' he asked.

Olaf scratched amongst his beard, his eyes skimming across the faces of those gathered on the benches in King Thorir's hall.

'What are you looking for?' Sigurd asked him.

'These fine sons of his,' Olaf said. He nodded at a group of drinking men. 'He is one without a doubt,' he said.

'What of it?' Sigurd asked.

'Perhaps the king is willing to let us . . . look after . . . one of them. For a little while.'

Sigurd felt the smile twitch in his lips like a fish on a line. He turned back to their host. 'King Thorir, are you certain the Freyja Maidens will take Runa and keep her safe?'

'As I say, we have an understanding,' the king said.

'And if we agree on the price for your most trusted hearthmen to deliver my sister to these maidens with all haste, what will you give me, seeing as we do not yet know each other well and I will have given you payment and my own sister who is more precious to me than anything in this life?'

The king's eyes narrowed. 'You want a hostage?'

Sigurd shook his head. 'A guarantee.'

'My sons are too old for fostering,' the king said.

'I find it is the young man who thinks he knows everything that is in most need of learning that he knows nothing much at all,' Olaf said.

Sigurd wondered if that had been aimed at him, but Olaf gave nothing away. The king was deep in thought by the looks and even raised a hand to hush the queen, who was trying to give her opinion on the proposition.

'Thidrek,' King Thorir called and a big-shouldered man stood from his bench, dragging a hand across his mouth.

'Father,' the man replied. He was not tall but he was stout as a boar in his prime.

'Could be useful,' Olaf muttered.

'Where's your brother?' King Thorir asked the young man.

'Thorberg,' Thidrek called over his shoulder to the man who had stood beside King Thorir on the wharf and who Sigurd and Olaf had known must be the king's son. This Thorberg half stood at his bench, spumy-bearded and frowning.

'No, damn it!' his father said. 'Thorbiorn! Where's Thorbiorn?'

Thidrek shrugged those impressive shoulders, spilling mead over the lip of his horn. His brother Thorberg sat down again.

'Here, Father,' someone said. All eyes turned to the far side of the hearth and a group of young bloods with mead in one hand and women in the other parted to give their king a line of sight to his son. Bare-chested, his fire-bright hair loose over his shoulders, Thorbiorn clambered out of a deep, fur-piled bench and the two naked bed thralls he had been sharing it with.

'Gods, boy, we have guests!' King Thorir roared, standing and hurling his horn across the hall at his son so that several men and women were spattered with mead.

Thorbiorn, who could not have been more than seventeen summers, stood on the rush-strewn floor as if he was on a ship in an angry sea.

'Maybe it was not such a good idea of yours, Olaf,' Solmund said under his breath.

'Shit of the gods,' Olaf rumbled into his beard.

'Do I have to come over and drag you up here by your balls?' King Thorir bellowed at the lad. This got a laugh from many but not from Thorbiorn, who grimaced and staggered across the hall, pulling on his tunic as he came. Then he stopped, bent double and spewed the contents of his stomach on to the floor, raising curses from the king's hirðmen and a stink that spread through the hall like a sea fog.

'Lad looks like you,' Olaf mumbled to Sigurd.

230

'Thorbiorn is my youngest son,' King Thorir told them. 'The gods know the boy has a lot to learn. When I was his age I had three or four good raids under my belt. I had stood in the shieldwall and weathered the storm of swords.' He shook his head. 'But Thorbiorn would rather swive himself half to death with any thrall who will open her legs for him than make a name for himself like his brothers.'

Whereas his brothers were wide and thick-necked, Thorbiorn was lean and knotty, though he did not look weak. His cheekbones were high and his eyebrows were darker than his hair, so Sigurd could see why Olaf had said that the young man looked like him. Even swaying on his legs like that, looking as if he might spew another steaming load.

'You want me to go with this . . . crew, Father?' Thorbiorn asked, gesturing at Sigurd and his companions. 'We do not know them. I will not be the hostage of some band of outlaws.'

'You will do what I tell you to do, boy!' the king said, flushing. But then he got a hold of his anger and looked to Sigurd. 'Still, Sigurd, my son has a point. We do not know what kind of man you are, other than a jarl-killer who worries about his sister.' He frowned. 'I want Thorbiorn to learn the ways of the warrior. We are at peace here and do not involve ourselves in petty fighting over sheep or cattle, so there is rarely an opportunity for him to taste the blood-fray.' He pointed a stubby finger at Sigurd and Olaf. 'How do I know that you are the right sort of men to teach him? And if you take him into a fight or two, how do I know that you can keep him alive?' He looked at Thorbiorn. 'He may be as much use as tits on a fish but he is my son.'

'Were you not listening to Sigurd's account of our blood feud with the oath-breaker and Jarl Randver of Hinderå?' Olaf asked him.

'A good story,' the king shrugged, which could not have been easy with those shoulders, 'but perhaps just a story,' he said.

'Wait for it,' Solmund mumbled.

The king looked at the queen. Halla gave a slight shake of her head but Thorir was already grinning.

'Wait for it,' Solmund said again.

'I have an idea, Sigurd Haraldarson,' King Thorir announced, loud enough to startle the mice in Skíringssalr's thatch.

'Here we go,' Solmund said through a grimace.

'I am listening,' Sigurd said.

'A fight, Sigurd. You against me.' His teeth looked good in that smile, Sigurd thought, which meant no one had ever managed to knock them out. 'A friendly little fight.'

The king's men were moving. Svein and Floki and the others began to rise but Sigurd stayed them with a hand.

'No blades of course,' King Thorir went on. 'Just a friendly grapple until one of us has had enough. What do you say?'

But before Sigurd could say anything at all, the king was out from his bench and on to the table, knocking platters and candles flying as he scrambled across the boards and jumped down on to the floor. Then he came at Sigurd like a rolling barrel and Sigurd had just got to his feet himself when the king grabbed hold of his belt and brynja and threw him into the middle of the hall. Even as he rolled across the floor he could hear Olaf bawling at the others to stay on their benches, but then the king was on him, bending low to wrap his brawny arms round Sigurd's thighs, his shoulder in Sigurd's crotch. Then the king drove upwards, lifting Sigurd off the floor, before slamming him down again, knocking the air from his lungs so that he could not have shouted *Stop* even if he'd wanted to. A fist hammered into his temple and another buried itself in his eye socket and white heat filled Sigurd's head.

He threw up his left hand, grabbing the king's beard rope, and savagely yanked on it, and the king's head had no choice but to follow so that Sigurd's right fist drove into it, hard enough to loosen Thorir's back teeth. Then Sigurd scrambled free and the two men got to their feet, circling each other like crabs at low tide, and Sigurd knew how Thorir had got the byname Gapthrosnir, one gaping in frenzy. The king's mouth was open and his eyes were round as arm rings. Then he came like a charging boar, wrapping his arms round Sigurd's waist and lifting him again. But this time Sigurd scrambled up and over the ledge of his shoulder and twisted, locking an arm round the king's neck and letting his own weight haul Thorir backwards until the king lost his footing and they hit the floor in a squall of flying fists and grappling arms.

The king was not a young man but he was wildly strong, and because he was so short all his strength was stuffed into those tree-trunk legs and thick, bulging arms, and it made him as good at wrestling as a mackerel is at swimming. There was blood in Sigurd's mouth and blood blurring the vision in his right eye but these things were the least of his problems, as the king wrapped a leg round his torso and an arm round his neck, binding him like Gleipnir, the fetter which held Fenrir Wolf.

Skíringssalr thundered as men hammered their heels against their benches, pounded their palms against sea chests and tables, and everyone in that shining hall clamoured either for the king or for Sigurd.

'Had enough?' Thorir growled in Sigurd's ear, his breath hot and meady.

Sigurd gasped for his own breath. 'No.' With sudden fury he straightened his legs and bucked, slamming his head back into the king's face. But Thorir's grip tightened again and his mouth was again by Sigurd's ear.

'Yield?'

This time Sigurd smelt metal on the king's breath. Blood. But darkness was flooding Sigurd now. He could not breathe. He could not see.

'Give it up, jarl-killer,' King Thorir growled, slackening his arm just enough to allow Sigurd's lungs to draw a whisper of air into them.

And Sigurd used that breath for one word.

'No.'

Sigurd bent his left arm round himself and felt the cold iron rings of King Thorir's brynja. Then his hand was under the brynja's hem and into the king's other, dearer treasures. He grabbed a handful of cock and balls and squeezed, and King Thorir bellowed like a gelded bull. Sigurd broke the fetters of bone and muscle and scrambled away on all fours, gasping like a man escaping a burning hall, but just as he tried to stand a hand clutched his left ankle and hauled him back and he fell again, kicking madly at the frothing beast who was clambering up his legs, that gaping mouth like a prow beast's.

They wrestled and grappled, punched and kicked, rolling round in the rushes and the dirt beneath those shimmering silks, as if for the amusement of the gods themselves, men and women cheering and banging cups against the boards. Just when it seemed King Thorir must choke the submission out of him Sigurd would somehow break free, only to be fettered again.

Twice more the king asked Sigurd if he would yield and twice more Sigurd said he would not. And if Sigurd was thinking at all, he was thinking that at his age the king must surely tire first, for wrestling in mail was a young man's game. Not that even young men keep that up long.

Then they were up and Thorir Gapthrosnir took three huge blows to the head as he came in low again, gripping Sigurd's belt in both hands and lifting to slam him down on his back, his solid weight driving the air from Sigurd. Crushing him. They stayed like this for a little while, Sigurd's strength countered by the weight pressing down on him, both men planning what to do next.

'You done?' Thorir rasped. He was blowing like a gale and his face was as grey as his beard rope.

'Are you?' Sigurd asked, fearing that some of his bones had snapped inside him.

And with that King Thorir laughed, his teeth bloody but all still planted firmly in his jaws. 'We're done, Sigurd,' he said, rolling off Sigurd's chest and springing up on to his feet with a nimbleness which must have been his last flourish for surely he was exhausted. 'Up you get, Sigurd jarl-killer,' he said, offering his hand for Sigurd to grasp. So Sigurd grasped it and the king pulled him on to unsteady legs and Sigurd spat blood into the rushes. 'That's one way to work up a thirst, hey?' The king loosened his massive shoulders and grinned at his people and then at Queen Halla. 'You see, wife! Still no one can beat me.'

Queen Halla shook her head and all but rolled her eyes and yet there was pride on her face too. And well there might be for her husband had just shown them all that experience was the master of youth.

'Olaf, give me a drink,' Sigurd called, staggering back to his bench, knuckling blood from his eye. 'Svein, fetch me some snow.'

'Well, jarl-killer, that was fun. Apart from when you crushed my bollocks.' King Thorir pointed at Sigurd accusingly. 'I am beginning to wonder if you kill your jarls when they are looking the other way, for that was cheating. Still, as my people will tell you, I have never been beaten and yet you did not give up. I think we could be rolling around in the cat shit until Ragnarök and still you would say you did not yield.' He winced, a hand going down to his groin. 'Only two other men before you have held out without saying they'd had enough. One of them had too much pride and so he is dead.' He wafted the honey-smelling air with a hand. 'We were not friends like you and I.' He grimaced again. 'The other my wife says was trying to yield. He was growling, I thought insulting me for my height, but Halla swears he was begging me to stop.' The king's sweat-glossed head wrinkled as his brow lifted. 'He is dead too.'

'Then it seems I was lucky,' Sigurd said and meant it.

'You see!' King Thorir said to his youngest son, who stood there looking as bored as if he had been forced to watch someone lay a new thatch. 'This is the sort of man who will show you what it means to be a warrior.'

Svein came up to Sigurd's bench, his upturned helmet full of snow. Sigurd clenched his fists and shoved his raw knuckles into the snow, relishing the icy chill that would soothe the pain and prevent the joints from swelling.

Svein leant in close to Sigurd. 'You made hard work of that, Sigurd,' he said. 'Gods but he's an old man!'

Sigurd grimaced.

'You think Sigurd should have put a king on his arse in his own hall?' Olaf asked Svein. 'You brainless ox. That would be a sure way to not get what we want.'

Svein frowned and Olaf glanced at Sigurd with a raised eyebrow, but Sigurd ignored them both. His body hurt in too many places to count but his pride was still in one piece. Truth was King Thorir was a formidable fighter, however old he was, and Sigurd was lucky that all his bones that were meant to be straight still were straight and that his skull was not cracked. Besides which Olaf was right in that it seemed his performance had done enough to impress the king.

'You will see my sister safely delivered to the Freyja Maidens, King Thorir?' he asked. He could see the king and queen only through his left eye now, his right having swollen shut.

'I will,' the king said, then pointed at Thorbiorn, 'and you will take Thorbiorn into your little fellowship. I hope that some of your grit rubs into him. We will be disappointed if, when you bring him back to Skíringssalr, he is still more familiar with tits and arse than with sword and shield.'

'Then we have an agreement, King Thorir,' Sigurd said, getting up again and limping over to take the king's hand which he proffered across the table.

'Let us drink to it, Sigurd Haraldarson.'

And they did, both of them to numb their pains as much as to approve the arrangement, and everyone in that shining hall took it as an excuse to celebrate: the Danes because their king had still never been out-wrestled, the king's hearthmen because they were getting rid of Thorir's useless son, and Sigurd's crew because Runa would be safe while they sailed east.

'Seems to me there are only two people not enjoying themselves in this hall,' Olaf said a little while later, throwing an arm round Sigurd's shoulder that made Sigurd curse with pain. Olaf was talking about him and Runa.

'She wants to stay with us,' Sigurd said. 'And I would rather she did,' he admitted, looking over at Runa who was with Valgerd, both of them on stools by the hearth. He had asked the shieldmaiden to tell Runa stories of her mother's mother, who had been a Freyja Maiden, in the hope that these stories might warm Runa to the idea of living amongst these warrior women for a time. After all, Runa had always loved the goddess. Even now she wore a silver pendant of Freyja the Giver and Sigurd knew she had invoked the goddess many times, had asked her to ride into battle beside him whenever Sigurd stood in the storm of swords.

'You know she can't come with us, Sigurd,' Olaf said. 'There'll be fighting and there'll be killing where we're going.' He shook his head. 'Wouldn't be fair on Runa and wouldn't be fair on the others.' He looked at their companions who were deep in their cups and horns and in good spirits enjoying the warmth of a hall after weeks at sea. 'It'd be only a matter of time before one of the idiots caught a spear in the ear while checking to see that the girl was all right.'

Sigurd nodded but he could not help feeling that he was failing. The oath-breaker King Gorm, the man who had betrayed his father, still lived. Hrani Randversson, who had brought death to Jarl Harald's people at Skudeneshavn, still lived. And now Sigurd had to admit that he could not keep his own sister, the last of his family, safe. He was an outlaw with less than a crew of warriors to call upon, for all that they were the finest Sword-Norse he could ever hope to fight beside. What were his father and brothers thinking, watching him from their mead benches in Valhöll?

'And yet it seems to me that Runa would be more useful to us than that streak of piss Thorbiorn,' Olaf said, nodding at the king's son who had returned to his bed thralls amongst the furs, no doubt keen to tup them while he could. He was yelling for mead as he slapped a naked arse, which evidently the thrall took as the command to get on all fours.

'If he becomes a pain in my arse I will hang him over *Reinen*'s side until his balls freeze off,' Svein put in, spilling mead as he leant across to have his say. 'And if his father does not like it then I will wrestle him myself and show you all how it is done.'

'Instead of boasting about winning a fight you'll never have, why don't you go and get me some more snow?' Sigurd said, wanting to press some against his eye around which the flesh was as juicy as an overripe plum.

'And find some more mead on your way back,' Olaf said, at which Svein grinned, picked up his helmet and drank the water in it, then set off through the crowd.

Sigurd looked at the king, who seemed no longer the worse for the fight, laughing with his hirðmen and drinking like Thór himself. 'Do you think Thorvard would've beaten him?' he asked. Sigurd's eldest brother had been an awe-inspiring warrior; strong as an ox and fast as an adder, though he had fallen to a spear and an axe in the ship battle which had begun this whole thing. Seemed a lifetime ago now, though it had not been two years.

'I think Thorvard would have strangled him with his own damn beard rope,' Olaf said, and far from feeling ashamed that he hadn't beaten the king himself, Sigurd felt hot pride swell in his chest so that he hardly noticed his injuries at all.

And so they would stay at Skíringssalr until King Thorir's messenger had been to the island of the Freyja Maidens and returned with their word that they would take Runa. Which of course they would, Sigurd knew, looking up at the silks which shimmered in the golden light. Because the short-arsed king who had just given him a rare pummelling was Freyja-favoured. No one in that shining place would deny that. And Runa was Freyja-favoured too, wasn't she? Or else that arrow might have gone into her eye and killed her. Perhaps the goddess had blown to divert the shaft's flight, letting it graze Runa's face to bring them all to this very place. For this very purpose. Was it not possible?

Anything was possible when the gods were involved, Sigurd thought, taking the mead horn which Svein offered him now and, with his other hand, scooping snow from the red-haired giant's helmet and holding it to his swollen eye.

Yes, anything was possible with the gods. But one thing was certain, and that was that there would be chaos and death.

Then he drank.

CHAPTER TEN

OF ALL THE CREW, ONLY TWO OF THEM SEEMED HAPPY TO be out on the fjord at this time of year. Ibor the blacksmith and his son and apprentice Ingel sat snugged up in the thwarts, talking or sleeping and grinning more often than not while the rest of King Thorir's men bent their backs to the oars or worked the sail of his ship, a broad-bellied, seaworthy looking knörr called *Storm-Elk*, moaning that they had been ordered to sea while their companions enjoyed their lord's hearth and hospitality.

Runa had caught Ingel's eyes on her at least a dozen times since they had left Skíringssalr, and his father Ibor's two or three times. Both men were respectful and handsome enough, yet she made sure not to cast even a fleeting glance in their direction when she felt their gaze upon her. Not that there wasn't a part of her which was buoyed, if only a little, by their attentions. She had thought no man would look at her again with that ugly scar carved across her face from her left eye to her ear. It seemed she was wrong about that. Unless it was pity or morbid curiosity which had got the better of the blacksmiths. At that thought she pulled her fur-lined hood down a little further so that it half covered the scar, at which Ingel looked across and smiled with his eyes before looking back to the game of tafl he was playing with his father.

'Not far now,' *Storm-Elk*'s skipper told her after a long day's sailing, jumping down from the mast fish from where he had been looking out across the fjord and the many tree-covered islands scattered along the grey coastline. Runa nodded back at him and felt her stomach roll over itself at the prospect of coming to this island that would be her home for the gods knew how long.

King Thorir's messenger had returned to Skíringssalr three days ago with word from the Freyja Maidens.

'Runa Haraldsdóttir is welcome. On our honour she will be safe with us until the king sends for her.'

That had been good enough so far as Sigurd was concerned and the king had begun the preparations. Every full moon he sent a ship to the island with supplies, offerings really, to buy the goddess's favour, such as smoked and salted meats, ale, barley and oats and other preserved foods. On occasion King Thorir also sent swords and spears, brynjur and helmets, along with the men who made them so that they might make alterations as necessary and help with any repairs that might be needed.

It would not be full moon for another three nights but Sigurd would not leave Skíringssalr until he saw Runa in the king's ship and the mooring ropes thrown into the thwarts, and so Thorir had agreed that *Storm-Elk* could set sail ahead of time. As generous as he was to the Freyja Maidens and the goddess herself, as a king Thorir was no doubt counting the cost of hosting Sigurd's crew day after day. His mead supply would have to last through till late summer, and with the likes of Svein, Bram, Moldof and Bjarni going at it like dogs at a stream on a ball-sweating day, he was wise to want them gone.

'You are my blood and my heart, sister,' Sigurd had said, embracing her on the slippery wharf before she went aboard. There had been tears in his eyes and that had made Runa even more determined that she would not cry. 'I will come back for you when it is safe.'

'It will never be safe, brother,' she had said.

He had smiled at that. 'No,' he admitted, 'but we will all be a little safer when our enemies are dead.'

'And then I shall pity them in the Allfather's hall,' Runa said, 'with our brothers waiting there for them.'

Gently, he had kissed the scar on her face, then tucked some escaped strands of her hair back over her ear. 'Do not leave me alone in this world,

Sigurd,' she said, and this was an order rather than a request. 'I shall hate you if you do.' That had been a heavy thing to say. A cruel thing. But she had wanted to hurt him a little then, as revenge for leaving her.

'The gods want me to avenge our father,' he said, which was not saying that he would die, but it wasn't saying that he would not. But then how could he promise that he would not leave her alone? By refusing King Gorm's offer of peace, Sigurd had raised his sail and set his course upon a red sea. A sea of blood.

'Learn what you can. Stay safe. I will be back soon enough,' he said.

Bram came up grinning. 'And if you meet a fierce beauty who wants to breed with a hero, then you tell her that Bram whom men call Bear will moor in her cove when we are done killing kings and jarls,' he said, which was just the kind of boast to take the cold edge off the parting so that there were smiles and waves as *Storm-Elk* slipped out into the cold water of the Viksfjord and turned her bows away from the kaupang, her crew pulling the oars with unhurried strokes, as those on the wharf, but for Sigurd, Olaf and Svein, trudged back up the hill towards the king's hall and its hearthfire.

Winter's grip at last was loosening. It was rare for the snow to sit so long on the coast as it had this winter. Even more so this far south, King Thorir had told them, clearly bored by it all and wanting to get outside again as all folk did. Now, clumps of snow were regularly falling from snow-laden pines or sliding from roofs when doors were slammed. The mantle lying like a fleece over the fields was glistening and wet-looking, ever a sign of the beginning of winter's end.

Runa longed for the spring, when the snow would have melted and only the mountaintops and north-facing hillsides would remain white. When spring flowers of every colour would rise, if only fleetingly, to cover the meadows like rewards from the gods for all living creatures which had survived the winter. But spring was also the time when jarls and kings hauled their boats from their nausts, stepped their masts, covered them in new pine resin, re-caulked them and fitted them with mended sails and new ropes and trimmed them with fresh paint above the water line: yellow, red and black. Men would resume blood feuds. They would go raiding and fight wars. For many new beards and many seasoned campaigners, this winter would have been their last.

'Fly, brother,' Runa whispered, looking south. 'Fly far, my eagle. So that they cannot kill you.'

And soon, with the sun in the west and *Storm-Elk*'s crew moaning about the prospect of a night spent out in the open, for unlike the blacksmiths Ibor and Ingel they were not permitted to set foot ashore, they came to the island which they called Kuntøy, but which the ship's skipper had told her was called Fugløy. Out of the two names Runa preferred Bird Island, though it was not hard to imagine why the men had given it a coarser name. And there, lining the rocks like a palisade to deter invaders, stood the Freyja Maidens in their battle gear, painted shields across their chests, spears pointing at the leaden sky, on some the dull grey of mail showing beneath cloaks and pelts. Runa counted thirty of them as *Storm-Elk* came gently up to the rocks – for there was no jetty – and some of her crew hurled ropes to the women whilst others used their oars to fend off the shore. Indeed, there was no other sign of the island being inhabited, which was surely intentional, Runa thought, imagining those rocks covered with birds: gull, terns and oyster-catchers, whose spring song would proclaim the end of winter.

Inland there were trees; birch and spruce and gorse, showing dark green where the snow had melted away. The spruce woods looked dark and inviting, the bare brown trunks promising shelter and firewood, and above them Runa thought there was perhaps a skein of smoke in the sky, but she had only noticed it because she had been looking for a sign that people lived in this place.

'Let's not linger,' the skipper said, gesturing at his crew to hurry up and get hold of a sea chest which needed to go ashore. Full of silver it was, if the rumours were to be believed. A gift from King Thorir to the goddess herself.

'Aye, this place puts the hairs up on the back of my neck,' a grizzled man said, and although Runa was not afraid as such, nevertheless she could feel the seiðr of this island, a magic which hung in the still air, as insubstantial as sea mist and yet as undeniable as the rock itself and the sea nuzzling it.

They laid a wide plank from the knörr's side to the shore and those in the thwarts began unloading; the barrels and sacks of supplies, the weapons which were King Thorir's gift to the Maidens, and that big sea chest which had the gangplank bending like a bow, so that if it really was full of silver then surely it would buy King Thorir and his queen a table in Freyja's hall come their deaths.

'Such a waste, all that lovely flesh. All those hungry holes,' one man said, ogling the women who had laid down their arms so that they could haul on the ropes to keep the ship still.

'You say that every time we come here,' another man said, helping Runa up on to the gangplank.

'Doesn't make it any less true,' the first man said, which no one could disagree with, and, her nestbaggin slung across her back, Runa thanked the skipper and walked across to the island, taking the hand of a striking red-headed woman who was there to help her.

'Welcome, Runa Haraldsdóttir,' the woman said. 'I am Skuld Snorradóttir, whom the Freyja Maidens call High Mother.' It was unusual but interesting to hear this woman name her mother rather than her father, and Runa wondered if Skuld's mother had also been, or still was, a Freyja Maiden. That Skuld shared a name with one of the Norns, those spinners who weave one's wyrd, was not lost on her either.

'I am honoured to be here, High Mother, and grateful for your hospitality,' Runa said, which drew a smile from the tight line of the red-head's lips. Then the woman, who wore her copper hair in two thick braids which hung over the iron rings of her brynja, turned and thanked *Storm-Elk*'s skipper and asked him to pay her compliments to good King Thorir whom Freyja the Giver watches over.

'I'll tell him, lady,' the man said with a nod, as Ibor and Ingel went ashore and his men then pulled the gangplank back into the thwarts.

'Give 'em one from me, you lucky shits,' one of the men growled after the blacksmiths.

'Ibor, you swine! If your sword snaps in the act, shout loud enough and I'll swim back here like a bloody otter,' another man said, though without conviction. But neither Ibor nor his son rose to the bait, Ibor hoisting a hand in farewell without looking back.

Some of the Maidens were now hefting the barrels and sacks, while others threaded spears through the short sleeves of the four brynjur to carry them more easily between them. They had brought a handcart too and into this the blacksmiths hefted the sea chest, huffing and puffing about it until the cart was creaking with the weight.

'Come, Runa,' the High Mother said. For a moment Runa's gaze lingered on those Spear Maidens who still lined the shore facing *Storm-Elk* as the rowers took to their benches to manoeuvre the knörr away from the rocks before setting the sail. 'They will stay until they are sure that the king's men have gone,' Skuld explained. 'You can imagine how tempting an island of women could be to them.'

'As tempting as a dragon's hoard, lady,' Runa said with a knowing smile.

'And yet harder to plunder,' Skuld said. 'Come, girl.'

So Runa went.

'While you are here among us you will live as we live,' Skuld said, as Runa descended the ladder from the loft where she would be sleeping. It was a small space and would likely get smoky on those days that the fire didn't draw well, but there was a bed with a straw-filled mattress and Runa was happy with the prospect of being somewhat apart from the other women, with only the mice and spiders and occasional roosting bird for company should she choose to retreat up that ladder.

'You will train as we do, work as we do, honour the goddess as we do,' Skuld went on, showing Runa around and letting the other Freyja Maidens get a good look at their young guest. Runa smiled at each face she saw, and the women greeted her with warm welcome as they took off their war gear, hanging sword belts and scramasaxes on pegs and shrugging off their brynjur. To look at them Runa was reminded of Valgerd, for like the shieldmaiden they were lean and well-muscled, broad of shoulder and fierce of eye.

'Have you learnt any sword-craft? Done any spear and shield work?' Skuld asked, taking Runa's shoulder in a strong grip and appraising her from head to foot.

'Yes, lady. My father was a great warrior, as were my brothers. I have trained with my brother Sigurd and even with a shieldmaiden.'

'Truly?' Skuld said, her eyes betraying surprise if not disbelief.

'Her name is Valgerd and she has joined my brother's hirðmen. She is a great warrior.' Runa considered mentioning that Valgerd's mother's mother had been a Freyja Maiden herself, but she decided against it. Better to wait a while before offering up such information.

'It is not often we hear of shieldmaidens, hey,' Skuld said with a wry smile, 'other than in fireside tales. But I believe you even if others would not.' She lifted her hand so that her finger brushed against the scar on Runa's cheek. 'Even so, perhaps you could be faster with the shield?' she said.

The longhouse was one of three standing side by side in a clearing in the pine woods, the clearing itself in something of a hollow with rock walls surrounding it on three sides down which fresh water trickled, finding its way into a narrow stream which burbled to the sea. Runa was shown inside all three houses and it struck her how strange it was to hear no gruff voices, no men cursing or boasting, laughing or mocking and taunting each other. There were no men drinking themselves stupid, wrestling between the benches, petitioning the jarl, giving vent to their grievances, pursuing pretty girls, comparing scars and old wounds, telling tall stories of war and dangerous journeys to far-flung lands, of fights won and loves lost.

In each house there were tables and benches at either end of the central hearth. Along the sides, between the roof support posts, were sleeping benches with mattresses and furs, whilst dozens of iron dishes filled with oil hung from the sloping roof, filling the place with flame and light and some sooty smoke which had blackened the roof timbers. The walls were almost entirely covered in tapestries depicting the goddess Freyja in all her guises: as the warrior riding in her cat-drawn chariot or upon her battle boar Hildisvíni, as a protector of the harvest in a field of golden rye, as a receiver of the slain in her hall Sessrymnir, as the lady of seiðr, war and death, and other forms with which Runa was as yet unfamiliar. But the tapestries which held Runa's eye were depictions of Freyja as the goddess of fertility and lust. In these weavings she was naked and wanton. She was big-breasted and open-legged. In some she was depicted in the act itself, rutting with naked warriors, her head thrown back as the men entered her.

'You like our work?' Skuld asked her, and Runa felt her cheeks flush for she realized she had been staring like a dead fish at those wall-hangings.

'They are like none I have seen before, lady,' she said. And neither were they, in their imagery or in the skill of their needlework. Who knew if these women could fight, but they could weave like the Norns themselves.

'We need our cattle for milk and our animals for food, and human victims to sacrifice are hard to come by here on our island,' Skuld said, 'so the Goddess does not receive many blood offerings from us. These tapestries are our offerings. When one of us dies, she is buried with one of her hangings, as well as with her weapons, as a gift to the Goddess and so that she knows here lies one who is pledged to her, who dreams of joining the Valkyries who choose the greatest warriors to fight beside the gods at the end of days.'

'I would wager that Freyja's hall is all the more beautiful for these gifts,' Runa said.

'And free of draughts by now,' Skuld said, casting her gaze along the numerous hangings, implying that many of her sisters had gone to Sessrymnir over the years. None of it, neither the hangings nor the way the houses were lit nor the buildings themselves, was anything like as impressive as King Thorir's mead hall. And yet these dwellings shared the same air of seiðr as Skíringssalr, a sense of the gods being close at hand, within earshot, watching these mortals but perhaps even on occasion moving amongst them, leaving a clue to their presence hanging in the flame-licked dark like a scent.

The only other buildings were a store house for grain, a cattle byre, a smithy, a smokehouse, and a hut that housed the cesspit, the ends of the longhouses themselves being given over to the usual occupations of weaving, butter- and cheese-making, brewing and milling. Pigs and hens wandered the woods at will, the pigs rooting and the hens pecking for food amongst the mud and carpet of pine needles, and given there was little in the way of pasture to be seen, Runa supposed the cattle must be brought hay from one of the stores or else taken to feed elsewhere on the island, perhaps on the fringes where the grass grew tall in summer.

'You will be safe here, Runa. Your brother has paid well, but know that we would have taken you in anyway, for the kings of Skíringssalr have long been friends of ours, none more so than Thorir.'

Runa knew that Sigurd had sent the Maidens seven swords and two of the four brynjur, which amounted to a hoard worth as much as a sea chest stuffed with hacksilver: a sum which must have impressed Skuld, though she was too proud to show it. Having been plundered from Jarl Randver's dead warriors, the brynjur would need to be altered, hundreds of their rings removed so that they would not drown their new owners, but that was one of the tasks for Ibor and Ingel, who would live on the island until *Storm-Elk* returned to collect them.

There were forty Freyja Maidens, seven of whom were too old to train with sword and shield these days and had been excused from coming down to the shore to meet Runa. The others were a mix of ages, but all looked strong and healthy, and Runa was eager to see them training for war. Even so, she could not help but wonder if they really had any steel in them, these Maidens, enough to face a real fight should they ever have to, yet alone the final battle at the twilight of the gods. It was one thing to hack at the trees, she thought, looking at an area in the woods where the pines had been sheathed in leather to use as targets for sword and spear practice, but it was quite another to face a shieldwall of spitting, growling, fearsome men who are worked up into the killing frenzy.

Runa studied the High Mother's strong but not unhandsome face. *Perhaps I have seen more of battle and the red chaos than you have*, she thought. But she said nothing, as they left the warm longhouse to pay a visit to the standing rune stone which the very first Freyja Maidens had put up many years before. She felt a gathering breeze and a mist of rain on her scarred cheek, even through the trees, and fancied she could hear *Storm-Elk*'s crew complaining about having to spend a damp night on some nearby island.

'Does the wound trouble you, girl?' the Freyja Maiden asked.

Runa had not realized that she had been running her fingers over the raised scar, and she pulled her hand away. 'No, High Mother,' she lied, then shrugged. 'I know it could have looked even worse had my brother or one of the others done the stitching rather than Valgerd.' The shieldmaiden had been so very careful with the fine bone needle and horsehair thread, her skill worthy of the embroidered hangings of which these warrior women were so proud.

'No,' she said again. 'I am not worried about it,' but Skuld stopped and turned to her. The woman was no fool.

'You must not be ashamed of this,' she said, gesturing at the wound which for all the neatness of the stitching was still new and angry-looking. 'And neither are you less beautiful for it.' Her eyes blazed in the gathering gloom. Night was upon them now. 'If I were you I would be proud. Such battle runes speak for us, Runa. They tell our tales as well as any skald. This rune of yours tells me that you are a survivor. A formidable young woman who possesses the strength for which you are named.'

Runa had not thought about it like that, and yet it was just the sort of thing that Valgerd might have said and she liked the sound of it. *A battle rune*, she thought, gently touching the puckered skin. *Yes, she liked the sound of that.*

‚'I will try not to hide it then, my lady,' Runa said, and Skuld nodded as they walked across the clearing amongst which several more oil lamps hung from the trees, their small flames hissing and spitting in the rain which was a little heavier now.

They passed the forge in which Ibor and Ingel were setting up so that they would be ready to begin work first thing in the morning. The two men were unwrapping tools from oiled leather sheets, piling up sacks of charcoal which they had brought from dry storage in the nearest longhouse, and tipping buckets of water which they filled from the nearby rocks into the plunge bath. And as Runa and Skuld walked on, Runa felt the weight of the younger man's eyes on her, heavy as a ringmail tunic.

By the third day on the island Runa knew very well why the father and son blacksmiths Ibor and Ingel had been grinning like mead-drunk fools while the other men aboard King Thorir's ship had looked so gloomy. It seemed the two men were useful for more than repairing weapons, making nails, riveting brynjur rings and all the other tasks which required more skill than simple iron-working. Runa had lost count of the times she had seen either Ibor or his son all but pulled into a Freyja Maiden's bed, or led up the ladder into one of the lofts by those women who preferred not to do their swiving in view of everyone else.

Freyja the battle maiden. Freyja the lover.

'The Goddess herself has such appetites, girl, and we are no different,' a tall, dark-haired woman with close-set eyes called Signy told Runa, who was watching Ingel being hauled out of his forge, his father laughing and waving that he should go and do what he must and that the bent sword he was working on would still be there when he returned.

Runa and another Maiden called Vebiorg had been fighting each other with wooden swords, going through the basic cuts and parries, when Runa's attention had been caught by the commotion across the clearing.

'Guthrun prefers the young bull to the old,' Vebiorg said now, slashing her practice sword through the air. 'Myself, I prefer Ibor. He makes the ride last longer and he knows what he is doing.'

'Yes but Ingel is getting better at it,' Signy said. 'The last time they were here he rode me like a man who has just heard that his jarl is putting on a feast and is serving his best mead.' Her lips curled into a smile. 'When he was done, I gave him a little while to catch his breath but told him I would cut off his snake if he didn't do it again.'

'Yes, you have told us this before, Signy,' Vebiorg said, waving a dismissive hand. 'The second time, you rode him and he lasted until the sun came up.'

'Well, it's true,' Signy said, 'and by the time we finished he was red raw but proud as a young stallion.'

Signy looked at Runa, who felt the colour in her face as a bloom of heat. She had never lain with a man and was not used to talking about such things, not that she was talking about it now. Perhaps if she'd had sisters instead of brothers.

'We are making our young guest uncomfortable,' Vebiorg said. 'Look,' she nodded at Runa, 'you could warm your hands on that face. All this talk has the girl as dewy as a spring morning. We'd best get back to sword and spear work before she wets her skirts.'

Runa could find no words to answer that and so she did the only thing she could. She raised her practice sword, tilting its point towards Vebiorg, and attacked.

CHAPTER ELEVEN

IT HAD COST FIONN MORE THAN HALF THE SILVER WHICH
King Gorm had given him to get to Birka. He had
bought passage on three different boats before going
aboard a trading knörr whose skipper was as eager
to reach Birka as Fionn was himself. The man had
a hold full of bear, wolf, marten and squirrel pelts
and feared the weather turning warmer before he
got the chance to sell them at twice their worth. His
name was Alver and he said he had seen too much
meltwater pouring into the fjord for it not to mean
that summer was around the corner. And so he
sailed that broad-bellied ship with an impatience
bordering on recklessness, or that was how it
seemed to Fionn who did not know that coast and
saw the rocks which broke the surface at low tide
like seals' backs and which threatened to rip out
Wave-Rider's belly, spilling men and furs into the sea.
But Fionn stood at the side and revelled in the song

of the wind through the lines because he was on the hunt. Did a stooping hawk, its talons extended, suddenly open its wings to slow its flight when it could almost taste the prey? No, it did not. Besides which, he could swim like an otter if needs be. Let them all drown, including his horses. Let it all sink to the fjord's bed and so long as he had his scían in his hand when he clambered up the rocks Sigurd Haraldarson would die.

And yet when *Wave-Rider* clumped up to her mooring and he had bid his farewells to Alver and gone off to get an eyeful of all the bays and berths which Birka had to offer, Fionn began to think that he had made a mistake. That he had been too hasty in killing the farmer and his family before he had taken ship into the Jutland Sea. He should have asked them more questions, made it even more clear what they stood to lose by lying to him, for as it was it seemed they had done just that. That fat sow. Because Sigurd Haraldarson and his crew-light ship were not in Birka.

No. They will come. Haraldarson will *come. In my haste I am here before him, that is all. Patience is the hunter's weapon*, he reminded himself.

And so he would wait.

'Well, I cannot even tell I have been drinking at all,' Bjarni said. He was standing on the table, an ale horn in each hand and a woman on his shoulders, just sitting there, her skirts up round her hips so that

Bjarni's beard bristles must have tickled her inner thighs. Though she looked happy enough with the arrangement. And Bjarni was naked.

'We started drinking properly at midday,' Svein said, a puzzled expression on his face, 'so I would wager we must have had one or two by now.' He grinned. 'But it would be a shame if we did not carry on a little while longer. It is not every day a man is drinking ale in such a place as this—' He frowned, trying to remember the name of the settlement.

'It is called Birka, you brainless ox,' Bjarni slurred.

'Ha! You had never heard of the place before we tied up to the wharf the other morning,' Olaf told him, downing the ale in his cup and dragging a hand across his beard and lips.

'This is true, Uncle,' Svein said, 'but now that we do know of Birka, I am thinking Birka should learn a little about us.' He grinned up at the woman on Bjarni's shoulders who was moving her arms up and down in undulating, languid strokes, as though she believed she was a bird flying through the sky. *A bird that was falling asleep*, Sigurd thought, looking at her eyes which were beginning to grow heavy. She had done her best to keep up with Bjarni and the others on the drinking and it had been a worthy effort, but there was more chance of those flapping arms lifting her up and out into the night.

'Tell your friend to get down,' the owner of the drinking house called across to Olaf, who waved a hand at the man as if to say he would get round to it in a moment.

'I am glad we are here,' Bjorn said. Along with Sigurd and Moldof and most of the others crammed into the benches of that fug-filled, reeking, flame-lit tavern, Bjorn, Hagal and Solmund were sitting on stools, leaning against the wall. Solmund had been asleep and snoring for a good while now, which at least got him out of the drinking. The only two missing were Aslak and Asgot who were down at the wharf with *Reinen*. There were harbour guards down there whose job it was to see that men did not steal from other men's ships, but Sigurd would not trust that job to Svearmen he did not know.

'This is what men like us should be doing when there is no one around who we ought to be killing,' Bjorn went on.

'You are lucky that Sigurd is so generous with his silver,' Olaf said, at which Bjorn and his brother both raised their ale horns to Sigurd by way of thanks for keeping the stuff flowing like a river in spate.

'When you want someone dead, we are your men,' Bjorn said, grinning. 'You just have to give us the word, Sigurd.'

At that moment the woman up on Bjarni's shoulders opened her mouth and spewed a hot, stinking gush on to the table, which had men jumping from the benches and cursing her to Hel's cold kingdom and beyond.

'At last we have found someone who holds their ale as well as Thorbiorn here,' Svein said, smacking King Thorir's son on the back as a foul-mouthed Bjarni deposited his burden. The woman cursed, spat and tried to grab Bjorn's ale horn but he held it beyond her reach and told her to fuck off, at which she cursed again and staggered away into the crowd.

Bram leant over to a stranger sitting on the bench behind and swiped the man's fur hat off his head, tossing it to Bjarni who was still standing on the table, though now he was wearing something at least, even if it was wet and foul and had recently been inside the girl.

'Where's my fucking h—' the stranger began, stopping when he looked up to see the well-muscled, well-scarred man wiping himself down with it.

'I would forget about the hat if I were you, friend,' Valgerd advised the stranger, who looked at her, then at Bram and Olaf and Sigurd, and promptly turned back round to his cup.

'I say we find somewhere else to drink,' Thorbiorn suggested, grimacing at the smell, though there were two thralls with water at the table now, trying to sluice the mess away without soaking anyone.

'Then it is too bad that no one gives a bag of bollocks about what you say, whelp,' Olaf told him.

'Get him off that table!' the drinking house's owner bawled again from beyond a press of men

who were even more drunk than Sigurd's crew. If
that were possible.

'Brave when he's all the way over there, isn't he?'
Black Floki muttered.

Again Olaf raised a hand in the man's direction,
then turned back to Bjarni. 'Down you get, lad,'
he said. 'If you don't hide that worm of yours soon
some bird is going to swoop in here and peck it off.'

'Just as soon as I have seen the girl I am looking
for, Uncle,' Bjarni slurred, sweeping his ale cup
across the crowded place, 'for up here you get the
best view.'

'And which one are you looking for, Bjarni?'
Sigurd asked him.

'The prettiest one of course,' Bjarni said, drinking.

'And by pretty he means blind,' Valgerd put in,
which had them all laughing.

They had been in Birka, on the island of Björko,
three days now and were still full of it, none of them
having ever seen a place like it. Unlike the kaupang
at Skíringssalr, Birka was a year-round trading
settlement, home to metal workers, bronze casters,
wood carvers, bone carvers and leather workers. It
buzzed with activity, with merchants and fur, hide
and ivory hunters, who had brought their goods in
readiness for the coming season and the arrival of
the trade knörrs which would mark the beginning
of summer. Iron mined all over Svealand was traded
at Birka, as were slaves, their captors bringing them
across the Baltic to the island where they exchanged

them for silver, glassware, cloth, jewellery, weapons, wine or any number of other goods. It was enough to make the palms itch for the feel of silver, as Sigurd's father might have said. But easier to get hold of that silver as a trading man than a raiding one, Sigurd had said.

Olaf had agreed. 'She's a sweet nut but she'd take some cracking,' he said as they took in the fortress surrounded by its earth and stone ramparts, which stood upon the great lump of bare rock due north of the settlement itself.

'Still, makes the mouth water just to think of it,' Moldof had put in. 'All the treasures in a place like that. The riches which make men build such walls to keep other men out.'

Birka's location was its greatest advantage, Sigurd knew, for it was protected from casual attack by a network of rivers, lakes and inlets, which would be guarded by ships full of Svear warriors. As it was they had been challenged by one such crew, whose skipper had wanted to see evidence of Sigurd's trade goods before granting him permission to enter the large harbour of Kugghamn at Björko's northern end. That itself had been no easy thing, requiring Solmund's experience at the tiller and Sigurd's own good eyesight, for the approach through the Skärgård and Løgrinn, the great bay of the Baltic Sea, had been strewn with rocks deliberately placed to make the way more difficult, hazardous even, for those new to Birka.

A commotion turned Sigurd's head now and he saw the main throng of drinking men part to allow the owner of the place and five big, ugly, broken-nosed men to come through, each of them brandishing a club of some sort. There were no blades, other than eating knives, allowed in the place, all swords and scramasaxes being left in the care of thralls outside.

'Only five?' Svein said. 'Now this whoreson is really nettling me. Five? What an insult.'

'I've told you enough times to get your friend down off my table,' the owner said, pointing a finger at Olaf, which was not, Sigurd thought, the best idea the man had ever had. 'And he can put some clothes on while he's at it. Gods but nobody in here wants to see all that flapping about like a fish in the bilge.'

That was when Olaf took hold of the man's finger and snapped it, and the man screamed and the fighting began. Olaf's fist in the man's mouth stopped him shrieking at least. 'It is hard to make so much noise when you are chewing on broken teeth and blood,' Svein said afterwards. But it took a purposeful blow to his jaw to shut the drinking house owner up completely.

It did not last long. Bram, Svein, Olaf and Bjorn were in the thick of it, breaking noses, hammering fists into jaws and eyes, kicking men in the balls and generally making a mess of the place while Sigurd and the others looked on, trying to avoid the flailing limbs and flying ale. He would not have admitted it but Sigurd's bones still ached from his fight with King Thorir all those weeks ago. Besides which, this fight was not of his making and he was content to keep out of the way and let the others have their fun.

Even Bjarni had jumped still naked into that seething cauldron, an unsettling sight as he grappled a man who was a head taller than he, until at Sigurd's word Olaf hauled him off, telling him to get his clothes back on before he earned Sigurd's crew the kind of reputation they did not want.

And yet no one seemed to be enjoying the fight more than Thorbiorn. He leant against the wall, grinning like a dead hare.

Solmund nodded in his direction. 'Maybe we should have left when the lad suggested it,' he said to Hagal, who for his part clearly did not think the fight worthy of one of his tales, for he seemed more concerned with emptying his ale cup down his throat while he still could.

Everyone in the place, all the other crews, the traders, the hunters and the craftsmen, were all watching, and many of them did not look happy about what was being done to the ale house owner and his companions by this crew whom many of them had never seen before. One of these spectators, a lean, dark-haired man with only a nub of skin where one of his ears used to be, caught Sigurd's eye. It wasn't just the missing ear that drew his attention. It was the tilt of his head and the way he held himself. He was no silversmith or wood turner this one. He was a warrior and it did not take any cleverness to see it.

Solmund noticed the man too. 'We are not going to make friends like this, Sigurd,' he said, turning back to see Svein pick up a discarded cudgel and walk over to a man who was on all fours, bloody spittle hanging from his beard as he tried to rise. Svein lashed the cudgel across the man's face and he dropped to the ale- and mud-slick floor.

No one was doing any killing, that they knew of anyway, but Solmund was right. It was not as though they needed any more enemies.

'Besides which, I doubt we will be served any more ale here,' Hagal said.

Bjarni nodded at the ale house owner who was a moaning heap of misery. 'Not unless that turd has pissed in it,' he said, stumbling into his breeks and trying, not altogether successfully, to pull them up.

'We're leaving,' Sigurd announced. 'Now.'

'S'pose we might as well,' Bram said, looking at the wreckage of dazed, crumpled men around them. He seemed disappointed that there was no one left to fight.

They downed the last of their ale and made for the door, other drinkers parting to let them leave, then poured out of the longhouse into the spring night, making their way past a line of warehouses, workshops and the jetties which provided access to them from the lake on the north-east of Birka. Dogs barked, horses in a nearby stable nickered and somewhere a baby screamed.

'Well, the owner of that place will never chew a good mutton stew again,' Svein said, looking up at the night sky and retying one of his braids which had come loose long before the fighting began. Grey cloud was scudding westward, breaking up here and there to reveal swathes of black in which stars beyond counting blinked like the sparks from some god's fire in Asgard. It was a good night to be alive, Sigurd thought.

'That is his own fault,' Olaf said. 'He was near enough picking my nose with that finger of his. A man should not shove his finger in another man's face unless he is certain he can put him on his arse.'

'Maybe he thought he could put you on your arse, Olaf,' Moldof said.

'He was an ugly swine but he wasn't blind,' Olaf said.

They turned on to a wider thoroughfare which led down to the harbour, passing between lines of houses leaking woodsmoke and snores and the sounds of folk swiving the night away. Most of these dwellings were wattle-and-daub affairs, but some were made of timber planks and still others were log houses caulked with clay; none of Sigurd's crew had ever seen a place where so many folk lived 'arse by arse', as Solmund had put it. 'A man with a long spear could poke his neighbour,' the helmsman said.

'Or his neighbour's wife,' Bjarni suggested with a wicked smile, and they all knew he was thinking about a different sort of spear.

'I am glad you young bone heads have had your fun,' Solmund said now, 'for we will likely be thrown out of Birka tomorrow.'

'Bollocks,' Bram gnarred.

'He's right,' Olaf said. 'This King Erik Refilsson sounds like a hard bastard. I heard some Svear cup-maker telling his friend that the king recently went hunting and killed a bear with nothing but a scramasax.'

'Ha! I have killed a bear with a fart,' Bram said. Which was not altogether unbelievable.

'There is no king in Birka now,' Hagal said. 'Erik is off fighting in the west somewhere.'

'How do you know this?' Sigurd asked, his eye drawn to the whirr of bats overhead.

'The most popular stories have kings in them,' Hagal said with a shrug. 'So if there is a king around the place I like to know about it so that I can put him in my tale.' He grinned at Olaf. 'I will get that bear story in there somewhere though. But . . .' he raised a finger, staggering almost sideways across the street, 'but King Erik has a man looking after Birka in his absence. A hersir called Asvith, whom men call Kleggi.'

Horsefly was a byname which told you all you needed to know about a man, so Sigurd was certain

that Solmund was right and that they would reap
the consequences of pummelling the ale house
keeper and his men. And a hersir, whilst not a
jarl, was still a powerful man, a warlord who was
usually rich in both silver and battle experience, so
this Asvith was not a man to be taken lightly. He
was likely up in the hill fort north of the town with
enough spearmen to defend Birka in case there was
a king or jarl with the ships, men and ambition to
sack the place. A half crew like Sigurd's would not
give them cause for concern, but then you could
hardly be accused of keeping the peace if outsiders
were free to go around breaking fingers and noses.

'No more fun tonight,' Sigurd said, glancing back
to see that Bjorn had fallen behind and was pissing
against the side of someone's house. 'We will sleep
aboard *Reinen* and wait on what tomorrow brings.'
There were some grumbles at this, because for
the last two nights they had slept wherever they
had drunk their last drop, and not all of them in
the same ale house, though Olaf had not let King
Thorir's son out of his sight, because of the lad's
reputation. The last thing they needed was some
man putting a sword in the boy for tupping his wife
or daughter.

'So who have you been fighting?' Aslak called
from *Reinen*'s side as they came down to the wharf
against which four other ships were moored. He
could tell just by the men's swagger that they had

been causing trouble and he looked sorry to have missed out.

'It was all Bjarni's fault so you will have to ask him about it,' Hagal said, gesturing at Bjarni who was twirling round and round, arms outstretched, his face turned up to the fleets of clouds skimming across the night sky, as though he alone could hear some music of horns and drums.

'You won't get much sense out of him,' Valgerd warned, as they jumped down into *Reinen* which was sitting low on the ebb tide.

'I will tell you all about it, Aslak,' Svein said, 'as soon as I have a horn of ale in my hand for I have a thirst that needs slaughtering.'

'No good story ever began with a dry mouth,' Hagal agreed.

Though it was cloudy, Asgot said it would not rain. They took their furs and skins and made their nests in the thwarts, each finding plenty of space, which was one good thing about being as crew-light as *Reinen* was. Sigurd had no sooner laid his head down on a rolled-up pelt than he was deeply and dreamlessly asleep.

And in the morning, Asvith, whom men call Horsefly, came down to the wharf to bite them.

Black Floki was the first to see them coming. He called to Sigurd, who was playing tafl with Solmund, the board and gaming pieces set up on a stool between two sea chests midships.

'Told you we'd be hoisting the sail today, lad,' Solmund muttered, disappointed to be finishing the game early, because he was winning.

'I have not said we're leaving,' Sigurd said, standing to look in the direction Floki had pointed, thinking that in truth they might not have much choice in the thing, judging by the forest of spears which was coming down to the harbour from the town.

'Keep your mouth shut, Bjarni. You too, Svein,' Olaf told them, muttering that it would have been nice to stay a few more days in Birka. 'The rest of you, try not to look like yourselves. Maybe we can convince this Asvith that the ale house owner started it.'

'You think the turd will believe a Norse crew over a bunch of Svearmen?' Solmund asked. 'That he'll take your side against a man from whom he likely gets his ale?'

'No,' Olaf admitted, 'but I'd wager that a man whose jaw I cracked won't be saying much of any sense to anyone this morning.'

This got a chuckle from the others just as this hersir Asvith came on to the wharf, which was unlikely to help their cause, Sigurd thought, nodding to the man in greeting. He had brought some thirty warriors down from the hill fort north of Birka, which made for both an impressive display and a clear warning, if not a threat. The ale house owner was there too, with two of his swollen-faced, sullen-looking men at his back. No doubt the other three had been in no fit state to come down to the harbour.

'Byrnjolf Hálfdanarson,' Asvith Kleggi called. He was not a big man, nor broad or otherwise physically impressive, but he made up for all that by looking rich. His black boots, green breeks and red tunic embroidered with gold thread were obviously expensive. So was his brynja, for it had some gold rings scattered throughout it, each of them gleaming against the iron grey, which must have looked even more striking on a sunny day. Over his chest hung a silver Thór's hammer on a gold chain.

'I am Byrnjolf,' Sigurd said, going over to the side. At least it was a rising tide, so that he was not having to crane his neck looking up at the man. Byrnjolf was the name Sigurd went by in Birka, for, far as they were from his enemies King Gorm and Hrani Randversson, it was safer if no one knew his real name.

'Who are you?' Sigurd asked, though he knew full well who the man was.

'I am the law here in Birka. My name is Asvith Grettisson. I speak for King Erik Refilsson.' The man's hand fell to rest on the pommel of his sword, a gesture clearly intended to ring louder than the words he had spoken.

'Well, if you have come with wergild for the injuries my men received at the hands of that ugly troll and his men, you did not have to. I am feeling generous this morning, Asvith Grettisson, and will let him off.'

There were some chuckles from the row benches at that, but Asvith did not look like a man who did much laughing. The muscle in his cheek was twitching as he glared at Sigurd with eyes that must have seen all types of men tie up their boats at his wharf, from outlaws and killers to boasters and drunkards. Here he had all those types in one ship.

The ale house owner gestured at one of his men to come forward, which he did, speaking in Asvith's ear whilst the hersir continued to stare at Sigurd. Then Asvith looked across at Olaf and nodded. 'I am told on oath that this man started the fight last night,' he said, pointing at Olaf.

'Are you?' Sigurd looked at Olaf. 'Did you?' he asked.

Olaf scratched his beard. 'Is that what *he* says?' Olaf asked Asvith, pointing at the ale house owner whose face was as lumpy as curds before straining. 'I want to hear it from him. If he is the man I am accused of fighting.'

This was a reasonable request had Olaf not guessed that the man's jaw was broken like a clay pot dropped on a rock, meaning he could not speak – and yet he tried his best. He stepped forward and attempted to accuse Olaf himself, but the words were mangled. They came out of the ruin of his mouth in a garbled mess of bloody spittle that hung from his beard. His eyes glistened with tears of pain or perhaps frustration.

Olaf held out his arms and looked from Sigurd to Asvith. 'Can someone tell me what he is saying? For I have heard more sense from a two-day-old bairn.'

Asvith looked resentful of the man and told him to stop mumbling because he was making a fool of himself. Then he looked back to Sigurd, gesturing for one of the ale house owner's men to come forward with the sack he was holding. This was the one whom Sigurd had last seen wrestling with a naked Bjarni, the two of them rolling round on the floor and Bjarni's arse shining like the moon. The man moved gingerly now, though at least he had the pride to try to hide his pains. He reached into the sack and pulled out a wooden cup, which might easily have been the one from which Sigurd had been drinking the previous day, then gave it to Asvith.

'Eight cups,' Asvith said. 'One for each of the six men your crew attacked. One for King Erik because you have broken the peace in his town. One for me . . .' he pointed to the boards beneath him, 'because I have had to come all the way down here to speak with you. You will fill all of them with silver, or amber if you have it.' He smiled then but it was as brittle as new ice. 'Fill these cups and that will be an end to it.'

'Will it now?' Sigurd said, glancing at Olaf.

All the silver that Sigurd had was in *Reinen's* hold and there was not much of it. He would need all of it and more, much more, and it would be a dry day in Rán's kingdom beneath the waves before he gave more than half of it to this shiny turd of a hersir.

'I had thought men called you Horsefly because you are annoying, flying around the place biting people, making a nuisance of yourself,' he told the man. 'But I see you also got the name because you spend your time around shit,' he said, gesturing at the ale house owner and his men.

Even Sigurd's crew thought this was a dangerous thing to say, for they stood up from their sea chests and bristled, looking for their spears and shields though not yet laying hands on them.

Asvith's face was all frown, as if he could not quite believe what he had just heard. 'Are you still full of ale, Byrnjolf?' he asked. 'Or have you come to Birka to die?'

'Neither, Horsefly,' Sigurd said. 'But nor will I give you eight cups of silver today.' He raised his hand. 'However, I will give you eight good pelts. Not as an admission that we began the trouble last night, but as a gift because I am a generous man and because we like it here and would stay a few more days if you are agreeable.'

'I do not want your rancid furs,' Asvith said. 'I will have my eight cups of silver or else I will have your ship.' His warriors, who stood in two lines across the wharf behind him, stirred like a forest in a gust, lifting shields and rolling shoulders and sensing that they might soon be called on to fight.

'You will get no silver from me, Horsefly,' Sigurd said. 'But I will gladly give you steel if that is what you want.' He glanced across to see that Solmund and Hagal were standing by the mooring ropes, axes in hand should Sigurd give the word to cut *Reinen* free of the wharf that they might fly from Birka. The others were picking up shields and spears now and coming over to the side.

'I can see now why you only have half a crew, Byrnjolf,' Asvith said. 'Either you got the rest killed, or else these are the only fools who are mad enough to sail with you.'

Valgerd gripped her bow and Svein his long-hafted axe. Aslak and Moldof were fetching oars from the trees, which they would use to push *Reinen* away from her berth before Asvith's warriors could leap aboard.

'You have struck the nail square with that,' Sigurd said. 'But you are forgetting that one Sword-Norse is worth two or three of you Svear.'

'Norse arsehole,' a warrior behind Asvith called.

'Sheep-swiving shits,' another man growled, but Asvith raised a hand to quieten them.

'How old are you, Byrnjolf?' he asked. 'You are barely into that beard of yours and yet you lead these men?' He glanced at Valgerd but did not correct himself. 'Are you a man of reputation, Byrnjolf?'

'I have always been a friend to the wolf and the raven,' Sigurd said, 'and have never been accused of letting them go hungry.'

'Give the word and we're gone,' Olaf said in a low voice. 'No point getting into a proper fight with this prick.'

'But I have an eye on that brynja of his, Uncle,' Sigurd said, loud enough for Asvith to hear.

'If you make an enemy of me, you make an enemy of King Erik Refilsson,' the hersir said. 'Not that that will concern you, for you will be dead.' He touched the silver Thór's hammer on his chest and Sigurd wondered why, until he looked over his shoulder and saw Asgot up on the mast step, staff raised, eyes closed as he communed with the gods in words as unfathomable as those which had come from the ale house owner's broken mouth.

'I will have the silver I came for,' Asvith said. 'And this is the last time I will say it.' With that he turned and gave a command and five men came forward with ropes and grappling hooks. They spread out on the wharf along *Reinen*'s length, uncoiling their ropes and making ready to hurl the hooks into the ship's thwarts.

'This Horsefly really is beginning to bother me,' Olaf grumbled into his beard, because Asvith seemed to know his business. If it came to a fight those men would hook *Reinen* like a fish. Yes, Sigurd's crew would cut the ropes, but it would be no easy thing to do it whilst also defending the ship from Asvith's thirty warriors *and* pushing off from the mooring. The chances were that a good number of these Svearmen would spill aboard in the first rush, and with Sigurd's lot fighting in the thwarts, more of Asvith's men would climb over the side and Sigurd's crew might never leave Birka.

'Asvith Grettisson,' someone called and the lines of Svear warriors parted to allow a knot of four men to come on to the wharf and approach the hersir. The one who had called the hersir's name was the lean, dark-haired, one-eared man Sigurd had seen watching the fight the night before. There was no mistaking him with his long hair tied back and that little piece of gristle on the left side of his head where his ear used to be. A sword stroke had likely done that, Sigurd thought, and if not for a good brynja the same blow might have cleaved into his shoulder, ruining the use of his shield arm at best.

'What do you want, Knut?' Asvith asked. 'I have heard you were at Fengi's place last night. Did these Norse scum cause trouble with you too?'

'Not with me,' this Knut said, shaking his head. 'But they dealt with Fengi and his men the way you or I would deal with a pack of unruly hounds.' All three men with Knut looked like grizzled fighters, scarred and dangerous, their arms adorned with silver rings and their beard braids knotted with more silver.

Asvith flicked a hand towards the men in *Reinen*. 'So these Norsemen started the fighting? Three of Fengi's men are in their beds with broken bones.'

Knut looked at Sigurd and nodded. 'Yes, they are to blame,' he said, 'and you should kill them now while you have the chance, and dump their bodies out in the fjord.' Asvith nodded and commanded his men to make ready to attack, but Knut lifted a hand and Sigurd noticed that two of the fingers on it were mostly missing, having been cut off at the knuckle joints. 'Or you could take four cups of silver as wergild and be done with it. These men will sail away and no one needs to die this morning.'

'If you had two ears, Knut, you would have heard this young fool tell me that he will not give me any silver. His best offer is some furs, and I have no need of furs.'

'I will fill four cups with my own silver,' Knut said. 'And I will take these men away from Birka. You will have made a handsome profit for little effort and King Erik will be happy with you.'

'What would you get out of it, Knut?' Asvith asked.

'You need not concern yourself with that, Asvith,' Knut replied, then he walked up to the edge of the wharf while his men stayed where they were, eyeballing those aboard *Reinen* with as much hostility as Asvith's men were.

'Are you agreeable to this arrangement, Byrnjolf?' he asked, and Sigurd had met enough killers to know that Knut was one of them. From the look of him he was a difficult man to kill, too, though clearly it had not stopped folk trying.

'What do you think you are buying with your four cups of hacksilver, Knut?' Sigurd asked him.

'Your sword, Norseman, and those of your crew. And your woman,' he added, nodding respectfully at Valgerd. 'I serve a man who has need of good fighters. It seems to me that you have not come to Birka to trade. Perhaps you are running from your enemies.' He shrugged. 'Or maybe you are out to make yourselves rich. Do a little raiding here and there when you think you can get away with it.' He hitched his cloak back over the sword at his hip and put his right foot up on to *Reinen*'s sheer strake. 'What I can be sure of,' he said in a lower voice, 'is that you did not come here to get yourselves killed by this preening cock behind me.' He grinned at Sigurd and then at Olaf. 'You Norse are not renowned for your cleverness. Even so, you must know you will die if you fight these men. Seeing as I do not think it is your wyrd to end your lives here in Birka, it must mean you will accept my offer.'

'Which is? Remind me,' Olaf put in.

Knut nodded. 'To fight for my lord Alrik against his enemies.'

'We have plenty of enemies of our own,' Sigurd said.

'What would we earn fighting for this Alrik?' Olaf asked.

'For a start, four cups of silver, the wergild for Fengi and his men. Give me your word that you will fight for Alrik and that debt is as good as paid. You will earn more silver for yourself soon enough and all of Alrik's men enjoy plenty of food and ale.' He scratched that little nub that was all that was left of his ear. 'You fight for Alrik, perhaps until autumn, perhaps longer, and you get rich on plunder.'

Sigurd looked at Olaf and could tell that he thought it was a proposition worth considering.

'It's not as though we have a great deal of choice,' Olaf said. This was true as far as Sigurd could see. 'And we are going to need more silver before this thing with the oath-breaker is done.' He gestured for Sigurd to follow him over to the mast step where they could talk without being overheard. 'We go with this Knut and we fight for his lord but we keep our heads down and maybe we make an alliance or two that might come in useful.' The rest of the crew were still poised for a fight, their shields forming a rampart along *Reinen*'s side. Sigurd knew they would fight if he gave the word and he was proud of them for it.

'What do you say?' Olaf asked him. 'If we meet this Alrik and he turns out to be a toad's arsehole who is not worth our sweat, we'll be on our way. If he tries to stop us . . .' Olaf shrugged. 'We kill him, then go on our way.'

Sigurd nodded and turned back to Knut. 'I will fight for your lord but I will not swear to him.

Neither will my crew for they are already sworn to me.'

'Are you a jarl then?' Knut asked.

'Not yet,' Sigurd said. 'But they are sworn to me. We will fight and you will see our worth, but I will not let your lord waste their lives.'

'So we are agreed? You will come with us? I have your word?'

Sigurd jumped on to the sheer strake and stepped across on to the wharf, gripping Knut's forearm as the one-eared warrior gripped his.

'You have my word, Knut,' Sigurd said.

'I am glad you have found some new meat for Alrik's shieldwall, Knut,' Horsefly said. 'I will be still more glad when I have my four cups of silver.'

'You know I'm good for it, Asvith,' Knut said.

'I do,' Asvith said. 'When will you sail?'

'Tomorrow? The day after? When we have the wind.'

Asvith nodded. 'Tell Alrik that King Erik wants that troll-swiving Jarl Guthrum dead before the Jól feast.'

Knut gave the man a warning look. 'You know as well as I do that my lord Alrik is not sworn to King Erik, nor any other king.'

'I like the sound of this Alrik,' Olaf muttered to Sigurd.

Asvith gave Knut a smile that was as greasy as swine fat. 'Not yet, perhaps,' he said. 'But once King Erik has got oaths from all of the western jarls, he will come east to mop up the last dregs from here south as far as Götaland. Your lord Alrik is no fool. He knows that resisting King Erik would be like trying to turn back the tide.'

'We will see what happens when that day comes,' Knut said. 'In the meantime we have our own fight.'

'You do,' Asvith said. 'We hear that it is not going well for you.' He turned back to Sigurd. 'Your crew is the caulking to stop Alrik's boat shipping water,' he said. Knut did not deny it.

'Then Alrik is a lucky man, for with caulking such as this, he could sail to the edge of the world,' Sigurd said, grinning.

'Let us hope there is more to you than a good boast, Byrnjolf, because you have already cost me enough silver,' Knut said, though there was a smile on his lips which looked at odds with his hard, battle-scarred face.

'Back to the borg then!' Asvith called, turning to his warriors, who if truth be told looked just as happy that they would not have to fight anyone that morning after all. They slung their shields across their backs, tucked hand axes back into their belts and began to head back to the town in loose order, their chatter a low hum in the dawn.

'So that's it for Birka then,' Svein said as they laid their own weapons down in the thwarts and removed their helmets. 'It was good while it lasted.'

'The wound-sea calls us,' Hagal said, meaning that they would be sailing a sea of blood before long, which was a dark way of looking at how the morning had turned out.

'I prefer to think that we are heading into an ice-sea,' Olaf said, which was not the best kenning for silver that anyone had ever heard, but they knew what Olaf meant and anyway they preferred it to Crow-Song's foretelling. For Knut had promised them fighting. And where there was fighting there was plunder.

CHAPTER TWELVE

_____

AS IT HAPPENED, THEY HAD SPENT ANOTHER THREE DAYS in Birka, waiting for a good wind and keeping out of trouble while Knut rounded up the last of those other men whom he had convinced to sell their swords to his lord Alrik and sail north with him. Some of these were men from outlying farms who had endured a hard winter and would need to earn enough silver to get their families through the next one. Most were Svearmen but some were Geats who had come north to Birka to make a name for themselves in trade or war. Rumour was that one man was from far-off Alba across the whale's road, which had men intrigued, at least until they laid eyes on him, for word had it the man was not much to look at. But wherever they were from Knut promised them fame as men of Alrik's war band, his fellowship, and they had swallowed the hook whole, and perhaps they _would_ earn fame in the sword-song. Still others were young men who would rather do anything than work the land like their fathers, or spend their days fishing, or turning wood, cutting peat to harvest bog iron, or felling trees in the forests. Few owned brynjur, helmets or swords, but most came with spears, short axes and heads full of fireside tales, and when they saw Sigurd and his crew they were round-eyed and as full of awe as men who have caught a glimpse of the world of the gods at the far end of Bifröst the shimmering bridge.

'Either you served a generous king or else you killed a rich one,' Knut had said to Sigurd, for even he had been impressed by the sight of them in all their war glory the day they had set off from Birka. It was not that Sigurd expected trouble, but he wanted Knut to see them in their mail and helmets, their spear blades gleaming, sword scabbards and belts oiled and lustrous, axe heads polished, and each of them looking as rich as a jarl and dangerous as death.

'No king gave us this war gear,' Sigurd had said, which was answer enough. Knut would know that he had brought battle-tested warriors to his lord's banner. He would also know better than to cheat them or waste them in some hopeless fight.

So they had sailed north across Løgrinn in the wake of Knut's ship, a sleek karvi named *Kráka*, which had Solmund muttering that *Crow* was a strange name for a ship, but then these men were

Svear, he said, which he supposed explained it. The crossing was easy enough, even when on the second day the wind died and they had to row, because although Løgrinn was not strictly a lake, for it drained into the Baltic Sea, it was as flat as a mead board. Terns, herring gulls, ducks and sandpipers thronged on the skerries. Now and then cormorants flew low over the water across *Reinen's* path, having returned to the north now that winter was over, which was a good thing to see, though young Thorbiorn was not so sure and would touch the Freyja pendant at his neck whenever he saw one. He believed that the birds were men who had been lost at sea, which had even Asgot muttering to himself. 'Those who drown but escape Rán's cold embrace end up on the island of Utrøst,' King Thorir's son told them. 'But the only way they can return to their homes to see their loved ones again is if they take the shape of cormorants.'

'And where is this Utrøst?' Solmund asked him. 'For I have never heard of it.'

Thorbiorn had shrugged and shot the helmsman a petulant look. 'You tell me, seeing as you are the one with salt water for blood and a beating sail for a heart,' he said. 'Besides, my mother told me the story when I was a boy and I cannot remember it all.'

'You must have a bad memory then, lad,' Solmund gnarred, which was well said because Thorbiorn was still a boy in many ways.

And when they came to the northern edge of Løgrinn, they followed *Kráka* east along the thickly forested shore until they arrived at the bay in which Alrik's other ships were moored. There were five of them in all: three knörrs, a big snekke as good for war as for riding the whale road, and another karvi similar to *Crow*, though to Sigurd's eyes none of them was as handsome as *Reinen*. The forest around the bay had been cleared, the timber having gone into several small buildings and the palisade of sharpened stakes which surrounded the settlement, enclosing it almost to the shore so that the ships at their moorings were protected. The rest of the place was a clutter of tents and animal pens, workshops and stores, and all of it roofed by a pall of smoke from the many fires around which men and women gathered. Though many of the men and women, at least fifty or sixty, came to the muddy shore to see *Kráka* and *Reinen* slide up to their moorings. They greeted Knut and those men they knew, exchanging news and hurling insults at one another the way men will when they are pleased to see that their friends are still in one piece.

Some of the camp men asked Knut how he had managed to get so many young men drunk enough to join him. Others told those wide-eyed strangers that they should have stayed in Birka where there were plenty of women and less chance of being gutted by a spear or bitten to death by the midges which swarmed round Løgrinn's shore in the summer. Most, though, eyed the poorly armed new men the way a gull watches a ship which it knows has its prow turned towards a storm.

'They've seen fighting, that lot,' Bram told Olaf, nodding towards a knot of men who, instead of clucking over the newcomers, were standing round a rack on which a wolf skin was stretched for scraping.

His arms full of his sea chest, Olaf glanced over at the men and nodded. They wore their experience of the spear-song like the cloaks on their backs. It was pride but weariness. It was callous cruelty but the indifference of a dull blade. It was fellowship.

'Take me to Alrik,' Sigurd told Knut when they had all disembarked and Knut had shown *Reinen*'s crew to their sailcloth shelter near the shore's edge.

'He is not here,' Knut said. 'But in a few days we will march north to Fornsigtuna. You will meet him then.'

There was no room in any of the log houses for now, but that could change at any time, Knut assured them. Not that Sigurd minded sleeping under sailcloth, for he did not want to be far from *Reinen* until he had got a better idea about this war-leader Alrik and his people.

'I don't think they have seen many shieldmaidens before,' Knut said to Valgerd, who must have felt the weight of men's eyes more than any of them. 'In truth I would have filled two of Asvith's cups just for you.' Even a grizzled, one-eared, finger-light

293

warrior like Knut was not invulnerable to Valgerd's fierce beauty, though unlike Bjarni – or Sigurd himself, truth be told – he was not vain enough to believe that she might be attracted to him. 'Alrik will see it as a good omen that I've brought him you.'

'His enemies will see it differently the first time they face her,' Sigurd said.

Knut nodded, tearing his eyes from Valgerd back to Sigurd. 'I will make sure I am nearby to see it,' he said. 'So . . . which of you will help me train these wet-behind-the-ears lads so that they don't turn and run off the first time they hear a shield din?'

'I'll help you,' Olaf said, coming back out of the tent. 'If one of them ends up beside me in the shieldwall I want to know he's not going to piss on my shoes.'

'Aye, I'll come,' Bram said.

'Me too,' Bjorn said, picking up his spear and shield.

'Good,' Knut said, turning towards the others. 'The rest of you make yourselves comfortable and try not to start any fights. You'll be earning the silver I paid for you soon enough.'

'Where will we find the ale?' Svein asked, throwing an arm over Bjarni's shoulder. 'If we are busy drinking then we are not busy fighting.'

For a moment Knut looked dubious, then he pointed to a tent of red cloth across the far side of the camp beside a modest log-built longhouse whose thatch leaked so much smoke that presumably it let in the rain too. 'You need to speak to a man called Trygir. He will give you the two skins which is your crew's daily measure. You want more, you pay for it.'

Svein and Bjarni seemed happy enough with that and off they went. The others continued lugging sea chests and war gear into the tent and making their nests with furs and fleeces, and Sigurd looked up to see a white-tailed eagle soaring high above the forest beyond the palisade.

We will sharpen our own talons for this Alrik, he thought, *and see where it leads us.* There would be fighting and the gods would be watching. And Sigurd would fill his sea chest with silver because silver would buy him a war host.

Fionn had begun to think he had lost the scent and yet he had never taken his eyes off the jetties and wharves, as though by imagining Haraldarson he could conjure the reality. Then one blustery day *Reinen* had slid up to her mooring and Fionn's quarry had been all but served up to him on a trencher. The farmer's wife had been telling the truth after all, which was worth knowing. Good to know his methods were effective, not that he'd ever really doubted them.

Ever since that day, Fionn had watched Sigurd the way a hunter stalks a bull elk, looking for the perfect opportunity to strike. Waiting for his prey to make some mistake, to reveal his weakness. Just one vulnerable moment would be enough, was all the hunter needed. But Fionn had stalked enough men in his time to know that patience itself is to a killer as important as a well-honed blade. Four winters past he had shared hearth, hall and three full moons with a man he was being paid to kill. They had even become friends so that his quarry was as shocked as any victim could be when Fionn had put a knife in him while the man squatted behind the reed screen with his breeks round his ankles. Perhaps Fionn could have taken him before that, but there was something about the waiting which excited Fionn, which put a bone in his own breeks truth be told.

And yet he did not have the luxury of time now. Having pledged himself to fight for Alrik the last thing he intended was actually doing so. Not for him the shieldwall and the chaos of battle. Nor death by some unseen arrow falling from the sky, or facing some thick-skulled giant waving a long axe around thinking he was the Thunder God. Not that anyone could call Fionn a coward, for it took balls to look into the eyes of a man you had shared a mead horn with and put your knife into his heart. A man needed iron in his spine to hunt and kill a man who was said to be god-kissed, favoured by Óðin whom these men around him now called Allfather, Spear-God, Battle-Wolf. But Fionn did not fear these northern gods. It was not that he doubted their existence, just that he did not think they cared one way or the other about mortals and their struggles. When Fionn's knife drank, men died. He had crossed the whale's road some five years ago now and no shining, spear-wielding god, no red-bearded or blaze-eyed Lord of Asgard had ever come down from the clouds to stop him cutting a throat.

But people? People sometimes got in the way. The big growler who watched Sigurd like a proud father was one to start with. Olaf his name was, and Fionn might not have revelled in the spear din like some men but he knew a formidable warrior when he saw one. This Olaf had the war gear and the bearing of a champion, a man who fears no other, but more than this, he was older than most of Haraldarson's crew and wiser too.

Yet, Olaf was not the only warrior between Fionn and Sigurd. There was a wolf-lean, black-haired young man who might as well have had 'raven-feeder' carved in runes on his head, for he was a killer and no mistake. Fionn had not caught this man's name but he and his hand axes were rarely far from Fionn's prey. And there was Moldof the one-armed, who used to be King Gorm's prow man and who might well recognize Fionn from his time at Avaldsnes.

And so Fionn, hunter of men, killer of men's enemies, had watched and waited and now, on the third night since they had come ashore to Alrik's camp, he was beginning to smell an opportunity like the iron scent of blood in the air.

Perhaps two skins of ale per day should have been enough for a half crew like them. But it was not. Svein, Moldof, Bjorn, Bjarni and Thorbiorn each drank two men's share. Bram drank three. And so long as they were not fighting or causing too much trouble Sigurd did not see the harm in keeping them well sluiced in the stuff. He was their leader, and whilst he could not be much of a ring giver yet, he could reward their loyalty with ale, which was just as good as far as most of them were concerned. Sigurd had done what he could to keep Alrik's ale flowing into their cups like meltwater off a cliff face, but they had run out again now, which was why he was walking through the camp in the pouring, freezing rain towards Trygir's red sailcloth tent. Men sat huddled in skins under what meagre shelter they could find, murmuring round hissing fires and looking miserable with it. Sigurd imagined that more than a few of the younger lads, who had followed Knut singing their own legends under their breath, were beginning to think they should have stayed in Birka where there was plenty of dry floor space and better ale than Trygir's to be had.

'I could see the fear in their faces,' Valgerd said through a grin as they walked together. 'They were terrified that I would not be able to carry as much.'

Sigurd laughed, slipping and sliding in the mud, his arms outstretched for balance. 'And yet not one of them was so terrified that he volunteered to go in your place,' he said, walking through a thick haze of smoke which leaked from a nearby shelter made of spears stuck in the mud with oiled skins for its roof.

'Fetch a drop for us, won't you, lad?' a voice from the smoke said, though Sigurd could not see the body to whom it belonged amongst those who huddled steaming and stinking in that shelter.

'You do look younger without your brynja and helmet and with your beard braided like that,' Valgerd said, amused by the man having addressed Sigurd as though he were some stripling running errands.

'And yet no less handsome, hey?' Sigurd replied, made bold by the ale already inside him warming his blood.

'Or vain,' Valgerd said, lifting an eyebrow then nodding through a gap between two tents because she had seen Trygir's place through the rain and the gloom.

When Sigurd had told the others he was off to fetch more ale he had glanced at Valgerd in the hope that she might offer to go with him. It was childish really, he thought, and the rest of them, those still halfway sober, had probably seen clean through it. And yet he did not care because before Svein had slurred three words Valgerd had stood, pushed her wet hair off her forehead and said she could do with walking a cramp out of her legs. And now they were alone, which meant that Sigurd's less than cunning plan had somehow worked.

It was dark inside Trygir's tent, the only light coming from two lamps which burnt foul-smelling fish oil, and the rain was pelting against the sailcloth which had been slathered in pine tar to keep Trygir and his barrels dry. In a corner of the tent a boy sat on a pile of furs carving a wooden sword. Trygir's son by the look of his reddish hair and upturned nose.

'*Reinen*'s crew, yes?' Trygir greeted them as they wiped the rain from their faces and shook water off their hands. A man like Trygir must come to know every new face in that camp, Sigurd thought. Sees them come, sees them go. 'Where's the big man with the red beard and his mouthy friend?' Trygir said. He was a big man himself, though a full head shorter than Svein.

'We drew the short straw tonight,' Sigurd said. Even his beard rope was dripping.

'Did you now?' Trygir asked, lifting his chin a little. He glanced at Valgerd and smiled. Unlike the man who had called to Sigurd outside, Trygir knew full well who led *Reinen*'s crew, brynja or no brynja. He knew that Sigurd was standing in his tent now because he wanted to be standing there.

'So what can I get you this fine night?' Trygir asked, putting both hands on the table before him and leaning towards his customers, ignoring the mud and water which they had traipsed across his reed- and grass-strewn floor. 'I'm hoping it's ale or else you've come to the wrong place.' Behind him were stacked two dozen barrels, with more partly visible beyond a hanging partition at the rear of the tent. Skin bags and wooden gourds hung from the central tent pole and a set of bronze scales hung over the table, suspended from the roof pole on thin chains. A collection of lead weights sat on the table along with Trygir's own cup and drinking horn, a cudgel to deter difficult customers, and a sharp-looking axe for those who needed a little more persuasion.

'Mead?' Sigurd asked with a grin.

'Ha! I wish,' Trygir said, rubbing his hands together for warmth. Readying himself to do business. 'I'll tell you what,' he said, his eyes smiling in the lamp glow, 'I'll do you a very good deal seeing as it's your first time in here.' He looked at Valgerd then. 'And because I don't often get beauties like you in here,' he added in a low voice, as if his wife might be behind that partition at the back of the tent.

They bought four skins from Trygir, who warned them that he would have to sell them less from now on because at this rate he would run dry and men would start killing each other for the stuff and Alrik would return to find half his army dead and the other half drunk. 'And don't tell anyone what a good deal I gave you or they'll be in here demanding the same,' he warned them.

Sigurd tied his two skins together and slung them over his shoulder. Valgerd did the same. 'We're off to find Alrik tomorrow anyway,' he said, at which Trygir nodded, understanding why the late-night visit, and wished them well. His merchant's mask almost hiding his disappointment to be losing his best customers, he then tried to sell Sigurd two more skins from what he alleged was Alrik's own stash.

'Four is enough,' Sigurd said, 'given the walk we've got ahead of us tomorrow.'

'We could try a little of Alrik's brew,' Valgerd suggested, moving further inside Trygir's big tent to avoid a stream of water which was pouring through a hole in the red cloth. She looked at Sigurd. 'Before we head back.'

Sigurd's stomach rolled over itself. He nodded. 'We could,' he said, rummaging in the scrip on his belt for a thumb-sized piece of silver. He did not owe Trygir anything like that much but it was his guarantee that he would be back in the morning, hopefully when it was dry, with the pelts he owed the man.

'You two looking for somewhere quiet?' Trygir asked. He looked from Sigurd to Valgerd and back to Sigurd. 'Some place to enjoy a drop of my best without your friends sticking their beaks in?'

Sigurd felt the heat in his face. 'We should get back—'

'Where do you suggest?' Valgerd asked Trygir. He had sent his boy into the back to fetch the good ale and now the lad handed Valgerd a leather flask and Sigurd two cups. Even the boy seemed taken with Valgerd, who pointed at the nearly finished sword tucked in his belt and said it was some of the finest work she had seen. The boy's teeth flashed in the gloom and he looked at his father with unbridled pride.

'You'll give the lad ideas and I'll lose him to some blade smith,' Trygir said, shaking his head, though his eyes were smiling because the boy looked so proud. He looked back to Sigurd. 'So, you go next door, to the back entrance, and you ask for a man named Brodd-Helgi. Can't miss him, face like a goat and broken teeth,' he said, putting fingers to his own mouth, 'like he's been eating rocks. Say Trygir sent you, that I said to give you the loft.' He nodded at the small ale skin which Valgerd held by the neck. 'You'll be able to enjoy that all to yourselves up there.'

'And what will that cost me?' Sigurd asked, thinking it would be worth any price to be alone with Valgerd. Just the two of them for once, without the rest of the crew around.

Trygir did his best to look offended. 'Nothing,' he said. 'You've been a good customer, Byrnjolf Hálfdanarson. And I wish you and your crew well.'

Sigurd nodded and shook the man's hand, then he and Valgerd turned and pulled their cloaks tight around their necks against the freezing rain which still hissed in the gloomy world beyond Trygir's tent.

'You make a good-looking pair,' Trygir said as Sigurd lifted the flap and they stepped outside, and Sigurd hoped Valgerd had not heard the man, though the curl of her lips told him that she had.

'There isn't enough of that good stuff to go round anyway,' Sigurd said quickly so that they would not have to deal with Trygir's parting words. The sly shit. 'So we might as well make the most of a dry spot while we drink it.' They stood there looking at the longhouse, whose thatch was shrouded in a thick haze, as if the whole place was steaming. The main door clunked open and two men stumbled out, one of them puking into the mud before he had made four paces. His companion fumbled at his breeks and began pissing on to the log pile under the eaves. Men's voices and a woman's shrill laughter leaked from the place before the door clumped shut again.

Valgerd lifted the flask and studied it. 'I for one would like to know how Alrik's ale compares with what we mortals have been drinking,' she said, and with that she trudged off down the side of the longhouse looking for the other door. And Sigurd followed, thinking that Tygir was a sly, scheming son of a she-troll. He was also thinking that in the morning, when he brought the man the pelts he owed him, he would tell Trygir to keep the hacksilver.

They waited beneath the dripping thatch, enjoying the last lungfuls of sweet, rain-cleansed air while the big-bellied man who had opened the door went off to find Brodd-Helgi, leaving another man blocking the threshold, swaying on a sea of ale.

Eventually, Brodd-Helgi came and he did not look happy about being dragged away from his women and his cup to deal with two strangers standing at his door.

He glared at Sigurd. 'Don't know your face,' he said, then lifted his chin. 'Fuck off.'

'Trygir sent us,' Sigurd said. 'He told me to tell you to give us the loft.' Sigurd grinned and patted one of the plump ale skins slung over his shoulder. 'We need to try a little of this before sharing it with our crew.'

Brodd-Helgi fixed his eyes on Valgerd. 'Wouldn't mind a taste of that myself,' he said, his stare lingering on the shieldmaiden. 'You friends of his, then?'

Sigurd shrugged. 'We are good customers.'

Brodd-Helgi's tongue poked out between the ragged remains of his teeth. 'I've seen you,' he said to Valgerd. 'You're the new crew that came in with Knut. Handsome ship you've got there. Too much ship for the crew as I recall.' He was not a big man but he was confident, which probably meant whoever had broken his teeth was most likely dead now. 'Shouldn't be here though,' he said, then threw an arm back towards the interior. 'Only men allowed in here are those who've been fighting for Alrik a season or more.'

Behind Brodd-Helgi, partly cast in the glow of the hearth, mostly shrouded in shadow, but fogged by smoke, Sigurd could make out men and women drinking and rutting on beds and on the fur-strewn floor. They fumbled and groped in the fire-played shadow, knots of limbs and bare flesh, writhing beasts made of tits and arse, beards and balls.

'Aye, I should be telling you to piss off and come back when you've broken a few skulls for Alrik.' Brodd-Helgi sniffed, leaning out of the door and peering up at the rain-filled gloom. Then he straightened and licked a drop of rain off his lip. 'But if Trygir vouches for you . . .'

Sigurd's stomach rolled over and he made to remove his sword belt but Brodd-Helgi flashed a palm.

'Keep it,' he said. 'No one starts trouble in here.' Then he turned to the man who had been guarding the door before. 'Kick that arse-leaf Stækar out of the loft. If he wants to swive that pretty thing of his without his wife knowing, he needs to pay for the privilege.'

The man nodded and went off and Brodd-Helgi shut the door behind Sigurd and Valgerd and led them through the musky fug, picking a well-practised path through the gloom-shrouded drinking and rutting and sleeping folk. Along the sides of the room, stretching from roof post to roof post, hung screens of canvas or wool, creating separate cells and privacy for those who wanted it. Some of these hangings were plain, but for the smoke and drink stains, whilst others were embroidered with birds, falcons whose feathers Freyja goddess of lovers wore as a cloak.

'It's just as well the others don't know about this place,' Valgerd said, stepping over the outstretched arm of a woman who held on to her ale cup despite being ridden like a fjord horse to a feast.

Sigurd's heart was hammering in his chest and his palms were slick with sweat, and he felt as if he were walking into an ambush as they waited for an angry-looking Stækar to descend the ladder followed by a blushing beauty who somehow managed to avoid everyone's eye before slipping off into the crowd.

'You miserable shit, Brodd-Helgi,' Stækar growled, raking his long fair hair back off his face. 'I was a cock's length from tupping her.'

Brodd-Helgi grimaced. 'Take her back to your tent and tup her there,' he said. 'I'm sure Hildigunn won't mind. If you're quiet she may not even wake up.' He turned a palm over. 'Or pay me to use the loft.'

'Prick,' Stækar growled, then shot Sigurd a filthy look and stormed off, calling to a friend to get him a drink.

'Enjoy the ale,' Brodd-Helgi said to Valgerd. 'I'll want you out long before dawn. If someone pays me for the bed you'll be gone before that.'

Sigurd wanted to tell the man they were only looking for somewhere to talk and drink, but

Brodd-Helgi would not believe him and what did it matter anyway? Then he was following Valgerd up the ladder and into the dark where the smoke had gathered, though someone had gouged a hole between two of the logs in the wall to let at least some fresh air in. As it happened there was no bed up there, just a thick pile of furs, two chests for leaning against, someone's rolled-up cloak – Stækar's perhaps – and a heavy dished stone lamp whose flame was sputtering on its cotton-grass wick.

'They'll worry about us,' Sigurd said, watching Valgerd bending over to shrug off her brynja. There was not enough room to stand and so Sigurd had crawled from the ladder on hands and knees towards the lamp glow.

'Olaf will come looking for you,' she said, picking up the discarded cloak and using it to dry her brynja to keep the iron rot out of it.

'Bram will come looking for the ale,' Sigurd said, removing his own sopping wet cloak and his sword belt. He held out the cups and watched Valgerd as she unstoppered the flask and poured the ale. The lamp only just caught her in its flickering bloom so that one side of her face was burnished gold and the other was cast in shadow. And Sigurd realized that this *was* Valgerd, half in the world and half . . . somewhere else. Lost. In the past perhaps.

'You think of her often?' he asked, dropping that into the silence between them. Not even knowing why he had done it, especially now of all times when they were alone with a flask of strong ale and a pile of soft furs.

She sipped from her cup and looked away, towards the glow and the clamour rising from the room below. 'Less than I did,' she said, seeming annoyed with him too for bringing it up. Then she turned her eyes on him, glacial blue even in this dim light, and a shiver ran down through Sigurd from head to arse.

Sygrutha, the spae-wife whom Valgerd had been sworn to protect, had been dead a day or two when Sigurd found Valgerd living apart from other folk by the sacred spring in the Lysefjord. The völva had been nothing but skin and bone, a wisp of a corpse lying in a bed, but that bed was the only one in the cabin and Sigurd had known that Valgerd and Sygrutha had been lovers. And since the day she had joined his crew, Valgerd had mourned the völva and hated the gods.

Valgerd shrugged and picked up the loose thread of it. 'Sygrutha knew she was dying. How could she not?' she said.

'Because she had the gift?' Sigurd asked.

'Because death stalked her,' Valgerd said. 'Because it worked on her like rot in the blade. And there was nothing we could do to fight it.' She drank again. Sigurd had not yet touched a drop. 'In the end she faded away. Like a dream.'

'Was there pain?' Sigurd asked.

'She tried to hide it from me. But yes. Eyes cannot lie about pain. Have you noticed that?'

He nodded. 'And you cannot forgive the gods?'

Valgerd shook her head. 'Nor Sygrutha,' she said. 'When she knew death was close, she told me she would come to me. After. She promised to come. She knew the ways, she said, to reach me through the birds or the wind. Or the waterfall.' For a moment Sigurd thought she would shed tears, but then those blue eyes sharpened. Valgerd had done all her crying unseen. 'She lied.'

'Maybe not. Maybe she tried,' he suggested.

'She lied,' Valgerd said. She drank again and this time Sigurd did too. 'Have your brothers come to you?' she asked him. 'Your mother? Your father?'

Sigurd frowned at the question because he did not know how to answer it. There had been times. A whisper amidst the sword-song. A feeling in the shield din. All in his own head perhaps.

'I don't know,' he said at last.

Valgerd shrugged. 'I don't think of her when I am fighting.'

Sigurd forced a smile. 'Then you have joined the right crew,' he said and with that lifted his cup and she did the same. 'Skál.'

Valgerd lifted her own cup. 'This *is* better than that,' she said, nodding at the four ale skins which they had put to one side.

Sigurd drank, then swept the back of his hand over his lips. 'Another reason it's a good thing we're leaving tomorrow,' he said, 'or else we'd be spending what little silver we have buying more of it.' The ale was rich and bitter, the flavours of the hops, juniper and bog myrtle combined in a fresh-tasting brew which hit Sigurd's stomach with a feeling not unlike the first thrill before a fight. Or maybe that was not the ale at all.

'So now we will fight another man's battles for him?' she said. 'Instead of our own.'

'You know we are not strong enough to face the oath-breaker,' Sigurd said, drinking again. 'By killing his messenger—' He frowned, searching for the man's name. Freystein. 'Freystein Quick-Sword.' *Not quick enough*, he thought. Gods but this ale was strong. 'Sending my father's jarl torc back to the oath-breaker around Freystein Quick-Sword's neck was all I could do to hurt Gorm. But we could not have stayed.'

Valgerd lifted one eyebrow, her hawk's eyes fastened on his.

'You think I should have accepted the oath-breaker's offer of land? I should have taken my father's torc as though it were the king's to give?'

'No,' Valgerd said. She shrugged. 'But perhaps there was another way. Perhaps we could have gained his trust and bided our time. Then, two, three summers from now, we put a blade in him when he least expects it.'

'Too late for that now,' Sigurd said, not even wanting to think that there might have been a cleverer way of doing things.

'Yes, too late now,' Valgerd agreed, picking up the flask and refilling their cups.

Neither said anything for a little while then. They sat in the near darkness, drinking and thinking, the sounds of men and women rutting louder now and then than the usual hum of the place.

Valgerd closed her eyes and sank down against the side of one of the sea chests and Sigurd took the opportunity to look at her without her knowing it. Her tunic was damp and without her mail on he could clearly see the swell of her breasts and the shape of her thighs and he could imagine what lay between them. She was not a fierce shieldmaiden now. She was just a woman. A beautiful, proud woman who had the courage to hate the gods and yet lacked the courage to ignore them.

He looked at her and wanted her. It really was like the battle thrill. There was a tremble in his legs and a fluttering in his chest like a bird up amongst the roof beams. His saliva was thick with ale and need, but it was need of her, not the wild joy of killing. He needed her and here she was. And would she have climbed up here with him if she had not known what was in his mind? No, she had led him up here. And what had he done? Talked! Because talking was like bailing, and if he stopped . . .

'Do you think I am a fool,' he asked, 'to believe I can avenge my father and balance the scales with the oath-breaker?'

Those piercing eyes opened, fixing on him again. 'You need silver and you need an army,' she said. 'But most of all, you need to believe that you can do it.' She leant over and picked up the flask. Sigurd had not realized her cup was empty again. He drained his own. 'Do you believe?' she asked.

He thought about it.

'Mostly,' he said.

She shook her head. 'Mostly is not enough,' she said. 'Any doubts you have are like loose caulking between the strakes. Water will get in and we shall all sink.'

He understood that, for those who had sworn an oath to follow him had done so because they saw something in him, a fire which burnt bright as a lightning flash. Perhaps he was Óðin-favoured as men said. As he told people himself. Or perhaps he was blinded by his own hatred for the man who had taken everything from him. Perhaps his crew mistook arrogance and audacity for something else. Something greater. Maybe they saw a destiny in him which was no more god-touched than any man's.

He took the flask himself now and emptied it into their cups.

'We kill his enemies and earn his silver,' Valgerd said. 'Then, when we are rich and *Reinen*'s ballast is all treasure instead of rocks, we put together our own war host and we sail north again to make war on the oath-breaker. We *will* kill him.' She smiled. 'And balance the scales.'

Sigurd nodded, grinning at her. 'So I am not a fool?' he said.

She drank until the cup was empty. 'Yes, you are. But not for that,' she said.

He finished his own cup, willing himself to do something but finding he was unable to move. He might as well have been a nail stuck in the floor boards.

Valgerd had been facing him but now she moved in the half-darkness, coming to sit beside him so that he felt the warmth of her body. He smelt the wet wool of her tunic and breeks mixed with the sweet scent of her sweat, a concoction unique to her amongst the crew and one which had his loins stirring now. And still he sat frozen, as petrified as a new beard on the eve of his first ship fight.

'So do you want to go back to the camp?' she asked him.

'No,' he said, swallowing.

'Do you want me?' she asked.

'Yes,' he said. There was no going back now.

She moved and he was suddenly more terrified than ever because he thought she was getting up to leave, but then she knelt and threw one leg over both of his so that she straddled him. Then her hands were in his hair, her fingers on the flesh of his neck and her thumbs in the short bristles of his beard. She pulled his face towards hers and their mouths came together and as he breathed her in he saw her eyes close.

They were stripped of it all now, the two of them. Unburdened of past and future, of duty and vengeance and all that it was to be the shieldmaiden and the would-be-jarl. No more bailing. *Let me sink now and worry after,* he thought, tasting her tongue and the ale on her breath, his body thrumming like a bow string.

Following Haraldarson and the shieldmaiden in the dusk and rain without them noticing him had been as easy as breathing. On such foul nights as this, folk did not tend to notice anything much, other than where to tread so as not to end up on their arses in the mud.

There had been no question in Fionn's mind that he should follow them, even if it meant leaving the fire around which he and a group of Birka men had been sitting getting soaked to the skin. For it was the first time that Haraldarson had strayed more than twenty paces from the others since they had all sailed across Løgrinn, Sigurd in *Reinen* and Fionn in *Crow*, Knut's own ship. They were close as arrows in a sheath, that crew. Tight as a fish's arse, and Fionn had sat under oiled skins with seven strangers for company, had even managed to regale them with tales from Alba as the rain scourged sea and shore, though all the while he had an eye on the young golden-haired, gods-favoured man not a stone's throw away.

And when Haraldarson had announced to his companions that he was heading off into the gloaming to fetch them more ale, Fionn had expected the giant with the red beard to go with him, or perhaps the broad, even more dangerous-looking one whom they called Bear. It had been a surprise when the shieldmaiden stood to go with him, but then, even through the rain-flayed gloom, Fionn had seen the flash of fire in Haraldarson's eyes and he understood completely. Haraldarson loved the woman. Or at the least he wanted her. And who could blame him, for she was something to behold in her brynja of polished rings, with her scramasax, sword and spear. She was beautiful, which was doubtless why she was rarely without her mail and never without her blades. He would be a fool who tried to force himself on her. He would also be a fool who thought that Haraldarson was as good as dead because a woman was all that stood between him and a knife in the heart.

But Fionn was no fool. So he had followed them across the camp to the red tent in which Trygir sold his ale. He had stood in the deluge outside Trygir's place, an ear close to the stinking sailcloth, sifting the words spoken within from the rain seething without. He had moved a little distance off and lingered in the shadows by the grain store, watching as Haraldarson and the shieldmaiden talked their way into the log house, and when the door closed behind them he had waited a while longer, about the time it takes to put an edge on a blunt sax. Or the time it takes to get soaked to the bone marrow.

Then Fionn had walked through the mud, following in his prey's tracks and pulling from his finger a silver ring which had once been worn by a Pictish king. He used the ring to buy his way into the log house, telling the fat man who had opened the door that it bought him entry as well as the man's silence, at which the man had grinned the way only a drunk man can, more than happy with the trade.

Now, he moved in the dark and the smoke, his blood pulsing in his ears and his chest tight with the thrill of what he was about to do. Of all the lives he had snuffed out, this one promised to stand out above the rest. And not because Haraldarson was rich or powerful, because he wasn't. Nor because Fionn stood to be paid a hoard's worth of silver for it – he had been paid more for others. There was just something about this one, about killing a man whom these Northmen believed to be gods-favoured.

He drew his scían, his hand relishing the feel of the stag-antler handle. It fitted his palm the way some men fitted some women. As if the two were always destined for each other.

Where were the gods when the knife went in? Where were they when the blade drank?

She was riding him, the hungry bitch, her arse grinding on his lap like a pestle in a mortar, her golden, sweat-drenched hair loose over her back and shoulders. Fionn drew a long, even breath, clenched his stomach muscles, breathed out and struck. Fast. Clamping his right hand over her mouth and pulling her head back, thrusting the long knife into her throat and forcing the blade out so there could be no scream. He shoved her aside and dropped his knees on to the naked groin and withering prick and his eyes locked with those of the man beneath him.

Fionn growled under his breath and plunged the scían down, again and again into the flesh, his left hand muffling his victim's cries which, if they were heard at all, would be taken as the normal sounds of a good swiving. Five, six, seven times Fionn thrust the blade deep and pulled it free and already the blood was pooling in the creases and folds of the furs beneath them both.

Then he ran the blade through a fistful of blanket and sheathed it, listening to the snoring and swiving and hushed, mumbled voices to ensure that no one was coming for him. He had to get out quickly, because the woman's bowels had disgorged their contents in death and the reek was filling the place, stinging his eyes with its sharpness. Others would smell it too, and if not that then the iron tang of fresh blood, and so Fionn had to go now before it was too late.

He looked once more at the mess he had made, then he slipped away, making for the same door through which he had entered, trying not to rush or draw attention to himself, drifting off unnoticed, like smoke through the roof hole.

Outside, he hauled the sweet, wet air into his lungs and plunged on through the mud, his mind reeling and his heartbeat thundering in his ears now. He had made a butcher's table in the dark. He had slaughtered the woman like a beast and he had let his long knife drink deep of her lover.

Now he cursed in the night, growled the foulest of insults at the rain and the cloud-veiled sky. Because the throat-cut woman was not the shieldmaiden Valgerd. And the dead man lying in a lake of his own blood was not Sigurd Haraldarson.

CHAPTER THIRTEEN

'THIS IS THE FURTHEST WE HAVE WALKED FOR AS LONG AS I can remember, and it does not help that I have to step over piles of horse shit reminding me that Knut and his friends are riding while we sprout blisters like toadstools,' Svein complained.

'Aye,' Solmund agreed, 'if you ask me, by the time we get wherever we are going we will have already earned the silver which Knut gave that arse-crack Asvith, and that is before we even get our swords wet.'

They had been walking for two days and it had been hard going because the pine forest was thick and in places still boggy from the meltwater running down from the hills. It would have been easier had they not been in all their war gear, the weight of their brynjur and helmets dragging them down with each plodding step, their shields and food-stuffed nestbaggins slung over their backs and each

320

of them carrying two spears or a spear and a long-hafted axe.

'Much more of this and we'll be too tired to do anything else after,' Bjarni said. '"Well then," this Alrik's enemies will say, "are we not going to fight after all? When you have come all this way?" "No," we'll say, "for we've just walked our arses off and now we are here we don't have it in us to fight you."'

Moldof muttered something foul, but whether it was aimed at Bjarni for his complaining, or whether the big man was expressing his own resentment at having to walk was impossible to say.

'I don't see why we couldn't have horses,' Thorbiorn said. 'It is not right that we should be walking with the rest of these nobodies.'

'Says the famous Thorbiorn at whose name men shake in their shoes,' Bram said.

'My father is a king,' Thorbiorn said, 'which is more than I can say for any of you.'

'A king he may be, but even a good fruit-rich tree can sprout a sour apple now and then,' Solmund said.

'Still, the lad is right about the horses,' Hagal Crow-Song said. 'Sigurd is Óðin-kissed, and we all have a reputation.' There were forty-four men in this war band which Knut was leading north through the forest, and many of them were striplings and untested men whom he had rounded up in Birka. Yet most of them seemed cheerful enough, even now brimming with a combination of the thrill and fear which squirms in a man's belly when he knows he will soon be fighting. 'Furthermore, it is going to rain. I can feel it in the air.'

'Knut said we will be there before midday tomorrow,' Olaf said, 'so in the meantime if you could stop whining like little girls I would be happier.' There were a few low grumbles but they soon died away and Olaf sighed with relief. 'That's better,' he said, lifting his helmet so that he could scratch his sweat-matted hair. 'Besides which, it is not going to rain, Crow-Song.'

No sooner had he said it than a low peal of thunder rolled across a sky which, seen through the gaps in the spruce and birch canopy, was the colour of old hearth ash. A dozen heartbeats later the rain lashed down, as though a god had tipped over his fresh-water barrel. It found its way through the trees and bounced off helmets and the shields on their backs, and it filled the world with seething noise which drowned out Olaf's cursing.

The men grumbled, the rain rushed down, and Sigurd immersed himself in the memory of that night with Valgerd, when they had given themselves to each other. But they had both taken, too, and afterwards Valgerd had shrugged her brynja back on, buckled her sword belt and braided her hair, barely looking at him in the dark of the log house loft. Like the water's surface closing over a dropped anchor stone, it was in some ways as if nothing at all had happened.

'We should get back to the others before they smash some other crew's heads and steal their ale,' Valgerd had said.

Sigurd had nodded, dazed, caught up in the seiðr which her scent on his skin wove around him.

She had not cried out in joy at the end, like some women did. But she had arched her back, driving her hips forward to bring him deeper inside her and she had trembled and bitten her bottom lip hard enough to draw blood. When they were finished, Sigurd had rolled on to his back feeling utterly spent, more tired than after most shieldwall fights he had been in.

'Are you coming? It will be dawn soon,' she had said, and he had opened his eyes to see that she was already clothed again. She had her boots on and he was in his breeks and tunic when the shouting and screaming began and they peered over the ledge of the loft to see that men had drawn blades. A knot of them, armed with steel and oil lamps, had gathered where one of the hanging partitions had been pulled back.

'Someone's been murdered,' Valgerd said, slinging a pair of ale skins over her shoulder and climbing on to the ladder.

Sigurd caught the stench of it then, had been amongst the crows after enough fights to know that smell, of blood and shit. Of death. They climbed down and pushed their way through the throng to see Brodd-Helgi standing over the bodies of a man and a woman, both slaughtered whilst they were at it, by the looks, her throat cut out and him stabbed half a dozen times in the stomach, under the breastbone and into the heart. If the knife had been long enough.

'What a fucking mess,' a man beside Sigurd growled.

'Did no one see anything?' Brodd-Helgi was asking them all, his eyes wide with the shock of what had happened. The dead woman's hair was long and golden and braided like Valgerd's.

'I'll wager Stækar's wife found out what he was up to,' one of Brodd-Helgi's henchmen said, at which Sigurd and Valgerd looked at each other, both recognizing the man who had been hauled out of the loft so that they might have it. 'She came in and caught them at it,' the man went on. 'That's what I reckon.'

'And did this?' Brodd-Helgi asked him, gesturing at the gore-slathered lovers. 'You think Hildigunn came in here and carved Stækar up like this? Don't be an idiot.'

'Aye, because if she did, then she's better with a blade than Stækar ever was,' another man put in, and this got a chuckle even in a blood- and shit-stinking moment like that.

The henchman shrugged. 'Who else would want him dead?' he asked, not ready to abandon his suspicions yet. There was a rumbling from the gathering at that. Still, no one came out with a name. Brodd-Helgi growled at a couple of big men to help him wrap the bodies in skins and carry them outside.

'Let's go,' Valgerd said to Sigurd, so they had, walking back through the rain, which was lighter now, neither of them talking about the murder or what had happened before it. When they came back to the camp most of the others were snoring in their tents. Most but not all.

'Where did you go for that? Asgard?' Olaf asked, opening one eye and catching Sigurd by surprise as he put the ale skins down inside the canvas shelter and took off his wet cloak for the second time that night. Olaf was wrapped in furs and leaning against his sea chest. Clearly he had been waiting up for Sigurd, who felt like a beardless, wayward boy then, rather than the leader of a war band, albeit one as small as this.

'There was a murder,' he said, making sure not to look at Valgerd as he spoke. But she was already heading off to her own tent. 'A man called Stækar and the woman he was tupping. Someone killed them in the log house.'

'The woman's husband, I'll wager,' Olaf said, arching an eyebrow as he pulled the furs up to his neck and shifted his great frame to get more comfortable. Sigurd thought he had gone back to sleep when he said, 'What were you two doing in the log house?'

Sigurd glanced at the massive pile of furs that was Svein, then across at Floki who lay along the other side of the tent, his two hand axes beside his head. They were both sleeping and yet Sigurd could not have felt more guilty if he'd been the one who had murdered Stækar and his pretty friend. 'We were drinking Alrik's ale,' he said, avoiding Olaf's eyes, wrapping the leather belt around Troll-Tickler which was sleeping in its scabbard. It was no lie, was it?

'Must be good stuff. Been gone half the night,' Olaf mumbled, closing his eyes again.

Better than you can imagine, Sigurd thought, though he said nothing as he sat on his own sea chest to pull off his mud-sheathed boots and get into his furs. Some sleep before the next day's journey would be no bad thing.

But he had lain there looking up at the canvas, listening to the rain drumming against it until dawn.

Now he was walking through the sopping woods on his way to meet Alrik. In body at least. In mind he was back in that loft. He would cloak himself in the memory of it, wrap it around him for as long as he could, for he had a feeling that it would never happen again.

And the next day they came soaked, cold and squelching in their shoes to the hill fort at Fornsigtuna.

Not that it was on much of a hill, as Bram observed when they came out of the forest on to the rolling, rock-strewn ground south of the palisade. All the way round the borg the trees had been felled to prevent enemies coming upon it unseen and to provide livestock with grazing. Now, the meadow before Knut's war band was a camp, with tents and men sitting round fires or perching on tree stumps. Horses cropped the new spring grass and sheep crowded in a pen, telling Sigurd that Alrik's enemies had not been expecting him for they had not taken the animals inside the borg.

'At least we'll be eating well,' Olaf said, and as soon as the words were out Sigurd caught the smell of mutton stew on the breeze.

'We'll have eaten those sheep and the horses too before we get in there,' Moldof said, taking in the borg. And there was probably some truth in that for the place looked formidable, even on that nothing hill.

'Aye, I begin to see why this Alrik sent Knut off looking for more men,' Solmund said. 'It would be easier for an old sod like me to get inside a pretty young wench than it will be to get inside that.' While there were undoubtedly bigger hills thereabouts, the palisade topped a steep earthen bank made higher and steeper still by the deep ditch before it.

Knut had explained how Alrik had a long-running feud with a jarl called Guthrum. It had started with the theft of a few sheep – Knut had not said who stole from whom – and grew from there, the way a snowball grows when you roll it in snow. Blood for blood. Murder for murder, as is the way with these things. Jarl Guthrum had risen high and fast, some saying he meant to raise enough spears to challenge King Erik Refilsson. He had taken this fort from another warlord and stuffed it with silver. 'He is raising an army,' Knut had said, 'but we mean to scupper his ambition and get back what he has taken from us over the years.'

Still, it did not look like it was going well for Alrik so far.

'You can see what has become of the men who have been knocking on that gate,' Asgot said, pointing his staff towards three mounds of newly turned earth over by the trees on the east side of the borg. Sigurd wondered how many men already lay in the ground for Alrik's ambition to take this place.

'If it was me I'd burn it,' Sigurd said. 'I would pile a great heap of dry wood against that gate and set fire to it at night. Then, while Jarl Guthrum's people were busy throwing pails of water and pissing out the flames, I'd get most of my men arrayed in a skjaldborg facing the gate, lit up by the fire for all to see.' He shrugged. 'While all this was happening, some of us would hop over the wall on the other side and start killing.'

'Good enough,' Olaf said with a nod.

'We cannot burn it,' Knut said, coming over to where Sigurd and the others stood. He nodded towards the borg. 'Alrik has forbidden it.'

'He might be one ear short of a pair but there's nothing wrong with the man's hearing,' Bram muttered to Svein.

'Why can't we burn it?' Sigurd asked.

'Because we might need that palisade,' Knut said. 'Only half of Guthrum's force is in there. The rest are with the jarl somewhere to the west, shaking taxes out of rich karls and raising spears.' He hawked and spat a wad of phlegm which was whipped away by the gathering breeze. 'The whoreson has promised his own arse King Erik's high seat.'

That made sense of why, back in Birka, Asvith had told Knut that King Erik wanted Jarl Guthrum dead by the Jól feast, Sigurd thought. This feud between Guthrum and Alrik was being fuelled by the king's silver, then.

'Gods but these things become tangled like yarn in a bairn's hands,' Olaf said.

'If the fire catches and too much of the palisade burns, we might not have the time to rebuild the defences before Guthrum himself shows up,' Knut said. 'Even if we cut the timber and fashioned the stakes to have them ready, they would not be properly bedded into the earth.'

'So we just sit here and wait for Guthrum's people to starve?' Olaf asked.

'That will be the easiest silver I have ever made,' Bjarni put in, grinning at his brother Bjorn.

'Is that Alrik's plan?' Sigurd asked. 'Because if Jarl Guthrum returns while we are sitting out here we will be caught between him and the borg, which does not strike me as a good thing.'

Olaf agreed with that. 'A shieldwall with enemies in front and behind does not tend to last very long,' he said.

'There is not much of Loki in this plan of Alrik's,' Sigurd said, turning back to Knut, 'and yet from the looks of those graves over there, perhaps starving them out will work better than whatever you have tried so far.'

Knut's lip curled and he seemed about to answer that accusation when his attention was drawn to a group of four warriors who were walking towards them, wet cloaks hitched over fine-looking swords, mail gleaming dully and sopping hair pulled back from weather-worn, battle-scarred faces. 'Here is your chance to come up with a better scheme, Byrnjolf,' he said, raising a hand in greeting to the newcomers. 'My lord Alrik, this is Byrnjolf Hálfdanarson and his crew, who have come to win this battle for us.' There was more than a touch of mockery in that, but only Bram bothered rising to the bait and growling something unpleasant in Knut's direction.

There was no contempt in Alrik's eyes though and neither would Sigurd expect there to be, what with them standing there in that camp looking like lords of war, albeit wet ones, in mail and helmets and the sort of gear you only normally saw on kings and the richest and highest of their hirðmen.

Few of Alrik's warriors were even half as well equipped by the looks.

'Welcome, Byrnjolf,' the warlord said, holding out his arm which Sigurd gripped, taking in the man before him. Alrik was a little shorter than himself but powerfully built. His hair was cropped close against his scalp on the sides but long enough on the top to be pulled back over his head and twisted into a rope, which hung down between his shoulder blades and was bound in leather thongs. 'I see Knut has brought me a crew who are no strangers to the blood-fray.' He glanced at Knut and nodded in appreciation. 'You've done well, Knut.'

'They can fight,' the one-eared warrior said. 'Even after drinking ale from sunrise to sunset they can fight. I'll vouch for that.'

'I do not doubt it,' Alrik said, looking from Sigurd to Olaf, his eyes widening as they moved on to Svein. It was not unusual for men, even battle-hardened warriors, to be impressed by Svein's size.

'Knut offered us silver to fight and so here we are,' Sigurd said, 'and just as well for that Asvith Horsefly and his men too,' he added, 'for I had just been thinking that Asvith's brynja would suit me well.'

'It's wasted on him, the soft sodding prick,' Alrik said. Clearly he was no friend of Asvith.

'I'll admit it was a fine brynja,' Olaf said. 'No matter. Knut assures us there is plenty of plunder to be had here fighting for you.'

331

'And he is right,' Alrik said. 'You and your men . . . and your woman will earn your fair share of the spoils.' He glanced at Valgerd who was sitting on a tree stump, her brynja laid across her knees as she polished the rings with a greasy cloth. 'Enough to make yourselves rich,' he said with a smile. 'Perhaps you will swear to me once we have killed Jarl Guthrum.'

'Perhaps,' Sigurd said. There was no harm in letting Alrik think Sigurd and his crew were there to be bought with the spoils of war.

Alrik held Sigurd's eyes, twisting one side of his moustaches, which were so long that they drooped past his chin. He seemed possessed of a war-leader's self-assurance, but Sigurd was the son of a jarl and he knew when a man's nerve was being tested, when his resolve had been damaged like a brynja which has shed rings. It was in the man's eyes, the strain of this long-running, root-deep feud of his with Jarl Guthrum.

'Why would anyone build a borg so far from the sea?' Sigurd asked. He had grown up with the scent of the sea and of his father's ships in his nose, the smell of pine resin and tarred ropes and damp sailcloth. He had lived with the sound of gulls and the suck and plunge of the clear water against the rocks and he could not imagine why men would choose to live far from all this. It was bad enough that they had come so far from *Reinen*.

'This borg is where Jarl Guthrum trains his warriors,' Alrik said. 'He has been building an army where he thinks no one can see him. He gathers spears from all over Svealand, demanding men's oaths and promising them silver and fame. The treacherous dog thinks he should be a king and have men from here to Uppland kiss his sword's hilt.'

'That may be so, but I like the sound of this silver of his,' Olaf said.

Alrik nodded at him. 'He has something else which is of great value to me. Something I crave even more than silver. And it's all in there,' he said, pointing at the borg.

'Gold?' Sigurd asked.

'Iron,' Olaf said.

Alrik's teeth flashed beneath those moustaches. 'There's enough iron behind those walls to make the rings for a Jötunheim-dweller's brynja. Or rivets for twenty ships. From good rauði too. Red earth which Guthrum's smiths have smelted and beaten into bars. Those bars sit in there waiting for me.' He grinned. 'At night they whisper to me, Byrnjolf. They beg me to have them forged into blades and helmets. Into swords that will cut down my enemies and write my reputation in their blood.' He threw out his arms to encompass his camp with its warriors and tents. 'That is why we are here. I will have Guthrum's iron.'

'First we have to get into the place,' Olaf said, 'and our beards will be white before that happens if you will not burn it. Or else we will be caught between the borg and Guthrum like the iron between the hammer and the anvil.'

'The man who commands in Guthrum's absence is called Findar,' Alrik said. 'He does not seem particularly clever, but I do not think he is a fool either.'

'He's still in there and you're still out here,' Olaf pointed out. It was not the most tactful thing he could have said and it got a frown out of Alrik.

'You will always find him in the heart of the fray,' Knut put in. 'No one can say the man lacks courage, though if you ask me, Findar will get himself killed sooner or later because he does not know when to pull his head in. Stands there to make a show of it as our arrows slice the air by his head.'

'So this Findar thinks he is something special,' Olaf said. 'That is good to know.'

'In the last attack on the wall I lost sixteen men,' Alrik said, as if pointing out to Olaf that he need not think it would be an easy thing to take the place, just because he and his friends had arrived in all their war glory. 'Twelve dead and the rest wounded,' the warlord went on. 'We used hooks and ropes at night. We got right into the ditch without any of them seeing us.' Alrik touched the Thór's hammer at his neck as if to ward off ill luck. 'But their dogs heard us. Or smelt us. Damned barking alerted the sentries and we threw the hooks and climbed and some made it over, but not enough. Those brave men were cut down. Corpses hurled back over the wall.' It was a sore memory by the looks and Alrik shook his head to rid himself of it. 'Anyway, you have come a long way and will be ready for something decent to eat and drink.'

'You are right about that,' Svein said, and so Knut led them off to find their patch of ground and some food to fill their bellies.

Sigurd had not expected the attack that night and neither had Alrik. Afterwards, Olaf would say to Sigurd that it was good war craft by Findar, who led the borg men himself, to sally from the fort. Before Alrik's new men had properly flattened the grass out there beyond the walls. While they were still tired after the trek from the lake camp and likely to be sleeping like the dead that first night in the new place. And they nearly were dead that night, no thanks to Alrik's sentries who gave no warning and two of whom had their throats cut and died without knowing it. A third had yelped before the blade had finished killing him, but afterwards two men would tell Alrik they had thought it the squeal of a fox, a vixen luring a male to mate with. Those two men were digging a new latrine trench for days after.

They came before the dawn, a raiding party of wraiths with spears. The night was not pitch black, winter showing its back now, but it did not need to be full dark, for once they had killed the two sentries nearest the borg, they were faced, if you can call it that, by men sleeping in their tents. It was an old warrior called Høther who raised the alarm eventually and it was his old bladder and his need to piss five times a night which saved a good number of lives.

'Shields!' old Høther yelled, admitting after that he had pissed down his own leg to see the borg men not in the borg. 'Shields, Alrik's men! We are attacked!'

Floki's hand gripping his shoulder roused Sigurd from a deep sleep and he got to his feet still foggy, watching through blurred eyes Floki trying to wake Olaf, which took him three or four good shakes, Olaf not being such a young man any more.

'The borg has come to us,' Bram said, poking his head into their tent and grinning even though he must have been half asleep himself.

Men were fighting now, dying too. The clamour of it had all of a sudden poured into the pre-dawn stillness, and Sigurd's first thought was of Valgerd. His second was that he would feel such a fool if they were killed now before ever throwing a spear or loosing an arrow at Guthrum's hill fort.

Still, they took the extra time to throw on their brynjur and tie their helmet straps and arm properly.

'No point rushing out there bare-arsed and still snoring,' Olaf said, making sure his helmet was a snug fit. 'Looking the part is half of it.' Then an arrow tore through the sailcloth and got fouled in the opposite wall, where it hung like an unanswered insult.

'Now I'm ready to kill the buggers,' Olaf said, hefting his shield, and with that they went out to face whatever had come.

Sigurd had barely drawn his first breath of night air when a throwing axe struck his shield like Thór's fist. It split the wood against the grain and jarred his arm in his shoulder joint, but from that moment he was wide awake.

'There,' Valgerd said, pointing her spear at the man who had thrown the axe, little more than a shape in the dim light. An arrow thumped into Olaf's shield and another glanced off the cheek of Svein's long-hafted axe, which he did not like much.

'On me,' Sigurd called, as the others closed round him. It was no shieldwall fight, this, with men fighting in loose order all around, but he did not want his crew off chasing kills in the dark. Besides which, it was no bad thing to show Alrik that they not only looked the part, but knew their business too. 'Forward,' Sigurd said, catching another arrow on his shield. 'Thorbiorn, you stay in the pack,' he growled. No one wanted King Thorir's boy getting sliced and tripping over his own guts in the dark. 'Move!' Sigurd shouted.

'You heard him,' Olaf bellowed, 'let's put these bold buggers back in their box.'

'Better still, kill them now and it'll save us a job later,' Bram said, which was true enough and with their shields up they strode into the fray, getting amongst the snarl of it all now that Alrik's men were fighting back. Those who were not dead in their tents, that was.

Svein ran ahead and started swinging that long axe, roaring his challenge in the night, not that anyone seemed interested in fighting him.

'Hard to know who's who,' Solmund said, his old eyes little more than slits as he peered at those fighting around them.

'If they're facing downhill, stick them. If they're facing uphill, don't,' was Moldof's answer, which was not altogether stupid, and as if to make his point he buried his spear blade, one-handed, in the belly of a man who had just thrown his own spear and was pulling the axe from his belt.

Bjarni and Bjorn speared a big warrior who died foaming at the mouth like a mad dog, and Valgerd stepped out of the loose formation to go up behind a man whom Knut was fighting and cut his hamstrings with her scramasax. The man fell in a heap and Knut hacked him to death, then glared at Valgerd before turning to find another enemy.

'Larboard, Sigurd,' Olaf said, and Sigurd looked to his left to see a wild-looking man coming for him, drawn by his war gear no doubt and leading a knot of borg men.

'Mine,' Bram said, discarding his shield and stepping in front of Sigurd to meet the attack. Coming fast, the borg man thrust his spear at Bram, who knocked it aside with his own spear and in the same movement drove it on into the man's belly, using the man's own momentum to lift him into the air. This got some roars of approval, for the strength it took as much as the spectacle of it, as Bram smashed the impaled man down into the ground so that bones must have broken in him like seashells under foot.

Sigurd stepped up and smashed his shield against another man's, stopping him in his tracks. The borg man growled and swung an axe over his shield and the blade struck Sigurd's shoulder, scattering brynja rings, but at the same time Sigurd thrust his spear down into his enemy's foot, pinning him to the spot. Olaf took off his head mid-scream.

'Alrik! Lord Alrik!' someone was yelling. But it was dark and men were still fighting all around them and it was hard putting voices to bodies.

'Where *is* Alrik?' Sigurd called back to Knut, who was leaning over a wounded man to cut his throat. The dead man flopped forward and Knut stood up, sword in hand, and shook his head as if to say he did not know.

'There!' another of Alrik's men yelled, pointing up the hill.

'Aye, it's him,' Crow-Song said.

A knot of five borg men had hold of Alrik and were dragging him up the hill towards the fort, though the warlord was not making it easy for them, kicking and flailing, frenzying against his captors.

'Whoresons want him alive,' Olaf said. 'They'll trade him to get us to piss off.'

'Or kill him on the wall for his men to see,' Sigurd said, for that was a more certain way of ending the siege, as without Alrik his army would disintegrate and scatter like chaff on the wind.

'Knut's got a fight on,' Solmund said, for though the sally had faltered, the borg men had regrouped and overlapped their shields in order to retreat back up the slope to safety. They had built a skjaldborg on the edge of the camp and Knut was trying to rein in his men to fight them, but many were busy looting the dead.

'Arse wipes would rather pick corpses for silver than fight,' Moldof said.

'Who wouldn't?' Thorbiorn asked and didn't get an answer.

Bram pointed up at Alrik, who'd had the fight knocked out of him now by the looks. 'Well, we need to get him back if we want paying,' he said, which was the truth of it.

'Floki, Bram, Svein, with me. Rest of you help Knut,' Sigurd said, and before Olaf could argue with that he was running up the hill. They loped like wolves, passing one of the sentries who had failed to warn the camp and now lay pale and bloodless in the grass.

'Findar!' Sigurd called, and hurled his spear as the borg man straightened at the challenge. Findar got his shield up in time but the spear's point punched through the limewood.

'Get him inside now!' Findar roared at his men, hurling his useless, spear-burdened shield aside and turning to face Sigurd who drew Troll-Tickler without missing a step. There was a blur in the darkness and Sigurd saw one of the men dragging Alrik fall to his knees with Floki's axe between his shoulder blades. Then, when he was ten feet from Findar, Sigurd stopped on his leading foot and hurled his shield. It flew hard and fast and struck Findar edge on in his left upper arm as he tried to haul his sword from its scabbard. The blow turned him but he got his sword up in time to block Sigurd's first cut, then attempted to throw a punch but perhaps his arm was broken because it flailed uselessly and Sigurd drove forward and butted his helmet into Findar's face. He staggered back but kept his feet, raising his sword as blood flooded from his nose into his beard.

'It took courage to leave the borg, Findar,' Sigurd said, 'but it was a mistake.' He pointed his sword up the hill to where Floki, Svein and Bram were slaughtering Findar's men, and when Findar had seen it he turned back to Sigurd and shrugged.

'A man gets bored hiding behind walls,' he said, then spat a wad of blood and phlegm into the grass.

Sigurd nodded. 'If you see my brother Sigmund Haraldarson in the Allfather's hall, tell him the shield throw worked. He laughed when I tried it on him once.'

'Tell him yourself,' Findar said. He came at Sigurd and his first cut took a bite out of Troll-Tickler and his second ripped Sigurd's brynja as he twisted aside, but his third was too wild and he put himself off balance. Troll-Tickler wanted its own revenge then and the blade snaked out, its point opening Findar's cheek before Sigurd pulled it back out of the way of the borg man's scything sword. Then Sigurd sank Troll-Tickler deep in the flesh of Findar's leg between the thigh and the knee joint. Findar went down and Sigurd considered sparing his life for three marks of silver.

'Finish it then,' Findar said, bleeding in the dark. Bleeding enough to know that he was a dead man one way or another.

Sigurd nodded. 'Sigmund Haraldarson, remember,' he said, then stepped up and hacked into Findar's neck.

'Gods you like to make a fight last, Sigurd!' Svein said, coming back down towards him. Floki and Bram were supporting Alrik between them, the warlord bleeding but shaking them off because he was too proud to be carried. Arrows were hissing down from the fort's ramparts now, thudding into the ground around them, so they moved back down the hill to avoid being killed by some lucky borg man.

'Protect Alrik,' Sigurd said, because the last of the borg men who had attacked the camp were now fleeing from Knut, who had put together his own skjaldborg and was marching up the hill.

Sigurd, Bram, Svein and Floki closed in around Alrik, nice and tight, blades raised just in case, but the borg men were no longer interested in them or Alrik. They ran past in the dark, yelling at their companions to let them back into the borg. And Sigurd let them go.

Life on Fugløy had settled into a pattern as predictable as the yellow and black of a plaid sailcloth or the squares of a tafl board. Runa woke each morning before dawn and took two pails to the byre and did not come out again until they were full to the brim with warm milk. Then she went to the ewes which foraged freely and took a pail of their milk too and all of this she brought to the hall to help Signy and Vebiorg make cheese, butter and skyr. There was still hay to be harvested and so she scythed it and raked it and stacked it against the byre wall for drying so that it would feed the animals come next winter. She teased wool which had been shorn or plucked the previous spring, and combed it diligently as she had learnt to under her mother's watchful eye, so that the tog fibres lay parallel to each other, crucial if you were to spin a strong warp thread. She worked the spindle and the distaff, she gathered fuel for the fires and she carried slops to the pigs. She practised with the bow, for the Freyja Maidens prided themselves on their skill with that weapon and could put an arrow through an arm ring at thirty paces seven times out of ten. Runa could not even do it one time out of ten in those first weeks, and yet she drew and loosed, drew and loosed, until her arms trembled and her fingers bled.

But mostly she fought. Sword, spear and shield work consumed her and all the other tasks were dreary by comparison, a means to an end which she rushed where she could in order to hold the shaft and the hilt again.

She was good, too. She knew it. Not as good as the others, but then most of them had practised the art of war for years. And yet what she lacked in experience she almost made up for with talent. Whenever she struck Signy's shoulder or snuck a blunted spear past Skuld's shield, neither of which happened often, she imagined that her father and brothers had seen it and were cheering for her. She imagined her mother looking on with disapproving eyes but being secretly proud.

'You are gifted, Runa,' Skuld had said one day, a compliment which Runa did not take very graciously because she was on her backside in the dirt trying to catch the blood which was pouring from her nose. She had been too slow in getting her shield in the way of Vebiorg's and had wrongly thought Skuld was mocking her.

My family were warriors, she thought afterwards, when she had done well enough to claw back a little pride at least. *My father was jarl. My brother is Óðin-kissed. Why shouldn't I be able to fight? Do we not share the same blood? The same will?*

It was a simple life stripped of the clutter of her past existence. Not on Fugløy the ale-fuelled fights of drunken men, the strutting and boasting of warriors chafing for a fight to prove themselves. Not on the island of the Freyja Maidens the poison that spreads when a woman swives another woman's man, or the serpent-toothed gossip or the bitter jealousy. Nor even the ever-present possibility of being raided, which hangs above most villages like a cloud which remains even if the sun is shining.

Though for all that it was not a life without pain. The practice swords were wooden or blunted so that they would not cut the flesh, but they left bruises which bloomed green, yellow and black, and now and then one of the warrior women would break a finger or an arm, or chip off a piece of bone which could be felt floating under the skin. Many of them had had their noses broken by their opponent's shield. Two had lost eyes, perhaps from spear work. All of them were hardened and honed, seasoned and sinewy and skilled, though still Runa could not help but wonder how they would fare at the Twilight of the Gods, for they were masters in practice but had never killed big, fierce, battle-tested men who were trying to kill them.

It was a half life in a way, spent in preparation for death, when each Maiden would be carried to Sessrymnir to fight for the Goddess. And yet Runa was almost happy. It was hard to think about your murdered mother and your slain father and brothers when you were taking hammer blows on your shield or trying to avoid some screeching woman's sword. It was hard to think of Sigurd and fret for him when you were slowing your heartbeat and drawing the bow, whispering to the arrow to fly true. When those fears came they came at night. Not every night. Sometimes she was too tired for them and would be asleep before they got their claws into her. Another reason to fight until she could hardly lift the shield to meet a high spear thrust. To shoot until she could no longer draw the bow string to her cheek.

Yes, a half life, hidden from the world and from its men. Though not all of its men. And therein lay the violent meeting of currents in an otherwise sleeping sea. She had noticed Ingel looking at her from his forge when she was practising with sword or spear. At first she had thought it was perhaps mere curiosity because she was a new face on Fugløy. That was what Runa told herself, even though she knew the truth of it really. A woman knows when a man wants her. It is all over him and it is in his eyes and it is not as if men even know how to hide it or even want to try.

It might not have been a problem had a woman called Sibbe not decided to be jealous about it. The first time Runa noticed this was when Sibbe, the cock-hunger upon her, had gone to the forge to pull the young blacksmith out of it and Ingel had abandoned his work and gone with her willingly enough, albeit his eyes had been on Runa from the moment he laid down his hammer to the moment he disappeared into the hall. And just as a woman knows when a man wants her, so she also knows when the man she is with wants someone else.

Sibbe had hated Runa from that day on. When she was not scowling at her across the hearthfire with eyes like knives, she was trying to fix it so that she was Runa's opponent in the practice bouts. During those fights she would come at Runa like a berserker so that it was all Runa could do to escape with cuts and bruises and nothing worse.

'You think because your father was a jarl you are better than the rest of us,' Sibbe growled at her during their first bout after Sibbe's roll in the hay with Ingel. 'But you are weak. A little girl sent away because your brother did not want the trouble of looking after you.' Perhaps she had heard this from the blacksmiths, for Runa had revealed almost nothing about her reasons for being there.

Sibbe's first attack had comprised a hail of sword blows which had deadened Runa's arm behind the limewood planks of her shield. The second attack

347

put Runa on the ground, a cut in her temple spilling crimson into her blonde braid.

'A little girl who would not know what to do with a man,' Sibbe sneered down at her, stepping back to allow Runa to rise just so that she could knock her down again.

Runa did not take the bait. She did nothing to let the bout spill over into a proper fight because she knew she would lose. But neither would she stay down amongst the twigs and the pine needles while she had the strength to rise, and this only infuriated the Freyja Maiden the more.

'Do not let her get to you,' Vebiorg had said. 'She grows more bitter with each new crease in her face.' She had smiled at Runa then. 'You are young and golden and beautiful, Runa, and there is nothing like that to remind us that we are getting old.'

'You are not old, Vebiorg!' Runa said, and neither was she. But then none of them was as young as Runa.

As for Ingel, all muscle and soot that he was, he looked, he stared, but actually speaking to Runa seemed beyond him. Eventually Runa grew tired of his games and did something which made him flush red as the metal he worked, and made Sibbe hate her with the fierce heat of the forge.

She stared back at him.

Alrik would have a new scar on his temple and another on his arm from where the poll of a hand axe had torn the skin, but other than that he was none the worse for having been all but carried off like a sheep in a spring raid. Yet he was furious and wanted everyone to know it.

He did not kill the sentries who had allowed Findar to come into his camp in the night and steal him from his tent, for he needed every man if he was going to beat Guthrum, but he raged and stormed about the camp, letting all know that if anyone should fall asleep on their watch again he would skin them and rub them with salt.

'You would think he'd be more grateful to us,' Thorbiorn said, jutting his chin towards Alrik who was amongst some other crew's tents wanting to know which of them had been looting the dead when they should have been the meat in Knut's shieldwall.

'What, for all the killing you did that night?' Solmund said to Thorbiorn, winking at Olaf, who tried not to grin.

Thorbiorn glowered. 'I would have done my share had I not been corralled like a prize bloody bull.'

'Bull, you say?' Svein's brow lifted.

'Goat, more like,' Bjarni suggested with a wicked smile.

'Still, the lad's on to something there,' Bjorn put in. 'We saved Alrik's arse and should see something for it.'

'Something that shines in the night like Fáfnir's eye,' Crow-Song said.

'Something drinkable at least,' Bram said, which had some murmurs of agreement.

'He knows what happened that night,' Sigurd said, 'and he knows what would have happened had we not fetched him back.'

'Within pissing distance of the gate, too,' Floki said.

'He'd be hanging from that wall by his neck,' Moldof rumbled, nodding at the borg from whose ramparts Guthrum's men stared out. Those men must know how close Findar had come to delivering them, to scattering Alrik's host like gulls before the plough. No doubt they felt Findar's absence now. Missed him the way Moldof missed his right arm.

'And the rest of us would be on our way back to our boats or else fighting each other for whatever silver Alrik keeps in his tent,' Solmund said, hands clasped, kneading the swollen flesh around his knuckles.

'Or . . .' Olaf said, 'we'd still be here scratching our beards trying to come up with a way of taking the place, for we still need silver if we are going to raise our own war host.'

'You don't have to remind me of that, Uncle,' Sigurd said and Olaf raised a hand to acknowledge it.

'Well, we didn't walk all this way to sit around scratching our backsides waiting for the end of days,' Svein moaned.

Olaf swept his arms wide. 'I'm all ears, Red,' he said. 'What is this Loki-worthy plan of yours to turf those shits out of their cosy borg? Don't be shy, lad, let's hear it.'

But Svein had nothing more to say on the matter and neither did any of them, and so they would just have to wait until someone did.

The next morning a gust of wind came out of the west. It was a wet wind laden with drizzle and it lifted the damp red cloth of one of Alrik's war banners which hung on a shaft stuck in the earth. It showed glimpses of some beast, that banner, a bear from what Sigurd had seen of it, standing tall on its hind legs, its forelegs stretched out. Reaching for something, Sigurd liked to think. Guthrum's silver probably.

'Here he comes again,' Valgerd said, nodding towards Alrik who had stopped to talk to some men by a fire but was clearly heading their way. The warlord had been hanging round their tents, comparing war gear, admiring the craftsmanship that had gone into Sigurd's helmet and Valgerd's brynja, and showing off his own gear, particularly his sword Sváva, of which he was very proud. It was a fine blade, the ghost in it like a swirl of Týr's breath on a cold day. Sleep-Maker was a good name for a sword, too, good enough to get a smile out of most men, though Bjarni asked Alrik if he had hit himself with his own blade, not to have woken when Findar came into his tent.

Alrik had told Bjarni to fuck himself. 'Leading a war host is tiring work,' he said. And it was, too,

Sigurd thought, having watched Alrik striding around the camp checking supplies, sending men off to buy bread, ale and cheese from any farmsteads within ten rôsts. Sending others foraging for meat: deer, boar and fowl if they could get it, squirrel, hare, nettles and leafy docks if they could not. All the while he was busy, listening to complaints from men who wanted what they believed Alrik owed them for sitting outside that borg, be it plunder or decent ale. Settling disputes. Rewarding men for their bravery. Whetting their silver-lust and reminding them of all the fights he had won in the past so that they might believe he would win this one too. All these jobs fell to Alrik, and none could deny that he was good at it.

'You could learn something from him,' Olaf had told Sigurd, who had dismissed that with a young man's arrogance, yet he had known Olaf was right. Which of them commanded a war host, after all? Being a dróttin, a warlord, was the same as being a jarl in some ways. Men wanted silver and loot in return for fighting. But it was different in that not all these men were oathsworn to Alrik, meaning they would pick up their nestbaggins and walk off if they thought they could do better fighting for someone else. And Alrik knew it, which was why he did his best to keep them fed and watered and was keen to remind them how much silver and iron was in Guthrum's borg if only they could get their hands on it.

And here he was again, coming like a weaver to the loom, to draw the threads of his army even tighter together.

'So you've finally come to reward us for saving your neck, Alrik,' Thorbiorn said. Being the son of a king, he thought he could speak to the man like that.

'You'll get your silver when you earn it, lad,' Alrik said, which got some dark looks from those who remembered all too well how close he had been to being dragged inside the borg and some unpleasant end. Alrik knew men and knew when he risked offending, and so he raised a hand at Sigurd and Olaf and Bram. 'You know your business. That's clear to everyone. Win me that borg and you will find me generous.' He glanced round to make sure he would not be overheard by his other men, then he came closer to the fire around which Sigurd's crew were scattered on the long flattened grass. 'Look, some of these men are happy enough taking my meat and ale and doing not much else,' he said. 'Gods, they'd be happy waiting all summer.' He looked at Sigurd now. One warrior to another. No. One leader to another. 'But you get me in there,' he said, thumbing at the fort up on the hill, 'and I'll make you rich.' He turned to Crow-Song, having got his measure for all that Hagal was not much of a skald these days. 'I mean rich enough to be worth a song or two,' he said.

Crow-Song nodded, happy to be noticed amongst men who were better with a blade than he.

'Does Jarl Guthrum have a banner?' Sigurd asked Alrik, pulling Troll-Tickler through a greasy cloth to stop the rust getting into the blade.

Alrik nodded. 'A white axe on a black cloth,' he said.

'Everybody seems to want a banner these days,' Solmund said.

'A banner can be a rag at the top of a stick,' Asgot said, retying a bone into his beard. 'Or it can be a powerful weapon.'

'Aye, well, I've yet to see a banner break down a gate,' Olaf said.

'Wiped my arse with a banner once,' Moldof said. 'I was not a proper warrior then. Don't think I'd even tupped a girl.' He grinned at the memory. 'Some jarl who refused to pay King Gorm what he owed came waving the thing about like he was somebody. We fed the crows that day and, after, my arse was squirting. Wiped it on that prick of a jarl's banner.' He looked at Hagal. 'That's in a song, now I think about it.'

Hagal grimaced. 'I'm sure the skald was a gifted man,' he said.

Sigurd felt Alrik's eyes on him now as he sat watching the dróttin's bear banner stirring in the wet wind. 'Why do you ask?' Alrik said, frowning, twisting the other tail of his long moustaches now as he stared at the borg's walls, which he seemed to do a lot. 'About Guthrum's banner.'

Sigurd looked to the west from where the wind came. From where Jarl Guthrum would come. 'I have an idea,' he said.

CHAPTER FOURTEEN

SIGURD AND HIS CREW WAITED AMONGST THE TREES ALONG with twenty of Alrik's warriors, all of them young men who had come north with Sigurd from the camp on the shore of Løgrinn. They were restless and most likely afraid, some of them having little or no experience of battle other than the night raid by Findar and the borg men. But they would play their part, Sigurd was sure, whether they liked it or not.

'Beardless buggers'll have no choice but to fight when it comes to it,' Olaf had remarked when Bjorn moaned that they looked as green as grass. 'There's no better way for a man to learn how to kill than by trying to stay alive.'

Furthermore, those twitchy young men with their shields, spears and axes must have taken heart from Sigurd's crew, who were eager and hungry for the fight, their blades honed to a wicked sharpness and their brynjur scrubbed free of rust. Even Thorbiorn looked the part in his war gear, which his father King Thorir had given him, comprising a brynja, a helmet whose brow band and nasal was silvered and decorated with knotted beasts, and a silver-hilted sword and scabbard to match, with gold and silver fittings which gleamed. Not that any of it looked to have ever been used, as Svein had pointed out, so that it was not surprising that all eyes were drawn to it, 'just like they are drawn to a pretty maiden who has never yet been swived,' as he had put it.

'Though underneath it all, the lad couldn't look more like Sigurd if he tried,' Sigurd overheard Bram mutter.

'He knows it too,' Svein said. 'But you never met Sigurd's brother Sorli,' he said to Bram. 'He was so pretty we called him Baldur.'

'Good lads. All of them,' Olaf put in, and Sigurd pretended not to hear because he did not want to start talking about his brothers now.

'Do you think the Allfather wants us to win?' a young man into his first proper beard asked Olaf, the knuckles of the hand gripping his spear bone-white as if he feared dropping the thing. 'There'll be many more of them than us,' he added, blinking too often, licking dry lips.

'What is your name, lad?' Olaf asked him. Sigurd guessed the young man was about his own age. But he had not lived Sigurd's life. He had not waded through blood to reach manhood.

'Kveld Ottarsson,' the young man said, standing a little taller at his mention of his father.

'Well then, Kveld Ottarsson, you are right in that there will probably be more of the goat-fuckers than there are of us, and that can be a problem in a fight.' Olaf pulled his scramasax from its sheath above his groin and pointed it at Kveld. 'But that is the best kind of problem because we are able to do something about it. Every man you kill is a man who will not be killing you. Or me come to that. So be a good lad and kill as many of those pieces of arse moss as you can. Keep killing them and then you'll find there are more of us than them. Simple as that.'

Kveld looked at Svein, who grinned and nodded, and then at Black Floki, who was showing nothing but contempt.

'Just don't get in our way, lad,' Bram said, slapping the cold iron cheek of the long-hafted axe he was leaning on. 'Because when this troll-shortening beauty is in full swing, she does not stop to ask whose side you are on.'

Kveld Ottarsson nodded, sharing a weak smile with some of the others who stood there sweating and invoking the gods, their arse cheeks flapping in their breeks.

'And the other thing,' Olaf went on, sheathing his long knife, 'now is the time to empty your bladders. Go for a shit if you can. Better to do it now than when you are facing some growler who will think you have ruined your breeks on his account.'

That was all the invitation most of them needed and they walked off into the trees, unslinging shields and pulling at belts as if they feared they might not get them undone in time.

'Make sure you don't get lost, Thorbiorn Thorirsson,' Olaf called after the king's boy. 'I wouldn't want you to miss the whole thing.'

'If you wanted to come and hold it for me, Olaf, you should've said,' Thorbiorn called over his shoulder, and if the lad was afraid he was doing a good job of hiding it.

'I remember my first fight,' Solmund said, watching them go.

'Ah yes, when Óðin still had two eyes and no beard to speak of,' Bjarni said, which got some laughs, though not from Solmund who was in the deep of his memory.

'My father took me on a raid. Some feud over sheep. Or was it goats? Anyway, the raid went bad as milk left in the sun. Our enemies had seen us coming across the fjord and prepared us a proper welcome. We'd lost three men in the time it takes to haul an anchor stone in, and that was three too many for a few sheep. Ended up haring back to our boat, braids flying in the wind. I had never seen my father run before.' He still seemed amazed by the sight of it in his mind. 'We never spoke again of our hurry that day.'

'Thank you, Solmund,' Sigurd said, jutting his chin at those men who had not gone off amongst the trees, 'for that is just the kind of story we all wanted to hear.'

'Enough stories,' Moldof growled, waving his half-arm in the direction of the borg. 'Let's get on with the thing so that we don't have to hear about the old goat's second fight.' Solmund shrugged and held his tongue and nor did any of the others have anything more to say but were content just to wait for the sound of the horn from the east, which was the signal Sigurd had agreed with Alrik.

For the three days since Sigurd had spun the plan in his head the warlord's men had been busy, cutting birch trees and making ladders in full view of those warriors on the borg's ramparts. To Guthrum's men it would look as if Alrik was readying to launch an all-out attack. As if he would throw his men at the palisade in the hope that they would break over it like a wave over a rock on the shore. It was likely the defenders would assume that Alrik had received word that Guthrum was nearby and that the warlord knew he must win the hill fort for himself now or else risk being caught out in the open and fighting on two fronts.

'There is every chance it will not work,' Alrik had said when Sigurd had come up with the scheme. 'But if it does, and we take the borg today, I will make you a rich man, Byrnjolf.'

If it didn't work, Sigurd considered now, he, his crew, and all the men standing amongst the trees with him now might easily die. No, not easily.

Never that, he thought, hoping that Óðin Geirtýr, the spear-god, was watching them, that Loki, too, was not far away, for surely that trickster would appreciate the low cunning in Sigurd's scheme.

And then there was no more time to think or hope, only to act, as the thin note of a horn made heads turn to the east, where Alrik's force would be taking up shields and drawing together, doing their best to look as if panic and fear were spreading amongst them.

'Now, king's son,' Sigurd said with a nod, at which Thorbiorn snatched up the war banner from where it had leant against a tree. Being the banner man was a position of honour and only fitting for the son of a king. Not that that was why Sigurd had given Thorbiorn the responsibility. He had done it because it would be no easy thing, carrying that banner aloft over sloping, uneven ground, which would leave less room in the young man's head for the fear which fills even experienced warriors at times like this. Being the merkismaðr might even stop Thorbiorn from doing something reckless. Not that he had given any impression of wanting to prove himself, other than when it came to women and ale.

'Stay with me, lad,' Olaf told him. 'That way I won't have to tell your father that you got yourself killed for some Svear warlord on some half-arsed hill in the middle of nowhere.'

Thorbiorn nodded, lifting the banner which had been nothing but a boar spear and a scrap of tent

cloth just two days before. Now, because they were
sheltered amongst the trees and there was anyway
little in the way of wind, the half-circle of black
cloth below the blade hung limp, so that only a flash
of the white shape embroidered on it could be seen.
Nevertheless, Jarl Guthrum's sign of the war axe
on a sea of black was clear enough on the shields
which Sigurd's crew and four of the others carried
now as they walked out of the tree line on to the
open ground to the west of the borg. Alrik and Knut
had confirmed that Guthrum's hearthmen boasted
shields painted like that because Guthrum had
famously killed his uncle, a jarl named Blihar, with
an axe. Guthrum wanted the torc for himself and
one day, when Blihar was dealing with a dispute
between two farmers in his own hall, Guthrum
struck him down in front of everyone. Anyone
would have thought that would be the end of
Guthrum then, and yet instead of avenging their
jarl, Blihar's hirðmen swore an oath to Guthrum
there and then, and he had taken the symbol of the
axe as his own from then on.

'The gods like a man to act boldly,' Asgot had
said, seeming to admire the Guthrum of that story,
and Sigurd had spun the scheme in his mind.
Those black-and-white-painted shields, along with
the war banner and the fact that Sigurd's crew
were relatively unknown to Guthrum's men, might
be enough to fool those in the borg now. From a
distance and in their mail and helmets, Sigurd's

crew might, if the gods were smiling on him, be taken for Guthrum's hirðmen rather than for Alrik's men, few of whom owned either.

'Keep this pace,' Sigurd said to those around him as they marched north-east across the bumpy ground, mail and fittings clinking, feet tramping, men puffing. Then he could hear shouting from the borg, as men on its ramparts spotted them. He could not hear what they were saying but he hoped it was not that they recognized him and his men from the other night when Sigurd had killed Findar on the hill below the gate. It was dark that night, he told himself. They saw nothing.

He growled at Thorbiorn to lift the banner so that what breeze there was might catch the cloth and make the axe on it dance. And he counted on the borg's men believing that they were looking at the vanguard of Jarl Guthrum's force, or even the jarl himself come out of the west to spin Alrik's doom.

'How will we know if they've swallowed the hook?' Kveld asked, keeping his shield high to partly obscure his face as Sigurd had told him.

'We'll know,' Sigurd assured him, looking to the south-east. Further down the slope, Alrik's men were forming into two shieldwalls, Alrik at the centre of one, Knut in the other, both men yelling commands and working their warriors into a battle fever. Another horn blast and then those shieldwalls were moving, one of them towards the borg, the other towards Sigurd, which was exactly as they had planned it. To those in the borg it would look as if Alrik was rushing to intercept the newcomers before they could reach the gate in the palisade on the borg's south side and safety. As for Knut's shieldwall, which was facing that gate, Guthrum's men would think that their enemies were trying to ensure that none from the borg came to the newcomers' aid.

They'll be hesitant. Unsure without Findar, Sigurd told himself as the sweat trickled down into his beard.

'Now, Sigurd!' Olaf hissed.

But the command was already on Sigurd's lips. 'Shieldwall!' he roared, stopping and planting the butt of his spear on to the ground, and those warriors in loose order around him stopped too, and formed two lines, with him at the centre, their shields overlapping, their spears threatening Alrik's men down the slope to their right. 'Move,' he yelled, and they were shuffling forward, trying to stay together over the uneven ground and through the long grass.

'And watch out for those arrows,' Olaf said, because two of Alrik's men had run forward with bows and were making ready to loose, which was not so dangerous from that range but would help the whole thing look right as far as the borg men were concerned. 'Here they come,' Olaf said as they lifted their shields to make the wall a little higher. Five heartbeats later an arrow hit Bram's shield and bounced off, and six heartbeats later Sigurd tramped on the other shaft, which was sprouting from the spring grass. Then Sigurd steered them to the right because he wanted to make it look as though he was willing to fight, that his skjaldborg and Alrik's would collide in a great clash of wood and steel, flesh and bone. Another arrow hissed overhead and Asgot caught its twin on his shield.

Sigurd looked left up the slope. They were close enough to the borg now to smell the mossy damp wood of the palisade and the smoke of the cook fires within. They could make out the shouts of those spearmen on the ramparts, and Sigurd liked what he heard. Some of the borg men were telling him and his men to slaughter Alrik and shit on their corpses. Others, the wiser ones amongst them, were warning Sigurd's war band that there were too many of the enemy for them to fight and that they should retreat back into the woods and wait for the rest of Guthrum's army. Which was good advice seeing as Sigurd's thirty-four faced a shieldwall sixty strong. Then there was Knut's skjaldborg of about the same number, and still more besides, for Alrik had left a number of warriors behind to guard the camp.

'Keep those shields up. Give the sods something to aim at,' Olaf said, for the risk of one of Alrik's bowmen putting an arrow in them was very real now that the men in the skjaldborg could not watch the shafts in flight and judge their arcing fall. From this range those arrows would be flying fast and almost straight. 'Here comes another,' Olaf warned, and two heartbeats later an arrow *tonk*ed off Sigurd's shield boss. A moment after that another whipped over their heads and Bjarni said he had heard it whisper Kveld Ottarsson's name, which was a cruel thing to say.

'Nearly there,' Sigurd said, as Alrik's men began to strike their shields with the cheeks and polls of their axes, the hilts of their swords and their spear shafts, and if this hadn't all been part of the ruse that thunderous beat might have had those young untested men behind Sigurd pissing down their legs. Perhaps it did even so.

'Now there's a face I have seen before,' Olaf said, 'six men to the right of Alrik as we look at them. See him?'

'The one with two beard ropes?' Sigurd asked, having picked out the warrior, who was hammering his shield with his sword's hilt.

'I've seen him around camp,' Sigurd said.

'Aye,' Olaf said. 'We know him.'

'I don't,' Sigurd said. To his eyes there was nothing familiar about the man and he glanced up the hill at the borg, which was behind him over his left shoulder now so that only the top of the main gate and the heads of two sentries could be seen above the crest of the hill.

'When we go, we go fast,' Sigurd called.

'As if Fenrir Wolf is snapping at our arses,' Olaf added, and they came on to the flatter ground an arrow-shot from the fort but only a spear-throw from Alrik's skjaldborg. Sigurd and Alrik locked eyes and the warlord roared a curse at him, calling him a dead man walking, which was the prearranged warning that chaos was about to slip its leash like Garm, the giant hound which guards the corpse-gate of Hel's freezing wastes.

'Kill them!' Alrik bellowed, lifting his spear and pointing the blade at Sigurd. Sixty voices clamoured in response as Alrik's shieldwall shattered and his men broke into a run.

'Stand!' Sigurd yelled, lifting his shield and bracing himself for the coming impact. 'Stand!' He sensed his own skjaldborg fragmenting around him, starting with the men at his rear. 'Stand, you swines!' he screamed, but they would not stand, because sixty warriors were running towards them, screaming death and butchery.

'Now, Sigurd,' Olaf growled, and Sigurd looked left and right, then over his shoulder, and saw that only six or so yet stood with him, grim-faced but steadfast. Thorbiorn was one of them, not bothering to lift the banner now as the cloth was as limp as an empty ale skin. The rest of them were running uphill towards the borg. Which was exactly what they were supposed to do.

'Now,' Sigurd agreed, then turned, screaming at his remaining warriors to run, and they did not need to be told twice. They fled up the slope towards the borg, which was lung-scalding work cumbered by mail, helmets, shields and weapons, and Solmund, who had been one of the first to flee, was already bent double and suffering, his old lungs creaking, but Valgerd grabbed hold of him and hauled him on.

'Thought you said it wasn't much of a hill, Bear,' Svein growled at Bram, huffing and puffing, the two of them gripping their big axes by their throats as they ran. Then a man beside Sigurd stumbled and fell, landing awkwardly because of the shield which he had foolishly strapped to his arm, but Sigurd ran on because he saw that the gates in the palisade were opening inwards.

'Come on! Hurry!' a man on the ramparts was yelling.

Sigurd looked behind him and saw that the man who had fallen was Kveld Ottarsson and he looked to have broken his arm by the way that his shield was lying in relation to the rest of him. On his knees and right elbow now, he had drawn his scramasax and was sawing at the shield straps. He must have known that Alrik's men were almost on him.

'Fool's going to scupper us,' Moldof said, looking over his shoulder as he leant on one leg dragging breath into his lungs because he was on the steepest part of the climb. Sigurd feared Moldof was right, but then Kveld hauled himself to his feet, pulled his sword from its scabbard and ran at those coming up the hill towards him, and it was Alrik himself who scythed the young man down with one swing of his massive sword, Sleep-Maker.

Sigurd turned and plunged up the slope, over the crest to see Valgerd and Floki leading the rest across the bridge over the ditch and through the gap in the bank. Then they were through the open gate and Sigurd knew it could all come to bloody ruin now if they did not get enough bodies inside the borg before Guthrum's men fathomed their trick.

He overtook Svein and Bram, Asgot, Solmund and Moldof, and thundered across the short bridge into the fort, where Jarl Guthrum's men were waiting. There were some twenty or thirty of them milling inside the gate, which some of them were already pulling closed so that Moldof and Svein had to turn sidewards to get in. And then those gates slammed shut and the locking beam was put in place and one of the men on the rampart above shouted down that Alrik's men had stopped halfway up the slope.

'Flea-ridden whoresons are just standing there scratching their arses!' he called.

'That's because the turds have no fight in them,' a black-bearded warrior shouted up at him, as those manning the ramparts jeered and hurled insults and waved the spears which they would have cast down on their enemies had the 'sheep-fuckers' and 'pale-livered nithings' the courage to come closer.

'Who are you?' one of Guthrum's men asked Floki, his eyes jumping from man to man and from their shields to the banner which Thorbiorn still gripped. Those eyes bulged when they took in Valgerd standing there like something from a legend, her braids like golden ropes lying on the grey rings of her brynja. 'Where is Jarl Guthrum?' the man asked. A tall, grey-bearded warrior with rings up his arms, he was one of the only borg men wearing a helmet, which likely meant he was in charge. 'I do not recognize any of you,' he said, his hand on the hilt of his sword, and it was clear he was beginning to have very bad thoughts. 'Well?' he demanded of Olaf. 'Who in Hel's cunny are you?'

Olaf looked at Sigurd, which was his way of giving Sigurd the great pleasure of dispelling Grey Beard's confusion. So, Sigurd stepped up to the man and grinned, dragging his right forearm across his head to wipe away the sweat. 'We are the men who you should not have opened your gate to,' he said, and then he cut the man down with one blow and brought the steel-chaos to Guthrum's borg.

Black Floki planted one of his short axes in a man's forehead, and Valgerd ran her spear through a warrior's chest before he had his sword half out of its scabbard. Asgot opened a big man's throat with his spear blade and Svein ran at Guthrum's men, giving himself room to swing that big axe and sowing panic amongst his enemies. Olaf slammed his shield against another man's, then hurled his spear which went into a man's open mouth and punched out the back of his skull, and Bram was cleaving shields and lopping off the arms behind them. Even Thorbiorn gave himself to the iron-storm, thrusting the boar spear banner into a man who came at him with an axe and driving him backwards into the press of his companions.

But Guthrum's men vastly outnumbered them, and once the initial shock had passed they were rallying, flooding from all over the borg towards the maelstrom at the gate. A rock struck Sigurd's shoulder and another smashed one of the Birka men's skulls, killing him instantly, and Sigurd lifted his shield up, looking round its rim to see that those up on the earthen rampart were trying to rain death on them from above. 'Shields!' he yelled, seeing Floki duck a sword swing and hack into a warrior's groin. His shield before him, Aslak forced a warrior back against the palisade, punching his scramasax into the man's neck over and over, so that blood sprayed across the timbers. 'Uncle! The gate!' Sigurd bellowed. Olaf nodded, wincing as a boulder the size of a man's head thumped into his shield which he held above him, causing him to stagger and go down on one knee in the mud.

Blood slapped Sigurd's face and he knew it was from another of Knut's recruits, whose head burst apart in a welter of blood, skull and grey brains. Svein, Bram, Moldof, and ten of the others had already formed a skjaldborg to defend the gate, and were holding off three times their number because since Findar was gone, Guthrum's men had no leader roaring orders at them and their own shieldwall was not properly built. And yet other borg men, in their desperation to retake the gate, were trying to come round the edges of Svein's wall, which lacked the bodies to bend back on itself and prevent them.

A thrown spear struck Bjorn's chest, knocking him down. A sword blow cleaved Valgerd's shield and then the borg man stepped up and rammed the hilt into the shieldmaiden's head, sending her reeling, but Bram strode forward and swung his long axe, hacking off both of the borg man's legs at the knee.

'Help them,' Sigurd ordered the men standing with him.

'Not you, Thorbiorn. You stay where I can see you, lad,' Olaf growled as Bjarni, Asgot, Crow-Song and Solmund ran to protect the skjaldborg's flanks. Still others of Sigurd's raiders were fighting to add their own shields to Svein's bulwark, and it was with grim pride that Sigurd saw the young adventurers who had marched north through the forests with them holding their own, trading blow for blow.

A spear streaked down but Sigurd got his shield to it and it glanced off to land in the mud, as Valgerd launched her spear up at the man on the ramparts who had thrown it, taking him in the belly so that he clutched the shaft and toppled down the bank into the borg, landing at Sigurd's feet. Then one of the other men up there yelled down at his companions that they must retake the gate and hold it, because Alrik was coming, at which all the men on the ramparts turned and began hurling their spears and rocks at those outside the borg. For they knew that if Alrik's men came through those gates the fort would be his before dusk.

Floki threw his shield aside, thrust his hand axe into his belt and scrambled up the earthen slope, pulling his scramasax free as he got to the top and punching it through the neck of a man whose back was to him as he loosed an arrow. Alert to the threat, another man turned and thrust his spear at Floki, which the former slave parried downwards with his knife, sending the spear blade into the earth and sweeping the scramasax back up along the shaft slicing off the man's hands at the wrists. The warrior staggered backwards, glaring at his spurting stumps, and Floki left him to it, pulling his axe free and planting it in another man's back a heartbeat before slicing his throat.

'Here we go,' Olaf said as he and Sigurd lifted the heavy beam from its brackets and dropped it on the earthen bank. The gates swung inwards and Alrik himself stalked in with his hearthmen around him. The eyes behind the helmet's guards were wild as he took in the scene: the dismembered bodies of his enemies strewn in the mud around the big gates, the butchered limbs and the bloody puddles. The intestines lying in the filth.

He grinned at Sigurd. 'Kill them!' he yelled to his warriors, hurling himself into the fray, running a man through with Sleep-Maker as his men poured into the borg, some of them throwing themselves into Svein and Bram's skjaldborg to bolster it. Others scrambled up the bank either side of the gate to deal death to those defenders on the ramparts, turning the borg into a slaughteryard.

'This won't last long,' Olaf said to Sigurd as they picked up their shields, hefted their weapons and strode forward to join the others. And neither did it, although no one could say that Jarl Guthrum's men did not fight bravely and as well as anyone might hope to who was in a battle they could not win. Knut's sixty men followed on the heels of Alrik's band, flooding through the gate like wolves to the scent of blood, eager to wreak their vengeance on those defenders who had until now held them at bay. And it was Knut's arrival which proved to be the weight that tipped the scales.

The fight went out of the enemy then; not individually – men still hacked and stabbed and struggled – but it was now a desperate instinct to survive which drove them, rather than a belief that they might hold out against Alrik and turn back the tide. Many broke and ran, haring off amongst the timber buildings, the byres and pens and workshops, the grain stores and reed-screened latrine pits, seeking to hide or hoping to regroup perhaps.

'Byrnjolf!' Alrik yelled, and it took Sigurd a heartbeat to realize that the warlord was shouting at him. 'Run them down! Kill them all!' Alrik said.

'We've not done enough?' Olaf said, spitting into the mud.

But Sigurd nodded at Alrik, then turned and ran after those fleeing men.

It was a common thing that the hunter admired his prey. How could he not respect the magnificence of the great bull elk? The ferocity of the bristling boar? The strength of the bear and the cunning of the fox? So Fionn was not surprised to find that he admired Haraldarson now. The young man's ruse had worked, much to Fionn and other men's surprise, and his band had got into the borg almost easily, something which Alrik had tried and failed to do so many times. If anything, Fionn had wished Haraldarson well as he saw him enter the place and heard the clamour of the ensuing fight. For he did not want Sigurd to die then. Had not followed his prey this far and into the maw of another man's war just to see him killed by another man's blade or arrow.

And as much as Fionn hated the idea of being meat in the blood-fray, relying on the man either side to keep him alive, he had watched with rising panic as he waited on the slope with the sixty warriors in Knut's band.

'We should go now,' he said, unable to rein in his frustration any longer as they watched Alrik lead his men through the gates.

'Aye, those arseholes will get all the plunder,' another warrior said, thinking that same fear was what had motivated the Alba man to speak up.

'We go when I say,' Knut had growled.

But eventually Knut *did* say and they hurried up the hill in loose order, confident that the fight inside the borg was almost won and hoping to get their hands on what they could before all the silver and copper, bronze and ivory, blades, brooches and amber had found their way into other men's purses and nestbaggins. Before the best of the dead men's shoes were on new feet and the dead men's cloaks were on new backs. Though Fionn was not interested in any of that. He wanted one thing and one thing only. Haraldarson.

And now he saw him. Haraldarson's crew had broken away from the main body of Alrik's force and were hunting amongst the borg's outbuildings, cutting men down in twos and threes. Knut's band had thrown themselves into the fight and this had broken Guthrum's men so that chaos was lord there now and it was hard to know who was who in the steel-storm. Fionn had put his sword in a man's side, hoping it was one of Guthrum's men, then some of Knut's men splintered off from the thickest fighting – the slaughter really, for that's what it was now – and Fionn took his chance. He rounded the grain store, his back brushing the planks as he moved across the thoroughfare to the side of a carpenter's workshop where he stopped for a moment, the sweet scent of pine shavings in his nose. Then he was moving again, following Sigurd from a distance, skirting the huge red-bearded warrior and the shieldmaiden who had cornered a broad-shouldered, big-bearded man who was growling insults at them as they closed in to kill him.

He saw one of Guthrum's men hiding in the pig pen, crouching against the woven hazel fence. Fionn ignored him, moving on past a great pile of felled timber: pine trunks stripped and smoothed ready to be used for building; and there he saw Olaf and Haraldarson's godi and the one they called Bear, along with two other men facing down a knot of borg men who had locked shields. For all the good it would do them, Fionn thought.

Then he caught sight of his prey again. It looked as though Haraldarson was making for the cattle byre and he only had one of his crewmen with him now. But that was the young man with the crow-black hair and he was dangerous, and so Fionn would have to be careful. And yet he might never get a better chance than this.

He drew his scían, thrilling as always to the feel of the stag-antler grip in his palm, and went to claim his kill.

Sigurd had long since lost his shield but he had picked up a discarded spear, so he held Troll-Tickler in his right hand and the spear in his left as he closed in on the bigger of the two men who had fled into the cattle byre. Floki was in there with him too, in that dark stinking barn, but he had gone down the opposite side after his man who was somewhere in amongst the cows themselves which were lowing in fear and panic. The beasts were thin and sorry-looking and perhaps starving, because since Alrik had come they had been moved inside the winter byre when they should have been outside on the hillsides feeding on the spring grass. Now their eyes shone in the dark and they emptied their bowels where they stood, terrified of the men with blades amongst them.

Coming into this dark place had stripped Sigurd of some of the battle thrill which had carried him up that hill, through the gate and into the maelstrom of the struggle for the borg. Now, the clamour of the fight muted and far away, alone but for Floki, the beasts and the men they were trying to kill, Sigurd felt the gnawing of doubt in his gut. What were these last borg men to him? Had he not played his part? He did not need some desperate man jumping out of the shadows to put a blade in his neck. Not now.

But then, he could not abandon Floki. Nor could he call out to tell him to leave these men with the cows without risking giving away Floki in the dark. So he walked deeper into that byre, which was longer than some rich karl's houses he had seen, and he told himself that this would be his last kill of the day.

No fame to be had here, boy, a voice growled in his head.

Then he felt it, almost like a change in the air behind him. Or eyes on his back, perhaps. He turned, lifting his spear, and peered through the stench-filled dark. But it was just one of Alrik's men, the Alba man who had joined up in Birka at the same time they had. The man put a finger to his lips and Sigurd nodded. No bad thing having another ally now, he thought, and gestured to the man that there were two enemies in there with them, hiding somewhere in all that dung and straw and lowing livestock. The Alba man nodded and peered off past Sigurd, lifting his long knife as he crouched and set off.

So Sigurd turned back round and began to move forward again, steeling himself against any sudden blade-swinging borg man rushing at him out of the dark.

Something made him glance behind him again, but too late to stop the blade which streaked through murk, slicing into the skin and following the line of his jawbone as he twisted and threw himself back. He fell against a cow which bellowed and skittered sidewards so that Sigurd fell into the filth. Then the man was on him and, having dropped his own weapons, Sigurd threw up his forearms to block, as the wicked long blade sliced again, across both arms, and the pain was searing. Yet somehow he got a grip of the hands which held the long knife's hilt, which were driving the blade down towards the hollow at the base of his neck.

Gods but he was strong for a man with barely the flesh to cloak his bones and it was all Sigurd could do to hold that knife at bay, as his own blood dripped on to his face, the coppery iron tang of it in his nose.

I'm losing, he thought. *This little man will kill me.*

The Alba man's face was two hand spans from his own, close enough to smell his breath through his teeth as he strained, forcing that strange knife of his down so that its point was against Sigurd's flesh. He could hear Floki fighting somewhere in the dark, but even if he wasted his strength calling out to him, Floki would never get to him in time. So Sigurd glared into the Alba man's wide eyes and put all his strength into trying to deny that thirsty blade the blood which it craved. But the Alba man all but lay upon the knife's hilt, bearing down with knotty strength and iron will, and Sigurd felt the skin of his throat give way to the blade's point.

Not like this, he thought. *Not in the dark like this with only the cows to see it. Killed by a man I did not even know was my enemy.*

He wrenched at those hands but they would not yield. If only he could push the knife to the side, just by an inch, he would have a chance. But this man wanted his death. He needed it.

'Shhh,' the Alba man hissed. 'It's over. Shhh, Haraldarson.'

Sigurd could not speak but his eyes spoke for him. *You're a dead man*, they said, because all Sigurd knew was defiance. *This is your end, not mine*, he silently promised the man. But he was losing and somewhere deep in the mire of his own mind he knew it.

'Shhh . . .'

Then a sword scythed in the dark and there was a wet *chop* and the Alba man's head toppled off the stem of his neck and rolled into the straw and cow shit. Sigurd gasped for breath, pain flooding him. There, looming like a one-armed giant in the dark, was Moldof, his teeth set in a wolf's grin, the faint light of the half-open byre door at his back.

Sigurd pushed the headless body off himself and took another breath, coughing from the straw dust clouding the air, then reached for the hand which Moldof offered him, letting the big man pull him to his feet. They both turned back to the dark interior to see another figure approaching. Moldof snatched up his gory sword and stepped forward, but then they saw that it was Floki emerging from the dusty gloom, his axes back in his belt because his hands were full.

'Who is that?' Floki asked, looking down at the head in the filth. It lay in a pool of cow piss. He had two heads himself, one in either hand, their hair snarled round his fists. Both bearded and staring with dead eyes. Both dripping.

'The Alba man,' Sigurd said, a hand clamped to his neck which was spilling hot blood as he bent to recover his sword and spear.

Moldof crouched and rolled the severed head over to get a better look at the face, grimacing at the stink of piss.

'Why would that piece of goat shit try to kill you?' Floki asked, tossing both his heads towards the door.

'Why don't you ask him?' Sigurd said. His head was swimming now and his legs were weakening. He had two long cuts on his forearms, the one between his jaw and his neck and another small one in the hollow of his throat, and he was losing enough blood now that his body was beginning to shiver.

'His blade is sharp and clean, I'll give him that,' Moldof said, thrusting the Alba man's long knife into its scabbard and handing it to Sigurd. He nodded at Sigurd's wounds. 'So long as we wash those out and thread them good and tight you'll live.'

Sigurd tucked the strange long knife, which had come so close to sending him to the afterlife, into his belt and took one last look at the head of the man who had wielded it.

Who was he? Why had he wanted Sigurd dead? Those questions would have to wait. For now Sigurd needed to get out into the light, was desperate to escape that reeking barn before his legs gave up on him and they had to carry him out.

'We've done our work today,' he said.

Moldof nodded. 'Let's get you back.'

Floki spat on the Alba man's headless corpse and he and Sigurd held each other's eye in silent

acknowledgement of how close Sigurd had come to
death in that nothing place.

'I need a drink,' Sigurd said, wincing at the pain,
keeping his blood-slick hand pressed against the cut
flesh of his neck.

'You've earned one,' Moldof said.

And with that they left the cows and the corpses
and walked through the byre back out into the day.

The butchery was great, the kind that even the gods
cannot ignore, and that dusk, when it was done and
Alrik's blood-thirst was sated, he called his war host
to heel.

They made a terrible sight, exhausted and gore-
spattered, their teeth white against their crimson
faces, their tunics and breeks blood-soaked as they
knelt in the mud robbing the dead, searching for
plunder like wolves, like crows and ravens stripping
carcasses to the bone.

As well as the wounded who had been unable to
fight on, some twenty-three of Guthrum's warriors
were alive at the end of it. Most of those had made
a last stand at the rear of the borg between two
longhouses, shields overlapped and seemingly
willing to fight to the death, which Sigurd said was
brave of them.

'Aye, it's brave,' Olaf agreed, 'but it also says
something about this Alrik who these men know
much better than us.' Which was true, for had Alrik
been a man known for his restraint and generosity

in victory, Guthrum's men might have thrown down their swords and spears and pleaded for their lives. As it was, Alrik formed two shieldwalls, each three men deep, one in front and one at the borg men's rear. He sent bowmen up on to the roofs of the longhouses either side of Guthrum's men to rain their shafts on to those doomed warriors.

Sigurd wanted no part in that final slaughter and led his crew away before the killing began, which Alrik himself did not seem to mind, not least when he saw Sigurd covered in his own blood and paling too.

'Nor should he mind, for we have given him this borg,' Sigurd said. He was sitting on a felled pine trunk while Valgerd stitched his wounds, glad that it was she and not Solmund doing it, for the old skipper might get his own back for the mess Sigurd once made of sewing him up. First, though, the shieldmaiden had cut his beard and shaved his chin so that she might see what she was doing, and the others laughed to see Sigurd looking like a much younger man again.

'I *am* a young man,' he said.

'Aye, but you've already lived a handful of lives,' Olaf said, and Sigurd could not disagree with that.

Of the others, more than half had taken cuts and sprains, though the real pain would come later, they knew. They stood around slaking their thirst, watching men picking the dead for plunder, listening to the spear din and letting the aftermath of the fight course through their veins as Alrik finished the borg men off.

When Valgerd's work was done, and fine work it was too, Thorbiorn led them to a rain barrel and they washed off the worst of the gore. Then they walked through the place, stepping over the half-naked corpses and blood pools, and Bram threw a stone at a dog which was licking the gore from a young man's face. Soon the crows and the rats would come to feed. The wolves, too, would come sniffing out of the forest, drawn by the scent of all that butchered meat, trying to work up the courage to sneak into the borg if they could.

'They've earned their places in the Allfather's hall,' Olaf said of Guthrum's one hundred and ten men, as the clash of arms and the screams of the dying followed them out of the gates.

And so they had.

They slept in a longhouse on dead men's benches, warmed by a raging hearth as the rain hissed in the black night outside where other men kept watch from the ramparts. Alrik had moved his entire force inside the borg as darkness cloaked the world, leaving all the dead where they lay. No one liked sleeping in those houses with so many corpses scattered like chaff in the mud outside, for men feared the ghosts of the dead. But with night coming and the choice needing to be made between dealing with the slain or moving the camp inside, most men would rather put up with the ghosts if it meant they had a dry place to sleep.

Sigurd's crew took the benches nearest the hearth in the longhouse they were in, and no one seemed to mind. Or if they did mind no one said anything. If his crew had not got the respect of Alrik's other warriors before the fight for looking like war gods in their fine gear, they had earned their respect now. Running into that borg had been a risky thing to do.

'It was bloody mad now that I think about it,' Olaf had said after. 'If Guthrum's men had held the gates shut behind us we would have been stuck like fish in a withy trap.'

None disagreed. They would have been too tired to do so anyway, for after a fight like that their very bones craved rest. No one spoke much at all. Each was on a journey through his or her own thoughts, recalling moments of the fight, men they had killed, men who had nearly killed them, the sight of the mutilated and the screams of the doomed. After the mad confusion of the fray, warriors would try to make sense of what they had lived through, weaving the tale of it in their minds like scenes on a tapestry.

I am getting used to it now, Sigurd thought with grim acceptance. It was always the same, he realized, looking into the fire whilst drinking the ale which Svein had given him. The muscle-trembling before a fight, the battle-rage and the blood-lust during it, and afterwards the flooding joy of knowing that you have survived. In the wake of all this came near-death exhaustion, a weariness of the body and soul which only a fjord-deep sleep could heal.

And yet he would likely be dead now had a one-armed man not saved him. Even worse that it was Moldof, who had been his enemy and against whom his father had fought a battle fit for skald-song.

'So who was he then, that shit from Alba who tried to slice you open at the gills?' Olaf asked.

Sigurd shook his head. 'He knew my name though. Called me Haraldarson,' he said.

'Maybe we can get some answers out of Knut, for he picked the man up in Birka,' Aslak suggested.

'And have Knut and Alrik asking questions about us and why the turd would want Sigurd dead?' Olaf said. 'Better to let it lie for now.'

Sigurd agreed with that. He drank again, then held a draught of ale in his mouth to sluice it clean of the bitter taste that lingers after so much death. He looked around. Svein was already asleep, leaning against a roof post, snoring like a troll. Olaf and Moldof were sitting on stools by an oil lamp playing tafl, which might have made for a strange sight even the previous day. But fighting shoulder to shoulder forges bonds between warriors, as does saving another man's life. It could not be said that Moldof hadn't proved himself, more so for being wolf-jointed and left-handed now.

Sigurd's gaze drifted over to Valgerd as it so often did. A green bruise staining her skin from her left temple down to her cheek, she sat on one of the benches, a pile of some fifty or more arrows on the fur beside her. She had gathered them from the mud and from Guthrum's dead and was examining each one by flamelight, checking that the iron heads were securely fixed and sharp, and that the fletchings, goose or eagle feathers by the looks, were undamaged. She was putting the best ones into her quiver and leaving the others aside to repair later.

Floki was working the edge of an axe against a whetstone, spitting on it now and then and holding it up to the light to inspect it. No surprise that it needed sharpening, after all the work it had been put to. The cleaving of shields, arm bones, necks, helmets, skulls.

Crow-Song was humming a sad melody to himself and Bjarni, Aslak, Bjorn and Bram were trying to out-drink each other, for the borg was not short of ale, thank the gods. Asgot was casting the runes, though for once Sigurd was not interested in what they had to say. Too tired for it.

Solmund had been sitting on the bench beside Sigurd, more asleep than awake, but now he stood, wincing and pressing a hand into the small of his back. The spear he had taken in the chest had ripped his brynja and bruised his flesh but the tough old helmsman was still in one piece. 'Gods but I'm old,' he said. 'Stiffer than a day-old corpse.' He swore. 'I'm going to find a dark corner and I'm going to lie down and none of you will disturb me if you know what is good for you.' He held a finger up to Sigurd. 'But do not let me die in my sleep, Sigurd. I will see *Reinen* again before I go.'

'I'll have no one else at her helm, old man,' Sigurd said, forcing a smile through the pain as his friend shambled off to find a good quiet place to get his head down. In truth only the gods and the Norns knew when they would see *Reinen* again. Sigurd looked at Thorbiorn who sat across from him staring into the crackling fire. 'You did well today, Thorbiorn Thorirsson,' he said. Sigurd had not heard the lad say a word since they had walked away from the slaughter of those last brave borg men by Alrik's warriors.

Thorbiorn looked up at him. There were tears in the young man's eyes. Tears which Thorbiorn did not blink away as he fixed his eyes on Sigurd's own. 'I have never wanted to lie with a woman more than I do now,' he said. But there were no women in Guthrum's borg because it was a place for warriors. It had been the forge in which Guthrum made his army, half of which now lay ruined in the mud outside.

'We will have to make do with ale,' Sigurd said, drinking until his cup was empty. Thorbiorn did the same, then looked back into the flames.

Sigurd did not want to think of the blood either, or the dead, or the Alba man or even the fight, which he had all but won for Alrik. Instead he thought of Runa, his brave, beautiful sister. He wondered where she was and what she was doing. And he wished she were with him now.

They came for Runa in the night, Vebiorg and a young fox-faced Freyja Maiden called Drífa, who despite being just a couple of years older than Runa was the best archer on Fugløy. They woke her roughly and Runa sat up, shedding a dream of her mother in which she and Grimhild were sailing a small færing north up the Karmsund Strait, knives in their hands for the oath-breaker king.

'Come, Runa!' Drífa hissed, tugging at the sleeve of her nightdress. 'She's back!'

'Who is back?' Runa asked, scrubbing the sleep from her face. She was usually a light sleeper but she had been fjord-deep in that dream and parts of it still clung to her like sea wrack. Perhaps the others had forgotten about her, she being up there in the loft with the smoke.

'The Prophetess!' Drífa said, her slanted fox eyes wide and shining in the light of the soapstone lamp which Vebiorg held before her. Drífa had been brought to Fugløy as a bairn, the rumour being that her father was King Thorir, he having begotten her on a bed slave then sent her to the Maidens to keep her out of the way.

'She has been gone since the winter before this one just past,' Vebiorg said.

'Come, Runa,' Drífa said. 'The others are there already.'

Runa shuffled to the end of her bed and looked down over the ledge at the hall below, at the empty benches and furs, and the hearthfire which was already dying because no one was around to feed it. Two of the older women were still there but they were wrapping themselves in blankets and readying to brave the night outside, like warriors going to battle.

By the time Runa had put on her over-dress, Vebiorg and Drífa were halfway down the ladder, and so she clambered on to it and followed them, their excitement having caught in her now so that she was almost trembling with it as she climbed down. At the foot of the ladder she stopped to tie her hair back, downed a wash of ale from an abandoned cup and ran through the hall out into the night.

As eager as she was to see this Prophetess, she could not help but glance over at the smithy, hoping to catch sight of Ingel, hoping that the commotion had woken him from his slumber in the makeshift shelter at the back of the forge. For while the blacksmiths were no strangers to the women's beds, they were forbidden to sleep anywhere else than in their furs with their tools for company and the constant heat from the furnace to keep them warm.

Suddenly Runa was falling, sprawling on to the ground because someone had shoved and tripped her. 'Climb back up to your nest, girl, and use your finger, for that is as close as you will get to a man's breeks snake.' It was Sibbe. She had come out of nowhere and Runa had not been ready. 'You are not one of us and have no right to hear what the Prophetess has learnt on her travels.'

'Leave her be, Sibbe,' Drífa said, coming back through the throng like a salmon swimming against the current and placing herself between Runa and Sibbe.

'Stay out of it, Drífa,' Sibbe spat, pointing at Runa. 'This jarl's brat is not a Freyja Maiden. She should not even be here.' Some of the other Maidens looked back but it was dark and they could not see what was happening and carried on into the tree line.

'That is up to the High Mother to decide,' Drífa countered, shouldering past the woman to help Runa up. Runa had cut her hand open on a stone but she clenched her fist on it because she did not want to give Sibbe the satisfaction.

'If you want to stop me, Sibbe, you had better draw your sword,' Runa said, squaring her shoulders to the woman and hoping Sibbe would not take her up on that challenge because she knew the Freyja Maiden would cut her down. Not least because the only blade Runa had on her was the scramasax she wore on her belt.

Sibbe's hand fell to her sword grip, her eyes boring into Runa's, and even Drífa half drew her own sword because she thought a fight was coming. But then Sibbe curled her lip, turned, and spat onto the ground to show what she thought of Runa.

'Not tonight,' she said. 'I want to hear the Prophetess. And after that I will rut with that man over there. I will ride that young buck until he cannot stand.' She grinned at the thought of that, then turned her back on Runa and Drífa and followed the others into the woods, where the Prophetess was waiting.

'It seems to me your family has a talent for making enemies,' Drífa said as she and Runa walked on.

Runa licked the blood from her cut palm. 'That may be so, Drífa, but believe me when I say that we are not the kind of people you want for enemies.'

Drífa grinned at her and Runa grinned back, the salty iron tang on her tongue, and then they came to where the others were assembled amongst the trees by a moon-flooded clearing. In that clearing, glimpsed now and then through the shifting tide of Freyja Maidens ahead, Runa caught sight of the Prophetess, short and slightly stooped, old certainly, her face cowled and a staff in her hand. The air was thick with seiðr, tainted by the stink of the filthy cat skins in which the silver-washed figure was cocooned, and it was that smell as much as the snatched sight of the woman which chilled Runa's insides like a drink of melted snow. And then the galdr rose on a plume of hot breath, a song-like chanting which silenced every other voice on Fugløy. It grew, this reed-thin crowing, lifting into the cold night, raising the hairs on Runa's arms and the back of her neck.

The witch. It was the witch whom Sigurd had found whilst out hunting wolves in the forest beyond Jarl Hakon Burner's old hall up in Osøyro. Runa had not seen the face beneath that cowl yet but she knew without a shred of doubt that it was the witch. She had lived in Burner's hall with them awhile. Watching. A darker shadow in a dark corner. And then she had gone, which no one had been sorry about.

Not a seiðr-kona now. The Prophetess spun her galdr like a yarn, drawing the listeners in like each new tuft of wool on a spindle, until they were all under her spell. Runa could not say how long they stood there bound by the strange enchantment, but by the time the galdr stopped, cut off suddenly like a shears-cut thread, she was shivering with cold and her feet were numb.

'We thank the Goddess that you are safely returned to us,' Skuld said, stepping forward to take the old woman's hands in her own. 'Let us all go back to the fire and hear your news.'

The Prophetess nodded and at the High Mother's command the Freyja Maidens, released from the spell now, it seemed, made their way back to the main longhouse, gathering by the hearth which was encouraged to roaring leaping life until every face was lit and Runa's feet prickled with welcome warmth.

Skuld the High Mother and the Prophetess talked for a while but being at the back Runa could not hear much of what they said. Yet she heard some of the others talking about her, caught their whispers in the smoke and more than one steely-eyed glance in her direction. It seemed Sibbe was not the only one amongst them who thought she should not be a part of this thing. They were right, she knew with sharp certainty. She was not a Freyja Maiden. She was an intruder. An interloper. Was it not bad enough that she had one enemy on that small island? Staying here to partake in this night, whatever it held in store, would earn her more, and that she did not need. And so she turned to sneak back to her own hall and her own bed, nevertheless hoping that Sibbe did not see her go because she would think it was Runa's fear of her that had driven her away.

But she had only taken three steps when a voice stopped her dead.

'And where are you going, Runa Haraldsdóttir?' Like an arrow in her back, that.

She felt the air move as every head in that longhouse turned towards her, felt all those eyes on her as she stood there suddenly wishing she had snuck away sooner.

'Creeping off like a forest cat when the hunter is around, hey?'

Runa turned round and looked along the channel which the women had opened to give the Prophetess a line of sight to her.

'Were you not going to say hei to your old friend?'

395

Some fish mouths at that, Runa saw, and round eyes too.

'I am not a Freyja Maiden,' she said, unsure how she should address the old crone who was clearly more than she had seemed up in Osøyro. 'This has nothing to do with me.'

'Ha! So you say, do you?' The Prophetess laughed then, a sound not dissimilar to the galdr and which turned Runa's blood cold again. 'It has everything to do with you, girl,' she said, and Runa did not have to look at Skuld to know that the High Mother was watching her the way an eagle watches a vole shivering in the grass.

'Should I stay then?' Runa asked, resisting the temptation to look at Sibbe whose gaze she also felt upon her.

'You could not now walk away if you tried, Runa Haraldsdóttir,' the crone said, pushing back her hood and hissing at one of the Freyja Maidens to pull up a stool so that she could rest her old bones. Then she sat down, shrinking in that ring of women which drew tight around her like a knot because everyone there knew that she had something important to say.

Runa was tempted to test the magic then, to see if she could walk away after all, but as if to prove the witch's seiðr she found herself pushing closer, eking into the gaps which the other women made for her because she was somehow now a part of this night, despite having known nothing about it until Vebiorg and Drífa had woken her. Had hauled her out of that dream she'd been sharing with Grimhild her mother, who waited for her in the afterlife. Almost without knowing how she had got there, she stood in the first ring now, looking into that known and yet unknown face, the stink of those cat skins, and of stale piss too perhaps, getting in her nose.

Her staff laid across her knees, the Prophetess looked up at Runa and nodded, took the cup which Skuld offered her, drank long and deeply, then put the empty cup on the ground and closed her eyes.

After a long while, during which the Freyja Maidens waited in patient silence, Runa thought that the old woman had fallen asleep. Not that Runa blamed her, for she was very old to have been wandering the world, as far north as Osøyro and then back here, and the gods only knew where in between.

But then the Prophetess exhaled a long, sour-smelling breath and began.

'I have walked far on these old feet since I was last here. More steps have I taken out there in the world than there are strands of hair on all of your heads together. I have walked with the wolf and the bear, the boar and the fox. I have soared with the eagle and talked with the gulls and the crows. I have seen the past and I have seen the future.' She shook her head then. 'And let me tell you that I prefer the past.'

Perhaps she was seeing it all now behind those closed eyelids. Who could say?

'The old ways are dying,' she said, her mouth puckering as she considered it. 'It is a slow death, yes, like that from a disease of the flesh. But there is no cure. Not that I have seen.'

She was quiet again, this time for so long that Runa could have easily slipped out to relieve herself as she needed to. She wished she had done when the old woman picked up the thread of it again.

'Our people are forgetting the ways of those who came before. They do not honour the gods as they should. And by not giving the Æsir their due, we weaken them. Do not the prize bull's ribs begin to show if he does not get good pasture?' Her dry lips pulled back from what few teeth she still had. 'There is a new god,' she said, as though the words were rancid. 'The White God. And his seiðr spreads like the roots of a great tree, a tree that will one day put Yggdrasil itself in the shade.'

Some of the Maidens shook their heads or mumbled that this could not be so. Skuld herself looked unsure, as though she suspected the Prophetess of having made some mistake.

'Shaking your heads will not change it,' the Prophetess told them. 'Just as the bear who lumbers off to his cave to sleep the winter away does not stop the winter coming. Nor does the fish who swims deep to stay warm stop the lake from freezing. This god already rules in distant lands where the old gods are long forgotten.' She extended an arm which looked like the branch of a silver birch. 'But now he reaches into the north. Even our King Thorir has dealings with this god's priests. He feasts them, shares his hall with them.'

'King Thorir would not turn his back on the Goddess,' Skuld said, shaking her head, making a stand on that point.

'No, he will not,' the Prophetess said, opening her eyes to look at Skuld. 'But many will. Not in your lifetimes perhaps, not here where the old gods still hold sway.'

'Then what has this to do with us?' the High Mother asked on behalf of them all. She looked like a goddess herself standing there amongst them, all bearing and beauty and fiery red hair.

'The time of kings and jarls is ending,' the old woman said. 'There will come a day when one king will rule everything beneath the sky as far in every direction as a raven can fly. And he will not support the Freyja Maidens. He will bend his knee to the White God.' She shook her head. 'All across the north, few kings and one god. That is what I have seen.'

'Are you talking about Ragnarök, Wise Mother?' Vebiorg asked, the first of the other Freyja Maidens to dare to speak directly to the old woman.

The old woman looked at her. 'Perhaps it is Ragnarök. Perhaps it is something else. But yes, the doom of the gods is coming.' She closed her eyes again, her claw-like hands white upon the staff across her legs. 'We and many before us have lived on this island, beyond the sight of men, our days given to prepare for when we might serve Freyja the Giver in the time of her greatest need. But I tell you now that we will be the last.'

A murmuring hum rose from the women then, and it was clear that this news was more terrifying than a failed harvest, or when a village hears that a ship full of her men has turned over in some wind-driven fjord.

'Quiet!' Skuld said, looking back to the Prophetess who had not finished yet.

'Even though all I have said is true, for I have seen it while you have been hiding from the world, the old gods are not without power,' the old woman said, opening her eyes and grinning. 'There are still those men . . . and women, whom the gods love. The way they used to love the kings and heroes in former times. There are still those in whose lives Óðin, Þór, Loki and Freyja like to meddle.' She moved a hand out before her, some invisible thing gripped between her thumb and forefinger. 'Making a move here and there as though these beloved mortals are pieces on a tafl board,' she said, then rested her hands on her staff again. 'One such woman is amongst us here this night.'

All eyes turned to Skuld now, but the High Mother had followed the Prophetess's eyes and those rested not on the Freyja Maiden but on Runa.

'Runa Haraldsdóttir and her brother are threads in the hem of the kyrtill of all this which I have spoken of.' She twisted her scrawny neck, her gaze raking over every pair of eyes in that place. 'But your time, my fierce children, is ending.' She nodded at Skuld, who looked defiant, as though she did not accept any of it. 'Yes, High Mother, rage against it. Why not? The Storm is coming,' the Prophetess said, 'when the Allfather and Freyja and all their great war host will ride because they have been summoned. And the wind from their passing will raise a tide of blood.'

The old woman bent and lifted the cup and one of the Freyja Maidens filled it from a jug. When the Prophetess had drained that cup she stood, planting her staff in the rushes.

'What are you telling us to do, Wise Mother?' Skuld asked.

'I am telling you what I have seen. Now you must decide what will become of us.'

'We will live as we have always lived,' Skuld said. 'What else is there?'

'Why not ask young Runa what she would do?' the Prophetess said, grinning at Runa.

'She is not one of us and does not have a say in it,' Sibbe put in and some of the others let it be known that they shared Sibbe's feelings about that. And nor did Runa want a say in it. What did she know about such things?

But Skuld looked at her and lifted her chin, a small gesture yet enough to make it clear that Runa was supposed to speak.

'I know a warrior woman,' Runa said, suddenly knowing how Sigurd must feel when he was giving the commands and acting the lord in front of seasoned warriors and full-beards who would have every right to doubt him. 'She is called Valgerd and her grandmother Ingun was a Freyja Maiden living here on this island.' A couple of the older Maidens looked at each other then. Perhaps they had been girls here in Ingun's time. And it struck Runa that the Prophetess might have been the one who had let Ingun leave the island with her lover, the champion who would become Valgerd's grandfather. If so, had she known who Valgerd was when she had stayed with them in Burner's hall?

'Valgerd lives in the world of men and she is respected wherever she goes because she is a great warrior. I have seen her fight in the shieldwall. I have seen men fall beneath her blade and I have seen them struck down by her arrows. She does not hide away. She is proud and brave, and you cannot tell me that the Goddess will not take her to Sessrymnir at the end of her days.' Some of the women looked excited, some looked confused. Most looked angry and Runa almost felt sick at the thought of the sword- and spear-training next day, for there were plenty of them in that longhouse who would repay her words with bruises.

'Our life is here,' Sibbe said. 'We are sworn to it, just as men swear to their jarls and kings.'

'More so!' another woman said. 'For an oath sworn to the Goddess is a heavier thing than one sworn to a man.'

There were murmurs of agreement with that.

'That may be so,' Runa said, 'but if what the Wise Mother says is true then perhaps you can serve the Goddess better out there in the world than you can here on this island. You can prove yourselves truly worthy of Sessrymnir.' She did not say that fighting real enemies was more proof of skill and courage than fighting practice bouts with wooden swords, but she did not need to, and Sibbe spat some or other insult in her direction though the words were lost amongst the rising hum as the Freyja Maidens began to argue amongst themselves. Some were hooked on this idea of leaving Fugløy and seeing something of the world beyond, as Valgerd's grandmother Ingun had done years before. Others claimed they did not have the right to abandon the way of life which had existed since the time of the Yngling kings. They would not be the ones to destroy it all, like a beautiful old mead hall burnt to ashes in one night's raiding. Still others could not believe what this night had dredged up, that there was even talk of leaving the island.

Drífa's eyes were alight though. She had lived on Fugløy her whole life and for her this new idea of going into the world shone like hacksilver in the scales.

'It cannot be just by chance that Runa has come amongst us,' she said. 'You all heard the Wise Mother.' She was looking from her companions to Runa, bringing all eyes with her. 'If Runa is beloved of the Goddess, then could it be that Freyja Giver *gave* her to us? Placed her amongst us for a reason? Perhaps to show us that we can better serve her out there like Runa's friend, this Valgerd.'

The Prophetess was silent now. She had delivered her message and seemed content to let Skuld and the others decide their futures. If there was even a choice where wyrd was concerned.

'Enough,' Skuld said, stilling every tongue. 'The Wise Mother has travelled far and needs her rest. All of you back to your beds. I will seek an answer from the Goddess. Then we will know what we must do.'

The women seemed content with that and began to leave the longhouse, more than a few of them looking at Runa with different eyes now.

'How will the High Mother learn Freyja's will?' Runa asked Vebiorg as they walked out into the night. Vebiorg had seemed less than sure about leaving the island, though Runa knew she would follow where Skuld led.

'She will go under the cloak,' Vebiorg said.

Runa had seen Asgot practise utiseta once, or sitting out as he had called it, for it involved sitting undisturbed in a wild place and then journeying either inwards to the very depths of self, or outwards to other worlds, perhaps even that of the Æsir.

When he had done it, Asgot had gone two days without food or water, until at last the answer to his question had come, though Runa could not for the life of her remember the question or the answer. What were the ways of the godi to a little girl? *Now look at me,* she thought, considering again how she had never imagined that she would see the seiðr-kona again. And yet, here she was talking of the gods and of Runa and her brother in the same breath.

'Look, there is Sibbe,' Drífa said, catching up with them. 'She meant what she said, then.' Runa looked over to the smithy and saw Sibbe standing there talking to Ingel, who looked half asleep, his face cast in shadow by the glow of the furnace behind.

'She cannot get enough, that one,' Vebiorg said as Runa strode across the dewy ground towards that fire glow. Towards Sibbe.

The Freyja Maiden heard her, or sensed her perhaps, and turned, her hand falling to the hilt of the sword at her hip even as Runa's fell to the handle of her scramasax.

'I do not care what the Wise Mother says about you—' Sibbe began, pulling the sword, but she said no more because Runa reversed the long knife and hammered its hilt into Sibbe's head beside her eye and the woman dropped like a stone, her mouth still full of words.

Ingel's own jaw dropped and if he had been half asleep before, he was awake now.

Runa looked down to see Vebiorg who had run over and was crouched over Sibbe.

'She's alive,' Vebiorg said, looking up into Runa's eyes, though Sibbe did not look alive.

Runa took Ingel's hand, felt his fingers curl round her own.

'You coming?' she asked.

The young man nodded. And together they walked off across the clearing, and Runa wondered how she would climb the loft ladder with her legs shaking so.

CHAPTER FIFTEEN

IN THE MORNING AFTER THEY HAD WON THE BORG, THEY gathered up the dead. Those of Alrik's men who had been killed, of which there were twenty-three, were to be buried side by side and with spears in a stone ship with a mound raised over them. Alrik promised to raise a rune stone in their memory too, which if he did was doing them a great honour.

'That's the least the lad deserves,' Solmund had said when Sigurd himself had gone to recover young Kveld Ottarsson's body from the slope below the borg where it had lain since Alrik had cut the lad down.

'He gave himself a good end,' Bram said, looking at the slashed corpse.

'A good end? The lad hadn't even lived yet,' Olaf said, shaking his head.

'The ruse would most likely have failed without him. If he had not gone for Alrik like that,' Sigurd said, keeping his neck stiff so as not to pull the stitches and reopen the wound. His slashed forearms hurt too, but there was no puffiness, no sign of the wound rot that took men to their graves in boiling, sweat-soaked agony.

To maintain their pretence of being Guthrum's men, Kveld had attacked Alrik's shieldwall knowing that the warlord would have no choice but to cut him down. It had been one of the bravest things Sigurd had ever seen, and from a young man in his first fight. 'If anyone won Alrik this borg and all the iron in it, it was Kveld,' he said.

Perhaps that stretched it a little, for there had still been plenty of killing to be done, but no one disagreed with him then, with Kveld lying there looking up at the sky. They made sure he had a sword with him in the grave, which was no small thing given that there were plenty of living breathing warriors in Alrik's host who did not own one themselves. Guthrum's dead they flung into three large pits to the north of the borg. No burial mound or standing stone for them, just the cold earth and the worms in it.

Despite their capture of the fort, the mood amongst Alrik's men was gloomy. This was not helped by a thick fog which smothered the new day and had men muttering that it was the ghosts of the dead wandering amongst the living. Men whispered that Guthrum's slain warriors could not accept that they had fallen for that trick. They would not rest or pass on to the afterlife knowing that they had been undone by such Loki cunning.

'You would think they had lost the fight,' Bram said, nodding at a knot of Alrik's warriors who were arguing over which of them was going to have to pick a severed head out of the stew of mud and brains it was resting in. 'Miserable, squeamish buggers.'

'They're tired, Bram. Like us,' Olaf said, for even amongst Sigurd's crew the mood was lower than it might have been. Bones and muscles ached from the fighting. Skulls were splitting from all the ale they had drunk the night before and which also made their stomachs queasy, a thing not helped by the stench of open bowels, blood, piss and filth which hung in the fog.

The stiff corpses were piled one upon another so that Sigurd asked Asgot how the Valkyries would know who was who, if those death maidens had not already chosen the best of them for Valhöll in the night. For Guthrum's men had fought bravely and surely Óðin and Freyja would welcome many of them, whatever the truth about ghosts wandering in the dawn.

'These warriors won't have been judged on yesterday's fight alone,' Asgot told Sigurd, 'but on every fight they have been in. The Spear-God will have been watching with his one eye those men who were born to the sword-song. The choosers of the slain have taken their fill, you can be sure. But they will return soon enough.'

'Your runes told you that?' Sigurd asked, recalling the godi casting them the night before.

Asgot tugged at one of the little bones knotted into his beard. 'Óðin watches you, Sigurd,' he said. 'But you drew Loki's eye too with that trick of yours yesterday. And now the Trickster cannot resist the temptation to play his part in all this. Let us keep our heads down for a little while.'

Sigurd looked at Olaf, who arched his brows. 'That's not like you, Asgot,' Olaf said. 'Did some sod drop a rock on your head? What happened to Sigurd having to keep the Allfather's attention now that he has it? Which means risking our lives a little too often as far as I'm concerned.'

Asgot curled his lip. He did not like the accusation that he was retreading his own path backwards on this matter. 'I am just saying that Loki has come aboard and when he is around things are not as simple as just slaughtering your enemies.'

'Well, Loki can piss off,' Olaf said, which had some of them touching their Thór's hammers to ward off ill-luck.

'Uncle,' Svein said, pointing to a group of men who were coming out of one of the other longhouses, each of them carrying a bar or two of iron. 'Isn't that the man you recognized yesterday?' Alrik had ordered every scrap of iron and silver to be brought to him so that he might know how rich he was and reward his warriors accordingly.

'Aye, that's him,' Olaf confirmed. 'Something about him, and I don't mean those beard ropes of his which no doubt he thinks the women get wet between the thighs for.'

'Come to think of it, I have seen him before too,' Hagal said, scratching his chin.

'You!' Olaf called out to the man, who stopped and turned towards them.

'Me?' he said.

Olaf nodded and beckoned him over, and the man shrugged, telling his companions that he would be back to work as soon as he had seen what Olaf had to say.

'I know you,' Olaf said. 'What's your name?'

The man hesitated. 'Kjartan Auðunarson,' he said.

Olaf shook his head. The name meant nothing to him and he turned to Sigurd. 'You still don't recognize him then?'

Sigurd did not and said as much.

'But I have seen you before, too,' Hagal said. 'And I do not forget a face.'

'Who are you?' the man asked him.

'Hagal, but they call me Crow-Song for I am a skald,' he said, 'and before I joined this crew I travelled all over.' He shrugged. 'I see a lot of faces. Still, I remember yours from somewhere,' he said, frowning.

'Well, I do not know you,' Kjartan told him, an iron bar cradled in his arms. 'Nor any of you,' he said

411

to Olaf and the rest, 'apart from by the reputation you are making for yourselves. That was bravely done yesterday.' He grinned. 'I would like to have been with you when you came through those gates and they realized they had let the wolves into the fold. It is just a pity that the worm Guthrum was not here himself. His face would have been something worth seeing.'

'His face will be worth seeing when he gets here and learns that this borg is no longer his and that half his army is buried in the earth,' Olaf said.

That gave Sigurd an idea. 'Thorbiorn, fetch the banner we made.' Thorbiorn nodded and went to get it.

'I have work to do,' Kjartan said and Olaf nodded as the man turned and walked off with the iron bar.

Olaf turned to Sigurd. 'I know what you're thinking,' he said, grinning.

'Want to share?' Svein asked, but it was Moldof who explained it.

'If Guthrum sees his banner flying above us, he might think his men still hold the place,' the one-armed warrior said.

Sigurd grinned. 'Worth a try,' he said.

They went to find Alrik, who agreed that Sigurd's idea was a good one. 'Though Guthrum is no fool, nor reckless like Findar was,' he said, glancing at Knut, who agreed with that. 'He did not rise so high so fast by not thinking a thing through. Look at this place. Guthrum is a man who does not put to sea until he knows that the wind is whispering his name and his strakes are tighter than a cat's arsehole.' He smiled then, smoothing his long moustaches with ringed fingers. 'Still, Byrnjolf, I am beginning to think the Allfather himself sent you to me.'

'I brought him, lord. Remember?' Knut said. 'So I will take some credit.'

Alrik laughed, raising a hand by way of admission. 'You did, Knut, you did. And I am grateful for it.'

'And are you grateful to us?' Sigurd asked him. 'You said you would make us rich men if we took this fort.' He fixed Alrik with a heavy stare. The dead lay in their stone ship in the newly raised mound. The fort was now Alrik's. It was time to remind the warlord what he had promised. It was time to pay Sigurd what he owed.

Alrik nodded. 'I did and I will,' he said, glancing from Olaf to Sigurd. 'No one can say I am a man who makes empty promises. Or empty threats,' he added, lifting an eyebrow. 'I will have your reward brought to your longhouse tonight, Byrnjolf. But first I must prepare the defences and make sure we are ready to receive Jarl Guthrum should he show up unannounced. I am also a man who knows how to treat my guests,' he said, spitting into the mud.

'Another thing, Alrik,' Sigurd said before the dróttin turned away. 'I have heard you are raising a runestone to your dead.'

Alrik nodded. 'They fought well and should be honoured. One of my men, Soti, whom we call Chisel, is skilled at that sort of thing.'

'Soti could carve runes on water,' Knut said.

Sigurd nodded. 'I would like it if the stone made mention of Kveld Ottarsson,' he said.

Alrik frowned and looked at Knut, who shrugged and gave a slight shake of his head.

'He was the young man you slaughtered on the hill when you led your men to the borg,' Sigurd said. 'He fell and he knew he must die or else Guthrum's men would see through our plan.'

'Ah yes,' Alrik said, remembering. 'Lad came at me like a berserker. I had no choice.' He laughed. 'He could have made himself a reputation if he'd cut me down.'

'He had never been in a real fight before,' Olaf said, 'but the boy had all the bravery in him you could want.'

Alrik considered this and after a long moment he nodded. 'I will have Soti put the lad's name on the stone,' he said.

Sigurd nodded, thinking of the young man who had been about his own age and who now lay in a pit in the ground, a decent sword by his side. Perhaps Sigurd would see him in Óðin's hall one day and if so he would thank Kveld for his courage and they would drink the Allfather's mead together and laugh.

Then Alrik and Knut were off giving commands and telling the men which of them would take that night's watch from the ramparts, and Sigurd and Olaf carried the banner they had made to fool Guthrum's men up the bank to fix it to the palisade beside the gates, in the hope that they might fool Guthrum himself when he came.

It was Hagal who remembered where he had seen Kjartan Auðunarson before.

'Örn-garð!' he blurted, crouched by the hearthfire which he was attempting to poke and prod into life with an iron because the logs were damp. 'The Eagle's Dwelling-place,' he said. Several heads came up at that, brows furrowed at the mention of Jarl Randver's hall back in Hinderå, which now of course belonged to his son Jarl Hrani.

'What of it,' Sigurd asked.

'That is where I've seen his face,' Hagal said, using the iron tool to roll a hissing log into what flame there was. 'That is where I've seen that man with the long moustaches, Kjartan Auðunarson.'

Sigurd glanced at Olaf, whose face looked like a thunder cloud.

'Are you sure, Crow-Song?' Sigurd asked the skald. There were other men in the longhouse but they were busy with tasks, sharpening blades and repairing gear, drinking and talking amongst themselves.

'Of course he's not sure,' Svein muttered.

Hagal nodded. 'I am certain of it,' he said, as a shower of bright sparks burst from one of the logs, making him start.

'When have you ever been certain of anything—' Aslak began.

'He's right,' Olaf put in, before any of the others could agree that Hagal was usually too blind drunk after one horn of mead to know his own name, let alone remember one man amongst a hall full. 'I have seen him at Hinderå. As have many of you, though you have forgotten it now. He was one of Jarl Randver's hearthmen. I remember him. He was one of those who helped Randver's other son, Amleth, away from the fight after Floki had cut him.'

'Then what in Óðin's arse is he doing here?' Bram asked, and Olaf gestured at him to keep his voice down.

There was a moment's silence but for the pop and spit of the damp logs while they thought about this, then Solmund said, 'Same as us, I suppose. Trying to earn himself some silver. He was Randver's hirðman you say? Then perhaps he did not want to fight for Hrani after Sigurd sent Randver's corpse to the bottom of the fjord.' He bit into a lump of hard cheese. 'I'll wager he ended up in Birka and was looking to make his fortune when Knut sniffed him out, same as he did us.'

No one could think of a better reason for Kjartan Auðunarson, if that was his real name, having left

Hinderå and come east into the lands of the Svear. The last of the other men who shared the longhouse were picking up their spears and shields now, off to take their turn on watch.

'Why he is here doesn't matter a spit,' Olaf said. 'What matters is that if we recognize him, there is no possibility that he does not recognize us.'

'No one can say we did not make an impression at that wedding celebration,' Svein said with a grin. For Hrani had taken Runa in a raid on Sigurd's village and had been part of Jarl Randver's scheme to marry her to Amleth his second son. He hoped this would help legitimize his family's claim to Jarl Harald's lands and smooth over the waters after his and King Gorm's betrayal of the Skudeneshavn folk. But the marriage had never taken place. Because Sigurd and his war band had gone to Hinderå and Sigurd had even sat in Jarl Randver's high seat, waiting for him to return. In the fight that followed, he had killed the jarl himself, but he had lost too many good men that day.

'Men say that the gods themselves fought beside you,' Moldof said. 'That is what they told King Gorm. I was there. I heard it.'

'And did he believe them?' Sigurd asked.

Moldof lifted the stump of his wolf-jointed arm. 'He said you are Óðin-touched.' He drank deeply, then lifted the jug from the stool beside him to refill his cup.

'If the gods fought beside us I did not see them,' Olaf said, remembering that bloody day and all

417

those brave men who had fallen. Then he looked at Sigurd. 'So what are we going to do about this Kjartan? What is to stop him going back to Hrani Randversson, or even King Gorm, and telling them where we are?'

'For all that Alrik is happy enough to share his mead with us, I cannot see him fighting Hrani or the oath-breaker for our sakes,' Asgot said. 'Not when one of them offers him a boatload of silver for our heads.'

'We will kill Kjartan,' Sigurd said. All eyes were on him and there were some nods. He had said it in a low voice, barely louder than the hiss of the wet logs in the hearth, and yet no one needed him to say the words again.

Olaf agreed. 'It is the only way to be sure,' he said. 'We'll do it tonight.'

'How?' Bram asked. 'We can't just go up to the man's bench and spear him when he's asleep.' Svein pursed his lips as if he didn't really see why not.

'Let me think about it,' Sigurd said. But he did not get much opportunity for thinking about how to bring about Kjartan's death, because just then the longhouse door opened, all but killing what feeble flames licked the damp hearth wood. Two of Alrik's warriors came in hefting a sea chest carved with ravens and eagles.

'Looks heavy,' Solmund told the men, who were huffing and puffing with the thing, not that either of them owned a pair of shoulders worth a mention.

With a grimace and a groan they put the chest on the ground before Sigurd.

'That's because it's full of silver,' one of the men replied to Solmund now that he had the breath to speak. He straightened, palming sweat off his forehead.

'Iron too,' said the other man.

And they were not wrong about that. The intake of breath amongst the others as Sigurd lifted the lid of that chest would have drawn the hearth flames had there been any.

'That is what I call keeping your word,' Olaf said, slapping Sigurd on his back.

'Aye, I am beginning to like this Alrik,' Bram added.

There were arm rings, whole ones like those many of Sigurd's crew already wore. There were small pieces of them too, hacksilver, and finger rings, sword and scabbard fittings, Thór's hammers, brooches, lengths of fine wire and solid ingots, all gleaming in the lamp-lit dark. Much of it had no doubt belonged to the men of the borg only days before, but now it belonged to Sigurd. Beneath the silver they found two roughly worked iron bars, which were themselves worth a fortune, as well as eight iron axe-head blanks, which could either be finished off by a half-decent smith or else used to trade with. There was a little gold in there too, just three finger-sized ingots wrapped in a cloth.

'I have never seen the like of it,' Bjarni said.

Neither had Sigurd. 'Fetch the scales,' he told Solmund, who went to dig them out of his own sea chest. 'Everyone gets a share,' he said, 'but the rest we will keep safe, for we will need it before we fight Hrani Randversson or King Gorm.' They seemed happy enough with that, as Solmund weighed out each portion against one of the heavier arm rings, and Bram said that the only thing wrong with silver was that you could not drink it. But when Thorbiorn Thorirsson came up last to get his share, Sigurd shook his head and closed the lid of the chest. 'Not you, Thorbiorn.' He gestured at Bram and Svein and the others. 'The rest of them have fought hard time and again and earned this silver and more besides. You do not get a share for waving a banner around in one little skirmish.'

Thorbiorn scowled like a boy who has had his backside whipped with a hazel switch. 'To be the merkismaðr is supposed to be an honour,' he said. 'Besides, how could I fight when I was busy holding that damn thing?'

'Had it been my banner it would have been an honour,' Sigurd said, 'but it was not.' He looked at Olaf, trying not to smile. 'I do not even have a banner, do I, Uncle?'

Olaf scratched his beard and frowned. 'No,' he said. 'There hasn't really seemed much point up to now, what with you not having a whole crew let alone a war host to worry anybody.'

Sigurd nodded and looked back at Thorbiorn. 'I will not deny you did a good job with Guthrum's axe banner,' he said, and shrugged. 'Perhaps you can ask to be his merkismaðr when he shows up.'

There were grins around the place but Thorbiorn did not like it. Not at all. He glowered like a spoilt child, which was fine by Sigurd.

'What would you do with it anyway, lad?' Olaf asked him, putting his own pieces of hacksilver in the purse at his waist. 'We have all the ale we could want and there are no women here to spend it on, unless Alrik has hidden them somewhere.'

But Thorbiorn was already skulking off with his wounded pride, whilst Bjorn and Bjarni, Hagal and Svein were discussing what they intended to do with their share.

'I would like a new smiting axe with silver and gold inlays,' Svein said. 'It will be so beautiful that women will be jealous of it. It will be such a fine axe that my enemies will enjoy being killed by it.' This raised some laughter, then Svein looked at Hagal. 'What about you, Crow-Song?'

Hagal did not have to think about it for more than a couple of heartbeats. 'One day I will own a handsome snekke,' he said, holding his arms out in front of him as though he could already see the ship riding Rán's white-haired daughters. 'I will buy the thralls to sail her and visit all the jarls and kings—' He stopped, frowning at Olaf and Sigurd.

'All those we have not killed by then,' he corrected, 'and they will pay me to weave their fame in story and song.'

'Ha! When was the last time any of us heard you come up with a story that we have not fallen asleep to twenty times before?' Olaf said.

'You see, it is talk like that which will make the Olaf of this tale I am currently spinning a spiteful, dwarf-like man with the manners of a troll,' Crow-Song said, getting a grin from Sigurd, 'and a shrivelled slug for a—'

'Careful, skald!' Olaf said, then pointed a finger at him that had a new silver ring on it. 'Well, let us see how good you are at telling your tales when you are being strangled with your own tongue,' he said, though he was half grinning when he threatened it. For they were still enjoying bathing in the silver glow and acting as if they had been up to the gills in mead all day. As for Sigurd, he fancied using a little of that gold to have a few rings made which he could rivet on to his brynja here and there. That hersir Asvith Kleggi at Birka had owned such mail and Sigurd had liked the look of it very much. Though he knew in truth he would save the gold and put it to better use. For he was rich now, rich as a jarl, which meant he could buy men and spears. He could begin to build a war host of his own. He could start to think about the day when he would sail back to Norway to challenge the oath-breaker king and have his revenge.

He leant back on his bench and closed his eyes, enjoying the insults and the chaffing and the boasts that were flying around the place. That would be a golden day, he thought, when he sailed back up the Karmsund Strait. When he had an army and a banner of his own. He smiled at the thought and opened his eyes to the reality. To the half crew before him. And yet Óðin himself could not have better than they in the centre of his shieldwall come Ragnarök. They were wolves, every one of them, and Sigurd was proud of them. Ha! He was in love with one of them, he thought, looking at Valgerd who had taken over the fire duty from Crow-Song and was at last getting some flame out of those wet logs.

But for now those wolves were dazzled by the lustre of that silver hoard, so that it was not until deep into the night that Valgerd sat up and said that they had forgotten about Jarl Randver's man Kjartan Auðunarson.

'It will have to wait till the morning now,' Olaf mumbled from his nest of furs, and the others agreed.

But in the morning, when they spread out through the borg looking for the Hinderå man, there was no sign of him. Nor could any of Alrik's other men say where he was.

Kjartan Auðunarson had gone.

CHAPTER SIXTEEN

'AND YOU ARE SURE IT IS HIM?' HRANI ASKED, LEANING over the cauldron to get a nose full of the steaming contents. Carrots and parsnips. Turnips, onions, hare and squirrel. Kjartan was eyeing the broth like one who has not eaten a proper meal for days. The man had too much pride to say he was hungry, or to expect the jarl's hospitality given how things stood.

'It's him, lord,' Kjartan said.

Not that Hrani was Kjartan's jarl, since Kjartan, who had been Jarl Randver's man, had left Hinderå at the end of last summer to seek his fortune to the east in Svealand.

'Tell me again why you left, Kjartan Auðunarson,' Jarl Hrani said.

Kjartan tore his eyes from the broth and fixed them on Hrani. 'My lad died in the ship battle against Jarl Harald,' he said. 'His mother . . . well, she wouldn't speak to me after that. Blamed me. Said I should've kept the lad safe. But what does a woman know of it?' His long drooping moustaches quivered, the only sign of the rage within. 'What does she know of the blood chaos? When it is raining spears and arrows. When axes are everywhere, cutting flesh the way lightning tears the night sky.'

Hrani gave no answer.

Kjartan shrugged. 'Gerutha would have nothing to do with me after that. I packed my sea chest and left.'

Still no apology from the man. Hrani sniffed the broth again, wondering if the good news which Kjartan had brought him made up for the offence he had given by leaving in the first place. A hirðman who knew Kjartan well had told Hrani that Kjartan had not wanted to swear the oath to him simply because he was Randver's son, that Hrani would first have to prove himself worthy of the jarl torc. The turd.

Prove myself to this flighty prick? Hrani thought now, slurping the hot liquid from a spoon. 'Salt,' he said to the woman who was standing nearby waiting for the jarl's verdict. 'More salt and it will be ready.' This got some enthusiastic rumbles from those of his hearthmen who were gathering in Örn-garð for food and ale, skald song and women. The door thumped open again and a gust licked into the hall far enough to get the hearth flames flapping like a loose sail. More men came in, rubbing their hands and skinning themselves of their furs and hats, the low hum of their voices filling the place.

'But now you are back again,' Hrani said, staring at Kjartan, 'like a fox sneaking back to its den.'

'Hardly sneaking, lord,' Kjartan said, gesturing to the spot upon which he was standing. 'I have travelled far to tell you what I know, when I could have stayed in Svealand earning silver for my sword-work.'

'Still, you think you will make more silver because you can tell me where to find Haraldarson and his flea-bitten pack,' Hrani said.

Kjartan said nothing, and nothing was not a denial.

'Lord, it is possible that someone else will kill them before you get the chance. They are stuck in that borg and this Jarl Guthrum will have his whole war host, what's left of it, surrounding the place by now.'

'And Alrik, what sort of a man is he?'

'He can fight. But he's too careful.'

'Well, that could be a good thing for us,' Hrani said to himself. Gods help this Alrik to hold that borg until he could get there, wherever *there* was. For Hrani wanted Sigurd dead but by his own sword, not some Svearman's as Jarl Guthrum's men flooded into the fort in a wave of steel and butchery.

'I'll take you to him, lord,' Kjartan said. 'Now if you want.'

He would as well, Hrani thought, with the cold still in his fingers, the filth of the journey on his clothes and the hunger griping in his belly.

'You will swear to me first,' Hrani said. A statement and question both. Truth be told he knew there were still other men who needed convincing about his right to wear the silver ring at his neck.

'I'll swear,' Kjartan said with a nod.

'Eat then, Kjartan Auðunarson. You are welcome in my hall,' Hrani said, proving that he was a generous man.

Kjartan nodded again and walked off to find a bench to sit at, and Hrani watched him go. Watched him sit and demand ale from a thrall, huffing warm air into his cupped hands. And Hrani happened to recall that Kjartan was sitting in the place he had favoured when he had served Hrani's father.

Let them eat well and drink well, he thought, and tomorrow we will load *War-Rider* with all that we will need for a long sailing.

The ship itself was ready, for he always kept her scrubbed and coated in resin and painted, even in winter when other jarls had their ships hauled up in their nausts waiting for spring. Perhaps some of the strakes could use some new caulking. And the ballast would need reorganizing once the cargo sank her a little deeper in the water. But he'd had the women make him a new sail with leather and hide criss-crossing the wool to help it keep its shape, and this sail sat neatly rolled by the wall behind his high seat, ready to be carried down to the wharf. He had enough wind-dried cod to last till Ragnarök, enough ale to put Thór himself under the table drunk, plenty of good rope, and at least half the oars were almost new, still pale and spruce-scented. So it would not take long. He would pack his ship with his best men, his hearthmen. His Sword-Norse. They would raise the new sail, which would stink of the tallow which was its proof against sea spray and rain. And they would go to Svealand to kill Sigurd Haraldarson and his friends.

GLOSSARY OF NORSE TERMS

the Alder Man: a spirit or elf of the forest

Asgard: home of the gods

aurar: ounces, usually of silver (singular: eyrir)

berserker: 'bare-shirt', or perhaps 'bear-shirt', a fierce warrior prone to a battle frenzy

bietas: a long pole used to stretch the weather leech when the ship is working to windward

Bifröst: the rainbow-bridge connecting the worlds of gods and men

Bilskírnir: 'Lightning-crack', Thór's hall

blood-eagle: a method of torture and execution, perhaps as a rite of human sacrifice to Óðin

bóndi: 'head of the household', taken to mean a farmer or land owner

brynja: a coat of mail (plural: brynjur)

bukkehorn: a musical instrument made from the horn of a ram or goat

draugr: the animated corpse that comes forth from its grave mound

dróttin: the leader of a war band

færing: literally meaning 'four-oaring'. A small open boat with two pairs of oars and sometimes also a sail.

Fáfnir: 'Embracer', a dragon that guards a great treasure hoard

Fenrir Wolf: the mighty wolf that will be freed at Ragnarök and swallow Óðin

Fimbulvetr: 'Terrible Winter', heralding the beginning of Ragnarök

forskarlar: the waterfall spirits

galdr: a chant or spell, usually recited rather than sung

Garm: the greatest of dogs, who will howl at the final cataclysm of Ragnarök

Gjallarhorn: the horn which Heimdall sounds to mark the beginning of Ragnarök

Gleipnir: the fetter which binds the wolf Fenrir

godi: an office denoting social and sacral prominence; a chieftain and/or priest

Gungnir: the mighty rune-carved spear owned by Óðin

hacksilver: the cut-up pieces of silver coins, arm rings, and jewellery

Hangaguð: the Hanged God. A name for Óðin.

haugbui: a living corpse. A mound dweller, the dead body living on within its tomb.

haugr: a burial mound

Haust Blót: autumn sacrifice

hei: 'hello'

Helheim: a place far to the north where the evil dead dwell

hersir: a warlord who owes allegiance to a jarl or king

Hildisvíni: the 'battle boar' on which Freyja rides

hirðmen: the retinue of warriors that follow a king, jarl or chieftain

hólmgang: a duel to settle disputes

hrafnasueltir: raven-starver (coward)

Hugin and Munin: 'Thought' and 'Memory', Óðin's ravens

huglausi: a coward

húskarlar: household warriors

jarl: title of the most prominent men below the kings

Jól feast: winter solstice festival

Jörmungand/Midgard Serpent: the serpent that encircles the world grasping its own tail. When it lets go the world will end.

Jötunheim: (giant-home) the realm of the giants

karl: a freeman; a landowner

karvi: a ship usually equipped with 13 to 16 pairs of oars

kaupang: marketplace

knörr: a cargo ship; wider, deeper and shorter than a longship

kyrtill: a long tunic or gown

lendermen: managers of the king's estates. Nobles.

merkismaðr: standard-bearer in a war band

meyla: a little girl

Midgard: the place where men live (the world)

Mímir's Well: the well of wisdom at which Óðin sacrificed an eye in return for a drink

Mjöllnir: the magic hammer of Thór

mormor: mother's mother

mundr: bride-price

naust: a boathouse, usually with one side against the sea and a ramp down to the water

nestbaggin: knapsack

Nídhögg: the serpent that gnaws at the root of Yggdrasil

Niflheim: the cold, dark, misty world of the dead, ruled by the goddess Hel

nithing: a wretch; a coward; a person without honour

Norns – Urd, Verdandi and Skuld: the three spinners who determine the fates of men

Ragnarök: doom of the gods

Ratatosk: the squirrel that conveys messages between the eagle at the top of Yggdrasil and Nídhögg at its roots

rauði: bog iron ore, related to rauðr meaning red

rôst: the distance travelled between two rest-stops, about a mile

Sæhrímnir: a boar that is cooked and consumed every night in Valhöll

scían: an Irish fighting long knife

scramasax: a large knife with a single-edged blade

seiðr: sorcery, magic, often associated with Óðin or Freyja

seiðr-kona: a seiðr-wife. A practitioner of witchcraft.
Sessrymnir: the dwelling place of the goddess Freyja
skál: 'cheers!'
skald: a poet, often in the service of jarls or kings
Skíthblathnir: the magical ship of the god Frey
skjaldborg: shieldwall
skyr: a cultured dairy product with the consistency of strained yogurt
Sleipnir: the eight-legged grey horse of Óðin
snekke: a small longship used in warfare comprising at least twenty rowing benches
svinfylkja: 'swine-array', a wedge-shaped battle formation
tafl: a strategy board game played on a chequered or latticed board
taufr: witchcraft
thegn: retainer; a member of a king or jarl's retinue
thrall: a serf or unfree servant
ting: assembly/meeting place where disputes are solved and political decisions made
utiseta: sitting out for wisdom. An ancient practice of divining knowledge
Valhöll: Óðin's hall of the slain
Valknuter: a symbol comprising three entwined triangles representative of the afterlife and Oðin
Valkyries: choosers of the slain
Varðlokur: the repetitive, rhythmic, soothing chant to induce a trance-like state
völva: a shamanic seeress; a practitioner of magic divination and prophecy

wergild: 'man-price', the amount of compensation paid by a person committing an offence to the injured party or, in case of death, to his family

wyrd: fate or personal destiny

Yggdrasil: the tree of life

THE NORSE GODS

Æsir: the gods; often those gods associated with war, death and power

Baldr, the beautiful; son of Óðin

Frey, god of fertility, marriage, and growing things

Freyja, goddess of sex, love and magic

Frigg, wife of Óðin

Heimdall, the watchman of the gods

Hel, both the goddess of the underworld and the place of the dead, specifically those who perish of sickness or old age

Loki, the mischief-monger, Father of Lies

Njörd, Lord of the Sea and god of wind and flame

Óðin, the Allfather; lord of the Æsir, god of warriors and war, wisdom and poetry

Rán, Mother of the Waves

Skadi, a goddess associated with skiing, archery and the hunting of game. Mother of Freyja.

Thór, son of Óðin; slayer of giants and god of thunder

Týr, Lord of Battle

Váli, Óðin's son, birthed for the sole purpose of killing Höðr as revenge for Höðr's accidental murder of his half-brother Baldr

Vanir, fertility gods, including Njörd, Frey and
    Freyja, who live in Vanaheim
Vidar, god of vengeance who will survive Ragnarök
    and avenge his father Óðin by killing Fenrir
Völund, god of the forge and of experience

ACKNOWLEDGEMENTS

Well here we are, up to our knees in Sigurd Haraldarson's saga. And what a joy it is to write these books and to live for a while in our Norsemens' world – a brutal and harsh world, yes, but one without smartphones and social media and reality TV and fitness trackers. And there's something to be said for that, I think. It can be refreshing to get away for a while. To go raiding with a fellowship. To stand at the sternpost of a longship and live a life that would be frowned upon these days, to say the least. I want you to 'feel' these stories as much as read them. I want you to abandon your twenty-first-century life and revel in the freedom and the danger, the grimness and the uncertainty – and the weather! – of late eighth-century Scandinavia. I hope you can revel too in the ideas and beliefs of Sigurd and his crew – men and women guided by capricious gods and tied one to another by bonds of loyalty and dreams of a shining reputation.

If you are reading this note, the chances are you already do these things. You are part of the crew and I humbly thank you. I could not write the books without you. Nor could I live my 'other lives' if it weren't for the host of professionals and friends who help get the stories out of my head and into your hands. Chief amongst these are Bill Hamilton, my agent, and Simon Taylor, my editor at Transworld. Thank you both for your insight, guidance and comradeship on these long journeys. To my little Vikings, Freyja and Aksel, thank you for distracting me from my work. Everything is for you, my dearest hearts. Even if you're not allowed to read these books till you're older. Much, much older. And to my wife, Sally, thank you for always helping when I need it (which is all the time) and for understanding the working weekends, the obsessions and the general chaos of the creative mind. Thanks also to Philip Stevens, my creative collaborator, for being the voice of the audiobooks for this series. I cannot wait to sit by the hearth fire and listen to your rendition of this saga, which is saying something given that I mostly know what happens.

But for now, far-wandering reader, hold on to your spear, because Sigurd and his wolves yet have the scent of prey in their noses. Vengeance must be had. Honour must be satisfied.

And we still have far to go, you and I.

Giles Kristian
January 2016

Family history (he is half Norwegian) inspired **Giles Kristian** to write his first historical novels: the acclaimed and bestselling 'Raven' Viking trilogy – *Blood Eye*, *Sons of Thunder* and *Óðin's Wolves*. For his next series, he drew on a long-held fascination with the English Civil War to chart the fortunes of a family divided by that brutal conflict in *The Bleeding Land* and *Brothers' Fury*. Giles also co-wrote Wilbur Smith's No.1 bestseller *Golden Lion*, but in his latest novels – *God of Vengeance* (a *Times* Book of the Year), *Winter's Fire* and now *Wings of the Storm* – he has returned to the world of the Vikings to tell the story of Sigurd and his celebrated fictional fellowship. Giles Kristian lives in Leicestershire.

To find out more, visit www.gileskristian.com

By Giles Kristian

The Raven Novels
Raven: Blood Eye
Sons of Thunder
Óðin's Wolves

The Bleeding Land
The Bleeding Land
Brothers' Fury

The Rise of Sigurd
God of Vengeance
Winter's Fire
Wings of the Storm

and published by Corgi Books

Turn the page to read the first chapter
of Giles Kristian's new novel

WINGS OF THE STORM

OUT NOW

CHAPTER ONE

———————————

THE HILL FORT AT FORNSIGTUNA BELONGED TO ALRIK NOW, AND SIGURD was Alrik's man. At least, he had won the place for the Svear warlord, tricking his way through the gates to sow death amongst the defenders, who were sworn to Alrik's enemy, a Svear jarl named Guthrum. Sigurd and his half crew, along with some of Alrik's men, had come to the borg under Guthrum's own banner of the white axe, and Guthrum's men, seeing that banner and thinking their lord had returned, had opened the gates. Only, that banner was not Guthrum's own. Nor could the jarl have ever laid eyes on it, seeing as it had been nothing but a scrap of sail cloth and a boar spear before Sigurd had Solmund get to work with his needle and thread.

With Loki-cunning and war-craft and in a welter of blood, Sigurd and his wolves had won Alrik the borg. But Sigurd would not swear an oath to the warlord, and if Alrik was sour about that he did a good job of hiding it. Mostly.

'He's had enough out of us without needing our oaths on top of it,' Olaf had told Knut, Alrik's most trusted man, when Knut had suggested that Sigurd and his men could do

445

worse than pledging their swords to the warlord and helping him defeat Jarl Guthrum himself, who was bound to turn up at the fort sooner or later.

Knut had looked from Olaf to Sigurd, wanting to hear the refusal from Sigurd's own mouth.

'We've made Alrik a rich man, Knut,' Sigurd said, which was understating it, as Knut well knew. Calling Alrik rich was like calling the sea damp, and Knut had nodded and raised a hand as if to say he would not press the matter further for now.

For the borg was full of silver and iron: sea chests crammed with hacksilver and stacks of iron already smelted and beaten into bars, enough to make the rivets for twenty ships, which was more iron than most people saw in their whole lives. And it had all been Guthrum's. The jarl had sat on this hoard while he built a war host large enough to take on King Erik, who was the real power in that part of Svealand, controlling the trading port of Birka and lands as far south as Götaland.

But Alrik, whilst he was not even a jarl, was an ambitious man and a hardened fighter, and he had grown powerful enough to challenge Guthrum, for all that he and his war host had then been stuck outside the borg as their beards grew long with the grass. Alrik had craved the place like a man who lusts after another man's woman, until Sigurd and his Sword-Norse had come and Sigurd had delivered the borg and its treasures to him. And so the warlord could make do without Sigurd's oath.

Not that Alrik was ungenerous. In the aftermath of the bloodletting he had given Sigurd a sea chest carved with ravens and eagles, and heavy it was too because it was stuffed with silver and iron: finger rings, sword and scabbard fittings, Thór's hammers, brooches, lengths of fine wire and solid ingots, iron bars, axe heads and even some gold, and in that one chest was a hoard as big as Sigurd's father Jarl Harald had ever owned. There would be more of the same, too, Alrik promised, if the Norsemen stayed and fought for him until Guthrum was carrion for the crows and his war host was scattered to the winds.

With such riches Sigurd could buy spearmen and maybe even ships. He could build his own war host and return to Norway to take on the oath-breaker King Gorm, and maybe he could have his revenge and so balance the scales which had been tipped against him and his kin since this whole thing began. That was the dream. And it was the gleam of all that plunder which blinded Sigurd and his crew to the presence of a man in Alrik's war band by the name of Kjartan Auðunarson, whom the skald Hagal Crow-Song – not that Crow-Song did much skalding these days – had recognized. Though it had taken him a while to pull that memory out of his thought box.

'He was Jarl Randver's man before he was Alrik's,' Crow-Song had said, turning all their thoughts back to that bloody fight in the fjord by Hinderå. Sigurd himself had killed Jarl Randver but now Hrani Randversson wore the torc and he wanted his revenge on Sigurd.

'What is to stop this Kjartan going home and making himself rich by telling Hrani Randversson where we are?' Olaf asked Sigurd when they had been thinking what to do about Kjartan.

'We kill him,' Svein had said with a shrug of his great shoulders, combing the fiery red beard of which he was so proud.

'He has to go,' Solmund agreed. The old skipper who had bound his wyrd to Sigurd's would rather hold a tiller than a sword, but even so he knew when someone needed killing.

447

'Of course he has to go,' Bram said. 'But the how of it. That's the question. We can't just go up to the man's bench and spear him when he's asleep.'

Sigurd and Olaf agreed it would take some thinking about, but then Alrik's men had brought that heavy sea chest in and all of them forgot about Kjartan Auðunarson.

Next morning, when they spread throughout the borg looking for the Hinderå man, there was no sign of him.

'What now then?' Olaf said when it was clear that Kjartan had gone, vanished 'like a fart in the breeze', as Bjarni put it.

'You are rich now, Sigurd,' Olaf went on. 'You've enough silver to put a proper crew together.'

'Not rich enough to take on the oath-breaker,' Solmund pointed out, which was true enough. Not that anyone liked hearing it.

'Seems to me we can stay here on this hill and earn more silver fighting for Alrik,' Bjarni said, lifting an eyebrow. 'There are worse places to live.'

'Even if Kjartan *has* slithered off back west to sell word of us to Hrani Randversson, it will be a long time before we have to concern ourselves about it,' Aslak said.

'True,' Olaf agreed, 'and weaving more reputation around here won't do us any harm.' For their war gear and the way they had won Alrik the borg had made the other men inside that ring of timber treat Sigurd's little crew warily and with the same respect as they did Alrik and Knut.

'Why get bogged down in a blood feud between two Svearmen when we have our own feud, which has a king in it?' Moldof put in, sweeping his one arm through the smoke-hung air. And this got some murmurs of agreement. They had avenged themselves on Jarl Randver by sending him to the seabed and many of his men to the afterlife sooner than they had thought to go. But Randver had only been a sword wielded by King Gorm. Gorm was the poison which tainted the very air for Sigurd. A nithing king who had shared mead and the feast table with Sigurd's father Harald. Who had laughed and hunted with the jarl and called him friend, but had in the end betrayed him, first in the ship battle in the Karmsund Strait, by not coming to Harald's aid when Harald was fighting Jarl Randver's ships, and then in the woods near Avaldsnes, by greeting Harald with swords and spears instead of with the mead he had promised.

'Moldof has a point there,' Bram admitted. 'Much as I am enjoying killing these Svearmen, we could end up stuck here. Going down with Alrik like the ballast stones in a sinking ship. And the oath-breaker king will be free to keep being the rancid goat's turd that he is for many years yet.'

That was not a happy picture in anyone's mind and so Sigurd told them he would think about it over the next days and decide what he would do.

But three days later the choice was taken away from him because Jarl Guthrum came. He brought with him the rest of his war host and it made for an impressive sight, spilling out of the tree line to the west of the borg, men's spear blades, axe heads and shield bosses glinting in the pink dawn light. Some of them owned helmets, fewer had mail, but it was the size of Guthrum's army which had Alrik's men cursing, fingering the Thór's hammers hanging at their necks and looking to their war gear. They checked that blades were sharp and shields were strong. They piled more spears and rocks against the palisade up on the earthen ramparts. They carried more pails of rainwater up the bank, setting them down around the perimeter twenty paces apart, ready to be flung at any fires should Guthrum try to burn the fence stakes.

'Silver or no, I am beginning to think we should have joined Guthrum instead of Alrik,' Solmund said, as still

449

more warriors came out of the trees. Alrik had ordered Sigurd to man the rampart above the gates as this was the most vulnerable part of the fort, where he wanted his best warriors.

'You won't be saying that when Guthrum strolls through those gates and gets a gut full of spear,' Olaf said as a horn sounded, formally announcing Guthrum's arrival.

Sigurd looked at the axe banner hanging on its long boar spear above the palisade, the wind stirring the cloth so that the white axe flickered, and in truth he did not think it would be as easy as Olaf said. The trick had worked once. Seeing that banner, which was the same as their jarl's, Guthrum's men in the borg had assumed their lord had come and they had opened the gates, inviting death into the borg. And now it was possible that Guthrum, having come at last, would see that banner and think that his men still held the fort. There was a chance, a hope at least, that Jarl Guthrum would walk into their trap and die easily.

But something told Sigurd that they would not be so lucky a second time.

Alrik had one of his men sound a horn in reply and those of his warriors not manning the ramparts thronged either side of the gates, shield and spear ready, waiting to spring their ambush.

It was worth trying, this ruse, but it was not without risk, as Bram pointed out. 'If enough of them get inside before we can shut the gates on the rest, their numbers will end up getting the better of us.'

'Not if we kill Guthrum,' Sigurd said. 'I have seen a hen run around after its head has been pulled off, but it does not know where it is going and soon falls down.' He shrugged. 'With Guthrum and his best men dead, the others will not know what to do.'

'I would like to see them all running around like your hen,' Bjarni said, grinning.

And perhaps they might have done, had Guthrum been fooled by that axe banner and walked into the borg to his death. But that did not happen and there was no steel-edged death for the jarl that day. He skirted the hill fort and came within an arrow-shot of the gate, close enough for Sigurd to see that he was a very big man, long-legged and broad in his brynja that reached almost to his knees. His silver jarl's torc glinted at his neck. His helmet had eye guards like Sigurd's own, so that they could not make out much of his face but for the big fair beard, and yet there was something about the man which told Sigurd that here was no fool. And sure enough Guthrum raised a hand and ordered his men to come no nearer to the borg. They waited, some two hundred Svearmen with their shields before them, because they smelt the fox in the coop.

'Whoreson knows,' Olaf said.

'He does,' Sigurd agreed. 'But look how he controls his temper.'

Olaf nodded. 'Ice in his veins this one,' he said. 'He knows that if Alrik is cosy up in his borg it means the rest of his men are most likely dead. Also knows he'll lose more men trying to kick us out.' Olaf pulled at his beard. 'That's a hard thing to swallow.'

It was, and yet Jarl Guthrum simply stood staring up at the borg. No cursing. No red-hot fury. No threats.

'Here we go,' Svein said as Guthrum took a spear from the man beside him who was even bigger than he was, and strode up the hill towards the gates.

'Guthrum is coming,' Sigurd called down to Alrik.

'I see him,' Alrik replied. He was standing on a barrel peering through a crack between the gate timbers.

451

'He's close enough,' Valgerd said, an arrow nocked on her bow string, the stave bent and straining. The shieldmaiden was the only woman in that borg, but there was no one in Alrik's war band or in Sigurd's crew who was better with a bow. Few better with a blade either. 'Want me to put this between his teeth?' she asked.

'No,' Sigurd said. 'If Alrik wanted to he could take three or four men out and pull Guthrum in here before the rest of his men got halfway up the hill. Let us hear what this jarl has to say.'

But Jarl Guthrum did not say anything. He ran a few steps and hurled the spear high and it soared over the palisade and Sigurd looked up at it before it plunged into the borg behind Alrik. It was the kind of throw that skalds sing about. More importantly, it meant that Guthrum was claiming the borg and every man in it.

'It'll be war then,' Olaf said.

'Did you think he would offer Alrik a horn of good mead and discuss a truce?' Solmund asked.

'I would have been disappointed in the man if he had,' Olaf said.

Jarl Guthrum turned his back on his enemies and walked back down the hill to rejoin his men. Then, protected by a shieldwall of fifty warriors, the remainder of his army made camp on the ground where Alrik's men had camped previously.

It was a grey, rain-filled day the first time Jarl Guthrum sent his warriors against the borg. Fifty attacked the eastern section of the palisade, fifty the west, and one hundred came at the southern perimeter, the bulk of them massing before the gate. Only, it wasn't really an attack. They brought ladders and ropes but never intended to climb. Instead they came close enough that Alrik's men had no choice but to throw spears and drop rocks, most of which did little more than split a few shields or send Guthrum's men away with cuts and bruises.

'Don't waste your spears,' Olaf said to those on the rampart above the gate, he being the first man in the fort to guess what Guthrum was up to. 'He's testing us, that's all,' he told Sigurd, 'and will be pleased with himself when we end up with nothing left to throw but clever insults and buckets of piss.'

The second time Guthrum attacked, his men did the same thing, and again the borg men tried to kill some of them, though they did not try as hard as before and did not throw many spears or shoot many arrows. The third time was different because this time some of Guthrum's men threw their ladders against the palisade and began to climb, their shields held over their heads, while archers on the ground loosed shafts at those on the ramparts. All the while Guthrum kept an impressive-looking skjaldborg facing the gate as a deterrent to Alrik leading a sortie out of the place. Some of the climbers made it over the top and on to the ramparts and fought ferociously too, but these brave men were soon sent on their way to Valhöll.

The fourth time the jarl attacked, the defenders did not know what he intended. They hurled their spears and dropped their rocks, killing seven of Guthrum's warriors and wounding a dozen more, which had Alrik's men cheering as though they expected Guthrum to turn round and lead his beaten army back into the forest.

Of course he did not do this.

'Why doesn't he come for the gate?' Thorbiorn asked, seeming disappointed. A prince amongst the Danes, Thorbiorn was more used to bed slaves and mead-soaked nights in his father's hall than days manning ramparts and dropping rocks on other men's heads, but King Thorir hoped his son would learn sword-craft and the warrior's way as part of Sigurd's crew, and in truth Thorbiorn seemed to be enjoying this new life. 'Why doesn't he just come?' he asked again.

'Because he's not a fool like you, that's why, boy,' Olaf gnarred.

'He knows we're here,' Sigurd explained to Thorbiorn, watching the fighting at the other walls. 'And he knows we are killers.'

'Well it's not right,' Svein said, gripping his big axe but having nothing to hit with it. 'It's like watching other men eating and drinking when you are hungry yourself.'

'He'll attack the gate tomorrow, Red,' Bram said, hopefully. 'Aye, he'll come at us tomorrow, if the gods want to watch the blood flying.'

What no one expected was another attack that very night when Guthrum should have been dealing with his own dead and, as Olaf put it, scheming about his next move. They came just before the dawn, men with ropes and grappling hooks, and they came from the north.

The first Sigurd and his crew knew about it was the shouting, followed by a moaning of horns from those sentries manning the northern ramparts.

'That Guthrum is a cunning shit,' Olaf grumbled, sitting up in his nest of furs and scrubbing the sleep from his face while the others groaned and cursed around him.

'I was beginning to like the man but he's ruined it now,' Bram said, downing a cupful of ale which someone had left on a stool by the hearth. 'Waking me up when I am dreaming about a beautiful woman is not the way to get on my good side.'

'Whoever the woman was, she owes Guthrum for sparing her your stinking clutches, Bear,' Valgerd told him, shrugging into her brynja and sweeping her golden hair back to tie it. A simple enough thing for a woman to do, and yet the watching of it hurt Sigurd like a blade in his flesh. In some ways . . . in one way . . . Valgerd was closer to him than any of them. They had been lovers, if only for a night. But he had less command over her than any in his crew. Valgerd was no more his than had the cascading water of the falls where he had found the shieldmaiden living been hers. She and the völva of the sacred spring had shared a life and perhaps Valgerd had belonged to the völva, but the seeress had withered and died, for which Valgerd blamed the gods. No, Sigurd thought now, watching Valgerd prepare for battle. He could no more claim that she was his than he could claim ownership of the hearth smoke which rose to leak out through the thatch above them.

'Ready?' Olaf said, giving Sigurd a newly sharpened spear and a look which was sharper still. Sigurd nodded.

They did not rush, as the other men sharing the longhouse did, tumbling out of the place half asleep, their bladders still full of ale and their blades as much a danger to themselves as the enemy. But when Sigurd's crew were fully into their war gear, some of them having relieved themselves in the ditch outside, Sigurd led them through the borg towards the fighting.

Guthrum's men had not got far into the borg, but there must have been thirty still alive out of those who had made it over the palisade and more were still clambering over, spilling into the place while their companions fought Alrik's men, half in the moonlight, half in the shadow of the north wall. They had won a good part of the ramparts in that spot, allowing the next in line to get over the wall with relative ease. The borg men manning the rest of the perimeter could do nothing to prevent it, since to leave their own stations would invite the enemy to flood over the wall from all sides.

'Wait!' Sigurd said, stopping Black Floki and Bram who would have walked right into the fight without breaking stride. The rest halted at Sigurd's shoulder while he stood there, eyes sifting the chaos ahead.

Alrik himself was in the thick of it, bellowing encouragement to his men and hammering shields with his sword. There were no shieldwalls as such, just two opposing tides which mingled here and there. Small knots of warriors making their own steelstorms.

'We take back the wall and let Alrik deal with these,' Sigurd said, gesturing with his spear at those enemy fighters already inside the place, and Olaf nodded because it was what he would have done. They split into two groups, six going with Sigurd, six with Olaf, and skirted round the mass of fighting men, resisting the urge to join the slaughter. Then they clambered up the bank either side of the point where most of Guthrum's men were coming over the wall, Valgerd stopping halfway up to draw her bow and put an arrow into the thigh of a warrior straddling the stakes. Pinned to the wall, the man screeched like a vixen and Sigurd knew that Valgerd had meant the shot, knowing the man's plight would put fear in the bellies of those on the other side who had yet to climb.

'Shieldwall!' Sigurd yelled, and those with him moved with the fluid ease of long practice, drawing level and overlapping their shields to form a rampart to which each of them entrusted their lives.

'Now kill the goat turds!' Svein roared as a spear clattered off his shield and Floki bent to put his axe into the skull of a man who sat with his back against the palisade having somehow snapped his leg coming over it.

They drove into Guthrum's men, hacking and stabbing, as Olaf's skjaldborg swept towards them along the rampart, two killing waves swamping all before them, trampling the dead, while Valgerd loosed arrow after arrow, the dull thud of shaft striking flesh announcing men's doom.

Sigurd speared a warrior in the shoulder then slammed his shield boss into the man's face, dropping him. Hagal cleaved a head in two and Bram spilled a man's guts. Holding his long axe halfway along the haft, Svein hooked the crescent head round his opponent's neck and hauled him on to Asgot's sword, which was quite a thing to see. And then there were no more living men between Sigurd's skjaldborg and Olaf's.

'Come then!' Bram yelled up at two of Guthrum's men who were half over the wall, but when they saw what was waiting for them they scrambled back down and were gone.

'You wait here in case any of those turds change their minds and want to die,' Olaf told Sigurd, pointing his gore-slick spear at the palisade. 'We'll help Alrik with this lot.'

Sigurd nodded and Olaf took Moldof, Bjarni, Bjorn, Floki and Svein back down the mound to hit Guthrum's men in their rear. But those men, knowing that they could expect no more reinforcements to come over the wall, did not fight on for long. One by one they threw down their swords and axes, clamouring to be spared, and some of them died on their knees, hacked to death before Alrik threw the leash over his own men and put an end to the butchery.

Men stood panting for breath, spitting, coughing, grimacing with pain or grinning at friends who had also survived. Some were already looting the dead, while others growled insults at Guthrum's men, the dead and the living. A handful of survivors stood around boasting that they had known their wyrds would not be severed that day, which Solmund muttered was a bold thing to claim.

The wounded were helped back to the dwellings where those most skilled in treating injuries waited with bone needles and horsehair thread, strong ale and herbs to numb the pain, and red-hot irons to seal cut flesh.

Sigurd looked out into the night and saw the backs of Guthrum's men as they retreated across the moon-silvered meadow and melted into the forest. Then he ordered some of Alrik's men to resume a watch from that place so that he and his crew would not have to, and no one questioned the order or refused it, even as weary as they were.

'Guthrum would be a fool to try that again,' Alrik told Sigurd, which was as much acknowledgement of Sigurd's part in that fight as he would give. The warlord was blood-spattered. There were beads of it on his long moustaches, glistening by flame and moonlight or dark against the pale skin of his neck where his Thór's hammer sat. His hair was cropped to the scalp at the sides but long enough on top to be braided into a rope which was pulled back over his head and tied between his shoulder blades.

'I would not put anything past Guthrum,' Sigurd said, and Alrik answered that by striking a kneeling prisoner across the temple with his sword hilt, dropping him. Then he turned and barked at his men to get on with the binding of the fourteen prisoners who, unlike the earlier boasters, must have sensed that they had come to the end of their wyrds now. The Norns, those spinners of men's futures, were poised with their shears.

'This feud you two have between you is a thirsty bitch, Alrik,' Olaf told him, looking at the carnage around them. 'She drinks blood like we drink ale.'

Alrik could not argue with that, though he did not like hearing it as he crouched to pull the silver rings from a dead man's fingers.

'It is a shame Guthrum did not have the courage to lead his men over the wall,' he said, running his sword through a scrap of wool torn from a tunic. 'He would be a corpse now and a good number of his men would pledge themselves to me.' With that he called to one of his men who looked up just in time to catch the two silver rings which Alrik threw. 'They would join my army because I am a more generous lord than Guthrum,' Alrik said, locking eyes with Sigurd. 'As you have seen for yourself, Byrnjolf,' he added, using the name by which Sigurd went amongst these Svearmen.

'Silver is of little use to dead men,' Sigurd said, which was not quite insulting Alrik's leadership but not far off. It was not that Sigurd disliked the man particularly, just that Alrik did not seem gods-favoured in any way, and that was disconcerting. Besides which, the strain of this feud was carved in Alrik's face like runes on a standing stone, which did not fill anyone with confidence.

'Byrnjolf has the right of that,' Olaf said. 'More nights like this and you won't have a war host to speak of,' he said, which was true. Sixteen of Alrik's men would never fight for him again, because they were dead or halfway dead: which was slightly better than Guthrum's losses, but still. Guthrum could afford to lose more men because he had more to begin with.

'Earn your keep, Norsemen, and we shall all come out of this silver-rich,' Alrik said, turning his back on them to greet Knut, his second in command, who had come to report how things stood across the other side of the borg. It seemed this at the north wall had been the only real assault, though Guthrum had made another feint at the gates to lure some of Alrik's men away from the proper fight.

'Earn our keep? Is that what he said?' Svein growled, clutching a fistful of arrows which he had gathered and now gave to Valgerd like a bunch of spring flowers. The shieldmaiden smiled and thanked him and Svein spat on his axe head and rubbed it with a handful of hay to get the blood off. 'If not for us Guthrum would be drinking mead from Alrik's skull by now.'

'At least he's a fighter, unlike my last lord,' Bram said with a shrug, which got some nods from the others who were milling around wondering what to do now. They had heard the story from Bram's own mouth, of how he had insulted his lord, a jarl named Otrygg, in his own hall because Otrygg had become a soft-bellied, hearth-loving jarl who had forgotten how to raid and live like a man should. And how Brak, Jarl Otrygg's champion, had had no choice but to defend his lord's honour and die for it too. Because Bram, whom men called Bear, was as skilled as he was strong and would fight Thór himself for the fame of it.

'Even so, this is not fighting,' Bram added, curling a lip at the sight of the prisoners who were being herded together by Alrik's men. 'You can all stay and watch this, but I am going back to sleep to see if that beauty in my dream is waiting for me.' He walked off, his shield slung across his back and his helmet under his arm.

'Wait for me,' Hagal called after. 'I do not want to watch these men get their throats cut.' Neither did any of the others, it seemed, and so they made their way back to the longhouse, leaving Alrik to do what he would with the prisoners. Not that anyone expected him to spare a single one.

The truth was that this attack had nearly succeeded, and almost certainly would have, had Sigurd's crew not retaken the rampart and turned the tide against Guthrum.

'Not that Alrik will admit it,' Olaf said as he and Sigurd wriggled out of their brynjur and laid them over a sea chest by their beds.

'Wager he expects this to buy him more dead enemies yet,' Sigurd said, touching the chest, which was carved with ravens and eagles, and leaning his shield against it. He drew his scramasax to check the blade. Wouldn't hurt to take a whetstone to it. His blood still thrummed with the battle thrill so it wasn't as if sleep would come to him any time soon.

'Aye, I think you're right with that,' Olaf admitted, yawning and taking the ale mug which Svein passed him. Nearby, Bram was already snoring, the sound of it like a rockfall.

Right he might be, but Sigurd suspected there was another reason for Alrik's having bitten his tongue rather than admit that Sigurd and his half crew of Norse had stopped Jarl Guthrum becoming king of that hill in Fornsigtuna. Alrik was beginning to feel the worm of jealousy squirming in his gut. As much as the warlord needed Sigurd's crew, he was a proud man, and whilst his own men were dying, it must have been a hard thing to recognize that here was a young warrior whose reputation was beginning to shine like a moon-washed blade.

Or a flame-licked blade, Sigurd thought, as by the flickering light of the hearth he ran the whetstone along the knife's edge.

Still, Alrik had more important things to worry about than reputation, either his own or Sigurd's. With Guthrum for an enemy they all did.

It was a golden day on Fugløy. A breeze rattled the birch leaves so that the rocks and long grass were dappled with dancing light. Bees threaded the air, going from flower to flower, the hum of them almost drowning out the distant clack of wooden swords as a group of Freyja Maidens practised in the clearing. The sky was endless and blue but for a few wisps of white, like a god's waking breath still lingering on the cool dawn air. The gulls soared and floated high above the island, at the edge of sight, seeming more inclined to revel in the day than dive for fish or scavenge snails and worms or leftovers from the midden.

But the sea was the richest treasure in the hoard of that day. It shone like a dented old helmet after a good polishing and was almost too bright to look at. A sleeping sea this morning, after the wind-tossed rollers of the previous day. Good for rowing, fishing, or taking a skiff to the shallow places to snatch up crabs or tempt them with meat on the end of a string. Good for washing in too, Runa thought now, squinting against the silver glare of it.

'I'm going to bathe,' she said. 'After that I must get back to milk the goats. A wash wouldn't hurt you, you know,' she told Ingel, raising an eyebrow at the man who lay back on his elbows in the grass beside her. The young smith was soot-stained and sweat-grimed, and yet from the way he grinned at Runa now anyone would think he was proud of his own stink. Not that Runa had minded it as she had straddled him in their nest of dewy grass, the two of them having sneaked away while the other women were beginning their daily tasks and Ingel's father Ibor was bringing the forge up to heat with the bellows.

But that was then. Now there was work to be done and, with the thrill of their coupling fading in Runa, receding like the tide, she was aware of the dirt on him, matted in his long hair and beard and ingrained in his skin so that the creases at the edges of his smiling eyes were as white as milk on the rare occasions he wore his serious face. Which he did now, though it took every effort by the looks.

'I'll bathe for you, Runa Haraldsdóttir,' he said, 'even though I do not see much point, for I will be covered in soot and grease again before midday.' He raised a callused finger. 'But only if we do it together. I swim like an anvil and will need to hang on to you so that I do not drown.'

Now the smile came to his lips and Runa struck his thigh with the back of her hand and tutted at his nonsense, for she had seen him swim like an otter more than once, the last time being when he and his father were off shore with the nets. She had watched Ingel jump over the side to cool down after rowing halfway round Fugløy and hauling in a bilge load of mackerel.

'You are a hopeless liar, blacksmith,' she said now, pursing her own lips on a smile she did not want to give him. She almost resented Ingel for his arrogance. For his knowing that he could have her, even looking like a black elf from one of the stories Runa's father Jarl Harald used to tell her when he wanted to frighten her.

No, when I wanted him to frighten me, she thought, remembering. 'Come then,' she said, climbing to her feet and looking back towards the tree line to make sure none of the other women had come looking for her, however unlikely that was. With the High Mother Skuld Snorradóttir off seeking guidance from the gods, there was a slackness to island life, the Freyja Maidens working with only half the usual purpose and endeavour. Skuld's absence was not the only reason for this. It was more than the mice playing while the cat was out of the way. Runa knew that the Prophetess's words about the future of their fellowship, her questioning of their way of life in uncertain times, had been like the serpent Nídhögg gnawing at the roots of the World Tree, so that the Freyja Maidens of Fugløy truly believed their way of life might come tumbling down.

And yet a good many of them were more than a little excited by the prospect of leaving the island and returning to the world. The idea of that had turned their heads and their thoughts from the everyday patterns which they had lived by up to now.

Runa's friend Drífa had been born on Fugløy and knew nothing else, no other life, but that only made her more eager to leave and she for one desperately hoped that the High Mother would return with the pronouncement that the Maidens were to leave this place and venture forth.

'It is hard to worry about next winter's hay when we may be living in King Thorir's hall by then,' Drífa had said when their friend Vebiorg announced that they should be cutting and drying what little grass grew on Fugløy while this good weather lasted.

'What makes you think the king will have us under his roof and share his meat with us?' Vebiorg had asked. 'He is happy to send us his smoked mutton, his weak ale and his blacksmiths, because he thinks it will buy him a place in Freyja the Giver's hall when he keels over, but he does not want a hall full of blade-wearing women.'

Drífa had frowned at her, but knowing nothing of the world beyond Fugløy's shores she could not put up an argument.

Still, with Skuld away there was more sword, spear and shield work going on than mundane tasks such as spinning shorn wool into thread or searching for gulls' eggs or scything grass to feed the animals next winter.

'Wait for me!' Ingel called after Runa, finally dragging himself to his feet now that Runa was up to her ankles in a rock pool a crab's scuttle from the lapping tide.

She shivered at the water's touch and looked out across the sea which shone like the silver of a jarl torc. Later in the day the air would be warm enough to bathe and not shiver half to death after, but she was up to her knees now and would not let Ingel see that she was cold. He already knew too much about her. Knew her body as well as a man could, which was itself such a shock to Runa; she wondered what her brother Sigurd would make of it were he to find out.

At least her thoughts and feelings were still her own. Ingel could not have that part of her. Not yet. Perhaps when they were married.

'It's cold,' he said, coming to stand beside her, bending to bring handfuls of water up and on to his skin to prepare his body for the plunge. Runa laughed and took his hand, leading him deeper, her feet gripping the weed-slick rocks as Ingel cursed the chill water and huffed and puffed.

Was she really thinking of marrying him? They had never brought it up, but neither had Ingel been with any of the other Freyja Maidens since he had lain with her. That must mean something. Certainly he did not seem to mind the scar which some nithing raider's arrow had carved in her face from just below her left eye to her ear. A disfigurement which Runa had been ashamed of but which Skuld the High Mother had told her to be proud of. 'Such battle runes speak for us, Runa,' Skuld had said. 'They tell our tales as well as any skald.'

Runa felt the sea breeze on the scar now, as gently as Ingel's lips had brushed against it earlier. A shiver ran through her and she tried not to think of what her brother would say if he could see her now, arse-naked and hand in hand with a filthy blacksmith who was cursing as the cold water shrivelled the snake between his legs.

You should not have left me behind, Sigurd, she thought, setting her jaw as the water shocked the skin between her hips and waist. Wondering where her brother was now and resenting him for abandoning her. Wishing he could see how good she had become with sword and spear, as much as she dreaded him knowing about Ingel.

'There,' the smith said, 'see there.' He was pointing with his free hand to the north beyond the pine-covered sliver of

GILES KRISTIAN

the island which jutted out into the sea. 'You see it? There! An arrow-shot off shore.'

'Too small for *Storm-Elk*,' Runa said, having been struck with the sudden fear that it was King Thorir's ship come to take Ingel and his father back to Skíringssalr. The blacksmiths were the only men permitted to set foot on the island, tasked with repairing the Freyja Maidens' weapons and forging what needed forging. But even they must return to Thorir's hall when the king sent for them.

No. Runa could see now that the boat being rowed towards the bay beyond that knife blade of land was just a færing. She sharpened her eyes upon it, which was no easy thing because of the glittering glare coming off the sea. Two pairs of oars, no more.

'Sibbe and Guthrun?' Ingel suggested, for those two had gone off fishing before sunrise. But Runa shook her head.

'They will be on the west side,' she said. She had lived on Fugløy long enough by now to know that if you wanted to make your arm ache from pulling in mackerel and, now and then something bigger like a codfish, you took the boat out to a place which the women called Flea Rock because the water there was as thick with fish as fleas on a dog.

'News from the king then,' Ingel said, his gaze lingering a moment on the distant craft before he turned to make his way back to dry land and his clothes and shoes which lay piled in the grass.

But Runa was already splashing through the rock pools then throwing her own tunic over her wet skin and thrusting her legs into her breeks. Because perhaps whoever was in that færing had word of Sigurd. What if he were dead? What if King Gorm or Jarl Hrani had caught up with him? No. She would not believe that. He had left her on this island because he would not make her endure the outcast's life he

466

had chosen for himself after King Gorm betrayed their father and Jarl Randver had brought slaughter to their village. But he would not leave her alone in this world, would not make the journey to the afterlife without her.

Runa thought all this as she ran across the rocks and long grass, scattering butterflies and bees before her and looking up to the bluff where one of the other women was on watch. That woman was standing on the rock at the edge of the bluff to get a better look at the boat and its crew, and Runa saw that it was her friend Vebiorg. She waved at Runa now to acknowledge that she had seen the craft, then turned and was gone, back to warn the others that they should expect visitors.

So Runa ran, leaping a fallen tree and ducking a spider's web which shimmered between two hazels. Then through the birch and thickets and up to the higher ground that would take her over the ridge and down into the bay where those in the rowboat meant to come ashore.

And Ingel, despite not yet owning the brawn that his father had earned from a lifetime in the forge, could not keep up with her.

Runa watched as the man pulled the little boat up the beach, the small stones crunching beneath its hull as he dragged it beyond the high-tide line with the woman still in it. Her brown hair had spilled from a white linen head-dress and her teeth worried her bottom lip as she sat on the bench, clinging on to the sides as the little færing jerked and bucked to a stop.

And then Runa realized why the woman had not leapt out of the boat into the shallows and either helped the man pull the boat up or else at least lightened the load for him. She was enormous with child and grimacing as she stood in the thwarts, holding out her hand so that the man could help her out of the boat, which almost tipped with her weight as she hoisted a leg over and set a foot on the strand. Runa was reminded of a whale she had once seen on the east coast of Karmøy. The beast had washed up on the shore and her father had sent a score of men and women to butcher it on the beach and bring the meat and fat and even strips of its skin back to Eik-hjálmr. She stifled a grin and felt mean for thinking of it now.

'You cannot come ashore here,' she told the man, still breathing heavily after the run. 'It is forbidden.'

The man raised a hand to her to show he had heard, but did not say anything as he helped the woman walk across the loose stones up the beach towards her.

'You must get back into your boat and row away from here. You cannot stay,' she said, and again the man raised a hand but kept walking towards her and Runa felt a stab of irritation. Was he deaf? Or just arrogant?

'She looks ready to drop it on the beach,' Ingel said, coming to stand beside Runa, breathing hard, eyes wide at the sight of the man half pulling, half pushing the woman up the slope.

'She can't,' Runa said. 'They should not even be here.'

Ingel shrugged. 'Then you'd better put her back in the boat and hope the seep water in the bilge isn't deep, for she will drop the bairn in there,' he said and Runa frowned because he had a point.

'Who are you?' she asked the couple, thinking that if the man raised his hand again she would draw her scramasax and cut it off, expectant wife or no.

'My wife is fit to burst,' the man said, letting go the woman's hand to come closer to Runa. She could smell the boat tar and sweat on him. 'She began the pains,' he said, 'the ones that come again and again like waves on the shore.' He frowned. 'But something is wrong. Or else the child is being stubborn, for it will not come.' Fair-haired, his face pitted with little scars, he was a man in his middle years and not rich by the looks of his clothes and his lack of a sword or any war gear to speak of, though he might have left his belongings in the færing. He had no beard to speak of, either, but for a few mossy patches and the dark bristles on his neck.

'I know little of such things,' Runa said, thinking that she should perhaps start to learn more given what she got up to with Ingel.

'My name is Varin and this is my wife Gudny,' the man said, looking from Runa to Ingel, arming sweat from his forehead and pressing hands into the small of his back. 'We have come far. Rowed through the night to get here.'

'Why here?' Ingel asked before Runa had the chance to.

'You can see that she is in pain,' Varin said, thumbing back towards his wife who stood there looking about as uncomfortable as a person could who was not either suffering from the runs or painful arse berries or serious over-eating. 'My wife needs help or the child will die inside her and kill Gudny with it.'

'But why come here? Surely there are women near your steading who can help her,' Runa said.

'I have heard about the old woman who lives here. The witch,' he said in a softer voice. He touched the little iron Mjöllnir which hung at his throat and knew from Runa's expression that she needed more explanation than that. 'My brother is a shipwright. He worked on *Storm-Elk*, King Thorir's ship, and he is a friend of her skipper, a man named Harthbren.' He raised that hand of his again but this time it was lifted like a shield against Runa's next question. 'This

Harthbren did not tell my brother where this island was . . . before you have King Thorir flay the skin from his flesh. But Biarbi was able to stitch the where of it together from what he learnt by talking to the man.' He forced a smile. 'My brother knows this sea better than he knows his own wife.'

He turned and beckoned to his woman to come closer. Her face was tear-stained and miserable-looking as she waddled forward, hands cradling her huge belly. There was blood near the hem of her kyrtill, Runa saw, which did not bode well for either her or the life inside her. Runa knew that much.

She looked at Ingel who shrugged as if to say he was just a blacksmith and who came and went was no business of his. She looked back at Varin and decided there was no point in telling him that men were not allowed on the island, not with Ingel standing there still flushed from their coupling in the grass.

'They will likely send you away,' she warned instead, this to Gudny, who was giving her such pathetic eyes that it was uncomfortable to look at her. 'Certainly they will not allow *you* to be here,' she said, turning back to Varin.

He set his face, the little muscles tensing beneath the pockmarked skin. 'I will not leave my wife,' he said. 'The bairn needs to come out of her. We need the old woman to weave her seiðr. She can help us. I know it. She will save Gudny and the child too, if the gods will it.' Gudny groaned then and swayed as if she might fall, and it was Ingel who stepped forward to steady her, earning the woman's mumbled thanks and a scowl from Varin, who took hold of his wife again though he did not refuse Ingel's help.

'Will you take us to her, girl?' Varin asked. 'Or will you stand there and watch my wife and bairn die?'

There was an edge of threat in the man's voice now, an air of violence about him, though it was not worth making a thing out of it, Runa thought, confident that she could handle him if she needed to; wondering why she had even thought about how she would take him down, this desperate and frightened man.

And so she nodded, turned her back on the sea and the couple who had come across it, and walked over the rocks towards the long grass and the birch and scrub beyond which lay the grazing meadows and, beyond them, the settlement where the Freyja Maidens lived their lives undisturbed.

'Come then,' she called over her shoulder.

Guthrum came three more times over the next six days. The last of those attacks brought terror to the borg, for as Sigurd knew only too well, few things frightened men more than fire in the night: ship-burning, hall-burning, man-burning fire.

Guthrum had bided his time, letting one rainless day follow another until the palisade, as well as the fuel he had gathered, was as dry as they were likely to get. Then, in the gloom of night, his men ran forward with arms full of sticks and dried moss tinder which they piled against the wall in four places, setting light to it. Alrik's men dowsed two of the four fires before they caught properly, but the other two, being fanned by a breeze coming out of the south-east, licked the stakes and then bit deep. It did not help that Guthrum, seeing the flames beginning to do their work, arranged all his archers before those two fires, so that they kept up a steady rain of arrows which, if they did not kill many, nevertheless kept Alrik's men's heads down when they should have been busy flinging water.

'What are we going to do about this, then?' Moldof asked Sigurd and Olaf, waving the stump of his right arm – all that was left of it since Sigurd's father had cut it off in a fight which the skalds sang of. A more grievous wound still because it had lost Moldof his position as King Gorm's champion and prow man, and this the warrior could not abide. Thinking he could reclaim his honour by killing his king's enemy Sigurd Haraldarson, Moldof had journeyed north alone, intent on finding Sigurd in his lair up in Osøyro. But in the event it was Sigurd who had offered Moldof a chance to rekindle his fame. Fame and the sword-song, or a bad death, cut into a stump and rolled into the fjord: that was the choice Sigurd had given him that white, frozen day on the fjord's edge. Moldof had chosen the first option and now the former champion fought for Sigurd, though Sigurd and the other Skudeneshavn men still felt the strange prickle of that like nettles on the skin, Moldof having been their enemy not so long ago.

Men were coughing now, choking on the smoke which billowed over the palisade into the borg, enveloping the huge mass of Moldof who scowled at it as if that would turn it back. And it might, given how ugly Moldof was.

Flame-glow showed like copper against the night sky.

'Now would be a good time to take your snake out of your breeks, hang it over the side and piss out that fire,' Svein told Bjarni, who was not above boasting about the size of the thing given any opportunity.

'I won't risk burning it. Not for the sake of this lot,' Bjarni said, gesturing at thirty of Alrik's men who stood with them on the ramparts, peering round their shields at Guthrum's war host massing on the slope.

It was one thing to make light of it all, Hagal said, but no one would be laughing when those burning stakes gave way and Guthrum's men poured into the place.

Alrik's men were bringing pails of water from all across the borg and tipping them over the wall, while their comrades shielded them from arrows and spears, and when a cheer went up fifty paces further along the rampart, Sigurd knew that the fire there had been put out. But the one eating the palisade where he stood was growing, tongues of flames now and then stretching above the pointed stakes to singe men's beards.

'Well, Byrnjolf?' Alrik said. 'What do we do?' The warlord was looking at the enemy rather than at Sigurd, and the question had leaked from the corner of his mouth like pus from a wound.

Sigurd had been asking himself the same question and had not liked the answer. But he shared it with Alrik anyway. 'A few of us slip over the wall and loot Guthrum's camp,' he said. Arrows streaked over their heads and thudded into men's shields around them. 'We burn his tents if we get the chance and we make a lot of noise about it.' He nodded towards the horde on the hillside, fully revealed in its war-glory now by the glow of the fire. He fancied he could make out Guthrum himself standing in the heart of that body of warriors, taller than those around him. 'If they think we are into their sea chests and slashing their ale skins they will hare back to the camp.' He shrugged. 'It may give your men a chance to deal with this fire at least.'

Alrik scowled, considering the idea. 'Anyone who makes it as far as those trees without being carved up will be tempted to keep going and not look back.'

'You think I would run?' Sigurd asked.

'You have sworn no oath to me,' Alrik said.

Here it was again. 'And neither will I,' Sigurd said. 'But tell me, Alrik, is my oath worth more to you than this borg?'

To his right Olaf cursed as an arrow *tonk*ed off his shield boss. He picked out the archer who had just tried to kill him and bellowed at him, calling the man a nithing son of a flea-ridden bitch. Then he turned back to Alrik.

473

'You won't have to worry about anyone leaving you here in the shit, Alrik,' he said. 'No one is going out there. Not us, not your oath-sworn.'

'What do you have in mind, Uncle?' Sigurd asked.

'We'll let the arse-leaves come to us instead. Only thing is, we need to lose this part of the wall to save the rest of it. If the fire spreads we're dead men.'

Sigurd knew what Olaf was thinking then.

Alrik knew too. 'But if there is just a small hole we will be able to plug it,' he said.

Olaf nodded, then called to Svein and Bram to bring their axes. Alrik ordered some others to help and they set to work, going at those flaming stakes like woodsmen while others went off into the borg to find the timbers they would need as replacements.

The first of the stakes fell with a shower of embers and the rest soon followed, and were kicked away down the slope from the palisade by Alrik's men, their shields raised against the heat as much as the arrows. Then Alrik himself stepped into the breach and his skjaldborg built itself around him. He was lucky in one way because the burning timbers lying on the bank checked Guthrum's advance. Yet he was unlucky in that those burning fence posts lit up his shieldwall so that Guthrum's archers could hardly miss.

'He can smell blood now,' Bram said. He meant Guthrum, who was pacing up and down in front of his men, yelling at them, inciting them to the coming slaughter, rousing them with promises of plunder and arm rings and fame. Men were flooding in from the surrounding darkness, swelling his numbers because they knew that this breach was their best chance of retaking the borg.

'All we have to do is hold!' Alrik called. 'We will kill them. We will bleed them and they will lose heart. Jarl

474

Guthrum will show himself for the pale-livered, pus-filled prick he is.' His men cheered this, thumping swords and axes against their shields, showing their defiance. One of them loosed an arrow at Guthrum which hit him square on the helmet between the eye guards. But Guthrum did not flinch. He pointed his sword at Alrik, roared something to Óðin Hrafnaguð, Ravengod, then led his army forward. They came up the slope as though they never doubted that they would win, as though they would punch through that gap in the fort's palisade like a rivet through a ship's strake.

But Alrik had not become a warlord by being an easy man to kill. Nor was he afraid to lead from the sharp end, and he held like a rock, striking men down, hammering them with his sword, splitting skulls and lopping limbs. Knut was there too and he was a deadly fighter, cunning and quick, his spear striking like a snake and laying men low.

'They're doing well,' Svein admitted grudgingly.

'Aye, they need to,' Solmund said. For now they stood back from the fighting because Alrik already had two lines of men filling the breach and there was no room for more.

'Hold your crew in reserve,' Alrik had told Sigurd. 'My men will fight harder knowing that you are at our backs. But if we break, you must hold the breach.'

'You won't break,' Sigurd had said, and so far he was right. And now those men they had sent off to find timbers were returning with their heavy loads, so that whilst Alrik and Guthrum's skjaldborgar clashed, their blades biting, Olaf took charge of the new defences. He had Sigurd's crew digging holes and setting the new posts in them, but not so that they made a new palisade, for being rushed it would be weak. Instead they set the timbers at a slant and supported them so that they pointed towards the breach. Old roof timbers, posts from the animal pens, even split planks from long tables were set in place, clustered thick as sea urchin spines, and then Olaf had them take axes and sharpen the ends of the timbers. And as they dug and hacked and sweated, they kept one eye on the battle in the breach, hoping that Alrik's shieldwall stood firm. Because if not, his men would be driven back on to those spikes and the enemy would surge in.

The sword-song rang out into the night, accompanied by the shrieks of the wounded and the gruff shouts of encouragement from men who knew only too well that they each depended on the other, that the shieldwall was only as strong as its weakest man. And it was a hard fight between those two warlords that night, with men falling on both sides, their bodies hauled back so that others could step up and take their place.

Still, try as he might, Guthrum could not break Alrik's shieldwall and force his way into the borg. And in the end, exhausted and bone-weary, Guthrum's men pulled back from the carnage in the breach, and Alrik's men up on the ramparts could not even sting them with arrows as they retreated down the hill, for they had long run out of shafts.

The mangled and the dismembered lay there like a grim burial mound, a testament to the savagery of that fight and to the stubbornness of both sides. But Alrik still held the hill, for all that he had paid a heavy price for it.

'I don't think we can take another night like that,' Svein said to Sigurd. Dawn was breaking and he had come with Sigurd to look at the hole in the palisade and see what Alrik was doing about it. 'I am thinking we should take our silver and iron and leave while we still can.' Svein had braided his thick red beard into one rope, which he pulled now as they watched three dogs licking the blood-smeared grass of the slope where the corpses had lain. Now Sigurd realized why Svein had got out of his bed to come with him while the rest were still half asleep in the longhouse. This was not the sort of thing his friend would say in front of anyone else. 'You know I would stay here and fight beside you until Ragnarök, Sigurd,' he said, tugging at that red rope, 'but how will that help us avenge our kin? This is a good fight but it is not our fight.'

They stood beside the sharp teeth of the makeshift defence, looking out across the rock-strewn meadow which was thick now with yellow flowers that showed even in the weak light, reminding Sigurd of home and Runa.

Now and then the breeze brought the low hum of men's voices from Guthrum's camp, but there was no sign that the jarl was going to attack the breach again. Which was why Knut was making the best of it and had his men digging out the last stumps of the ruined timbers, like rotting teeth from raw gums, so that they could be replaced properly.

'You think Guthrum would let us walk out of here and back to *Reinen*?' Sigurd asked.

'I think he would be glad to see us go. Glad to see Alrik spilling men like a wound spilling blood,' Svein said, then held his tongue while two of Knut's men walked past hefting a long timber between them. 'Guthrum has lost too many warriors already,' Svein went on when the men were out of earshot. 'He wants this borg and the iron in it. He won't sacrifice more of his men fighting us if he doesn't have to. Not if we show him our backs.'

'It wouldn't be much of a fight. Not out there in the open,' Sigurd said, which was true enough. Even armed like Týr, Lord of Battle, they were just fourteen, whilst Guthrum still commanded as many as one hundred and fifty warriors. Even so, he suspected Svein was right and that Guthrum would just be glad to see Sigurd's crew fly the coop, leaving Alrik in the mire of it.

'We will never kill the oath-breaker if we die here,' Svein said, his mention of King Gorm like the stab of a cold blade

477

in Sigurd's guts. There was no argument Sigurd could make against that and so he said nothing, which allowed a silence to spread between them like a bloodstain.

It had taken a lot for Svein to suggest that they turn their backs on Alrik and leave his men to Guthrum's army. And yet Svein was right, this was not their fight.

'Alrik will think we are cowards,' Sigurd said after a while.

'Alrik will not be alive for long after we leave so what does it matter what he thinks?'

But Óðin will know, Sigurd thought, *and I have not come this far, having got old One-Eye's attention, just to prove unworthy of it now.*

Sigurd looked along the rampart and saw Alrik doing his rounds, walking the perimeter and talking to the clusters of men manning the palisade. Down in the borg his other warriors were spilling out of their dwellings now, stretching aching muscles and preparing for whatever the day might bring. They were good men. Loyal men.

'We just have to beat Guthrum,' Sigurd said. Svein raised one thick red eyebrow but Sigurd pressed on. 'We beat Guthrum and we leave here as rich men.'

Svein nodded, which was his way of saying that whatever Sigurd decided, that was fine by him.

Sigurd nodded too. All he had to do was come up with a way of killing Jarl Guthrum and he would earn silver, fame and the Spear-God's respect. He was still wondering how this might be done when Svein tramped back down the bank into the borg to find something to eat.

It was not until four days later that the answer came to him. And it was Guthrum himself who came up with it, laying it before Sigurd like a gift.

*

'The horse prick is trying to put the worm of fear in our bellies, breathing down our necks like this,' Knut said. After three days of rain it had dawned bright and golden. The breeze itself was warm and what little cloud there was drifted through the blue sky like unspun wool.

Alrik, Knut, Sigurd and Olaf had gathered on the ramparts above the gates because the sentries there had called down into the borg that Guthrum was coming.

But the jarl was not attacking. Rather he was moving his whole camp up the hill towards the borg so that it was more than a spear-throw but less than an arrow-shot from the walls. Not that he need fear Alrik's archers taking long-range shots, because they were saving what few arrows they had scavenged or made for Guthrum's next attack.

'He thinks that if he puts his war host in full view, my men will lose heart at the sight,' Alrik said.

Olaf nodded in agreement. 'He wants this thing over with,' he said, 'and is coming at us like a hand round a throat. And his own men are going to want to finish it sooner rather than later for they will be fed up with living on a hillside and rolling out of their beds.'

It took most of the day, but by the time the sun fell behind the mountains in the west the enemy had set up their tents again and were sitting round fires, or rather lying because of the slope, drinking and talking, laughing and singing, and all of them ready in their war gear, shields and spears within reach. It was a sight which had Alrik's one hundred and ten fit men gripping sword pommels, spear shafts, axe hafts and Thór's hammer amulets with sweaty palms. But of all of it, one thing had Alrik spitting curses and telling anyone who would listen that he was going to pull Guthrum's head out of his arse, stick it on a pole and leave it for the birds. That was the sight of the jarl's own tent sitting nearer the borg than any of the others, as if Guthrum were announcing to gods and men that he was a man without fear of death. That he could snore the night away almost within spitting distance of his enemies and have no concern that he might wake with a blade in his belly.

Guthrum's tent was of red sail cloth and the upper ends of its cross-timber supports were carved to resemble snarling wolves; the whole thing now being where it was made for a decent insult. It was Jarl Guthrum saying that Alrik was too afraid to come out and fight him amongst the spring flowers, man against man, skjaldborg against skjaldborg.

And it was a sight which had Sigurd's heart pounding against the anvil of his breastbone. When *he* looked at Guthrum's red tent he saw opportunity, a chance to win this fight for Alrik and cut out the despair which was spreading through the borg like rot in damp wood.

'What is on your mind then?' Olaf asked him. They were sharing bread and some cheese and a skin of ale that was only a little sour. 'When you are quiet like this it usually means you are waist-deep in some scheming.'

'Not this time, Uncle,' Sigurd said.

But that was a lie.